THE
MIDDLE KINGDOM

David Wingrove is the Hugo Award-winning co-author (with Brian Aldiss) of *Trillion Year Spree: The History of Science Fiction*, and co-author of the first three *Myst* books – novelizations of one of the world's bestselling computer games. He is also author of *The Roads to Moscow* trilogy. He lives in north London.

THE
MIDDLE KINGDOM

BOOK 3

DAVID WINGROVE

FRAGILE
BOOKS

The Middle Kingdom was first published in Great Britain in 1989 by New English Library.

A revised and updated edition published in special edition hardback, trade paperback, and eBook in Great Britain in 2012 by Corvus, an imprint of Atlantic Books Ltd.

This edition published in trade paperback and eBook in Great Britain in 2017 by Fragile Books.

A CIP catalogue record for this book is available from the British Library.

Trade paperback ISBN: 978-1-912094-69-1
eBook ISBN: 978-1-912094-68-4

Printed in Great Britain by 4edge Ltd.

Fragile Books
5a Arundel Square
London
N7 8AT

www.fragilemedialtd.com

CONTENTS

For Hilary and Clarissa –
for nursing this ungainly epic into being,
and for your endless kindnesses.

INTRODUCTION

Where did it all begin? When was the first step taken on that downward path that led to Armageddon? Perhaps it was on that fateful June day in 2043 when President James B. Griffin, last of the sixty presidents of the United States of America, was assassinated while attending a baseball game at Chicago's rebuilt Comiskey Park.

The collapse of the sixty-nine states of the American Empire that followed and the subsequent disintegration of the allied Western economies brought a decade of chaos. What had begun as 'The Pacific Century' was quickly renamed 'The Century of Blood' – a period in which the only stability was to be found within the borders of China. It was from there – from the great landlocked province of Sichuan – that a young Han named Tsao Ch'un emerged.

Tsao Ch'un had a simple – some say brutal – cast of mind. He wanted to create a utopia, a rigidly stable society that would last ten thousand years. But the price was high. In 2062, Japan, China's chief rival in the East, was the first victim of Tsao Ch'un's idiosyncratic approach to *realpolitik* when, without warning – following Japanese complaints about Chinese incursions in Korea – the Han leader bombed Honshu, concentrating his nuclear devices on the major population centres of Tokyo and Kyoto. When the dust cleared, three great Han armies swept the smaller islands of Kyushu and Shikoku, killing every Japanese they found, while the rest of Japan was blockaded by sea and air. Over the next twenty years they would do the same with the islands of Honshu and Hokkaido, turning the 'islands of the gods' into a wasteland, while the crumbling Western nation states looked away.

★

The eradication of Japan taught Tsao Ch'un many lessons. In future he sought 'not to destroy but to exclude' – though his definition of 'exclusion' often made it a synonym for destruction. As he built his great City – huge, mile-high spider-like machines moving slowly outward from Pei Ch'ing, secreting vast, tomb-like hexagonal living sections, three hundred levels high and a kilometre to a side – so he peopled it, choosing carefully who was to live within its walls. As the City grew, so his servants went out among the indigenous populations he had conquered, searching among them for those who were free from physical disability, political dissidence or religious bigotry. And where he encountered organized opposition, he enlisted the aid of groups sympathetic to his aims to carry out his policies. In South Africa and North America, in Europe and in the People's Democracy of Russia, huge movements grew up, supporting Tsao Ch'un and welcoming his 'stability' after decades of chaos and suffering, only too pleased to share in his crusade of intolerance – his 'Policy of Purity'.

Only the Middle East proved problematic. There, a great Jihad was launched against the Han – Muslims and Jews casting off centuries of enmity to fight against a common threat. Tsao Ch'un answered them as he had answered Japan just five years before. The Middle East and large parts of the Indian subcontinent were reduced to a radioactive wilderness. But it was in Africa that his policies were most nakedly displayed. There, the native peoples were moved on before the encroaching City and, like cattle, they starved or died from exhaustion, driven on by the brutal Han armies. Following historical precedent, City Africa was reseeded with Han settlers.

In terms of human suffering, Tsao Ch'un's pacification of the globe was unprecedented. Contemporary estimates put the cost in human lives at well over four billion. But Tsao Ch'un was not content merely to eradicate all opposition, he wanted to destroy all knowledge of the Western-dominated past. Like the First Emperor, Ch'in Shih Huang-ti, twenty four centuries before, he decided to rewrite the history books. Tsao Ch'un had his officials collect all books, all tapes, all recordings, allowing nothing that was not Han to enter his great City. Most of what they collected was simply burned, but not all. Some was adapted.

One group of Tsao Ch'un's advisors – a group of Scholar-Politicians who termed themselves 'the Thousand Eyes' – persuaded their master that it would not be enough simply to create a gap. That, they knew, would attract curiosity. What they proposed was more subtle and, in the long term, far more persuasive. With Tsao Ch'un's blessing they set about reconstructing the history of the world, placing China at the centre of everything – back in its rightful place, as they saw it. It was a lie, of course, yet a lie to which everyone subscribed... on pain of death.

But the lie was complex and powerful, and people soon forgot. New generations arose who knew nothing of the real past and to whom the whispers and rumours seemed mere fantasy in the face of the solid reality they saw all about them. The media fed them the illusion daily, until the illusion became, even for those who worked in the Ministry responsible, quite *real*, and the documents they dealt with some strange aberration – a mass hallucination, almost a disease that had struck the Western peoples of the great Han empire in its latter years. The officials of the Ministry even coined a term for it – 'racial compensation' – laughing among themselves whenever they came across some clearly fantastic reference in an old book about quaint religious practices or races of black – think of it, *black!* – people.

Tsao Ch'un killed the old world. He buried it deep beneath his glacial City. But eventually his brutality and tyranny proved too much even for those who had helped him carry out his scheme. In 2087 his Council of Seven Ministers rose up against him, using North European mercenaries, and overthrew him, setting up a new government. They divided the world – Chung Kuo – among themselves, each calling himself T'ang, 'King'. But the new government was far stronger than the old, for the Seven made it so that no single one of them could act on any major issue without the consensus of his fellow T'ang. Adopting the morality of New Confucianism, they set about consolidating a 'peace of ten thousand years'. The keystone of this peace was the Edict of Technological Control, which regulated and, in effect, prevented change.

Change had been the disease of the old, Western-dominated world. Change had brought its rapid and total collapse. But Change was alien to the Han. They would do away with Change for all time. Their borders were secured, the world was theirs – why should they not have peace and stability until the end of time? But the population grew and grew, filling the vast

City and, buried deep in the collective psyche of the European races, something began to stir – some long-buried memory of rapid evolutionary growth. Change was needed. Change was wanted. But the Seven were set against it.

For more than a century they succeeded, and their great world-spanning City thrived. If a man worked hard, he could climb the levels into a world of space and luxury; if he failed in business or committed a crime he would be demoted – down toward the crowded, stinking Lowers. Each man knew his place in the great scheme of things and obeyed the diktats of the Seven. Yet the pressures placed upon the system were great and as the population climbed toward the forty billion mark, something had to give.

DAVID WINGROVE, May 2012

PROLOGUE Yin/Yang

WINTER 2190

'Who built the ten-storeyed tower of jade?
Who foresaw it all in the beginning,
when the first signs appeared?'

'Tien Wen' ('Heavenly Questions') by Ch'u Yuan, from
the Ch'u Tz'u ('Songs Of The South'), 2nd century BC

YIN

I n the days before the world began, the first *Ko Ming* Emperor, Mao Tse Tung, stood on the hillside at Wu Ch'i Chen in Shen-hsi Province and looked back at the way he had come. The Long March, that epic journey of twenty-five thousand li over eighteen mountain ranges and through twelve provinces – each larger than a European state – was over and, seeing the immensity of China stretched out before him, Mao raised his arms and addressed those few of his companions who had survived the year-long trek.

'Since P'an Ku divided heaven from earth, and the Three Sovereigns and the Five Emperors reigned, has there ever been in history a long march like ours? In ten years, all China will be ours. We have come this far – is there anything we cannot do?'

China. *Chung Kuo*, the Middle Kingdom. So it had been for more than three thousand years, since the time of the Chou, long before the First Empire.

So it had been. But now Chung Kuo was more. Not just a kingdom, but the Earth itself. A world.

In his winter palace, in geostationary orbit 160,000 li above the planet's surface, Li Shai Tung, T'*ang*, Son of Heaven and Ruler of City Europe, stood on the wide viewing circle, looking down past his feet at the blue-white globe of Chung Kuo, thinking.

In the two hundred and fifty-five years that had passed since Mao had stood on that hill in Shen-hsi province, the world had changed greatly. Then, it was claimed, the only thing to be seen from space that gave evidence of Man's existence on the planet was the Great Wall of China. Untrue as it was, it said something of the Han ability to plan great projects – and not merely to plan them, but to carry them out. Now, as the twenty-second century entered its final decade, the very look of the world had changed. From space one saw the vast Cities – each almost a continent in itself; great sheets of glacial whiteness masking the old, forgotten shapes of nation states; the world one vast, encircling megalopolis: City Earth.

Li Shai Tung stroked his long white beard thoughtfully, then turned from the portal, drawing his embroidered silk *pau* about him. It was warm in the viewing room, yet there was always the illusion of cold, looking down through the darkness of space at the planet far below.

The City. It had been playing on his mind much more of late. Before, he had been too close to it – even up here. He had taken it for granted. Made assumptions he should never have made. But now it was time to face things: to see them from the long perspective.

Constructed more than a century before, the City had been meant to last ten thousand years. It was vast and spacious and its materials needed only refurbishing, never replacing. It was a new world built on top of the old; a giant stilt village perched over the dark, still lake of antiquity.

Thirty decks – 300 levels – high, each of its hexagonal, hive-like stacks two li to a side; there had seemed space enough to hold any number of people. Let Mankind multiply, the Planners had said; there is room enough for all. So it had seemed, back then. Yet in the century that followed, the population of Chung Kuo had grown like never before.

Thirty-four billion people at last count, Han and European – Hung Mao – combined. And more each year. So many more that in fifty years the City would be full, the storage houses emptied. Put simply, the City was an ever-widening mouth, an ever-larger stomach. It was a thing that ate and shat and grew.

Li Shai Tung sighed then made his way up the broad, shallow steps and into his private apartment. Dismissing the two attendants, he went across and pulled the doors closed.

It was no good. He would have to bring the matter up in Council. The Seven would have to discuss population controls, like it or no. Or else? Well, at best he saw things stabilized: the City going on into the future; his sons and grandsons born to rule in peace. And at worst?

Uncharacteristically, Li Shai Tung put his hands to his face. He had been having dreams. Dreams in which he saw the Cities burning. Dreams in which old friends were dead – brutally murdered in their beds, their children's bodies torn and bloodied on the nursery floor.

In his dreams he saw the darkness bubble up into the bright-lit levels. Saw the whole vast edifice slide down into the mire of chaos. Saw it as clearly as he saw his hands, now, before his face.

Yet it was more than dreams. It was what would happen – unless they acted.

Li Shai Tung, T'ang, ruler of City Europe, one of the Seven, shuddered. Then, smoothing the front of his *pau*, he sat down at his desk to compose his speech for Council. And as he wrote he was thinking.

We didn't simply change the past, as others tried to do, we built over it, as if to erase it for all time. We tried to do what Mao, in his time, attempted with his Cultural Revolution. What the First Han Emperor, Ch'in Shih Huang-ti, tried to do, two thousand four hundred years ago, when he burned the books and built the Great Wall to keep the northern barbarians from the Middle Kingdom. We have not learned from history. We have preferred to ignore its counsel. But now history is catching up with us. The years ahead will show how wise a course we set. Or blame us for our folly.

He liked the shape of his thoughts and set them down. Finished, he got up and went back down the steps to the viewing circle. Darkness was slowly encroaching on City Europe, drawing a stark, dividing line – a terminator – across its hollowed geometric shape, north to south.

No, he thought. *We haven't learned. We have been unwise. And now our own Long March is fast approaching. The bright days of ease – of unopposed rule – lie in our past. Ahead lies only darkness.*

The old man sighed again, then straightened, feeling the imaginary cold in his bones. Chung Kuo. Would it survive the coming times? Would a son of his look down, as he looked now, and see a world at peace? Or was Change come again, like a serpent, blighting all?

Li Shai Tung turned, then stopped, listening. It came again. An urgent pounding on the outer doors. He made his way through and stood before them.

'Who is it?'

'*Chieh Hsia!* Forgive me. It is I, Chung Hu-Yan.'

Coming so hard upon his thoughts, the tone of panic in his Chancellor's voice alarmed Li Shai Tung. He threw the doors open.

Chung Hu-Yan stood there, his head bowed low, his mauve sleeping gown pulled tightly about his tall, thin frame. His hair was unbraided and uncombed. It was clear he had come straight from his bed, not stopping to prepare himself.

'What is it, Chung?'

Chung fell to his knees. 'It is Lin Yua, *Chieh Hsia*. It seems she has begun...'

'*Begun?*' Instinct made him control his voice, his face and his breathing. But inside, his heart hammered and his stomach dropped away. Lin Yua, his first wife, was only six months into her pregnancy. How could she have begun? He took a sharp breath, willing himself to be calm.

'Quick, Chung. Take me to her at once.'

The doctors looked up from the bedside as he entered, then bowed low and backed hastily away. But the fear in their eyes told him more than he wanted to know.

He looked beyond them, to her bed. 'Lin Yua!'

He ran across the room, then stopped, his fear transformed into an icy certainty.

'Gods...' he said softly, his voice breaking. 'Kuan Yin preserve us!'

She lay there, her face pale as the harvest moon, her eyes closed, a blue tinge to her lips and cheeks. The sheets were rucked up beneath her naked legs, as if from some titanic struggle, their whiteness stained almost black with her blood. Her arms lay limply at her sides.

He threw himself down beside her, cradling her to him, sobbing uncontrollably, all thought of sovereign dignity gone from him. She was still warm. Horribly, deceptively warm. He turned her face and kissed it, time and again, as if kissing would bring the life back to it, then began to talk to her, his voice pleading with her.

'Lin Yua... Lin Yua... My little peach. My darling little one. Where are you, Lin Yua? The gods help us, where *are* you?'

He willed her eyes to open. To smile and say that this was all a game – a test to see how much he loved her. But it was no game. Her eyes stayed closed, their lids impenetrably white; her mouth devoid of breath. And, at last, he knew.

Gently he laid her head against the pillow, then, with his fingers, combed her hair back lovingly from her brow. Shivering, he sat back from her, then looked up at his Chancellor, his voice hollow with disbelief.

'She's dead, Hu-Yan. My little peach is dead.'

'*Chieh Hsia*...' The Chancellor's voice quivered with emotion. For once he did not know what to do, what to say. She had been such a strong woman. So filled with life. For her to die... No, it was an impossibility. He stared back at the T'ang, his own eyes filled with tears, and mutely shook his head.

There was movement behind him. He turned and looked.

It was a nurse. She held a tiny bundle. Something still and silent. He stared at her, appalled, and shook his head violently.

'No, Excellency,' the woman began, bowing her head respectfully. 'You misunderstand...'

Chung Hu-Yan glanced fearfully at the T'ang. Li Shai Tung had turned away; was staring down at his dead wife once again. Knowing he must do something, Chung turned and grabbed the woman's arm. Only then did he see that the child was alive within the blankets.

'It lives?' His whisper held a trace of disbelief.

'*He* lives, Excellency. It's a boy.'

Chung Hu-Yan gave a short laugh of surprise. 'Lin Yua gave birth to a boy?'

'Yes, Excellency. Four catties he weighs. Big for one born so early.'

Chung Hu-Yan stared at the tiny child, then turned and looked back at the T'ang. Li Shai Tung had not noted the woman's entrance. Chung licked his lips, considering things, then decided.

'Go,' he told the nurse. 'And make sure the child is safe. Your life is forfeit if he dies. Understand me, woman?'

The woman swallowed fearfully, then bowed her head low. 'I understand, Excellency. I'll take good care of him.'

Chung turned back, then went and stood beside the T'ang.

'*Chieh Hsia*?' he said, kneeling, bowing his head.

Li Shai Tung looked up, his eyes bleak, unfocused, his face almost unrecognizable in its grief.

'*Chieh Hsia*, I...'

Abruptly, the T'ang stood and pushed roughly past his Chancellor, ignoring him, confronting instead the group of five doctors who were still waiting on the far side of the room.

'Why was I not summoned earlier?'

The most senior of them stepped forward, bowing. 'It was felt, *Chieh Hsia*...'

'Felt?' The T'ang's bark of anger took the old man by surprise. Pain and fury had transformed Li Shai Tung. His face glowered. Then he leaned forward and took the man forcibly by the shoulder, throwing him backward.

He stood over him threateningly. '*How did she die?*'

The old man glanced up fearfully, then scrambled to his knees again, lowering his head abjectly. 'It was her age, *Chieh Hsia*. Forty-two is late to have a child. And then there are the conditions here. They make it dangerous even for a normal labour. Back on Chung Kuo...'

'You incompetent butchers! You murderers! You...'

Li Shai Tung's voice failed. He turned and looked back helplessly at his dead wife, his hands trembling, his lips parted in surprise. For a moment longer he stood there, lost in his pain. Then, with a shudder, he turned back, his face suddenly set, controlled.

'Take them away from here, Chung Hu-Yan,' he said coldly, his eyes filled with loathing. 'Take them away and have them killed.'

'*Chieh Hsia?*' The Chancellor stared at him, astonished. Grief had transformed his master.

The T'ang's voice rose in a roar. 'You heard me, Master Chung! Take them away!'

The man at his feet began to plead. '*Chieh Hsia!* Surely we might be permitted...'

He glared at the old man, silencing him, then looked up again. Across from him the others, greybeards all, had fallen to their knees in supplication. Now, unexpectedly, Chung Hu-Yan joined them.

'*Chieh Hsia*, I beg you to listen. If you have these men killed, the lives of all their kin will be forfeit too. Let them choose an honourable death. Blame them for Lin Yua's death, yes, but let their families live.'

Li Shai Tung gave a visible shudder. His voice was soft now, laced with pain. 'But they killed my wife, Chung. They let Lin Yua die.'

Chung touched his head to the floor. 'I know, *Chieh Hsia*. And for that they will be only too glad to die. But spare their families, I beg you, *Chieh Hsia*. You owe them that much. After all, they saved your son.'

'My son?' The T'ang looked up, surprised.

'Yes, *Chieh Hsia*. You have a son. A second son. A strong, healthy child.'

Li Shai Tung stood there, frowning fiercely, trying hard to take in this latest, unexpected piece of news. Then, very slowly, his face changed yet again. The pain pushed through his mask of control until it cracked and fell away and he stood there, sobbing bitterly, his teeth clenched in anguish, tears running down his face.

'Go,' he said finally in a small voice, turning away from them in a gesture of dismissal. 'Order it as you will, Chung. But go. I must be alone with her now.'

YANG

t was dark where they sat, at the edge of the terrace overlooking the park. Behind them the other tables were empty now. Inside, at the back of the restaurant, a single lamp shone dimly. Nearby, four waiters stood in shadow against the wall, silent, in attendance. It was early morning. From the far side of the green came the sounds of youthful laughter; unforced, spontaneous. Above them the night sky seemed filled with stars; a million sharp-etched points of brilliance against the velvet blackness.

'It's beautiful,' said Wyatt, looking down. 'You know, sometimes just the sight of it makes me want to cry. Don't you ever feel that?'

Lehmann laughed softly, then reached out to touch his friend's arm. 'I know...'

Wyatt let his head tilt back. He was drunk. They were all drunk, or they wouldn't be speaking like this. It was treason. The sort of thing a man whispered, or kept to himself. Yet it had to be said. Now. Tonight. Before they broke this intimacy and went their own directions.

He leaned forward, his right hand resting on the table, the fist clenched tightly. 'And sometimes I feel stifled. Boxed in. There's an ache in me. Something unfulfilled. A *need*. And when I look up at the stars I get angry. I think of the waste, the stupidity of it. Trying to keep it all bottled up. What do they think we are? Machines?' He laughed; a painful laugh, surprised by it all. 'Can't they *see* what they're doing to us?'

There was a murmur, of sympathy and agreement.

'They can see,' said Berdichev, matter-of-factly, stubbing out his cigar, his glasses reflecting the distant image of the stars.

Wyatt looked at him. 'Maybe. But sometimes I wonder. You see, it seems to me there's a whole dimension missing. From my life. From yours, Soren, and yours, Pietr. From *everyone's* life. Perhaps the very thing that makes us fully human.' He leaned forward dangerously on his chair. 'There's no place for growth any more – no more white spaces on the map.'

Lehmann answered him drily. 'Quite the contrary, Edmund. There's nothing *but* white.'

There was laughter, then, for a short time, silence. The ceiling of the great dome moved imperceptibly, turning about the illusory axis of the north star.

It had been a good night. They had just returned from the Clay, the primitive, unlit region beneath the City's floor. Eight days they had been together in that ancient netherworld of rotting brick and savage half-men. Days that had marked each of them in their own way. Returning, they had felt good, but now their mood had changed. When Wyatt next spoke there was real bitterness in his voice.

'They're killing us all. Slowly. Irreversibly. From the inside out. Their stasis is a kind of poison. It hollows the bones.'

Lehmann shifted uneasily in his chair. Wyatt turned, then saw his friend's discomfort and fell silent. The Han waiter came out from the shadows close by, holding a tray before him.

'More *ch'a*, sirs?'

Berdichev turned sharply, his face dark with anger. 'Have you been listening?'

'Sir?' The Han's face froze into a rictus of politeness, but Wyatt, watching, saw the fear in his eyes.

Berdichev climbed to his feet and faced the waiter, leaning over him threateningly, almost a head taller than the Han.

'You heard me clearly, Old Hundred Names. You were listening to our conversation, weren't you?'

The waiter lowered his head, stung by the bitterness in Berdichev's voice. 'No, honoured sir. I heard nothing.' His face remained as before, but now his hands trembled, making the bowls rattle on the tray.

Wyatt stood. 'Soren, please...'

Berdichev stood there a moment, scowling at the man, his resentment like something palpable, flowing out across the space between them. Then he turned away, glancing briefly at Wyatt.

Wyatt looked across at the waiter and nodded. 'Fill the bowls. Then leave us. Put it all on my bill.'

The Han bowed, his eyes flashing gratitude at Wyatt, then quickly did as he was asked.

'Fucking chinks!' Berdichev muttered, once the Han was out of earshot. He leaned forward and picked up his bowl. 'You have to watch what you say these days, Edmund. Even small Han have big ears.'

Wyatt watched him a moment, then shrugged. 'I don't know. They're not so bad.'

Berdichev laughed scornfully. 'Devious little shit-eaters. That's what they are.' He stared out across the green, pulling his silk *pau* tighter about his neck. 'I'd rather hand all my companies over to my bitterest rival than have a single one of them in a senior management position.'

Lehmann sighed and reached out for his bowl. 'I find them useful enough. In their own way.'

'As servants, yes...' Berdichev laughed sourly, then finished his *ch'a* and set the bowl down heavily. 'You know what they call us behind our backs? Big noses! The cheek of it! Big noses!'

Wyatt looked at Lehmann and both men laughed. He reached out and touched Berdichev's nose playfully. 'Well, it's true in your case, Soren, isn't it?'

Berdichev drew his head back, then smiled, relenting. 'Maybe... But I'll be damned if I'll have the little fuckers taking the piss out of me while they're drawing from my pocket!'

'But isn't that true of all men?' Wyatt insisted, feeling suddenly less drunk. 'I mean... it's not just the Han. Our race – the *Hung Mao* – aren't most of us like that?'

'Speak for yourself,' Lehmann said, leaning back, his whole manner poised, indifferent. 'However, the Han rule this world of ours, and that changes things. It makes even the most vulgar little Han think he's a T'ang.'

'Fucking true!' said Berdichev, wiping at his mouth. 'They're arrogant little shits, one and all!'

Wyatt shrugged, unconvinced, then looked from one of his friends to the other. They were harder, stronger men than him. He recognized that. Yet there was something flawed in each of them – some lack of sympathy that marred their natures, fine as they were. He had noted it, down there in the Clay: had seen how they took for granted what he had found horrifying.

Imagination, he thought. It has to do with imagination. With putting yourself in someone else's place. Like the waiter, just then. Or like the woman I met, down there, in the awful squalor of the Clay.

He shivered and looked down at his untouched *ch'a*. He could still see her. Could see the room where they had kept her. Mary, her name had been. Mary…

The thought of it chilled his blood. She was still there. There, in the room where he had left her. And who knew which callous bastard would use her next; would choose to beat her senseless, as she had been beaten so often before.

He saw himself again. Watched as he lifted her face to the light and traced the bruise about her eye with his fingers. Gently, aware of how afraid she was of him. He had slept with her finally, more out of pity than from any sense of lust. Or was that fair? Wasn't curiosity part of what he'd felt? She'd been so small, her arms so thin, her breasts almost non-existent. And yet pretty, strangely pretty, for all that. Her eyes, particularly, had held some special quality – the memory, perhaps, of something better than this she had fallen into.

He had been wrong to leave her there. What choice did he have? That was her place, this was his. So it was fated in this world. And yet there must be something he could do.

'What are you thinking, Edmund?'

He looked up, meeting Lehmann's eyes. 'I was thinking about the woman.'

'The woman?' Berdichev glanced across at him, then laughed. 'Which one? There were hundreds of the scrawny things!'

'And boys…'

'We won't forget the boys…'

He looked away, unable to join their laughter, angry with himself for feeling as he did. Then his anger took a sudden shape and he turned back, leaning across the table.

'Tell me, Soren. If you could have one thing – just one single thing – what would it be?'

Berdichev stared across the darkened green a while, then turned and looked back at him, his eyes hidden behind the lenses of his glasses. 'No more Han.'

Lehmann laughed. 'That's quite some wish, Soren.'

Wyatt turned to him. 'And you, Pietr? The truth this time. No flippancy.'

Lehmann leaned back, staring up at the dome's vast curve above them. 'That there,' he said, lifting his arm slowly and pointing. 'That false image of the sky above us. I'd like to make that real. Just that. To have an open sky above our heads. That and the sight of the stars. Not a grand illusion, manufactured for the few, but the reality of it – for everyone.'

Berdichev looked up solemnly, nodding. 'And you, Edmund? What's the one thing you'd have?'

Wyatt looked across at Berdichev, then at Lehmann. 'What would I want?'

He lifted his untouched bowl and held it cupped between his hands. Then, slowly, deliberately, he turned it upside down, letting the contents spill out across the table's top.

'Hey!' said Berdichev, moving backwards sharply. Both he and Lehmann stared at Wyatt, astonished by the sudden hardness in his face, the uncharacteristic violence of the gesture.

'Change,' Wyatt said defiantly. 'That's what I want. Change. That above everything. Even life.'

PART SIX   A Spring Day at the Edge of the World

SPRING 2196

'A spring day at the edge of the world.
On the edge of the world once more the day slants.
The oriole cries, as though it were its own tears
Which damp even the topmost blossoms on the tree.'
—Li Shang-yin, *Exile*, 9th century AD

CHAPTER 26

FIRE AND ICE

Flames danced in a glass. Beyond, in the glow of the naked fire, a man's face smiled tightly.

'Not long now,' he said, coming closer to the fierce, wavering light. He had delicate, oriental features that were almost feminine; a small, well-shaped nose and wide, dark eyes that caught and held the fire's light. His jet black hair was fastened in a pigtail then coiled in a tight bun at the back of his head. He wore white, the colour of mourning – a simple one-piece that fitted his small frame loosely.

A warm night wind blew across the mountainside, making the fire flare up. The coals at its centre glowed intensely. Ash and embers whirled off. Then the wind died and the shadows settled.

'They've taken great pains, Kao Jyan.'

The second man walked back from the darkness where he'd been standing and faced the other across the flames, his hands open, empty. He was a much bigger man, round-shouldered and heavily muscled. His large, bony head was freshly shaven and his whites fitted him tightly. His name was Chen and he had the blunt, nondescript face of a thousand generations of Han peasants.

Jyan studied his partner momentarily. 'They're powerful men,' he said. 'They've invested much in us. They expect much in return.'

'I understand,' Chen answered, looking down the moonlit valley towards the City. Then, unexpectedly, he laughed.

Jyan narrowed his eyes. 'What is it?'

'See?' Chen pointed off to his right. 'There! Up there where the mountains almost touch the clouds.'

Jyan looked. Thin strands of wispy cloud lay across the moon's full circle, silvered by its intense light. Beyond, the sky was a rich blue-black. 'So?'

Chen turned back to him, his eyes shining in the firelight. 'It's beautiful, don't you think? How the moonlight has painted the mountain tops white.'

Jyan shivered, then stared past the big man towards the distant peaks. 'It's ice.'

'What? Plastic, you mean?'

Jyan shook his head. 'No. Not the stuff the City's made of. Real ice. Frozen water. Like the ch'un tzu put in their drinks.'

Chen turned and looked again, his broad face wrinkling. Then he looked away sharply, as if the very thought disturbed him.

As it should, thought Jyan, aware of his own discomfort. The drugs he'd been given made all of this seem familiar – gave him false memories of such things as cold and clouds and moonlight – yet, beneath the surface calm of his mind, his body was still afraid.

There was a faint movement against his cheek, a sudden ruffling of his hair. At his feet the fire flared up again, fanned by the sudden gust. *Wind*, thought Jyan, finding it strange even to think the word. He bent down and lifted a log from the pile, turning it in his hand and feeling its weight. Then he turned it on its end and stared at the curious whorl of its grain. Strange. Everything so strange out here, outside the City. So unpredictable. All of it so crudely thrown together. So unexpected, for all that it seemed familiar.

Chen came and stood by him. 'How long now?'

Jyan glanced at the dragon timer inset into the back of his hand. 'Four minutes.'

He watched Chen turn and – for what seemed like the hundredth time – look back at the City, his eyes widening, trying to take it in.

The City. It filled the great northern plain of Europe. From where they stood, on the foothills of the Alps, it stretched away northward a thousand five hundred *li* to meet the chill waters of the Baltic, while to the west the great wall of its outer edge towered over the Atlantic for the full three thousand *li* length of its coastline, from Cape St Vincent in the south to Kristiansund in the rugged north. To the south, beyond the huge mountain ranges of the Swiss Wilds, its march continued, ringing the Mediterranean like a giant bowl of porcelain. Only to the east had its growth been checked in a jagged line that ran from Danzig in the north to Odessa in the south. There the plantations began; a vast sea of greenness that swept into the heart of Asia.

'It's strange, isn't it? Being outside. It doesn't seem real.'

Chen did not answer. Looking past him, Jyan saw how the dark, steep slopes of the valley framed a giant, flat-topped arrowhead of whiteness. It was like a vast wall – a dam two li in height – plugging the end of the valley. Its surface was a faintly opalescent pearl, lit from within. Ch'eng, it was. City and wall. The same word in his mother tongue for both. Not that he knew more than a smattering of his mother tongue.

He turned his head and looked at Chen again. Brave Chen. Unimaginative Chen. His blunt face rounded like a plate, his bull neck solid as the rocks surrounding them. Looking at him, Jyan put aside his earlier misgivings. Chen was kwai, after all – a trained knife – and kwai were utterly reliable. Jyan smiled to himself. Yes, Chen was all right. A good man to have at your back.

'You're ready?' he asked.

Chen looked back at him, his eyes firm, determined. 'I know what I have to do.'

'Good.'

Jyan looked down into his glass. Small tongues of flame curled like snakes in the darkness of the wine; cast evanescent traces on the solid curve of transparency. He threw the glass down into the fire, then stared into the flames themselves, aware for the first time how evasive they were; how, when you tried to hold their image clear in mind, it slipped away, leaving only the vaguest of impressions. Not real at all, for all its apparent clarity. Perhaps that's how the gods see us, he thought; as mere traces, too brief for the eye to settle on.

There was a sharp crack as the glass split and shattered. Jyan shivered, then looked up, hearing the low drone of the approaching craft.

'They're here,' said Chen, his face impassive.

Jyan looked across at the kwai and nodded. Then, buttoning their one-pieces at the neck, the two assassins made their way towards the ship.

★

'Your pass, sir?'

Pi Ch'ien, Third Secretary to Junior Minister Yang, glanced up at the camera, noting as he did the slow, smooth movement of the overhead trackers, the squat, hollowed tongues of their barrels jutting from the mouths of stylized dragons. Bowing low, he took the card from his robe and inserted it into the security slot. Placing his face against the moulded pad in the wall, he held his left eye open against the camera lens, then stepped back, looking about him.

He had never been into one of the Imperial Solariums before. Even as District Magistrate, responsible for the lives of the twenty thousand people in his deck, he had lacked the status to enter such a place. Now, however, as Third Secretary to Yang Lai, he had been permitted to place his name on the list. But the list was a list, like all the others in this world – interminable. It would be many years and several more promotions before he would find himself inside for reasons of leisure.

The outer doors slid back.

An armed guard barred his way, indicating with his gun that Pi Ch'ien should go into the antechamber to his left. With a bow, Pi Ch'ien did as he was bid. Inside, in front of a vast, brightly coloured tapestry that filled the whole of the back wall, an official sat at a desk. The man scanned the screen in front of him, then looked up, smiling.

'Good evening, Third Secretary Pi. I am First Steward Huong. Might I ask the purpose of your visit?'

Pi Ch'ien bent his head respectfully.

'Greetings, First Steward Huong. I have but a trivial message to deliver. For his serene excellency, Junior Minister Yang Lai. Ten thousand pardons for imposing on you like this, for it is a matter of the least urgency.'

He looked up, holding out the almost translucent message card for the Steward's inspection. Both men knew it was immensely important.

'Forgive me, Third Secretary Pi, but might I have that?'

Again Pi Ch'ien lowered his head. 'My deepest apologies, First Steward Huong. Nothing would please me more than to oblige you, but I am afraid that is not possible. I was instructed to place the message, unimportant as it is, only in the hands of the most illustrious Junior Minister himself.'

Steward Huong stood, then came round his desk to stand beside Pi Ch'ien. 'I understand, Third Secretary Pi. We are but our masters' hands, neh?' He smiled again, all courtesy now. 'If you would be so kind as to permit me, I shall inform the Junior Minister.'

Pi Ch'ien bowed, feeling a pang of disappointment. He was not to go inside, then?

'Please, follow me, Third Secretary,' the Steward said, making the slightest bow, his head barely lowered as befitted their relative positions. 'Junior Minister Yang is with the Minister himself and may not be disturbed. However, I will have a maid come and serve tea for you while you wait.'

Pi Ch'ien bowed again, delighted by the courtesy he was being shown. He followed the official out and down a wide, high-ceilinged corridor on the walls of which hung a series of huge *shanshui*, landscape paintings, depicting rugged peaks and pleasantly wooded valleys.

Where the corridor turned he had a brief glimpse of another, more ornate passageway lined with bronze statues of gods and dragons, and at its end a huge, brightly lit chamber – the solarium itself. They walked on until they came to a small but plushly decorated room, hung with colourful tapestries.

First Steward Huong turned to him and smiled, indicating that he should enter and take a seat. 'Please be assured, I will keep you no longer than I must, Third Secretary. The maid, meanwhile, will see to all your needs.' Then, with a bow, he was gone.

Almost at once a maid entered from a door to one side. She was wearing powder blue er-silks with a pattern of tiny yellow sunflowers. Smiling, she set down the tray she was carrying on a low table at Pi Ch'ien's side, then knelt and bowed low to him. Straightening up, she poured the *ch'a* and offered it to him, her eyes averted. He took the cup, studying her closely. She was a pretty little thing, her skin almost white, her dark, fine hair tied with silk ribbons of blue and yellow. He looked down at her feet and saw, with satisfaction, how petite she was.

'You would like something else, sir?'

He leaned forward and gently drew back the hair to reveal her neck. It was as he had thought. There was a small circular mark low down on the left hand side of the neck, close to the collar bone. A Capital G with a smaller S inside, the letters English, but the style – the brushwork of the design – pure Han. She was GenSyn. Artificial.

He hesitated, not knowing how long the Junior Minister would be, or what etiquette prevailed here. Then he remembered the First Steward

Huong's words. 'The maid will see to all your needs.' Screwing up his courage, he told the girl to close the door.

As she turned to face him again, he beckoned her back. Then, making her bow before him, he opened the front of his cloak and drew her head down into his naked lap.

'Here, girl. See to me.'

The three men in the craft had been masked and silent; even so, Kao Jyan had recognized them as *Hung Mao* – whites – from the sour, milky scent of their sweat. It had surprised him. His own guesses had taken him in another direction. But even as the craft set down on the roof of the City he was adding this new fragment to what he already knew.

When the door hissed open he went through quickly, followed by Chen. The dome of the Imperial Solarium was directly ahead of them, no more than a li – five hundred metres – distant; a vast hemispherical blister, lit from within. Half a li further on was the maintenance shaft. The two assassins ran, side by side, in silence, knowing that if others hadn't done their work properly they were already as good as dead.

But it would be okay. Jyan sensed it. Every step he took made him more certain of it. He was beginning to see how things connected, could even begin to make guesses as to names and motives.

There were those who would pay well to know such things. Who would grant amnesties, perhaps, to those who were merely the tools of other men.

Coming closer to the dome, Jyan slowed, looking about him. The moon was much lower now, over to the right of them. In its light it seemed as though they were running on the surface of a giant glacier.

'Circle left,' he said softly to Chen. But it was unnecessary. Chen was already moving out around the dome towards the shaft. It was his job to secure it while Jyan was at work.

Jyan stopped, looking down at the dragon on his wrist. Timing was crucial now. He had four minutes to climb the outer wall, then three minutes apiece after that to position and set each of the four charges. That left nine minutes to get into the shaft and away. If all went well it would be easy.

If all went well. Jyan took a deep breath, steeling himself.

He knelt, then reached behind him. Four catches fastened the lightweight parcel. Gently his fingers released the catches and eased the cloth-wrapped package from his back. Carefully he laid it in his lap and, with delicate, practised movements, drew back the thin folds of cloth.

The four plate-sized hoops had been bound together tightly with a hair-fine wire. They were a dull bronze in colour, unmarked except in one place, where it seemed the finger-thick cords joined upon themselves, like snakes swallowing their tails. Quickly, carefully, he untied the wire knots and separated the hoops into two piles on his upper thighs. They were warm to the touch, as if alive. With the slightest shudder he pulled two of them up over his left arm, looping them gently over his shoulder, then did the same with the others, securing them about his right shoulder.

Taking a deep breath, he stood again. Chen was out of sight, behind the dome. Quickly Jyan ran the final distance to the dome's base and crouched there, breathing easily. From the pocket over his heart he took out the claws and clicked them open. Separating them, he eased them onto his hands, respecting the razor-sharpness of their tips. That done, he began to climb.

Lwo Kang, son of Lwo Chun-Yi and Minister of the Edict, sat back in his tall-backed chair and looked around the circle of men gathered about him. The folds of his salmon pink *pau* hung loosely about him and his olive flesh glistened damply in the dome's intense light. He had a strong, but some-how ugly face; his eyes too big, his nose too broad, his ears too pendulous. Yet when he smiled the faces of the dozen men seated about him returned his smile like mirrors. Just now, however, those men were silent and watchful, conscious that their lord was angry.

'You talk of accommodation, Shu San, but the Edict is quite clear on this. We are not here to interpret but to implement. We do as we are told, neh?'

To Lwo Kang's left, Shu San bowed his head abjectly. For a moment all eyes were on him, sharing his moment of shame. Minister Lwo sniffed, then spoke again.

'Only this afternoon two of these businessmen – Lehmann and Berdichev – came to me. We talked of many things in the course of our audience, but finally they presented me with what they termed an "ultimatum".' Lwo Kang looked sternly about the circle of his junior ministers. 'They said that certain factions were growing impatient. *Hsien Sheng* Lehmann even had the impudence to claim that we have been subjecting them to unnecessary delays. He says that our officials have been overzealous in their application of the Edict's terms.'

There was an exchange of glances between the seated men. None had missed that the Minister had used the term *Hsien Sheng* for Lehmann – plain *Mister* Lehmann, not even the commonplace *Shih* or *Master* – when proper etiquette demanded the use of his full title, Under Secretary. It was a deliberate slight.

Lwo Kang laughed sharply, sourly, then shook his head in an angry gesture. 'The impertinence of these men! Because they have money they think themselves above the laws of other men!' His face formed a sneer of disgust. '*Hsin fa ts'ai!*'

This time there was mild laughter from some quarters. Others, not understanding the term, looked about them for guidance, and formed their faces into smiles, as if half-committed to the joke.

Again Lwo Kang sniffed and sat back a little in his chair. 'I'm sorry. I forgot. We are not all *ch'un tzu* here, are we?'

Lwo Kang looked about him. *Hsin fa ts'ai*. Social upstarts. *Ch'un tzu*. Gentlemen. These were *Kuan hua*, or Mandarin terms. But not all were bred to the tongue who sat about him. More than half the men here had come up through the levels; had schooled themselves in the five Confucian classics and climbed the ladder of the examination system. He did not despise them for that; quite the contrary, he prided himself on promoting men not through connection but because of their natural ability. However, it sometimes made for awkwardnesses. He fixed his gaze on Shu San.

'We will say no more of this, Shu San. You know now how I feel. We will have no further talk of accommodation. Neither will I see these men again.'

Shu San bowed his head, then met his lord's eyes, grateful for this second chance. He had come expecting less.

Lwo Kang smiled and looked away, his whole manner changing, relaxing. He had the reputation of being a scrupulously fair man, honest beyond reproach and incorruptible. But that was not to say he was liked. His appointment, three years earlier, had surprised some who saw family connection as a more important quality in a man than honesty or competence. Nonetheless, Lwo Kang had proved a good choice as Minister responsible for the implementation of the Edict.

While his subordinates talked among themselves, Lwo Kang sat back, contemplating what had happened earlier that day. It did not surprise him that there were those who wanted to subvert the Edict's guidelines. So it had ever been, for the full 120 years of the Edict's existence. What disturbed him more was the growing arrogance of those who felt they knew best – that they had the right to challenge the present order of things. These *Hung Mao* had no sense of place. No sense of *Li*. Of *propriety*.

The problem was one of race. Of culture. Though more than a century had passed since the foundation of Chung Kuo and the triumph of Han culture, for those of European stock – the *Hung Mao*, or 'redheads' as they were commonly known – the ways of the Han were still unnatural; were at best surface refinements grafted on to a cruder and less stable temperament. Three thousand years of unbroken civilization – that was the heritage of the Han. Against that these large-nosed foreigners could claim what? Six centuries of chaos and ill-discipline. Wars and further wars and, ultimately, collapse. Collapse on a scale that made their previous wars seem like oases of calm. No, they might seem like Han – might dress and talk and act like Han – but beneath it all they remained barbarians. The New Confucianism was rooted only shallowly in the infertile soil of their natures. At core they were still the same selfish, materialistic, individualistic species they had ever been; motivated more by greed than duty.

Was it so surprising, then, that men like Lehmann and Berdichev failed to understand the necessity of the Edict?

Change, they wanted. Change, at any cost. And because the Edict of Technological Control was the Seven's chief means of preventing the cancer of change, it was the Edict they tried to undermine at every turn.

Lwo Kang leaned back, staring up at the roof of the dome high overhead. The two great arches of the solarium met in a huge circular tablet, halved by a snake-like S into black and white. *Yin* and *Yang*, he thought. Balance. These Westerners have never understood it; not properly – not in their bones. It still seems some kind of esoteric game to them, not life itself, as it is to us. Change – the empty-headed pursuit of the new – that was the real enemy of civilization.

He sighed, then leaned to his right, listening, becoming at once the focus of their talk.

They are good men, he thought, looking along the line of faces. Han, every one of them. *Men I could trust my life with.*

Servants passed amongst them, dumb mutes who carried trays of ch'a and sweetmeats. GenSyn eunuchs, half-men in more senses than one. Yet even they were preferable to the likes of Lehmann and Berdichev.

Yang Lai was talking now, the tenor of his words strangely reflective of Lwo Kang's thoughts.

'It's a disease that's rife amongst the whole of this new generation. Things have changed, I tell you. They are not like their fathers, solid and dependable. No, they're ill-mannered brutes, every last one of them. And they think they can buy change.'

Lwo Kang stretched his bull neck and nodded. 'They lack respect.'

There was a murmur of agreement. Yang Lai bowed, then answered him. 'That's true, my lord. But then, they are not Han. They could never be ch'un tzu. They have no values. And look at the way they dress!'

Lwo Kang smiled, sitting back again. Though only in his late thirties he was already slightly balding. He had inherited his father's looks – a thick-set body already going to fat at waist and upper chest – and, like his father, he had never found the time for exercise. He smiled, knowing how he looked to them. *I am not a vain man*, he thought; *and in truth I'd be a liar to myself if I were. Yet I have their respect.*

No, it was not by outward show that a man was to be judged, but by his innermost qualities; qualities that lay behind his every action.

His father, Lwo Chun-Yi, had been born a commoner; even so, he had proved himself worthy and had been appointed Minister to Li Shai Tung in the first years of his reign. Because of that, Lwo Kang had been educated to the highest level and had learned the rudiments of service in his earliest years. Now he in his turn was the T'ang's Minister. He looked about him again, satisfied. No, there was not one here who did not know him for their master.

'What these *Hung Mao* need is a lesson,' he said, leaning forward to take a shrimp and snow pickle sweetmeat from the tray on the footstool next to him. He gulped it down, savouring the sweet, spicy *hoisin* sauce on his tongue, and belched appreciatively. 'A lesson in manners.'

Jyan clung to the outside of the dome like a small, dark insect. Three of the hoops were set. It remained only to place and arm the last charge.

Where he rested, one hand attaching him to the dome's taut skin, the slope was relatively gentle. He could look out over the capped summit of the dome and see the distant, moon-washed peaks. It was a beautiful night. Clear, like glass. Above him the stars shone like polished jewels against the blackness. So many stars. So vast the blackness.

He looked down. *Concentrate*, he told himself. *You've no time for stargazing.* Even so, he took a final glimpse. Then, working quickly, he placed and fastened the hoop, taping it at four points. That done, he tugged gently but firmly at the joint.

Where he pulled at it, the hoop came apart, a thin thread joining tail to mouth. Like a snake's wire-thin tongue. Fully extended, the thread was as long as his little finger. Already it was being coiled back into the body of the hoop. Eventually the ends would join up again and the hoop would send out a trigger signal. When all four were primed, they would form a single, destructive harmonic. And then...

Slowly, carefully, he backed away, edging back down the steepening wall of the dome. Like all else in the City its skin was made of the super-plastic, ice. Normal charges would scarcely have dented the steel-tough, fire-resistant skin, but these would eat right through it before they detonated.

He was balanced at the point where the dome wall fell sharply away when he stopped, hearing a noise beneath him. He turned his head slowly, scarcely daring to breath. *Who in the gods' names...?*

The figure was directly underneath, staring up at him. As Jyan turned his face a brilliant beam of light shone directly into his eyes.

'You! What are you doing up there?'

Jyan looked away, momentarily blinded, then looked back in time to see Chen coming up behind the man.

The man turned quickly, sensing something behind him. As Chen struck out with his knife, the man raised the big torch he was carrying and deflected the blow.

Chen's knife went clattering across the roof.

For a moment the two faced each other warily, then Chen moved, circling the newcomer. He feinted, making the other back off, then dropped to his knees, searching for his knife in the shadows at the base of the dome.

The man looked at his torch, considering whether to use it as a weapon and go for Chen, then turned and ran off to the right, where a faint patch of light revealed a second maintenance hatch.

'*Pien hua!*' swore Jyan under his breath. Loosening the claws, he dropped the last five metres and rolled. Crouched there, he looked about him.

He saw Chen at once, to his right, running after the stranger. But the man was already at the hatch and climbing down.

'Shit!' he said desperately, trying to ease the claws from his hands as quickly as he could. If the bastard got to an alarm they would both be done for.

He looked up in time to see Chen disappear down the hatch.

'Hurry, Chen!' he murmured anxiously, folding the claws and tucking them away in his pocket. He turned, looking back up the dome's steep slope, then glanced down at the dragon timer in his wrist. Six minutes. That was all that remained.

And if Chen failed?

He swallowed drily, then began to run towards the second shaft, his heart pounding in his chest. 'Shit!' he kept saying. 'Shit!'

He was only twenty *ch'i* from it when a figure lifted from the hatch and turned to face him.

He pulled up sharply, gasping with fear, but it was Chen. The *kwai* looked up, the broad shape of his face and chest lit from beneath, his breath pluming up into the chill air.

'Where is he?' hissed Jyan anxiously, hurrying forward again. 'Oh, gods! You didn't let him get away, did you?'

Chen reached down and pulled the man up by the hair. 'He's dead,' he said tonelessly, letting the corpse fall back. 'There was no other way. He was trying to open a Security panel when I came on him. Now we'll have to find somewhere to hide him.'

Jyan shuddered, filled with relief. 'Thank the gods.' He turned and glanced back at the dome. 'Let's go, then. Before it blows.'

'Yes,' said Chen, a faintly ironic smile lighting his big, blunt face. 'The rest should be easy. Like the bamboo before the blade.'

The maid had gone. Pi Ch'ien sat alone in the room, his *ch'a* long finished, contemplating the fifteen-hundred-year-old painting of Wen Ti that hung on the wall above the door. It was Yen Li-pen's famous painting from the *Portraits of the Emperors*, with the Han Emperor attended by his Ministers.

Every schoolboy knew the story of Wen Ti, first of the great Emperors. It was he who, more than twenty-three centuries before, had created the concept of Chung Kuo; who, through his thorough adoption of the Confucian virtues, had made of his vast but ragtag land of warring nations a single State, governed by stern but just principles. Wen Ti it was who had first brought commoners into his government. He who had changed the harsh laws and customs of his predecessors so that no one in the Middle Kingdom would starve or suffer cruel injustice. Famine relief, pensions and the abolition of punishment by mutilation – all these were Wen Ti's doing. He had lowered taxes and done away with the vast expense of Imperial display. He had sought the just criticism of his Ministers and acted to better the lot of the Han. Under his rule Chung Kuo had thrived and its population grown.

Eighteen hundred years later, the Manchu Emperor, K'ang Hsi, had established his great empire on Wen Ti's principles. Later still, when the Seven had thrown off the yoke of the tyrant, Tsao Ch'un, they too had adopted the principles of Wen Ti's reign, making him the First Ancestor of Chung Kuo. Now Wen Ti's painting hung everywhere in the City, in a thousand shapes and forms. This, however, was a particularly fine painting – a perfect reproduction of Yen Li-pen's original.

Pi Ch'ien got up and went over to the painting, remembering the time when his father had stood there with him beneath another copy of the portrait and told him the story of the finding of the handscroll.

For centuries the *Portraits of the Emperors* roll had been housed in a museum in the ancient town of Boston, along with much more that had rightly belonged to the Han. When the American Empire had finally collapsed much had been lost. Most of the old Han treasures had been destroyed out of spite, but some had been hidden away. Years had passed. Then, in the years when the Han were building their City over the old land of America, skilled teams had been sent across that continent to search for any remaining artifacts. Little was found of real value until, in an old, crumbling building on the shoreline of what had once been called California, they had found a simple cardboard box containing the scroll. The handscroll was remarkably preserved considering its ill-use, but even so, four of the original thirteen portraits had been lost. Fortunately, the painting of Wen Ti was one of those that had emerged unscathed.

He turned away and went back to his seat. For a second or two longer he contemplated the painting, delighted by the profound simplicity of its brushwork, then leaned across and picked up the handbell. He was about to lift the tiny wooden hammer to ring for more ch'a when the door swung open and Yang Lai came hurriedly into the room.

Pi Ch'ien scrambled to his feet and bowed low.

'Well, Pi Ch'ien?' Yang Lai barked impatiently. 'What is it?'

His expression showed he was far from pleased by his Third Secretary's intrusion.

Pi Ch'ien remained bowed, the card held out before him.

'I have an urgent message for you, Excellency. I was told to bring it here at once.'

'Give it here!' Yang Lai said irritably.

Pi Ch'ien handed the card across. Yang Lai stared at it a moment, then turned away. With upturned eyes Pi Ch'ien watched him tap his personal code into the Instruct box and place his thumb against the Release.

There was a moment's silence from Yang Lai, then he gasped. When he turned to face Pi Ch'ien again, his face was ashen. For a moment his mouth worked silently, then, without another word, he turned and left the room, his silk cloak flapping as he ran.

Pi Ch'ien lifted his head, astonished. For a moment he stood there, rooted to the spot. Then he rushed across the room and poked his head out into the corridor.

The corridor was empty. There was no sign of Yang Lai.

He looked back into the room. There, on the floor, was the message card. He went across and picked it up, then turned it in his hand, studying it. Without Yang Lai's thumb on the Release pad the surface of the card was blank; even so, it might prove interesting to keep.

Pi Ch'ien hesitated, not certain what to do. Yang Lai had not formally dismissed him; but then, he had fulfilled his duty – had delivered the message. Surely, then, it was all right for him to go. He went to the door and looked out again. The corridor was still empty. Careful now, conscious of the watching cameras, he stepped outside and pulled the door shut behind him. Then, composing himself, trying to ignore the strong feeling of wrongness that was growing in him by the moment, he began to walk towards the entrance hall.

*

There was movement up ahead. Chen crouched in the narrow circle of the horizontal shaft, perfectly still, listening. Beside him, tensed, his breathing like the soft hiss of a machine, Jyan waited.

Chen turned, smiling reassuringly. In the dim overhead light Jyan's face seemed more gaunt than normal, his cheekbones more hollow. The roseate light made him seem almost demonic, his cold, black eyes reflecting back two tiny points of redness. Chen wanted to laugh, looking at him. Such delicate features he had; such neat, small ears. He could imagine how Jyan's mother would have loved those ears – back when Jyan had yet had a mother.

He looked away, sobered by the thought. *It's why we're here*, he realized, waiting, knowing the noise, the movement would go away. *If we had loved ones we would never have got involved in this. We're here because we have no one. Nothing to connect us to the world.*

Chen kept his thoughts to himself; like a good *kwai* he cultivated the appearance of stupidity. Like all else, it was a weapon. He had been taught to let his enemies underestimate him; to always keep something back – something in reserve. And lastly, to make no friends.

Ahead it went silent again. He waited, making sure, then began to move up the access tunnel once more, his right hand feeling his way along the tunnel wall. And as he moved he could sense Jyan immediately behind him; silent, trusting.

Minister Lwo pulled himself up out of his chair and stretched his legs. It was almost time to call it an evening, but first he'd dip his body in the pool and cool off. His Junior Ministers had risen to their feet when he had stood. Now he signalled them to be seated again. 'Please, gentlemen, don't break your talk for me.'

He moved between them, acknowledging their bows, then down three steps and past a lacquered screen, into the other half of the dome. Here was a miniature pool, its chest-deep waters cool and refreshing after the heat of the solarium. Small shrubs and potted trees surrounded it on three sides, while from the ceiling above hung a long, elegant cage, housing a dozen songbirds.

As he stood there at the pool's edge two attendants hurried across to help him undress, then stood there, heads bowed respectfully, holding his clothes, as he eased himself into the water.

He had been there only moments when he heard the pad of feet behind him. It was Lao Jen.

'May I join you, Excellency?'

Lwo Kang smiled. 'Of course. Come in, Jen.'

Lao Jen had been with him longest and was his most trusted advisor. He was also a man with connections, hearing much that would otherwise have passed the Minister by. His sister had married into one of the more important of the Minor Families and fed him juicy titbits of Above gossip. These he passed on to Lwo Kang privately.

Lao Jen threw off his *pau* and came down the steps into the water. For a moment the two of them floated there, facing each other. Then Lwo Kang smiled.

'What news, Jen? You surely have some.'

'Well,' he began, speaking softly so that only the Minister could hear. 'It seems that today's business with Lehmann is only a small part of things. Our friends the Dispersionists are hatching bigger, broader schemes. It seems they have formed a faction – a pressure group – in the House. It's said they have more than two hundred Representatives in their pocket.'

Lwo Kang nodded. He had heard something similar. 'Go on.'

'More than that, Excellency. It seems they're going to push to reopen the starflight programme.'

Lwo Kang laughed. Then he lowered his voice. 'You're serious? The starflight programme?' He shook his head, surprised. 'Why, that's been dead a century and more! What's the thinking behind that?'

Lao Jen ducked his head, then surfaced again, drawing his hand back through his hair. 'It's the logical outcome of their policies. They are, after all, Dispersionists. They want breathing space. Want to be free of the City and its controls. Their policies make no sense unless there is somewhere to disperse to.'

'I've always seen them otherwise, Jen. I've always thought their talk of breathing space was a political mask. A bargaining counter. And all this nonsense about opening up the colony planets, too. No one in their right mind would want to live out there. Why, it would take ten thousand years to colonize the stars!' He grunted, then shook his head. 'No, Jen, it's all a blind. Something to distract us from the real purpose of their movement.'

'Which is what, Excellency?'

Lwo Kang smiled faintly, knowing Lao Jen was sounding him. 'They are *Hung Mao* and they want to rule. They feel we Han have usurped their natural right to control the destiny of Chung Kuo, and they want to see us under. That's all there is to it. All this business of stars and planetary conquest is pure nonsense – the sort of puerile idiocy their minds ran to before we purged them of it.'

Lao Jen laughed. 'Your Excellency sees it clearly. Nevertheless, I...'

He stopped. Both men turned, standing up in the water. It came again. A loud hammering at the inner door of the solarium. Then there were raised voices.

Lwo Kang climbed up out of the water and without stopping to dry himself, took his *pau* from the attendant and pulled it on, tying the sash at the waist. He had taken only two steps forward when a security guard came down the steps towards him.

'Minister!' he said breathlessly, bowing low. 'The alarm has been sounded. We must evacuate the dome!'

Lwo Kang turned, dumbstruck, and looked back at Lao Jen.

Lao Jen was standing on the second step, the water up to his shins. He was looking up. Above him the songbirds were screeching madly and fluttering about their cage.

Lwo Kang took a step back towards Lao Jen, then stopped. There was a small plop and a fizzing sound. Then another. He frowned, then looked up past the cage at the ceiling of the dome. There, directly above the pool, the smooth white skin of the dome was impossibly charred. There, only an arm's length from where the wire that held the cage was attached, was a small, expanding halo of darkness. Even as he watched, small gobbets of melted ice dropped from that dark circle and fell hissing into the water.

'Gods!' he said softly, astonished. 'What in heaven's name... ?'

Then he understood. Understood, at the same moment, that it was already too late. 'Yang Lai,' he said almost inaudibly, straightening up, seeing in his mind the back of his Junior Minister as he hurried from the dome. 'Yes. It must have been Yang Lai...'

But the words were barely uttered when the air turned to flame.

★

The patrol craft was fifteen li out when its tail camera, set on automatic search-and-scan, trained itself on the first brief flicker from the dome. On a panel above the navigator's head a light began to flash. At once the pilot banked the craft steeply, turning towards the trace.

They were almost facing the dome when the whole of the horizon seemed to shimmer and catch fire.

The pilot swore. 'What in *Chang-e*'s name is that?!'

'The mountains...' said the navigator softly, staring in amazement at the overhead screen. 'Something's come down in the mountains!'

'No...' The pilot was staring forward through the windscreen. 'It was much closer than that. Run the tape back.'

He had barely said it when the sound of the explosion hit them, rocking the tiny craft.

'It's the dome!' said the pilot in the stillness that followed. 'It's the fucking solarium!'

'It can't be.'

The pilot laughed, shocked. 'But it's not there! It's not fucking there!'

The navigator stared at him a moment, then looked back up at the screen. The image was frozen at the point where the camera had locked onto the irregular heat pattern.

He leaned forward and touched the display pad. Slowly, a frame at a time, the image changed.

'Gods! Look at that!'

Near the top of the softly glowing whiteness of the dome two eyes burned redly. Slowly they grew larger, darker, the crown of the dome softening, collapsing until the crumpled face of the solarium seemed to leer at the camera, a vivid gash of redness linking two of the four holes that were now visible. For a single frame it formed a death mask, the translucent flesh of the dome brilliantly underlit. Then, in the space of three frames, the whole thing blew apart.

In the first it was veined with tiny cracks – each fissure a searing, eye-scorching filament of fire, etched vividly against the swollen, golden flesh of the dome. As the tape moved on a frame, that golden light intensified, filling the bloated hemisphere to its limit. Light spilled like molten metal from the bloodied mouths that webbed the dome, eating into the surrounding darkness like an incandescent acid. Then, like a flowering wound, the whole thing opened up, the ragged flaps of ice thrown outward violently, flaming like the petals of a honey gold and red chrysanthemum, its bright intensity flecked with darkness.

He reached forward and pressed to hold the image. The screen burned, almost unbearably bright. He turned and stared at his colleague, seeing at once how the other's mouth was open, the inner flesh glistening brightly in the intense, reflected light, while in the polished darkness of his eyes two gold-red flowers blossomed.

'Gods... That's awful... Terrible...'

The flat, Han face of the navigator turned and looked up at the screen. *Yes*, he thought. *Awful. Terrible. And yet quite beautiful. Like a chrysanthemum, quite beautiful.*

CHAPTER 27

THE SILKWORM AND THE MULBERRY LEAF

At the mouth of the narrow, low-ceilinged corridor they had been following, Chen stopped and placed his hand against Jyan's chest, looking out into the wide but crowded thoroughfare beyond.

Pan Chao Street teemed with life. Along both sides of the long, broad avenue ran balconies, four of them, stacked like seed trays one atop another, their low rails packed with people, the space between them criss-crossed with a vast unruly web of lines from which enormous quantities of washing hung, like giant, tattered veils, dripping endlessly onto the crowds below.

A hundred smaller corridors led into Pan Chao Street, the regular pattern of their dark, square mouths peppering the walls behind the balconies, like the openings to a giant hive.

Chen reached out and touched the smooth surface of the hexagonal, graffiti-proof plaque on the wall close by. 'Level Eleven', it read; 'South 3 Stack, Canton of Munich'. Relieved, he looked back, ignoring the curious stares of passers-by. That much, at least, was right. But were they in the right place? Had they come out at the right end?

He glanced at Jyan, then nodded. 'Come on. Let's find that lift.'

It was a noisy, boisterous place And it stank. The sharp, sour-sweet smell of spiced soymeats and overcooked vegetables was mixed inextricably with the sharper scent of human sweat and the damp, warm smell of the washing. Jyan looked at Chen, and grimaced.

'It's worse than beneath the Net!'

Chen nodded. It was true. The air was a rich, unwholesome soup. After the freshness of the higher tunnels it made him feel like retching. Each breath seemed to coat the lungs.

Chen pushed out into the middle of the press, aware of Jyan at his back. Young children, naked, many of them streaked with dirt, ran here and there through the crowd, yelling. Some tugged at their clothes as they passed.

'Ch'ian!' one tiny, shaven-headed boy yelled, pulling at Chen's tunic, then putting his hand out aggressively. *Money!* He could have been no more than three at most. Chen glared at him and raised his hand threateningly, but the child only laughed and ran away, making a sign with his hand that was unmistakable. *And you*, thought Chen. *And you.*

People jostled this way and that, using their elbows and shoulders to force a way through the press. In the midst of it all a few of them simply stood and talked, making deals or just passing the time, oblivious of the noise, the crush, the rickshaws jostling to get by. Some turned and eyed the two men as they made their way through, but most ignored them, intent on their own business.

At the edge of things, small groups of women stood in doorways watching the multitudes, their arms folded over their breasts, their lips moving incessantly, chattering away in the pidgin dialect of these levels. Nearby, traders pushed their barrows through the crowd, crying out in the same strange, sing-song tongue as the watching women. Small MedFac screens were everywhere, on brackets fixed to walls and in shop fronts, on the sides of rickshaws or pushed along in handcarts, their constant murmur barely distinguishable above the general hubbub, while from every side countless PopVoc Squawks blared out, some large as suitcases, others worn as earrings or elaborate bracelets. All added to the dull cacophony of sound.

Chen moved through it all slowly, purposefully, trying not to let it overwhelm him after the empty silence of the maintenance tunnels. His eyes searched for Security patrols, conscious all the while of Jyan at his side, matching him pace for pace. He allowed himself a brief, grim smile. It would be all right. He was sure it would all be fine.

They were mostly Han here, but those *Hung Mao* about were almost indistinguishable in dress or speech. These were Chung Kuo's poor. Here, near the very bottom of the City, you could see the problem the City faced – could touch and smell and hear it. Here it hit you immediately, in the constant push and shove of the crowds that milled about these corridors. Chung Kuo was overcrowded. Wherever you turned there were people; people talking and laughing, pushing and arguing, bargaining and gambling, making love behind thin curtains or moving about quietly in cramped and crowded rooms, watching endless historical dramas while they tended to a clutch of bawling children.

Chen pushed on dourly, swallowing the sudden bitterness he felt. To those who lived a quieter, more ordered life in the levels high above, this would probably have seemed like hell. But Chen knew otherwise. The people of this level counted themselves lucky to be here, above the Net and not below. There was law here and a kind of order, despite the overcrowding. There was the guarantee of food and medical care. And though there was the constant problem of idleness – of too many hands and too few jobs – there was at least the chance of getting out, by luck or hard work; of climbing the levels to a better place than this. Below the Net there was nothing. Only chaos.

Below this level the City had been sealed. That seal was called the Net. Unlike a real net, however, there were no holes in it. It was a perfect, supposedly unbreachable barrier. The architects of City Earth had meant it as a quarantine measure: as a means of preventing the spread of infestation and disease. From the beginning, however, the Seven had found another use for it.

They had been wise, that first Council of the Seven. They had known what some men were; had seen the darkness in their hearts and had realized that, unless they acted, the lowest levels of the City would soon become ungovernable. Their solution had been simple and effective. They had decided to use the Net as a dumping ground for that small antisocial element on whom the standard punishment of downgrading – of demoting a citizen to a lower level – had proved consistently unsuccessful. By that means they hoped to check the rot and keep the levels pure.

To a degree it had worked. As a dumping ground, the Net had served the Seven well. Below the Net there was no citizenship. Down there a man had no rights but those he fought for or earned in the service of other, more powerful men. There was no social welfare there, no healthcare, no magistrates to judge the rights or wrongs of a man's behaviour. Neither was there any legitimate means of returning from the Net. Exile was permanent, on pain of death. It was little wonder, then, that its threat kept the citizens of Pan Chao Street in check.

Chen knew. It was where they came from, he and Jyan. Where they had been born. Down there, below the Net.

And now they were returning.

At the mouth of one of the small alleyways that opened onto Pan Chao Street, a group of young men had gathered in a circle, hunched forward, watching excitedly as a dice rolled. There was a sudden upward movement of their heads; an abrupt, exaggerated movement of arms and hands and shoulders accompanied by a shrill yell from a dozen mouths, a shout of triumph and dismay, followed a moment later by the hurried exchange of money and the making of new bets. Then the young men hunched forward again, concentrating on the next roll.

As they passed the entrance, Jyan turned and stared at the group. He hesitated, then, catching their excitement, began to make his way across.

'Kao Jyan!' Chen hissed, reaching out to restrain him. 'There's no time! We must get on!'

Jyan turned back, a momentary confusion in his face. His movements seemed strangely feverish and uncontrolled. His eyes had difficulty focusing. Chen knew at once what was wrong. The drug he had taken to tolerate the conditions outside the City was wearing off.

Too soon, Chen thought, his mind working furiously. *You must have taken it too early. Before you were told to. And now the reaction's setting in. Too soon. Too bloody soon!*

'Come on, Jyan,' he said, leaning closer and talking into his face. 'We've got to get to the lift!'

Jyan shivered and seemed to focus on him at last. Then he nodded and did as Chen said, moving on quickly through the crowd.

Where Pan Chao Street spilled out into the broad concourse of Main, Chen stopped and looked about him, keeping a grip on Jyan. The bell tower was close by and to his left, the distribution lift far to his right, barely visible, more than a li distant.

Shit! he thought. *I was right. We've come out the wrong end!*

He glanced at Jyan, angry now. He knew they had been in there too long. He had told him they had come too far along the shaft, but Jyan wouldn't have it. 'The next junction,' Jyan had said when Chen had stopped beside the hatch: 'Not this one. The next.' Chen had known at the time that Jyan was wrong, but Jyan had been in charge and so he'd done as he'd said. Now he wished he'd overruled him. They had lost valuable time. Now they'd have to backtrack – out in the open where they could be seen. Where Security could see them. And with Jyan going funny on him.

He leaned close to Jyan and shouted into his ear. 'Just stay beside me. Hold onto my arm if necessary, but don't leave my side.'

Jyan turned his head and looked back at him, his expression vacant. Then, as before, he seemed to come to. 'Okay,' he mouthed. 'Let's go.'

Main, the huge central concourse of Eleven, was a Babel of light and sound, a broad, bloated torrent of humanity that made Pan Chao Street seem a sluggish backwater. Along its length people crowded about the stalls, thick as blackfly on the stem, haggling for bargains, while high above them massive viewscreens hung in clusters from the ceiling, filling the overhead. On the huge, five-level walls to either side of the concourse a thousand flickering images formed and reformed in a nightmare collage. Worst of all, however, was the noise. As they stepped out into the crush the noise hit them like a wave, a huge swell of sound, painful in its intensity, almost unbearable.

Chen gritted his teeth, forcing his way through the thick press of people, holding on tightly to Jyan's arm, thrusting him through the crowd. He looked about him, for the first time really anxious, and saw how the long-time natives of Eleven seemed to ignore the clamour; seemed not to see the giant, dreamlike faces that flickered into sudden existence and followed their every movement down the Main. They knew it was all a clever trick; knew from childhood how the screens responded to their presence. But to a stranger it was different. Nowhere in the City was quite like Eleven. Here, in the first floor above the Net, life seemed in perpetual ferment; as if the knowledge of what lay sealed off just below their feet made them live their lives at a different level of intensity.

Jyan was turning his head from side to side as he moved through the crush, grimacing against the brute intensity of the noise, the awful flickering neon brightness of the screens. Then, abruptly, he turned and faced Chen, leaning into him, shouting into his face.

'I can't stand it, Chen! I can't hear myself think!'

Jyan's face was dreadful to see. His mouth had formed a jagged shape; his round and frightened eyes held a neon glimpse of madness. It was clear he was close to cracking up. Chen held his arms firmly, trying to reassure him through his touch, then leaned close, shouting back his answer. 'Two minutes, Jyan, that's all! We're almost there!'

Jyan shuddered and looked up, away from Chen, his eyes wide. From one of the larger screens a huge head turned and focused on him. It was a classically beautiful oriental face, the eyes like almonds, the skin like satin, the hair fine and straight and dark. Meeting Jyan's eyes she smiled and, somewhere else, a computer matched the face she looked down into against its computer memory of all the faces in that sector of the City.

'You're a stranger here,' she said, after barely a pause, the wire-thin stem of a speaker appendage snaking down to a point just above their heads. 'Are you just visiting us, or have you business here?'

Jyan had frozen. Chen too had turned and was looking up at the screen. 'Come on,' he said tensely. 'It's dangerous here.'

As the seconds passed, and Jyan did not move, the computers spread their search, looking to match the face and find a name. It was good sales technique. This time, however, it came up with nothing. Fourteen near likenesses, but nothing to match the retinal print of the man standing beneath its screen. In a Security post five levels up a warning message flashed up on a screen.

'Come on, Jyan!' Chen said urgently, tugging Jyan away; ignoring the curious looks of passers-by, pulling him along roughly now.

At the end of Main, only a quarter *li* away, the doors to one of the huge delivery lifts were opening. Chen increased his pace, glancing from side to side. As the doors slid slowly back, a number of Ministry of Distribution workers – *chi ch'i* – stepped out, their dark, uniformed figures dwarfed by the huge doors.

Nearer the lift the crowd thinned and the going grew easier. Chen slowed, then stopped and drew Jyan round to face him. The doors were almost fully open now. Already a number of the low-slung electric carts were spilling out into Main, unloading the code-marked crates.

'You know what to do?' Chen asked, his hands gripping the collar of Jyan's jacket tightly. 'You remember what we rehearsed?'

Jyan nodded, his eyes suddenly much clearer. 'I'm all right,' he shouted. 'It was only...'

Chen put his hand to Jyan's mouth. 'No time!' he yelled back. 'Let's just do it!'

There were about thirty *chi ch'i* working the lift. All of them were wearing wraparounds – the bulky headpieces blinkering them from all distractions. Their close-shaven heads and the heavy, black, full-face masks gave them a sombre, distinctly mechanical appearance; an impression which their routine, repetitive movements enhanced. Chen walked towards them casually, aware of Jyan moving away from him, circling towards the lift from the other side.

There were two *pan chang* or supervisors. One of them stood only a few paces from where Chen had stopped, his back to the overhead screens, his headphones making him deaf to the surrounding noise. From time to time he would bark an order into his lip-mike and one of the *chi ch'i* would pause momentarily, listening, then respond with a brief nod.

Chen nodded to himself, satisfied. To all intents and purposes the *chi ch'i* could be discounted. Their awareness was limited to the colour-coded crates they were shifting from the lift: crates that stood out in simple, schematic shapes of red and green and blue against the intense blackness in their heads.

He looked across. Jyan was in position now, directly behind the second *pan chang*. At a signal from Chen, they would act.

Chen had made Jyan practise this endlessly; ripping the mike away quickly with his left hand, then chopping down against the victim's windpipe with his right. Now he would discover if Jyan had learned his lesson.

Chen brought his hand down sharply, then moved forward, grabbing his man. Savagely he ripped the mike from the *pan chang*'s lips and brought the heel of his right hand down hard against the man's throat. He felt the man go limp and let him fall, then looked across.

Jyan was still struggling with his man. He had ripped away the lip-mike, but had failed to finish things. Now he was holding the *pan chang* awkwardly, his right arm locked around the middle of his head, his left hand formed into a fist as he flailed frantically at the man's chest. But the *pan chang* was far from finished. With a shout he twisted out and pushed Jyan away, then turned to face him, one hand reaching up to pull his headphones off.

Chen started forward, then saw something flash in Jyan's hand. A moment later the *pan chang* staggered backward, clutching his chest. At the same time some of the *chi ch'i* straightened up and looked about blindly, as if suddenly aware that something was going on.

Chen ran for the lift. At the doorway he turned and looked back.

Jyan was kneeling over the *pan chang*, one foot pressing down into the dead man's shoulder as he tried to pull the long-handled knife from his chest.

'Jyan!' Chen screamed, his voice almost lost in the background noise. 'Leave it!'

Jyan looked up sharply. Then, as if coming to himself again, he stood up and began to run towards the lift, skirting the unseeing *chi ch'i* and their carts. He had made only eight or nine paces when the first shot rang out.

Instinctively, Chen ducked. When he looked up again he couldn't see Jyan. He took a step forward, then stopped, backing up. There, a half *li* down the Main, were three Security guards. They were approaching in a widely spaced line across the corridor, moving people out of their way brusquely, almost brutally as they walked towards the lift. Chen cursed beneath his breath and slammed his hand hard against the lift's control panel.

Slowly – very slowly – the doors began to slide shut.

'Jyan!' he screamed. 'Jyan, where are you?'

A second shot rang out, ricocheting from the back of the lift. Out in the corridor there was chaos as people threw themselves down. Only the three Security men and the masked *chi ch'i* were standing now. As Chen watched, one of the electric carts trundled towards the narrowing gap. Angry with Jyan, Chen pulled out his gun and aimed it at the cart, then lowered it again.

It was Jyan. He was crouched over the cart, making as small a target of himself as possible.

There were two more shots, closely spaced. The second ricocheted, clipping a crate on its exit from the lift, and flew up into a nest of screens. There was a sharp popping and spluttering and a strong burning smell. Glass and wiring cascaded down amongst the unseeing *chi ch'i*.

With a painful slowness the cart edged between the doors. Seeing what was about to happen, Chen slammed his hand against the controls once, then again. The huge doors shuddered, made to open again, then slammed shut. But the delay had been enough. The cart was inside.

Jyan climbed down quickly and went to the panel.

Chen's voice was low and urgent in the sudden silence. 'Hurry! They'll bring up burners for the locks!'

Jyan got to work. Pulling the panel open, he put his fingernails underneath the edges of the thin control plate and popped it out. Behind it was an array of smaller plates, like tiny squares of dark mirror. Only two of them were important. Gingerly, he eased them out, careful not to damage the delicate circuitry behind. At once a voice boomed out from an overhead speaker, warning him not to tamper. Ignoring it, Jyan felt in his pocket for the two replacement panels and carefully fitted them. Then he slipped the top plate back and closed the panel.

'Going down!'

Jyan hammered the manual override and felt the huge lift shudder. For a moment there was a terrible groaning noise, as if the machine was going to grind itself to bits. Then came the sound of something very big and very solid breaking underneath them. With that the floor beneath the lift floor gave way and the lift plunged a body's length before jerking to a halt. For a moment there was silence. Then, with a click and a more normal-sounding hum, it continued its descent.

Across from Jyan, Chen picked himself up. 'We're through!' he said elatedly. 'We've broken through the Net!'

Jyan turned. 'That should keep them busy, neh, Chen?'

Alarms were sounding overhead, back where they had come from. Jyan could almost see what it was like up there. Right now they would be panicking, afraid of the sudden darkness, the blaring sirens; packing the lightless corridors that led to the transit lifts; screaming and fighting one another blindly; trying to get up and out, away from the breach, before the quarantine gates – the Seals – came down.

Jyan counted. At fifteen the lift juddered again. The sound was like a huge, multiple explosion, muffled and distant, yet powerful enough to shake the foundations of the City. 'There!' he said, grinning at Chen. 'The Seals! They've brought down the Seals!'

Chen stared back at Jyan blankly, the elation draining from him. He was sobered suddenly by the thought of what they had done. 'That's it, then,' he said softly. 'We're safe.' But he was remembering the feel of a small, dirty hand tugging at the sleeve of his one-piece as he walked down Pan Chao Street; the sight of a woman nursing her baby in a doorway; the faces of ordinary men and women going about their lives.

'We did it!' said Jyan, laughing now. 'We fucking well did it!' But Chen just looked away, giving no answer.

★

Eight hours later and two hundred and fifty lǐ to the north-west, two Security officers waited outside the huge doors of a First Level mansion. Here, at the very top of the City, there was space and silence. Here the only scent was that of pine from the crescent of miniature trees in the huge, shallow bowl at one end of the long, empty corridor; the only sound the soft, shimmering fall of water from the ornamental fountain in their midst.

Major DeVore faced his ensign, his eyebrows raised. He had seen the look of surprise on the young officer's face when they had stepped from the lift.

'You'd like to live here, Haavikko?'

The ensign turned and looked back at the broad, empty corridor. The floor was richly carpeted, the high walls covered with huge, room-sized tapestries, the colouring subdued yet elegant. Bronze statues of dragons and ancient emperors rested on plinths spaced out the full length of the hallway. At the far end the doors of the lift were lacquered a midnight black. A solitary guard stood there, at attention, a *deng* 'lantern gun' strapped to his shoulder.

'They live well, sir.'

DeVore smiled. He was a neat, compact-looking man, his jet black hair nearly Han in its fineness, his shoulders broad, almost stocky. On the chest of his azurite-blue, full dress uniform he wore the embroidered patch of a third ranking military officer, the stylized leopard snatching a bird from the air. He was a full head shorter than his ensign and his build gave him the look of a fighter, yet his manners, like his face, seemed to speak of generations of breeding – of culture.

'Yes. They do.' The smile remained on his face. 'These are extremely rich men. They would swallow up minnows like us without a thought were the T'ang not behind us. It's a different life up here, with different rules. Rules of connection and influence. You understand?'

Haavikko frowned. 'Sir?'

'What I mean is... I know these people. I know how they think and how they act. And I've known Under Secretary Lehmann's family now for almost twenty years. There are ways of dealing with them.'

Haavikko puzzled at the words momentarily. 'I still don't understand, sir. Do you mean you want to speak to him alone?'

'It would be best.'

Haavikko hesitated a moment, then, seeing how his Major was watching him, bowed his head.

'Good. I knew you'd understand.' DeVore smiled again. 'I've harsh words to say to our friend, the Under Secretary. It would be best if I said them to him alone. It's a question of face.'

Haavikko nodded. That much he understood. 'Then I'll wait here, sir.'

DeVore shook his head. 'No, boy. I want you to be a witness, at the very least. You can wait out of earshot. That way you'll not be breaking orders, neh?'

Haavikko smiled, more at ease now that a compromise had been made.

Behind them the huge double doors to the first level apartment swung open. They turned, waiting to enter.

Inside, the unexpected. A tiny wood. A bridge across a running stream. A path leading upward through the trees. Beside the bridge two servants waited for them, Han, their shaven heads bowed fully to the waist. One led the way before them, the other followed. Both kept their heads lowered, eyes averted out of courtesy. They crossed the bridge, the smell of damp earth and blossom rising to greet them. The path turned, twisted, then came out into a clearing.

On the far side of the clearing was the house. A big, two-storey mansion in the Han northern style, white-walled, its red tile roof steeply pitched.

DeVore looked at his ensign. The boy was quiet, thoughtful. He had never seen the like of this. Not surprising. There were few men in the whole of Chung Kuo who could afford to live like this. Eighty, maybe ninety thousand at most outside the circle of the Families. This was what it was to be rich. Rich enough to buy a whole ten-level deck at the very top of the City and landscape it.

Pietr Lehmann was Under Secretary in the House of Representatives at Weimar. A big man. Fourth in the pecking order in that seat of World Government. A man to whom a thousand lesser men – giants in their own households – bowed their heads. A power broker, even if that power was said by some to be chimerical and the House itself a sop – a mask to brutal tyranny. DeVore smiled at the thought. Who, after all, would think the Seven brutal or tyrannous? They had no need to be. They had the House between them and the masses of Chung Kuo.

They went inside.

The entrance hall was bright, spacious. To the left was a flight of broad, wood-slatted steps; to the right a sunken pool surrounded by a low, wooden handrail. The small, dark shapes of fishes flitted in its depths.

Their guides bowed, retreated. For a moment they were left alone.

'I thought...' Haavikko began, then shook his head.

I know, DeVore mused; *you thought he was* Hung Mao. Yet all of this is Han. He smiled. Haavikko had seen too little of the world; had mixed only with soldiers. All this was new to him. The luxury of it. The imitation.

There was a bustle of sound to their right. A moment later a group of servants came into the entrance hall. They stopped a respectful distance from the two visitors. One of them stepped forward, a tall Han who wore on the chest of his pale green one-piece a large black pictogram and the number 1. He was House Steward, Lehmann's chief servant.

DeVore made no move to acknowledge the man. He neither bowed nor smiled. 'Where is the Under Secretary?' he demanded. 'I wish to see him.'

The steward bowed, his eyes downcast. Behind him were lined up almost half of Lehmann's senior household staff, fifteen in all. They waited, unbowed, letting the steward act for them all.

'Excuse me, Major, but the master is out in the pagoda. He left explicit orders that he was not to be disturbed.'

DeVore half turned and looked at his ensign, then turned back. 'I've no time to wait, I'm afraid. I come on the T'ang's business. I'll tell your master that you did his bidding.'

The steward nodded, but did not look up, keeping his head down as the Major and his ensign walked past him, out across the terrace and onto the broad back steps that led down to the gardens.

Lotus lay scattered on the lake, intensely green against the pale, clear water. Huge, cream slabs of rock edged the waterline, forming a perfect oval. To the left a pathway traced the curve of the lake, its flower-strewn canopy ending in a gently arching bridge. Beyond the bridge, amidst a formal garden of rock and shrub and flower, stood a three-tiered pagoda in the classic Palace style, its red-tiled roofs unornamented. Further round, to the right of the lake, was an orchard, the small, broad-crowned trees spreading to the water's edge. Plum and cherry were in blossom and the still air was heavy with their fragrance.

It was early morning. From the meadows beyond the pagoda came the harsh, clear cry of a peacock. Overhead, the light of a dozen tiny, artificial suns shone down from a sky of ice painted the pastel blue of summer days.

Standing on the topmost step, DeVore took it all in at a glance. He smiled, adjusting the tunic of his dress uniform, then turned to his ensign. 'It's okay, Haavikko. I'll make my own way from here.'

The young officer clicked his heels and bowed. DeVore knew the boy had been ordered by the General to stay close and observe all that passed; but these were his people; he would do it his way. Behind Haavikko the senior servants of the household looked on, not certain what to do. The Major had come upon them unannounced. They had had little chance to warn their master.

DeVore looked back past Haavikko, addressing them, 'You! About your business now! Your master will summon you when he needs you!' Then he turned his back on them.

He looked out across the artificial lake. On the sheltered gallery of the pagoda, its wooden boards raised on stilts above the lake, stood three men dressed in silk *pau*. The soft murmur of their voices reached him across the water. Seeing him, one of them raised a hand in greeting, then turned back to his fellows, as if making his excuses.

Lehmann met him halfway, on the path beside the lake.

'It's good to see you, Howard. To what do I owe this pleasure?'

DeVore bowed his head respectfully, then met the other's eyes. 'I've come to investigate you, Pietr. The General wants answers.'

Lehmann smiled and turned, taking the Major's arm and walking beside him. 'Of course.' Light, filtering through the overhanging vines, turned his face into a patchwork of shadows. 'Soren Berdichev is here. And Edmund Wyatt. But they'll understand, I'm sure.'

Again DeVore gave the slightest nod. 'You know why I've come?'

Lehmann glanced his way, then looked forward again, towards the pagoda. 'It's Lwo Kang's death, isn't it? I knew someone would come. As soon as I heard the news, I knew. Rumour flies fast up here. Idle tongues and hungry ears make trouble for us all.' He sighed, then glanced at DeVore. 'I understand there are those who are misconstruing words spoken in my audience with the Minister as a threat. Well, I assure you, Howard, nothing was further from my mind. In a strange way I liked Lwo Kang. Admired his stubbornness. Even so, I find myself... unsurprised. It was as I thought. As I *warned*. There are those for whom impatience has become a killing anger.'

DeVore paused, turning towards the Under Secretary.

'I understand. But there are things I must ask. Things you might find awkward.'

Lehmann shrugged good-naturedly. 'It's unavoidable. The Minister's death was a nasty business. Ask what you must. I won't be offended.'

DeVore smiled and walked on, letting Lehmann take his arm again. They had come to the bridge. For a moment they paused, looking out across the lake. The peacock cried again.

'It is being said that you had most to gain from Lwo Kang's death. His refusal to accommodate you in the matter of new licences. His recent investigations into the validity of certain patents. Most of all his rigid implementation of the Edict. That last, particularly, has harmed you and your faction more than most.'

'My faction? You mean the Dispersionists?' Lehmann was quiet a moment, considering. 'And by removing him I'd stand to gain?' He shook his head. 'I know I've many enemies, Howard, but surely even they credit me with more subtlety than that?'

They walked on in silence. As they reached the pagoda, the two men on the terrace came across and stood at the top of the slatted steps.

'Soren! Edmund!' DeVore called out to them, mounting the narrow stairway in front of Lehmann. 'How are you both?'

They exchanged greetings then went inside, into a large, hexagonal room. Black, lacquered walls were inset with porcelain in intricate and richly coloured designs. The ceiling was a single huge mosaic, a double-helix of tiny, brightly coloured pythons surrounded by a border of vivid blue-white stars. Four simple, backless stools with scrolled, python-headed feet stood on the polished block-tile floor, surrounding a low hexagonal table. On the table was a small green lacquered box.

Despite the heaviness, the formality of design, the room seemed bright and airy. Long, wide, slatted windows looked out onto the lake, the orchard and the surrounding meadows. The smell of blossom lingered in the air.

It was almost more Han than the Han, DeVore observed uneasily, taking a seat next to Lehmann. A rootless, unconscious mimicry. Or was it more than that? Was it Han culture that was the real virus in the bloodstream of these *Hung Mao*, undermining them, slowly assimilating them, 'as a silk-worm devours a mulberry leaf'? He smiled wryly to himself as the words of the ancient historian Ssu Ma Ch'ien came to mind. *Ah yes, we know their history, their sayings. These things have usurped our own identity. Well, by such patience shall I, in turn, devour them. I'll be the silkworm delving in their midst.*

'So how's the Security business?'

DeVore turned on his stool, meeting Edmund Wyatt's query with a smile. 'Busy. As ever in this wicked world.'

Despite long years of acquaintanceship, Wyatt and he had never grown close. There had always been a sense of unspoken hostility beneath their surface politeness. It was no different now.

Wyatt was a slightly built man with an oddly heavy head. Someone had once commented that it was as if he had been grafted together from two very different men, and that impression, once noted, was hard to shake. At a glance his face revealed a strong, unequivocal character: aristocratic, his dark green eyes unflinching in their challenge, his chin firm, defiant. But looking down at the frame of the man it was noticeable at once how frail he seemed, how feminine. His hands were soft and thin and pale, the nails perfectly manicured. Slender *tiao tuo*, bracelets of gold and jade, hung bunched at both wrists. Such things made him seem a weak man, but he was far from that. His father's ruin might have destroyed a lesser man, but Wyatt had shown great courage and determination. He had gambled on his own talents and won: rebuilding his father's empire and regaining his place on First Level.

DeVore studied him a moment longer, knowing better than to underestimate the intelligence of the man, then gave the slightest bow.

'And you, Edmund – you're doing well, I see. There's talk your company will soon be quoted on the Index.'

Wyatt's eyes showed a mild surprise. He was unaware how closely DeVore kept himself briefed on such things. 'You follow the markets, then?'

'It makes sense to. Insurrection and business are close allies in these times. The Hang Seng is an indicator of much more than simple value – it's an index of power and ruthlessness, a club for like-minded men of similar ambitions.'

He saw how Wyatt scrutinized him momentarily, trying to make out the meaning behind his words. The Hang Seng Index of Hong Kong's stock market was the biggest of the world's seven markets and the most important. But, like the House, it was often a front to other, less open activities.

DeVore turned slightly in his seat to face Berdichev, a warm smile lighting his features. 'And how are you, Soren? I see far too little of you these days.'

Soren Berdichev returned the smile bleakly, the heavy lenses of his small, rounded glasses glinting briefly as he bowed. He was a tall, thin-faced man with pinched lips and long, spatulate fingers; a severe, humourless creature whose steel-grey eyes never settled for long. He was a hard man with few social graces, and because of that he made enemies easily, often without knowing that he did; yet he was also extremely powerful – not a man to be crossed.

'Things are well, Howard. Progressing, as they say.'

DeVore smiled at Berdichev's understatement. SimFic, his company, was one of the success stories of the decade. It had been a small operation when he had bought it in eighty-eight, but by ninety-one it had been quoted on the Hang Seng 1000 Index, along with Chung Kuo's other leading companies. Since that time he had made great advances, leading the market in the production of HeadStims and Wraps. In five short years SimFic had achieved what had seemed impossible and revolutionized personal entertainment. Now they were one of the world's biggest companies and were quoted in the Top 100 on the Index.

For a while they exchanged pleasantries. Then, as if at a signal, Berdichev's features formed into a cold half-smile. 'But forgive me, Howard. I'm sure you haven't come here to talk market.' He turned away brusquely, and looked pointedly at Wyatt. 'Come, Edmund, let's leave these two. I believe they have business to discuss.'

Wyatt looked from Lehmann to DeVore, his whole manner suddenly alert, suspicious. 'Business?'

There was a moment's awkwardness, then DeVore smiled and nodded. 'I'm afraid so.'

Wyatt set down his glass and got up slowly. Giving a small bow to Lehmann, he made to follow Berdichev, then stopped and turned, looking back at Lehmann. 'Are you sure?' he asked, his eyes revealing a deep concern for his friend.

Lehmann gave the slightest of nods, meeting Wyatt's eyes openly as if to say, *Trust me*. Only then did Wyatt turn and go.

DeVore waited a moment, listening to Wyatt's tread on the steps. Then, when it was silent again, he got up and went to the table, crouching down to open the small green box. Reaching up to his lapel, he removed the tiny device that had been monitoring their conversation and placed it carefully inside the box. Lehmann came and stood beside him, watching as he switched on the tape they had recorded three weeks before. There was the cry of a peacock, distant, as if from the meadows beyond the room, and then their voices began again, continuing from where they had left off. DeVore smiled and gently closed the lid, then he straightened up, letting out a breath.

'The simplest ways are always best,' he said, and gave a short laugh. Then, more soberly, 'That was unfortunate. What does Wyatt know?'

Lehmann met DeVore's eyes, smiling, then put an arm about his shoulders. 'Nothing. He knows nothing at all.'

DeVore peeled off his gloves and laid them on the table.

'Good. Then let's speak openly.'

The Stone Dragon was a big, low-ceilinged inn at the bottom of the City; a sprawl of interconnected rooms, ill-lit and ill-decorated; a place frequented only by the lowest of those who lived in the ten levels below the Net. A stale, sweet-sour stench permeated everything in its cramped and busy rooms, tainting all it touched. Machines lined the walls, most of them dark. Others, sparking, on the verge of malfunction, added their own sweet, burning scent to the heavy fug that filled the place. Voices called out constantly, clamouring for service, while shabbily dressed waitresses, their make-up garishly exaggerated, made their way between the tables, taking orders.

The two men sat in the big room at the back of the inn, at a table set apart from the others against the far wall. They had come here directly, two hours back, unable to sleep, the enormity of what they had done playing on both their minds. To celebrate, Kao Jyan had ordered a large bottle of the Dragon's finest Shen, brought down from Above at an exorbitant price, but neither man had drunk much of the strong rice wine.

Jyan had been quiet for some while now, hunched over an untouched tumbler, brooding. Chen watched him for a time, then looked about him.

The men at nearby tables were mainly Han, but there were some Hung

Mao. Most of them, Han and *Hung Mao* alike, were wide-eyed and sallow-faced, their scabbed arms and faces giving them away as addicts. Arfidis was cheap down here and widely available and for some it was the only way out of things. But it was also death, given time, and Chen had kept his own veins clear of it. At one of the tables further off three Han sat stiffly, talking in dialect, their voices low and urgent. One of them had lost an eye, another was badly scarred about the neck and shoulder. They represented the other half of the Stone Dragon's clientele, noticeable by the way they held themselves – somehow lither, more alert than those about them. These were the gang men and petty criminals who used this place for business. Chen stretched his neck, and leaned back against the wall. Nearby, a thick coil of smoke moved slowly in the faint orange light of an overhead panel, like the fine, dark strands of a young girl's hair.

'It's like death,' he said, looking across at Jyan.

'What?' Jyan said lazily, looking up at Chen. 'What did you say?'

Chen leaned forward and plucked a bug from beneath the table's edge, crushing it between his thumb and forefinger. It was one of the ugly, white-shelled things that sometimes came up from the Clay. Blind things that worked by smell alone. He let its broken casing fall and wiped his hand on his one-piece, not caring if it stained. 'This place. It's like death. This whole level of things. It stinks.'

Jyan laughed. 'Well, you'll be out of it soon enough, if that's what you want.'

Chen looked at his partner strangely. 'And you don't?' He shook his head, suddenly disgusted with himself. 'You know, Jyan, I've spent my whole life under the Net. I've known nothing but this filth. It's time I got out. Time I found something cleaner, better than this.'

'I know how you feel,' Jyan answered, 'but have you thought it through? Up there you're vulnerable. Above the Net there are Pass Laws and Judges, taxes and Security patrols.' He leaned across and spat neatly into the bowl by his feet. 'I hate the thought of all that shit. It would stifle the likes of you and me. And anyway, we hurt a lot of people last night when the quarantine gates came down. Forget the assassination – someone finds out you were involved in *that* and you're dead.'

Chen nodded. It had meant nothing at the time, but now that the drug had worn off he could think of little else. He kept seeing faces; the faces of people he had passed up there in Pan Chao Street. People who, only minutes later, would have been panicking, eyes streaming, half-choking as Security pumped the deck full of sterilizing gases. Children, too. Yes, a lot of them would have been just children.

He hadn't thought it through; hadn't seen it until it was done. All he'd thought about was the five thousand yuan he was being paid for the job: that and the chance of getting out. And if that meant breaking through the Net, then that's what he would do. But he hadn't thought it through. In that, at least, Jyan was right.

The Net. It had been built to safeguard the City, as a quarantine measure to safeguard the Above from plague and other epidemics, and from infiltration by insects and vermin. *And from us*, thought Chen, a sour taste in his mouth. *From vermin like us.*

He looked across, seeing movement in the doorway, then looked sharply at Jyan. 'Trouble...' he said quietly.

Jyan didn't turn. 'Who is it?' he mouthed back.

Chen groomed an imaginary moustache.

'Shit!' said Jyan softly, then sat back, lifting his tumbler.

'What does he want?' Chen whispered, leaning forward so that the movements of his mouth were screened by Jyan from the three men in the doorway.

'I owe him money.'

'How much?'

'A thousand yuan.'

'A thousand!' Chen grimaced, then leaned back again, easing his knife from his boot and pinning it with his knee against the underside of the table. Then he looked across again. The biggest of the three was looking directly at them now, grinning with recognition at the sight of Jyan's back. The big man tilted his head slightly, muttering something to the other two, then began to come across.

Whiskers Lu was a monster of a man. Almost six ch'i in height, he wore his hair wild and uncombed and sported a ragged fur about his shoulders like some latterday chieftain from a historical romance. He derived his name from the huge, tangled bush of a moustache that covered much of his facial disfigurement. Standing above Jyan, his left eye stared out glassily from a mask of melted flesh, its rawness glossed and mottled like a crab's shell.

The right eye was a narrow slit, like a sewn line in a doll's face. Beneath the chin and on the lower right-hand side of his face the mask seemed to end in a sunken line, the normal olive of his skin resuming.

Ten years back, so the story went, Whiskers Lu had tried to come to an arrangement with Chang Fen, one of the petty bosses of these levels. Chang Fen had met him, smiling, holding one hand out to welcome Lu, his other hand holding what looked like a glass of wine. Then, still smiling, he had thrown the contents of the glass into Lu's face. It was acid. But the man had not reckoned with Whiskers Lu's ferocity. Lu had held on tightly to the man's hand, roaring against the pain, and, drawing his big hunting knife, had plunged it into Chang Fen's throat before his lieutenants could come to his aid. Half-blinded he had fought his way out of there, then had gone back later with his brothers to finish the job.

Now Whiskers Lu was a boss in his own right; a big man, here beneath the Net. He stood there, towering over Kao Jyan, his lipless mouth grinning with cruel pleasure as he placed his hand on Jyan's shoulder, his single eye watching Chen warily.

'Kao Jyan... How are you, my friend?'

'I'm well,' Jyan answered nervously, shrinking in his seat. 'And you, Lu Ming-Shao?'

Whiskers Lu laughed gruffly, humourlessly. 'I'm fine, Kao Jyan. I killed a man yesterday. He owed me money.'

Jyan swallowed and met Chen's eyes. 'And he couldn't pay you?'

Lu's grip tightened on Jyan's shoulder. 'That's so, Kao Jyan. But that's not why I killed him. I killed him because he tried to hide from me.'

'Then he was a foolish man.'

The big man's laughter was tinged this time with a faint amusement. His eye, however, was cold, calculating. It stared challengingly at Chen from within its glass-like mask.

Chen stared back at it, meeting its challenge, not letting himself be cowed. If it came to a fight, so be it. Whiskers Lu would be a hard man to kill, and the odds were that Lu and his two henchmen would get the better of Jyan and him. But he would not make it easy for them. They would know they had fought a *kwai*.

Whiskers Lu broke eye contact, looking down at Jyan, his thin lips smiling again.

'You owe me money, Kao Jyan.'

Jyan was staring down at his tumbler. 'I have a week yet, Lu Ming-Shao. Don't you remember?'

'Oh, I remember. But I want my money now. With interest. Twelve hundred yuan I want from you, Kao Jyan. And I want it now.'

Almost unobtrusively, Whiskers Lu had slipped the knife from his belt and raised it to Jyan's neck. The huge, wide blade winked in the faint overhead light. The razor-sharp tip pricked the flesh beneath Jyan's chin, making him wince.

Chen let his hand slide slowly down his leg, his fingers closing about the handle of his knife. The next few moments would be critical.

'Twelve hundred?' Jyan said tensely. 'Surely, our agreement said...'

Jyan stopped, catching his breath. Whiskers Lu had increased the pressure of the knife against his flesh, drawing blood. A single bead trickled slowly down Jyan's neck and settled in the hollow above his chest. Jyan swallowed painfully.

'You want it now?'

'That's right, Kao Jyan. I've heard you've been borrowing elsewhere. Playing the field widely. Why's that, Kao Jyan? Were you planning to leave us?'

Jyan looked up, meeting Chen's eyes. Then, slowly, carefully, he reached up and moved the knife aside, turning to look up into Whiskers Lu's face.

'You mistake me, Lu Ming-Shao. I'm happy here. My friends are here. Good friends. Why should I want to leave?' Jyan smiled, then swept his hand over the table, indicating the empty chairs. 'Look, you're a reasonable man, Lu Ming-Shao. Why don't we talk this through? Why don't you sit with us and share a glass of *Shen*?'

Whiskers Lu roared, then grabbed Jyan's hair, pulling his head back viciously, his knife held threateningly across Jyan's throat.

'None of your games, Kao Jyan! I'm an impatient man just now. So tell me and have done with it. Do you have the money or not?'

Jyan's eyes bulged. Lu's reaction had startled him. His hand went to his pocket and scrabbled there, then threw three thick chips out onto the table. Each was for five hundred yuan.

Chen forced himself to relax, loosening his tight grip on the knife's handle. But he had seen how closely Lu's henchmen had been watching him and knew that they'd had orders to deal with him if it came to trouble. He

smiled reassuringly at them, then watched as Whiskers Lu let go of his grip
on Jyan. The big man sheathed his knife, then leaned forward, scooping up
the three ivory-coloured chips.

'Fifteen hundred, eh?' He grunted and half turned, grinning at his men.
'Well, that'll do, wouldn't you say, Kao Jyan?'

'Twelve hundred,' Jyan said, rubbing at his neck. 'You said twelve hundred.'

'Did I now?' Lu laughed, almost softly now, then nodded. 'Maybe so, Kao
Jyan. But you made me work for my money. So let's call it quits, neh, and
I'll forget that you made me angry.'

Chen narrowed his eyes, watching Jyan, willing him to let it drop. But
Jyan was not through. He turned and looked up at Lu again, meeting his eye.

'I'm disappointed in you, Lu Ming-Shao. I thought you were a man of
your word. To ask for your money a week early, that I understand. A man
must protect what is his. And the extra two hundred, that too I understand.
Money is not a dead thing. It lives and grows and must be fed. But this
extra...' He shook his head. 'Word will go out that Lu Ming-Shao is greedy.
That he gives his word, then takes what is not his.'

Whiskers Lu glowered at Jyan, his hand resting on his knife. 'You'd dare
to say that, Kao Jyan?'

Jyan shook his head. 'Not I. But there are others in this room who've seen
what passed between us. You can't silence them all, Lu Ming-Shao. And you
know how it is. Rumour flies like a bird. Soon the whole Net would know.
And then what? Who would come and borrow money from you then?'

Lu's chest rose and fell, his single eye boring angrily into Jyan's face. Then
he turned sharply and barked at one of his henchmen. 'Give him three hundred! Now!'

The man rummaged in the pouch at his belt then threw three slender
chips down in front of Jyan.

Jyan smiled. 'It was good to do business with you, Lu Ming-Shao. May
you have many sons!'

But Whiskers Lu had turned away and was already halfway across the
room, cursing beneath his breath.

When he was gone, Chen leaned forward angrily. 'What the fuck are you
playing at, Jyan? You almost had us killed!'

Jyan laughed. 'He *was* angry, wasn't he?'

'Angry!' Chen shook his head, astonished. 'And what's all this about you borrowing elsewhere? What have you been up to?'

Jyan didn't answer. He sat there, silent, watching Chen closely, a faint smile on his lips.

'What is it?'

Jyan's smile broadened. 'I've been thinking.'

'Thinking, eh?' Chen lifted his tumbler and sipped. The calculating gleam in Jyan's eyes filled him with apprehension.

Jyan leaned forward, lowering his voice to a whisper. 'Yes, thinking. Making plans. Something that will make us both rich.'

Chen drained his tumbler and set it down, then leaned back in his chair slowly, eyeing his partner. 'I've enough now, Jyan. Why should I want more? I can get out now if I want.'

Jyan sat back, his eyes filled with scorn. 'Is that all you want? To get out of here? Is that as high as your ambitions climb?' Again he leaned forward, but this time his voice hissed out at Chen. 'Well, I want more than that! I want to be a king down here, in the Net. A big boss. Understand me, Chen? I don't want safety and order and all that shit, I want power. Here, where I can exercise it. And that takes money.'

Heads turned at nearby tables, curious but lethargic. Chen looked back at one of them, meeting the cold, dispassionate stare that was the telltale symptom of arfidis trance with a cold look of loathing. Then he laughed softly and looked back at Jyan.

'You're mad, Jyan. It takes more than money. You can't buy yourself a gang down here, you have to make one, *earn* one, like Whiskers Lu. You're not in that league, Jyan. His kind would have you for breakfast. Besides, you're talking of the kind of sums you and I couldn't dream of getting hold of.'

Jyan shook his head. 'You're wrong.'

Chen looked down, irritated by Jyan's persistence. 'Forget it, neh? Take what you've got and get out. That is, if you've still got enough after paying Whiskers Lu.'

Jyan laughed scornfully. 'That was nothing. Small change. But listen to me, Chen. Do you really think you *can* get out?'

Chen said nothing, but Jyan was watching him closely again.

'What if all you've saved isn't enough? What if the permits cost more than you can pay? What if you run into some greedy bastard official who wants a bit more squeeze than you've got? What then? What would you do?'

Chen smiled tightly. 'I'd kill him.' But he was thinking of Pan Chao Street and the quarantine gates. Thinking of the huge, continent-spanning City of three hundred levels that was there above the Net. He had hoped to get a foothold on that great social ladder – a place on the very lowest rung. But he would have to go higher than he'd planned. Up to Twenty-One, at least. And that would cost more. Much, much more. Maybe Jyan was right.

'You'd kill him!' Jyan laughed again and sat back, clearly disgusted with his partner. 'And be back here again! A *kwai*. Just a *kwai* again! A hireling, not the man in charge. Is that really what you want?'

Chen sniffed, then shook his head.

Jyan leaned across the table again. 'Don't you understand? We *can* be kings here! We *can*!' His voice dropped to a whisper. 'You see, I know who hired us.'

Chen met the other's eyes calmly. 'So?'

Jyan laughed, incredulous. 'You really don't see it, do you?'

Chen let his eyes fall. Of course he saw it. Saw at once what Jyan was getting at. Blackmail. Games of extreme risk. But he was interested, and he wanted Jyan to spell it out for him. Only when Jyan had finished did he look up, his face expressionless.

'You're greedy, Jyan. You know that?'

Jyan sat back, laughing, then waved a hand dismissively. 'You weren't listening properly, Chen. The tape. It'll be my safeguard. If they try anything – anything at all – Security will get the tape.'

Chen watched him a moment longer, then looked down, shrugging, knowing that nothing he said would stop Jyan from doing this.

'Partners, then?'

Jyan had extended his left hand. It lay on the table's surface beside the half-empty bottle; a small, almost effete hand, but clever. An artisan's hand. Chen looked at it, wondering not for the first time who Jyan's father might have been, then placed his own on top of it. 'Partners,' he said, meeting Jyan's eyes. But already he was making plans of his own. Safeguards.

'I'll arrange a meeting, then.'

Chen smiled tightly. 'Yes,' he said. 'You do that.'

★

Edmund Wyatt stopped beneath the stand of white mulberry trees at the far end of the meadow and looked back at the pagoda. 'I don't trust him, Soren. I've never trusted him.'

Berdichev looked sideways at him and shrugged. 'I don't know why. He seems a good enough fellow.'

'Seems!' Wyatt laughed ironically. 'DeVore's a *seeming* fellow, all right. Part of his Security training, I guess. All clean and smart on the outside – but at core a pretty dirty sort, don't you think?'

Berdichev was quiet a moment. He walked on past Wyatt, then turned and leaned against one of the slender trunks, studying his friend. 'I don't follow you, Edmund. He is what he is. Like all of us.'

Wyatt bent down and picked up one of the broad, heart-shaped leaves, rubbing it between thumb and finger. 'I mean... he works for them. For the Seven. However friendly he seems, you've always got to remember that. They pay him. He does their work. And as the Han say – *Chung ch'en pu shih erh chu* – You can't serve two masters.'

'I don't know. Do you really think it's that simple?'

Wyatt nodded fiercely, staring away at the distant pagoda. 'They own him. Own him absolutely.'

He turned and saw that Berdichev was smiling.

'What is it?'

'Just that you let it worry you too much.'

Wyatt smiled. 'Maybe. But I don't trust him. He's up to something.'

'Up to what?' Berdichev moved away from the tree and stood beside Wyatt, looking back across the meadow. 'Look, I'll tell you why he's here. Lwo Kang was murdered. Last night. Just after eleventh bell.'

Wyatt turned abruptly, shocked by the news. 'Lwo Kang? Gods! Then it's a wonder we're not all in the cells!'

Berdichev looked away. 'Maybe... And maybe not. After all, we're not unimportant men. It would not do to persecute us without clear proof of our guilt. It might make us martyrs, neh?'

Wyatt narrowed his eyes. 'Martyrs?'

'Don't think the T'ang underestimates us. Or the power of the Above. If he had all of us Dispersionists arrested, what then? What would the Above make of that? They'd say he was acting like a tyrant. He and the rest of the Seven. It would make things very awkward.'

'But Lwo Kang was a Minister! One of Li Shai Tung's own appointees!'

'It makes no difference. The T'ang will act properly, or not at all. It is the way of the Seven. Their weakness.'

'Weakness?' Wyatt frowned, then turned back, looking across at the pagoda. 'No wonder DeVore is here. I'd say he's come to find a scapegoat. Wouldn't you?'

Berdichev smiled then reached out, putting his hand on his friend's shoulder. 'You really think so, Edmund?' He shrugged, then squeezed Wyatt's shoulder gently. 'Whatever else you might think about him, DeVore's *Hung Mao*, like us. He may work for the Han, but that doesn't mean he thinks like them. In any case, why should he be interested in anything but the truth?'

Wyatt stared at the pagoda intently for a time, as if pondering some mighty problem, then he shivered and touched his tongue to his teeth in a curiously innocent, childlike gesture. He turned, looking back at Berdichev. 'Maybe you're right, Soren. Maybe he is what you say. But my feelings tell me otherwise. I don't trust him. And if he's here, I'd wager he's up to something.' He paused, then turned, looking back at the pagoda. 'In fact, I'd stake my life on it.'

'Yang Lai is dead, then?'

DeVore turned from the window and looked back into the room. 'Yes. The Junior Minister is dead.'

Lehmann was silent a moment. 'I see. And the lieutenant in charge of the Security post?'

'Dead too, I'm afraid. It was... unavoidable.'

Lehmann met his eyes. 'How?'

'By his own hand. The dishonour, you see. His family. It would have ruined them. Better to kill oneself and absolve them from the blame.'

'So we're clear.'

DeVore gave a short laugh. 'Not yet.'

'You think there's still a chance they'll find something?'

The Major's eyes met Lehmann's briefly. 'Remember how long this took us to plan. We've been careful, and such care pays off. Besides, we have the advantage of knowing all they do. There's not a move General Tolonen can make without me hearing of it.'

He was quiet a moment, staring off across the meadow. It was true what he had said. He had spent years recruiting them; young men like himself who had come, not from First Level, from the privileged top deck of the City – the *supernal*, as they liked to term themselves – or from the army families – the descendants of those North European mercenaries who had fought for the Seven against the tyrant Tsao Ch'un a century before – but ordinary young men without connection. Young men of ability, held back by a system modelled on the Manchu 'banners' – an archaic and elitist organizational structure where connection counted for more than ability. Misfits and malcontents.

Like himself.

He had become adept at spotting them; at recognizing that look, there at the back of the eyes. He would check out their backgrounds and discover all he could about them. Would find, invariably, that they were loners, ill at ease socially and seething inside that others had it so easy when army life for them was unmitigatedly hard. Then, when he knew for certain that it was so, he would approach them. And every time it was the same; that instant opening; that moment of recognition, like to like, so liberating that it bound them to him with ties of gratitude and common feeling.

'Like you, I am a self-made man,' he would say. 'What I am I owe to no one but myself. No relative has bought my post; no uncle put in a word with my commanding officer.' And as he said it, he'd think of all the insults, all the shit he'd had to put up with from his so-called superiors – men who weren't fit to polish his boots. He had suffered almost thirty years of that kind of crap to get where he was now, in a position of real power. He would tell his young men this and see in their eyes the reflection of his own dark indignation. And then he would ask them, 'Join me. Be part of my secret brotherhood.' And they would nod, or whisper yes. And they would be his: alone no longer.

So now he had his own organization; men loyal to him before all others; who would neither hesitate to betray their T'ang nor lay down their lives if he asked it of them. Like the young officer who had been on duty the night of Lwo Kang's assassination. Like a hundred others, scattered about the City in key positions.

He looked back at Lehmann. 'Are the trees real?' He pointed outward, indicating the stand of mulberries at the far end of the meadow.

Lehmann laughed. 'Heaven, no. None of it's real.'

DeVore nodded thoughtfully, then turned his face to look at Lehmann. 'You're not afraid to use Wyatt?' His eyes, only centimetres from Lehmann's, were stern, questioning.

'If we must. After all, some things are more important than friendship.'

DeVore held his eyes a moment longer then looked back at the figure of Wyatt down below. 'I don't like him. You know that. But even if I did – if it threatened what we're doing... If for a moment...'

Lehmann touched his arm. 'I know.'

DeVore turned fully, facing him. 'Good. We understand each other, Pietr. We always have.'

Releasing him, DeVore checked his wrist-timer then went to the middle of the room and stood there, looking down at the box. 'It's almost time to call the others back. But first, there's one last thing we need to talk about... Heng Yu.'

'What of him?'

'I have reason to believe he'll be Lwo Kang's replacement.'

Lehmann laughed, astonished. 'Then you know much more than any of us. How did you come by this news?'

'Oh, it isn't news. Not yet, anyway. But I think you'll find it reliable enough. Heng Chi-Po wants his nephew as the new Minister, and what Heng Chi-Po wants he's almost certain to get.'

Lehmann was quiet, considering. He had heard how high the Heng family currently rode. Even so, it would use all of the Minister Heng's quite considerable influence to persuade Li Shai Tung to appoint his nephew, Heng Yu. And, as these things went, it would be a costly manoeuvre, with the paying-off of rivals, the bribery of advisors and the cost of the post itself. They would surely have to borrow. In the short term it would weaken the Hengs quite severely. They would find themselves beholden to a dozen other families. Yet in the longer term...

Lehmann laughed, surprised. 'I'd always thought Heng Chi-Po crude and unimaginative. Not the kind to plan ahead. But this...'

DeVore shook his head. 'Don't be mistaken, Pietr. This has nothing to do with planning. Heng Chi-Po is a corrupt man, as we know to our profit. But he's also a proud one. At some point Lwo Kang snubbed him. Did something to him that he could not forgive. This manoeuvring is his answer. His revenge, if you like.'

'How do you know all this?'

DeVore looked across at him and smiled. 'Who do you think bought Yang Lai? Who do you think told us where Lwo Kang would be?'

'But I thought it was because of Edmund...' Lehmann laughed. 'Of course. Why didn't you tell me?'

DeVore shrugged. 'It didn't matter until now. But now you need to know who we are dealing with. What kind of men they are.'

'Then it's certain.'

'Almost. But there is nothing – *no one* – we cannot either buy or destroy. If it is Heng Yu, then all well and good, it will prove easy. But whoever it is, he'll remember what happened to Lwo Kang and be wary of us. No, they'll not deal lightly with us in future.'

'And Li Shai Tung?'

DeVore spread his open hands, then turned away. There, then, lay the sticking point. Beyond this they were guessing. He, and the others of the Seven who ran the Earth, were subject to no laws, no controls but their own. Ultimately it would be up to them whether change would come; whether Man would try once more for the stars. DeVore's words, true as they were for other men, did not apply to the Seven. They could not be bought – for they owned half of everything there was – neither, it seemed, could they be destroyed. For more than a century they had ruled unchallenged.

'The T'ang is a man, whatever some might think.'

Lehmann looked at DeVore curiously but held his tongue.

'He can be influenced,' DeVore added after a moment. 'And when he sees how the tide of events flows...'

'He'll cut our throats.'

DeVore shook his head. 'Not if we have the full weight of the Above behind us. Markets and House and all. Not if his Ministers are ours. He is but a single man, after all.'

'He is Seven,' said Lehmann, and for once he understood the full import of the term. Seven. It made for strength of government. Each a king, a T'ang, ruling a seventh of Chung Kuo, yet each an equal in Council, responsible to his fellow T'ang; in some important things unable to act without their firm and full agreement. 'And the Seven is against Change. It is a principle with them. The very cornerstone of their continued existence.'

'And yet change they must. Or go under.'

Lehmann opened his mouth, surprised to find where their talk had led them. He shook his head. 'You don't mean...'

'You'll see,' said DeVore, more softly than before. 'This here is just a beginning. A display of our potential, for the Above to see.' He laughed, looking away into some inner distance. 'You'll see, Pietr. They'll come to us. Every last one of them. They'll see how things are – we'll open their eyes to it – and then they'll come to us.'

'And then?'

'Then we'll see who's more powerful. The Seven, or the Above.'

Heng Chi-Po leaned back in his chair and roared with laughter. He passed his jewel-ringed fingers across his shiny pate, then sniffed loudly, shifting his massive weight. 'Excellent, Kou! Quite excellent! A good toast! Let's raise our glasses, then.' He paused, the smile on his face widening. 'To Lwo Kang's successor!'

Six voices echoed the toast enthusiastically.

'Lwo Kang's successor!'

There were eight men in the spacious, top-level office. Four were brothers to the Minister, three his nephews. Heng Yu, the subject of the toast, a slender man in his mid-twenties with a pencil moustache and a long but pleasant face, smiled broadly and bowed to his uncle. Kou, fourth son of Heng Chi-Po's father Tao, clapped an arm about Yu's shoulders, then spoke again.

'This is a good day, first brother.'

Heng Chi-Po nodded his huge, rounded face, then laughed again. 'Oh, how sweet it was to learn of that weasel's death. How sweet! And to think the family will profit from it!'

There was laughter from all sides. Only the young man, Yu, seemed the least bit troubled.

'He seemed a good man, uncle,' he ventured. 'Surely I would do well to be as he was.'

The laughter died away. Chi-Po's brothers looked among themselves, but Heng Chi-Po was in too good a mood to let Yu's comments worry him. He looked at his nephew good-naturedly and shook his head in mock despair. Yet his voice, when he spoke, had an acid undertone. 'Then you heard wrong, Yu. Lwo Kang was a worm. A liar and a hypocrite. He was a foolish, stubborn man with the manners of the Clayborn and the intelligence of a GenSyn whore. The world is a better place without him, I assure you. And you, dear nephew, will make twice the Minister he was.'

Heng Yu bowed deeply, but there was a faint colour to his cheeks when he straightened, and his eyes did not meet his uncle's. Heng Chi-Po watched him closely, thinking, not for the first time, that it was unfortunate he could not promote one of his nearer relatives to the post. Yu, son of his long-dead younger brother, Fan, had been educated away from the family. He had picked up strange notions of life. Old-fashioned, Confucian ideals of goodness. Things that made a man weak when faced with the true nature of the world. Still, he was young. He could be re-educated. Shaped to serve the family better.

Kou, ever-watchful, saw how things were, and began an anecdote about a high-level whore and a stranger from the Clay. Giving him a brief smile of thanks, Chi-Po pulled himself up out of his chair and turned away from the gathering, thoughtful, pulling at his beard. Under the big, wall-length map of City Europe he stopped, barely aware of the fine honeycomb grid that overlaid the old, familiar shapes of countries, thinking instead of the past. Of that moment in the T'ang's antechamber when Lwo Kang had humiliated him.

Shih wei su ts'an.

He could hear it even now. Could hear how Lwo Kang had said it; see his face, only inches from his own, those coldly intelligent eyes staring at him scornfully, that soft, almost feminine mouth forming the hard shapes of the words. It was an old phrase. An ancient insult. *Impersonating the dead and eating the bread of idleness.* You are lazy and corrupt, it said. You reap the rewards of others' hard work. Chi-Po shuddered, remembering how the others there – Ministers like himself – had turned from him and left him there, as if agreeing with Lwo Kang. Not one had come to speak with him afterwards.

He looked down, speaking softly, for himself alone. 'But now the ugly little pig's arse is dead!'

He had closed those cold eyes. Stopped up that soft mouth. And now his blood would inherit. And yet...

Heng Chi-Po closed his eyes, shivering, feeling a strange mixture of bitterness and triumph. Dead. But still the words sounded, loud, in his head. *Shih wei su ts'an.*

★

Big White brought them a tray of ch'a, then backed out, closing the door behind him.

Cho Hsiang leaned forward and poured from the porcelain bottle, filling Jyan's bowl first, then his own. When he was done he set the bottle down and looked up sharply at the hireling.

'Well? What is it, Kao Jyan?'

He watched Jyan take his bowl and sip, then nod his approval of the ch'a. There was a strange light in his eyes. Trouble. As he'd thought. But not of the kind he'd expected. What was Jyan up to?

'This is pleasant,' said Jyan, sitting back. 'Very pleasant. There's no better place in the Net than Big White's, wouldn't you say?'

Curbing his impatience, Cho Hsiang placed his hands on the table, palms down, and tilted his head slightly, studying Jyan. He was wary of him, not because he was in any physical danger – Big White frisked all his customers before he let them in – but because he knew Jyan for what he was. A weasel. A devious little shit-eater with ambitions far above his level.

'No better place in the Net,' he answered, saying nothing of the excellent Mu Chua's, where he and others from the Above usually spent their time when they were here, or of his loathing of the place and of the types, like Jyan, with whom he had to deal. 'You'd best say what you want, Kao Jyan. I've business to attend to.'

Jyan looked up at him, a sly, knowing expression in his eyes. 'I'll not keep you long, mister contact man. What I have to say is simple and direct enough.'

Cho Hsiang stiffened slightly, bristling at the insult Kao Jyan had offered him in using the anglicized form of Hsien Sheng, but his mind was already working on the question of what it was Jyan wanted. As yet he saw no danger in it for himself, even when Jyan leaned forward and said in a whisper, 'I know who you work for, Cho Hsiang. I found it out.'

Jyan leaned back, watching him hawkishly, the fingers of his right hand pulling at the fingers of the left. 'That should be worth something, don't you think?'

Cho Hsiang sat back, his mind working quickly. Did he mean Hong Cao? If so, how had Jyan found out? Who, of Hsiang's contacts, had traced the connection back? Or was Jyan just guessing? Trying to squeeze him for a little extra? He looked at the hireling again, noting just how closely the other was watching him, then shrugged.

'I don't know what you mean. I am my own man. I'm not a filthy hireling.'

He made the insult pointed, but Jyan just waved it aside. 'You forget what you hired me for this time, mister contact man. It was way beyond your level. I knew at once you were working for someone else. And not just anyone. This one had power. Real power. Power to make deals with Security, to trade with other, powerful men. With money to oil the cogs and sweep away the traces. That's not your level, Cho Hsiang. Such people would not deign to sit at table with such as you and I.'

Cho Hsiang was quiet a moment, then, 'Give me a name.'

Jyan laughed shortly, then leaned forward, his face now hard and humourless. 'First I want a guarantee. Understand? I want to make certain that I'm safe. That they'll not be able to come for me and make sure of my silence.'

He made to speak, but Jyan shook his head tersely. 'No, Cho Hsiang. Listen. I've made a tape of all I know. It makes interesting listening. But tapes can go missing. So I've made a copy and secured it in a computer time-lock. Never mind where. But that time-lock needs to be reset by me every two days. If it isn't, then the copy goes directly to Security.

Cho Hsiang took a deep breath. 'I see. And what do you want in return for your silence?'

In answer, Jyan took the tape from the pocket of his one-piece and pushed it across the table to him. 'I think they'll find a price that suits us both.'

Smiling, Jyan refilled his cup from the bottle, then, sitting back again, raised it in salute. 'You said you wanted a name.'

Cho Hsiang hesitated, his stomach tightening, then shook his head. He hadn't seen it at first, but now he saw it clearly. Jyan's talk of safeguards had brought it home to him. It was best he knew nothing. Or, if not nothing, then as little as possible. Such knowledge as Jyan had was dangerous.

'Suit yourself,' said Jyan, laughing, seeing the apprehension in Cho Hsiang's face. When he spoke again his voice was harsh; no longer the voice of a hireling, but that of a superior. 'Arrange a meeting. Tomorrow. Here, at Big White's.'

Cho Hsiang leaned forward, angered by Jyan's sudden change of tone, then sat back, realizing that things had changed. He picked up the tape and pocketed it, then got up from his chair and went to the door. 'I'll see what I can do.'

Jyan smiled again. 'Oh, and, Cho Hsiang... pay Big White for me on your way out.'

Lehmann turned sharply, the low, urgent buzzing of the desk alarm sending his heart into his mouth. Four symbols had appeared on the screen of his personal comset, Han pictograms that spelt *Yen Ching* – Eye – the codeword for his Mid-Level contact, Hong Cao.

That it had appeared on his personal screen indicated its urgency. No computer line, however well protected, could be guaranteed discreet. For that reason, Hong Cao had been instructed to use the personal code only as a last resort.

Placing his right forefinger to the screen, Lehmann drew an oval, then dotted the centre of it. At once the message began to spill out onto the screen.

It was brief and to the point. Lehmann read it through once, then a second time. Satisfied he had it memorized, he pressed CLEAR and held the tab down for a minute – time enough to remove all memory of the transmission. Only then did he sit back, stunned by the import of the message.

'Shit!' he said softly, then leaned forward to tap in DeVore's personal contact code.

Someone knew. Someone had figured out how it all connected.

DeVore was out on patrol. Part of his face appeared on the screen, overlarge, the signal hazed, distorted. Lehmann realized at once that DeVore was staring down into a wrist set.

'Pietr! What is it?'

Lehmann swallowed. 'Howard. Look, it's nothing really. Just that you... you left your gloves. Okay? I thought you might want to pick them up. And maybe have a drink.'

DeVore's face moved back, coming into clearer focus. There was a moment's hesitation, then he nodded. 'I'll be off duty in an hour. I'll come collect them then. Okay?'

'Fine.' Lehmann cut contact at once.

The package from Hong Cao containing the tape and a sealed message card arrived a half bell later by special courier. Lehmann stared at it a moment, then put it unopened in the top drawer of his desk and locked it.

His first instinct had been right. They should have erased all traces that led back to them. Killed the killers. Killed the agents and the contact men. Killed everyone who knew. DeVore had argued against this, saying that to do so would only draw attention, but he, Lehmann had been right. And now they would have to do it anyway. If they still could.

When DeVore arrived they took the package straight through to Lehmann's Secure Room and listened to the tape through headphones. Afterwards they sat there looking at each other.

DeVore was first to speak. 'He may have got it wrong, but he was close enough to do us damage. If Security investigate Berdichev at any depth they'll uncover the links with you. And then the whole structure comes crashing down.'

'So what do you suggest?'

'We kill him.'

'What about the copy tape?'

'Leave that to me.' DeVore reached across and took the message card. He looked at it, then handed it to Lehmann.

Lehmann activated the card, read it, then handed it back across to DeVore.

'Good. This Kao Jyan wants a meeting. I'll see to that myself. Meanwhile I've something you can do.'

Lehmann frowned. 'What's that?'

'Yang Lai's alive. He tried to make contact with Wyatt. My men have found out where he is, but he'll only speak to you or Wyatt. It seems you're the only ones he trusts.'

Lehmann felt his stomach flip over for the second time that morning. Yang Lai had been one of the Ministers of the Edict, Lwo Kang's chief officials. They had thought he was among the dead.

'Then he wasn't in the dome when it went up?'

DeVore shook his head. 'I only heard two hours back. All of the internal Security films were destroyed in the explosion, but the door tally survived. The body count for the solarium came out two short. It seems Junior Minister Yang is one.'

'Then who's the other?'

DeVore shrugged. 'We don't know yet. But Yang Lai might. Go see him. Do what you must.'

Lehmann nodded. This time he would act on his instincts. 'Okay. I'll deal with him.'

DeVore stood up. 'And don't worry, Pietr. We can handle this.' He glanced down at the tape and card, then back at Lehmann. 'Destroy those. I'll see to the rest. Oh, and, Pietr...'

'What?'

'My gloves...'

Jyan had spent two hours at Big White's after Cho Hsiang had gone. A meal of real pork and vegetables, a bottle of good wine and a long session with two of the house's filthiest girls – all on Cho Hsiang's bill – had put him in a good mood. It was all going his way at last. Things were happening for him. About time, he thought, turning the corner and entering the corridor that led to his apartment.

In the noise and crush of the corridor he almost missed it. Almost went straight in. But something – some sense he had developed over the years – stopped him. He drew his hand back from the palm-lock and bent down, examining it. There was no doubt about it. The lock had been tampered with.

He put his ear to the door. Nothing. At least, nothing unusual. He could hear a soft machine purr coming from within, but that was normal. Or almost normal...

He turned and looked back down the busy corridor, ignoring the passers-by, trying to think. Had he left any of his machines on? Had he? He scratched at his neck nervously, unable to remember, then looked back at the marks on the lock, frowning. They looked new, but they might have been there some while. It might just have been kids.

It might have. But he'd best take no chances. Not in the circumstances.

He placed his palm flat against the lock, then, as the lock hissed open, drew back against the wall, away from the opening.

As the door slid back slowly, he looked into the room for some sign of an intruder. Then, drawing his knife with one swift movement, he stepped into the room.

The knife was knocked from his hand. He saw it flip through the air. Then a hand was clamped roughly about his mouth.

Jyan struggled to turn and face his assailant, one arm going up instinctively to ward off a blow, but the man was strong and had a tight grip on him.

Then, suddenly, he was falling backward.

He looked up, gasping. Kuan Yin, goddess of mercy! It was Chen!

Chen glared down at him angrily. 'Where have you been?'

Two or three faces appeared in the doorway behind Chen. Jyan waved them away, then got up and moved past Chen to close the door. Getting his breath again, he turned to face the *kwai*, a faint smile returning to his lips. 'I've been arranging things. Making deals.'

He went to move past him again, but Chen caught his arm and sniffed him. 'You've been whoring, more like. I can smell the stink of them on you.'

Jyan laughed. 'A little pleasure after business, that's all.' He moved into the room, then sat down heavily on the bed, facing Chen. 'Anyway, what are you doing here?'

Chen sheathed his big hunting knife and crossed the room. There, in a corner recess, was an old-fashioned games machine. Turning his back on Jyan, he stared at the screen. 'I thought I'd come and find out what was happening. You were gone a long time.'

Jyan laughed, then pulled off his left slipper. 'As I said, I was making deals. Working for both of us.'

Chen toyed with the keys of the games machine a moment longer, then turned back. 'And?'

Jyan smiled and kicked off the other slipper, then began to peel off his onepiece. 'We've another meet. Tomorrow, at Big White's. We fix the price then.'

Oblivious of the other man, Jyan stripped naked, then went over to the corner shower and fed five ten *fen* tokens into the meter beside it. Drawing back the curtain, he stepped inside and, as the lukewarm water began to run, started to soap himself down.

Chen watched Jyan's outline through the plastic a moment, then turned back to the machine.

It was an ancient thing that had three standard games programmed into it; *T'iao Chi, Hsiang Chi* and *Wei Chi*. Jyan had set it up for a low level game of *Wei Chi*, and the nineteen by nineteen grid filled the screen. He was playing black and had made only twenty or so moves, but white was already in a strong position.

Chen looked about him once again. He had never been in Jyan's room before today – had, in truth, never been interested in Jyan's homelife – but now the situation was getting deep. It had seemed best to know how things stood.

Cheap tapestries hung on the walls. Standard works by Tung Yuan and Li Ch'eng; scenes of mountains and valleys, tall pine trees and gentle-flowing rivers. The sort of crap one saw everywhere in the Net. On the bedside table was a small shrine to Wen Ti, the evidence of burnt candles in the tray revealing a side of Jyan he would never have guessed. A small rug covered part of the bare ice floor at the end of the single bed, but otherwise the only furnishings were a pair of cheap fold-up chairs that weighed nothing.

Some of the things there had surprised him. In a box under the bed he had found a recent generation SimFic HeadStim: a direct-input job that linked up to wires implanted in the brain. That alone must have cost Jyan at least five hundred yuan at current black market prices – maybe even the full thousand he had borrowed from Whiskers Lu – but unlike the two wrap-arounds he had, it was a useless item – a status symbol only – because Jyan, like most in the Net, hadn't had the operation.

A huge blue and gold er-silk eiderdown covered the bed. Underneath it, two bright red cotton blankets were spread out over the normal ice-cloth sheets of the bed – as if for a wedding night. For some reason it had reminded Chen of that moment on the mountainside when Jyan had pulled the wine bottle and the glasses from his sack. There was something dangerously impractical about that side of Jyan. Something hideously self-indulgent. It was a flaw in him. The kind of thing that could kill a man.

Chen cleared the board and switched off the machine, his sense of disenchantment coming to a head. All this – it was so ostentatious. So false. Jyan ached to be better than he was. Richer. More powerful. More cultured. Yet his attempts at mimicry were painful to observe. He was a cockroach imitating a turtle. And this latest scheme... Chen shuddered. It was doomed to failure. He knew that in his bones. You could not make deals with these people; could not be partner to them, only their hireling.

He looked about him one last time, watching the thinly fleshed shape of Jyan bend and stretch behind the plastic curtaining. Then, his mind made up, he left quietly. It wasn't toys he wanted. He wanted something real. A new life. Better than this. More real than this. A child, maybe. A son.

He was tired of being *wang pen* – rootless, his origins forgotten. It was time he was connected. If not to the past, then to the future. He sighed, knowing he could do nothing about the past. But the future – that was unwritten...

As he walked back to his own apartment the thought went through his mind like a chant, filling his head, obsessing him – A child. A son. A child. A son – the words coursing through him like the sound of his feet as they pounded the bare ice flooring of the corridors. A child. A son.

Yang Lai knelt at Lehmann's feet, his head bowed low, his hands gripping the hem of Lehmann's pau tightly.

'You're a good man, Pietr Lehmann. A fine man. I've been so scared. So frightened that they would find me before you or Edmund came.'

Lehmann looked about him. The room was filthy. It looked as if no one had tidied it in years. Had Yang Lai fallen this low? Had he no friends of higher rank to help him in his need? He drew the man to his feet and freed his hand, then reached across to lift his chin, making Yang Lai look at him.

'I'm glad you called, Yang Lai. Things are difficult. If Security had found you...'

'I understand.'

'How did you get out?'

'Does it matter?'

Lehmann noted the undertone of suspicion in Yang Lai's voice. The man had had time enough to work it out. Yet he wasn't certain. His trust in Wyatt had acted like a barrier against the truth. It had prevented him from piecing things together. Well, that was good. It meant things would be easier.

'I'm interested, that's all. But anyway...' He feigned indifference, changing tack at once, moving past Yang Lai as he spoke. 'The Minister's assassination. It wasn't us. Someone pre-empted us.' He turned and looked back at the Han. 'Do you understand me, Yang Lai? Do you see what I'm saying? Whoever it was, they almost killed you.'

'No!' Yang Lai shook his head. 'That's not how it was. They... warned me. Told me to get out of there.'

Yang Lai shuddered violently and looked away. He was red-eyed and haggard from lack of sleep, and his clothes smelt. Even so, there was something in his manner that spoke of his former authority.

For a moment Yang Lai seemed lost in thought. Then, like someone suddenly waking, he looked up at Lehmann again, a smile lighting his face. 'Then Edmund had nothing to do with it?'

'Nothing.' This time it was the truth.

Lehmann pondered the connection between Wyatt and the Han. Why did Yang Lai trust Edmund so explicitly? Was it only friendship? Or was it deeper than that? Were they lovers?

'Who warned you?' he asked, moving closer. 'You have to tell me, Yang Lai. It's very important.'

Yang Lai glanced up at him, then looked down sharply, his shame like something physical. 'A messenger came. My Third Secretary, Pi Ch'ien.'

Pi Ch'ien. Lehmann caught his breath. Pi Ch'ien hadn't been on the list of names DeVore had given him. Which meant he was probably still alive. Lehmann turned away, pressing his left hand to his brow, trying to think. 'This *Pi Ch'ien*... where is he?'

Yang Lai shrugged. 'I don't know. I assume he was killed.' He looked away, his voice going very quiet. 'I think I was the last to get out.'

Lehmann was still a moment, then, abruptly, he turned and made to go.

Yang Lai rushed after him and caught him at the door, holding tightly to his arm.

'What's happening? Please, Pietr, tell me what's happening!'

Lehmann turned back, taking Yang Lai's hands in his own. 'It's all okay, Yang Lai. It will all be all right. Trust me. Trust Edmund. But there are things we have to do. For all our sakes.'

Yang Lai studied his face intently for a moment. Then he looked down. 'All right. Do what you must.'

Outside, Lehmann paused and glanced across at the two men standing against the far side of the corridor. Behind him he heard the door slide shut and the lock click into place.

It would not help Yang Lai. His men had the combination to the lock.

It's necessary, Lehmann told himself. *All of this. All the killing and the lying and the double-dealing. All necessary.*

He met the eyes of the taller man and nodded, then turned away, making his way quickly to the waiting transit lift.

Necessary. For all our sakes.

★

Cho Hsiang put the envelope on the table in front of Jyan, then leaned back, watching him carefully.

'What's this?' Jyan looked up guardedly.

'Open it and see. I'm only the messenger.'

Cho Hsiang saw how suspicious Jyan was of the envelope. He had not seen anything like it before. It was all tape or mouth-work down here. No subtleties.

'You tear it open,' he explained. 'The message will be written on the sheet inside.'

Jyan hesitated, then picked up the envelope and examined it. On one side of the whiteness was written his name. The other seemed to have been slit open diagonally, then sealed with something hot that had left the imprint of a double-helix. Seeing that, he laughed.

'I guessed right, then?'

Cho Hsiang said nothing, merely inclined his head towards the envelope.

Jyan tugged gently at the seal, trying to prise it open. Then, more brutally, he tore at the silken paper. The seal gave suddenly and the message spilled out onto the table, coming to rest beside Cho Hsiang's hand. It was a single folded sheet. Gingerly, using only his fingertips, Cho Hsiang pushed it across to him.

On the paper was a figure. Jyan studied it a moment, then whistled softly.

'Will it do?'

There was the faintest trace of sarcasm in Cho Hsiang's voice.

Jyan had folded the paper. He unfolded it and stared at the figure again. Then he looked up over the paper at Cho Hsiang.

'Do you know what it says?'

Cho Hsiang shook his head slowly. 'As I said, I'm only the messenger. But I know this. There'll be no haggling. Understand? You either take what's offered or you get nothing.'

'Nothing...' Jyan laughed tensely. 'That would be rather stupid of them, don't you think?'

Cho Hsiang leaned forward. 'You heard me. Take it or leave it.'

'And if I leave it? If I take what I know elsewhere?'

Cho Hsiang allowed himself a cold smile. 'You're an imaginative man, Kao Jyan. Work it out for yourself.'

Jyan looked down, unfolding the paper yet again. Cho Hsiang watched him, amused. They knew how to deal with such types up Above. Theirs was the way of ultimatum. Take it or leave it – it was all the same to them. Either way they would come out on top. He reached out and took his glass, draining it, then reached across and pressed the button on the wall that would summon Big White.

'I have to go now, Kao Jyan. What shall I say to my friends?'

Jyan looked up. From his face Cho Hsiang could see he was still undecided. He pressed him. 'Well?'

There were sounds outside. The doorlock popped softly and the door began to slide back. Jyan looked past Cho Hsiang, then back at him.

'Okay. We'll take it. And tell your man...'

He stopped, seeing Big White there.

'Yes?' Cho Hsiang stood up, letting Big White help him into his big mock-beaver coat.

'Tell him he'll have no more trouble. Okay?'

Cho Hsiang smiled tightly. 'Good.' He turned, as if to leave, then turned back. 'I'll be seeing you then, Kao Jyan.'

Jyan nodded, all the cockiness gone from him.

'Oh, and, Jyan... See to the bill for me, neh?'

'What have we got?'

The technician tapped at the keys, running the recording back for analysis. Then he leaned back, letting DeVore read from the screen for himself.

Fifty-one words total. Fourteen repetitions. Total vocabulary 37 words.

'It's not enough.'

The technician shook his head. 'Maybe not for direct speech transposition. But we could generate new words from the sounds we have. There's a considerable range of tones here. The computer can create a gestalt – a whole speech analogue – from very little. We've more than enough here to do that. You write the script, the machine will get him to say it. And not even his mother would know it wasn't him saying it.'

DeVore laughed. 'Good. Then we'll move quickly on this.' He took a hard-file from his jacket pocket and handed it to the technician. 'Here's what I want our friend Jyan to say.'

The technician hesitated fractionally, then nodded. 'Okay. I'll get to work on it right away. Will tomorrow be too late? Midday?'

DeVore smiled and slapped the technician's back. 'Tomorrow's fine. I'll collect it myself.'

He went out, heading back down towards the Net. It was early evening. In under four hours he was due to meet the General to make his report. There was time enough, meanwhile, to set things up.

In the Security lift, descending, he made contact with the two men he had left outside Big White's.

'How's our man?'

The answer came back into his earpiece. 'He's still inside, sir.'

'Good. If he comes out, follow at a distance. But don't make a move. Not yet. I want them both, remember.'

He had barely closed contact when an urgent message came through on his wrist console. It was Lehmann again, his face taut with worry.

'What is it, Pietr?'

Lehmann hesitated, conscious that he was speaking on an open channel, then took the risk. 'The missing body. I know who it is. It's Yang Lai's man, Pi Ch'ien.'

'I see. So where is he?'

Lehmann laughed anxiously. 'That's just it. I've been checking up. There's no trace of him. He hasn't been seen since the assassination.'

'So he's in hiding?'

'It seems so.'

'Right. Leave it to me.' He paused. 'All's well apart from that?'

Lehmann hesitated, then gave the coded answer. 'It's a cloudless sky, Howard. I... Well, I'll see you some time, yes?'

DeVore closed contact. So Yang Lai was dead. Good. That was one thing less to worry about.

The lift slowed, then came to a halt. For a moment DeVore stood there, his hand almost touching the Door Open pad, his skin, beneath the simple one-piece he was wearing, tingling from the decontamination procedure. Then, clear in mind what he had to do, he hit the pad and went outside, into the Net.

CHAPTER 28

A GAME OF STATIC PATTERNS

Fifth bell was sounding when Major DeVore reported to General Tolonen in his office at the top of the vast fortress-like barracks that housed Security Central. The General stood as he came into the room and came round his desk to greet DeVore, a broad smile on his chiselled face.

'Good morning, Howard. How are things?'

DeVore bowed at waist and neck, then straightened up, meeting the old man's eyes. 'Not good, sir. Our investigation of the Minister's death is proving more difficult than I thought.'

The General looked at him, then nodded. Briefly he rested a hand on the Major's arm, as if to reassure him, then turned and went back behind his desk. Ensconced in his chair again he leaned forward, motioning to DeVore to take a seat. 'Still nothing, eh?'

DeVore gave the smallest hint of a bow then sat. 'Not quite, sir.'

Tolonen tilted his chin back, interested. 'I see. What have you got?'

'Nothing certain. Only rumour. But it may prove a lead.'

'Anything I should know about?'

DeVore took the tiny tape from his tunic pocket, wiped it on the cloth then handed it across the desk. Tolonen sat back and pushed the wafer-thin cassette into the input socket behind his left ear. For a minute or two he sat there, silent, his eyes making small, erratic movements in their sockets. Then, as if coming to again, he looked directly at his Major.

'Interesting, Howard. Very interesting.' Tolonen squeezed the narrow slit of skin behind his ear and removed the tape. 'But how reliable is this?'

DeVore tilted his head slightly, considering. 'Normally I'd say it was highly reliable. But the circumstances of this case – particularly its political importance – make it more complex than usual. It would be unwise to take things at face value. For now I'm having the sources checked out. Playing ear. However...' He hesitated, then spoke again, studying the General more closely than before. 'There is something else, sir. Something perhaps more important in the long run.'

'Go on.'

'Well, sir. I'm almost certain this involves Security. Maybe at Staff level.'

Tolonen nodded soberly, his expression unchanged. 'I agree. Though with great reluctance, I must say. The very thought of it makes me shudder.'

'Then...'

Tolonen stopped him with a look. 'Let me outline the situation as I see it, Howard. Then we'll see how this new information fits with what we have.'

DeVore sat straighter in his chair, his eyes watching the older man intently as he outlined the situation.

'First – what kind of weapon was used, and where and by whom was it manufactured?' Tolonen pulled broad, long fingers through neatly cut grey hair, his deeply blue eyes fixing DeVore. 'We're working on the assumption that it was some kind of ice derivative. An ice-eater. Research into ice derivatives has been banned by the Edict, but we're not dealing with legitimate activity here. It's possible that someone has come up with such a thing.

'Second – who knew Lwo Kang would be there at that time? Most of those we might have suspected – Lwo's own Junior Ministers – died with him. Only Yang Lai is unaccounted for.'

'No trace yet, sir. But we're still looking.'

'Good. Now, third – who took the Security squad off duty? Are we safe in assuming it was the duty captain, or was someone higher up the chain of command behind the decision?' Tolonen paused and shook his head. 'It seems almost inexplicable to me that the officer concerned acted independently. His record was without blemish and his suicide would seem to confirm it. But he was a frightened man, Howard. I believe he was acting under threat.'

'I agree, sir. I knew the man as a cadet and I'd vouch that he would not have acted as he did without good reason. Our assumption is that his immediate family was threatened. We haven't yet located them – but whether that's because he placed them in hiding or whether they were taken we don't know. Even so, we mustn't rule out another motive. Gambling debts, perhaps. Or some kind of addiction. Women, maybe. Even the best men have their weaknesses. In any case, I have a squad investigating it.'

'Good. Then, fourth – who were the actual assassins? As you know, our first idea was that it was done from the air – from a craft over-flying the dome. But now we've ruled that out.'

'Sir?' DeVore tensed slightly, suddenly more alert.

'A search of the area surrounding the dome has brought a number of new items to light, chief amongst which is a corpse.'

'A corpse?'

'Yes. We found the body crammed into a narrow feed tunnel, not far from a ventilation shaft that comes out close by the dome. A *Hung Mao*. Male. Aged thirty-five. He'd been stabbed twice with a large-bladed knife. Very expertly, so I'm told.'

'Then we've got one of the assassins?'

Tolonen shrugged. 'I wouldn't rule that out, but it's more likely that the man simply stumbled onto things. His ID shows him to have been a maintenance engineer, cleared for First Level Security.'

DeVore considered that. 'It sounds the ideal profession for gaining access to the dome.'

'My own first thought, only it doesn't check out with anything else. We can account for his movements up to the time he got into that ventilation tunnel. We've checked. He's on camera, climbing into the access hatch only twelve minutes before the dome went up. He made one check – timed and logged – halfway up the tunnel. That accounts for the first five minutes. That would leave him only seven minutes to climb the rest of the way, meet his partner, set the charges and get back down.'

'Time enough. And anyway, what if his partner set the charges?'

'That's possible. But then why would he be needed? And why killed? It doesn't fit. And anyway, we have something else.'

DeVore blinked. 'You have been busy, sir.'

Tolonen laughed. 'Yes, well, I did try to get you, Howard. Anyway, it's possible we have our men. Two low-level sorts. They were involved in an incident with Security guards in one of the nearby stacks at Level 11. A CompCam unit noticed that one of the men had no ID match and had Security investigate. There was an exchange of shots and the two men got away.'

'But you have them now?'

'No. Not yet. But listen to this, Howard. You'll never believe it. Do you know how they got out?'

DeVore shook his head.

'Well, our men thought they had them cornered in a Distribution lift. They'd called up a burner, ready to melt the doorlocks, but the two suspects did something to the lift. They overrode its circuits, then rammed the whole thing through the floor and into the Net! The whole deck had to be sealed and cleaned out. A messy business. Thousands hurt. More than a hundred and fifty dead. We've had to put out a story about systems failure. But think about it, Howard. Our two friends must have had inside information. There aren't that many people who know those lifts go down another ten levels. Just as important, however, is the fact that they had a device that overrode the circuitry.' He paused. 'It makes sense of other things, too. My guess is that they were dropped in. Picked up at one of the under-Net gates – perhaps near one of the agricultural processing stations – and landed on top of the City. They did the job, made their escape down the ventilation shaft – killing our maintenance man on the way – then emerged at Eleven.'

DeVore nodded. 'It makes sense.'

'I'm glad you think so. In which case there are a few other questions that need answers. Who were their contacts? Who gave them the information? Who trained them? Who physically landed them on the roof? This kind of operation would have needed a lot of planning. A substantial number of people would have been involved.'

Again DeVore nodded, but this time there was an air of distraction about him.

Tolonen leaned forward excitedly. 'Just think. If we could get to just one of those involved – just one! – we could blast the whole thing open!' He laughed, then slammed his hands down firmly on the desktop. 'And in order that we can do just that, I've been to see the T'ang.'

'Sir?' DeVore seemed surprised by this new development.

'Yes, and the T'ang has given me the authority to cut through bureaucratic tape, to make deals, grant pardons, whatever's necessary, providing we get information on the people who were behind this.' He smiled broadly. 'So you see, Howard. What you brought me was of great interest. If Wyatt was involved, either as principal or as agent... Well, I want him. Understand? I want to know what his motive was, who his connections were.'

'So you think it might be him?'

The General shrugged. 'I don't know. I thought... Well, you know what I thought. I listened to the tape of your conversation with Lehmann. He's an unpleasant specimen, but I agree with you. He's too bluff, too careless in what he says to have been behind this. As for Wyatt, I've met him more than once, and I liked him.' Again he shrugged. 'Still, do what you must. The T'ang wants answers, and he wants them fast.'

When DeVore had gone, Tolonen summoned his ensign, Haavikko.

Axel Haavikko was a tall, broad-shouldered young man of nineteen years, his blond hair cut severely short. On his jacket he wore the insignia of the elite military school from which he had graduated only eight months previously, on his chest the embroidered sea horse patch of a ninth-grade military officer. He marched briskly across the room and came to attention before the desk.

'Sir?'

The General smiled. 'At ease, boy. Have you got the tape?'

'Yes, sir. But I thought...'

Tolonen raised an eyebrow. 'I know. But I decided against it. Major DeVore doesn't need to know everything. He's tired. I could see it myself. He's taking on too much, trying to keep abreast of everything.'

He leaned back in his chair, studying the young man; observing that he too was showing signs of strain. 'We could all do with some rest, neh, Haavikko? A break from things. But the evil of this world goes on, whether we're there to deal with it or not.' He smiled kindly. 'Okay, let's see what we have.'

The cadet bowed, then turned and went over to the viewer, placing the flimsy transparent card he was carrying onto the viewing surface. Immediately the wall-screen above his head lit up, showing two men pushing their way through a broad but crowded corridor. The tape sheet had been put together from segments of hundreds of individual tape sheets, then edited to make it seem as though a single camera had followed the suspects the whole length of the Main.

'These are the two men, sir. The one on the left was addressed as Jyan. The other is unnamed. There's no entry on either in Security Central Records.'

The General sniffed. 'Hold that a moment.'

The image froze. A sign behind the first of the men read 'Level 11, South 3 Stack, Canton of Munich', the English in blocked black figures above the blood-red Mandarin pictograms. Crowds packed the Main. The second man – better built than the first; the telltale bulge of a knife at his waist – had turned to left profile, revealing a short, livid scar on his neck just below the ear.

'Interesting types, neh, Axel? From the Net. There's no doubt about it. If Security Central has nothing, then I'm certain these are our men. Can we tell where they appeared from?'

Axel tapped the controls. At once the picture changed – showed a smaller corridor; dimly lit, almost empty.

'Where's this?'

'Up five levels, sir. At Sixteen. It's a maintenance corridor, not used by the public. Watch.'

As they watched, a hatch dropped down from the ceiling and two men lowered themselves into the corridor, one after the other. The two Han from the other shots.

'Where does that lead?'

'There's a long vertical shaft, about twenty ch'i back from that hatch. It comes out at Forty-One. There we lose them.'

'Any reason why?'

'Camera malfunction. Vandalism. It seems genuine. They'd been having trouble with that section for weeks.'

'Okay. So let's get back to Eleven. See what kind of men we're dealing with.'

For the next ten minutes they watched in silence as the situation unfolded. They saw the fight. Saw Jyan draw and use his knife, then drive the loader into the lift. Then, less than a minute later, the screen went blank.

'That's all that survived, sir. When the quarantine seals came down most of the cameras blew. We've pieced this together from Central Records' copies.'

Tolonen nodded, satisfied. 'You've done a good job, Haavikko. It should-n't be difficult to trace these two. We have arrangements with certain of the

Triad bosses beneath the Net. They'll find them for us. It's only a question of time.'

'Then we do nothing, sir?'

'Nothing until we hear from our contacts. But I want us to be ready, so I've arranged something. It'll mean that we'll have a squad down there, under the Net in Munich Canton, when news comes. It'll allow us to get to them at once. I've put Fest in charge. He has strict orders to take the men alive if possible. You and Hans Ebert will make up the squad.'

'What are we to do down there?'

'Until you're called on, nothing. You can treat it as a paid holiday. Ebert knows the place quite well, apparently. I'm sure he'll find something for you to do. But when the call comes, be there, and fast. All right?'

Haavikko bowed his head. 'Anything else, sir?'

'Yes. One last thing.'

'Sir?'

'I want you to compile a list of all those who might have planned this, anyone who might conceivably have been involved. Not just those with a clear motive but anyone who might have had the right contacts.'

'Anyone?'

The General nodded sternly. 'Leave no one out, however absurd it might seem.'

The cadet bowed deeply, then clicked his heels together. 'Sir.'

Alone again, Tolonen stood, then went to the window. Far below, the wide moat of the Security Fortress seemed filled with an inky blackness. In the early morning light the two watchtowers at the far end of the bridge threw long, thin shadows across the apron of the spaceport beyond.

He would not act. Not yet. For a while he would trust to instinct and let Wyatt be. See if Wyatt's name appeared on Haavikko's list. Wait for DeVore to gather something more substantial than the tattle of Above. Because deep down he didn't believe that Wyatt was involved.

He turned back to his desk, putting his fingers lightly to the intercom pad.

His secretary answered at once. 'General?'

'Play me that tape again. Major DeVore and Under Secretary Lehmann. The part where Lehmann talks about suffocating and bad blood. A few lines, that's all.'

'Yes, General.'

He turned back to the window, looking down. As he watched a tiny figure emerged from the shadow and marched quickly but unhurriedly across the bridge. It was DeVore.

Major DeVore was a clever officer. A good man to have on your team. There was no fooling him; he saw things clearly. Saw through the appearance of things. And if he believed that Lehmann wasn't involved...

'The tape's ready, General.'

'Good,' he said, not looking round; continuing to watch the figure far below. 'Let me hear it.'

At once Lehmann's voice filled the room, urgent and passionate.

'We're suffocating, Howard! Can't they see that? Biting at the leash! Even so, violence... Well, that's a different matter. It hurts everyone and solves nothing. It only causes bad blood, and how can that help our cause? This... act. All it does is set us back a few more years. Makes things more difficult, more...'

The voice cut out. After a moment the General sniffed, then nodded to himself. He had heard the words a dozen times now, and each time they had had the power to convince him of Lehmann's innocence. Lehmann's anger, his callousness, while they spoke against him as a man, were eloquent in his defence in this specific matter. It was not how a guilty man behaved. In any case, he was right. How would this serve him? Li Shai Tung would merely appoint another Minister. Another like Lwo Kang.

Down below, DeVore had reached the far end of the bridge. Two tiny figures broke from the shadow of the left-hand tower to challenge him, then fell back, seeing who it was. They melted back into the blackness and DeVore marched on alone, out onto the apron of the spaceport.

The General turned away. Perhaps DeVore was right. Perhaps Wyatt was their man. Even so, a nagging sense of wrongness persisted, unfocused, unresolved.

'I'm tired,' he said softly to himself, sitting himself behind his desk again. 'Yes, tiredness, that's all it is.'

'Wait outside, at the junction. You know what he looks like?'

The Han nodded. 'Like my brother.'

'Good. Then get going.'

The Han did as he was told, closing the door behind him, leaving DeVore alone in the room. DeVore looked around, for the first time allowing himself to relax. Not long now. Not long and it would all be done. This was the last of it. He looked at the sealed bag on the floor by the bed and smiled, then sat on the end of the bed next to the corpse's feet.

The *kwai*, Chen, had been hard to kill. Stubborn. He had fought so hard for life that they had had to club him to death, as if strangling the man hadn't been enough. His head was a bloodied pulp, his features almost unrecognizable. The Han had enjoyed that. DeVore had had to drag him off.

Like animals, he thought, disgusted, promising himself he'd make the Han's death a particularly painful one.

For a while he sat there, head down, hands on knees, thinking things through. Then he looked up, looked about himself again. It was such a mean, shabby little place, and like all of this beneath the Net, it bred a type that matched its circumstances. This Kao Jyan, for instance; he had big dreams, but he was a little man. He didn't have the skill or imagination to carry off his scheme. All he had was a brash impudence; an inflated sense of self-importance. But, then, what else could be expected? Living here, a man had no perspective. No way of judging what the truth of things really was.

He got up and crossed the room. Inset into the wall was an old-fashioned games machine. A ResTem Mark IV. He switched it on and set it up for *Wei Chi*; an eighth-level game, the machine to start with black.

For a time he immersed himself in the game, enjoying the challenge. Then, when it was clear he had the advantage, he turned away.

The General was sharper than he'd thought he'd be. Much sharper. That business with the dead maintenance engineer. His discovery of Kao Jyan and the other *kwai*. For a moment DeVore had thought their scheme undone. But the game was far from played out. He'd let the General find his missing pieces. One by one he'd give them to him. But not until he'd done with them.

He glanced at the machine again. It was a complex game, and he prided himself on a certain mastery of it. Strange, though, how much it spoke of the difference between East and West. At least, of the old West, hidden beneath the levels of the Han City, the layers of Han culture and Han history. The games of the West had been played on similar boards to those of the East, but the West played between the lines, not on the intersecting points. And the games of the West had been flexible, each individual piece given breath, allowed to move, as though each had an independent life. That was not so in *Wei Chi*. In *Wei Chi* once a piece was placed it remained, unless it was surrounded and its 'breath' taken from it. It was a game of static patterns; patterns built patiently over hours or days – sometimes even months. A game where the point was not to eliminate but to enclose.

East and West – they were the inverse of each other. Forever alien. Yet one must ultimately triumph. For now it was the Han. But now was not forever.

He turned from the screen, smiling. 'White wins, as ever.'

It had always interested him; ever since he had learned how much the Han had banned or hidden. A whole separate culture. A long and complex history. Buried, as if it had never been. The story of the old West. Dead. Shrouded in white, the Han colour of death.

DeVore stretched and yawned. It was two days since he had last slept. He crossed the room and looked at his reflection in the mirror beside the shower unit. Not bad, he thought, but the drugs he had taken to keep himself alert had only a limited effect. Pure tiredness would catch up with him eventually. Still, they'd keep him on his feet long enough to see this through.

He looked down. His wrist console was flashing.

DeVore smiled at his reflection. 'At last,' he said. Then, straightening his tunic, he turned to face the door.

Jyan came laughing into his room. 'Chen...' he began, then stopped, his eyes widening, the colour draining from his cheeks. 'What the...?'

He turned and made to run, but the second man, following him in, blocked the doorway, knife in hand.

He turned back, facing the stranger.

'Close the door,' DeVore said, looking past Jyan at the other. Then he turned to face Jyan again. 'Come in, Kao Jyan. Make yourself at home.'

Jyan swallowed and backed away to the left, his eyes going to the figure sprawled face down on the bed, the cover over its head. It was Chen. He could tell it from a dozen different signs – by the shape of the body, the clothes, by the black, studded straps about his wrists.

For a moment he said nothing, mesmerized by the sight of those two strong hands resting there, lifeless and pale, palms upward on the dark red sheet. Then he looked up again. The stranger was watching him, that same cruel half-smile on his lips.

'What do you want?' Jyan asked, his voice barely audible.

DeVore laughed, then turned to face the games machine, tapping in his next move. Jyan looked at the screen. The machine was set up for *Wei Chi*, the nineteen by nineteen grid densely cluttered with the small black and white stones. From the state of the game it looked as though the stranger had been waiting for some time.

DeVore turned back, giving Jyan a strangely intense look. Then he dropped his eyes and moved closer. 'It's a fascinating game, don't you think, Kao Jyan? Black starts, and so the odds are in his favour – seven out of ten, they say – yet I, like you, prefer to play against the odds.'

He stepped closer. Jyan backed against the wall, looking away.

'You have the envelope, Kao Jyan?'

Jyan turned his head, meeting the other's eyes. Only a hand's width separated them now. He could feel the other's breath upon his cheek. 'The... envelope?'

'The offer we made you.'

'Ah...' Jyan fumbled in the inside pocket of his one-piece, then drew out the crumpled envelope and handed it to him. The stranger didn't look at it, merely pocketed it, then handed back another.

'Go on. Open it. It's our new offer.'

Jyan could see the body on the bed, the man waiting at the door, knife in hand, and wondered what it meant. Was he dead? He looked down at the sealed letter in his hand. It was identical to the one Cho Hsiang had given him.

His hands shaking, he opened the envelope and took out the folded sheet. This time there was nothing on it. The pure white sheet was empty.

DeVore smiled. 'You understand, Kao Jyan?'

Jyan looked from one man to the other, trying to see a way out of this. 'The tape...' he began, his voice trembling now. 'What about the tape?'

The stranger turned away, ignoring his comment, as if it had no significance. 'I'm sorry about your friend. It was unfortunate, but he was no part of this. The deal was with you, Kao Jyan.'

Jyan found he was staring at the body again. The stranger saw where he was looking and smiled. 'Go on. Look at him, if you want. He'll not mind you looking now.' He went across to the bed and pulled the cover back. 'Here...'

The stranger's voice held a tone of command that made Jyan start forward, then hesitate, a wave of nausea passing through him.

DeVore looked up from the body. 'He was a hard man to kill, your friend. It took both of us to deal with him. Chu Heng here had to hold him down while I dressed him.'

Jyan shuddered. A cord had been looped about Chen's bull neck four or five times then tightened until it had bitten into the flesh, drawing blood. But it was hard to judge whether that had been the cause of death or the heavy blows he'd suffered to the back of the head; blows that had broken his skull like a fragile piece of porcelain.

He swallowed drily then looked up, meeting the stranger's eyes. 'Am I dead?'

DeVore laughed; not cruelly, but as if the naivety of the remark had genuinely amused him. 'What do you think?'

'The tape...' he said again.

'You don't understand, do you, Kao Jyan?'

The Han in the doorway laughed, but shut up abruptly when DeVore looked at him.

Jyan's voice was almost a breath now. 'Understand what?'

'The game. Its rules. Its different levels. You see, you were out of your depth. You had ambitions above your level. That's a dangerous thing for a little man like you. You were greedy.'

Jyan shivered. It was what Chen had said.

'You've... how should I say it... *inconvenienced us.*'

'Forget the whole thing. Please. I...'

DeVore shook his head. 'I'm sorry,' he said quietly, looking at Jyan with what seemed almost regret. 'It's not possible.'

'I'll say nothing. I swear I'll say nothing.'

'You give your word, eh?' DeVore turned and picked up the bag on the floor by the bed. 'Here. This is what your word means.'

DeVore threw the bag at him. Jyan caught it and looked inside, then threw the bag down, horrified. It was Cho Hsiang's head.

'You understand, then? It's necessity. We have to sacrifice some pieces. For the sake of the game.'

'The game...?'

But there were no more explanations. The Han's knife flashed and dug deep into his back. Kao Jyan was dead before he hit the floor.

In Mu Chua's House of the Ninth Ecstasy it was the hour of leisure and the girls were sprawled out on the couches in the Room of the Green Lamps, talking and laughing amongst themselves. Mu Chua's House was a good house, a clean house, even though it was below the Net, and catered only for those who came here from Above on business. Feng Chung, biggest of the local Triad bosses and Mu Chua's one-time lover, gave them his protection. His men guarded Mu Chua's doors and gave assistance when a customer grew troublesome. It was a good arrangement and Mu Chua had grown fat on it.

Mu – it meant mother in the old tongue, though she was no one's mother and had been sterilized at twelve – was in her fifties now; a strong, small woman with a fiery temper who had a genuine love for her trade and for the girls in her charge. 'Here men forget their cares,' was her motto and she had it written over the door in English and Mandarin, the pictograms sewn into every cushion, every curtain, every bedspread in the place. Even so, there were strict rules in her House. None of her girls could be hurt in any way. 'If they want that,' she had said to Feng Chung once, her eyes blazing with anger, 'they can go down to the Clay. This is a good house. A loving house. How can my girls be loving if they are scared? How can they take the cares of men away unless they have no cares themselves?'

Mu Chua was still a most attractive woman and many who had come to sample younger flesh had found themselves ending the night in mother's arms. Thereafter there would be no other for them. They would return to her alone, remembering not only the warmth and enthusiasm of her embraces, but also those little tricks – special things she kept a secret, even from her girls – that only she could do.

Just now she stood in the arched doorway, looking in at her girls, pleased by what she saw. She had chosen well. There were real beauties here – like Crimson Lotus and Jade Melody – and girls of character, like Spring Willow and the tiny, delicate-looking Sweet Honey, known to all as 'little Mimi', after the Mandarin for her adopted name. But there was more than that to her girls; she had trained them to be artisans, skilled at their craft of lovemaking. If such a thing were possible here in the Net, they had breeding. They were not common *men hu* – 'the one standing in the door' but *shen nu* – 'god girls'. To Mu Chua it was an important distinction. Her girls might well be prostitutes, but they were not mere smoke-flowers. Her House was a land of warmth and softness, a model for all other Houses, and she felt a great pride in having made it so.

Crimson Lotus and Sweet Honey had settled themselves at the far end of the room and were talking with another of the girls, Golden Heart. Mu Chua went across to them and settled herself on the floor between them, listening to their talk.

'I had a dream, Mother Chua,' said Golden Heart, turning to her. She was Mu Chua's youngest girl, a sweet-faced thing of thirteen. 'I was telling Crimson and little Mimi. In my dream it was New Year and I was eating cakes. *Nian-kao* – year cakes. Above me the clouds formed huge mountains in the sky, lit with the most extraordinary colours. I looked up, expecting something, and then, suddenly, a tiger appeared from out of the West and came and mated with me.'

The other girls giggled, but Golden Heart carried on, her face earnest. 'Afterwards I woke, but I was still in the dream, and beside me on the bed lay a pale grey snake, its skin almost white in places. At first it moved, yet when I reached out and touched it it was cold.'

Mu Chua licked at her lips, disturbed. 'That is a powerful dream, child. But what it means...' She shrugged and fell quiet, then changed the subject. It would not do to worry Golden Heart. 'Listen. I have a special favour to ask of you girls. We are to have visitors. Three important men from the Above. Soldiers.'

Crimson Lotus clapped her hands in delight. 'How wonderful, Mother Chua! Soldiers! They keep themselves so fit, so trim!' She gave a low, seductive laugh and looked across at Sweet Honey. 'If Mother Chua weren't here to look after us I'm sure I'd do it for nothing with a soldier!'

Mu Chua joined their laughter. 'Yes. But these are not just any soldiers. These are the Great General's own men, his elite, and you will be paid three times your usual fee. You will entertain them in the Room of Heaven and you will do whatever they ask.'

'Whatever they ask?' Sweet Honey raised an eyebrow.

Mu Chua smiled reassuringly at her. 'Within the rules, of course. They have been told they are not to harm you in any way.'

'And if they are not pleased?' asked Golden Heart, her face still clouded from the dream she'd had.

Mu Chua reached out and stroked her cheek tenderly. 'They are men, child. Of course they will be pleased.'

Ebert stopped at the curtained doorway and turned to face them. 'Here we are, my friends. Mu Chua's. The finest beneath the Net.'

Fest laughed, delighted, but at his side Haavikko looked uncertain. 'What is this place?'

Fest clapped his shoulder and pointed up at the sign of the lotus and the fish above the doorway. 'What does it look like, Axel? We're in Flower Streets and Willow Lanes here. In the land of warmth and softness. At home with the family of the green lamps.' He saw comprehension dawn on Haavikko's face and laughed again. 'Yes, Axel, it's a Sing-Song House. A brothel.'

He tried to go forward, his arm still about Haavikko's shoulder, but the young ensign held back.

'No. I don't want to go in.' Haavikko swallowed. A faint colour appeared in his cheeks. 'It... isn't my thing.'

Ebert came back to him. 'You're a man, aren't you, Haavikko? Well, then, of course it's your thing.'

Haavikko shook his head. 'You go in. I'll wait for you.'

Ebert looked at Fest and raised an eyebrow. Then he looked back at Haavikko. 'That's impossible. I've booked us in for the night. We're staying here. This is our billet while we're down here. Understand?'

'You mean they do more than...?'

Ebert nodded exaggeratedly, making Fest laugh once more, then he grew more serious. 'Look, Haavikko, if you don't want to screw one of the girls you don't have to. But come inside, eh? Mu Chua will bring you a meal and show you to a room. You can watch a trivee or something while Fest and I enjoy ourselves.'

Haavikko looked down, angered by the slightly mocking tone in Ebert's voice. 'Isn't there somewhere else I could stay?'

Ebert huffed, losing his patience suddenly. 'Oh, for the gods' sake, Fest, order him inside! Don't you understand, Haavikko? We're a squad. We need to be together when the call comes. What's the fucking good if you're somewhere else?'

Haavikko looked to Fest, who smiled apologetically. 'It's true, Axel. My orders are to keep us together at all times. Look, why don't you do what Hans has suggested? Come inside and take a room. Then, if you change your mind, you've not far to go.'

'I've told you...'

'Yes, yes. I understand. Now come inside. I order you. All right?'

Inside Mu Chua greeted them expansively, then led them through to a large room at the back of the House where three girls were waiting. As they entered the girls knelt and bowed their heads, then looked up at them, smiling, expectant, as if waiting for them to make their choice. Axel stared at them, surprised. They were not at all what he had expected, neither was this place the gaudy den of harlotry he had so often seen in vid dramas.

'What is this room called?' he asked, surprising both Ebert and Fest by being the first to speak.

The girl on the far left looked briefly across at her companions, then looked up at Axel, smiling radiantly. 'This is the Room of Heaven. Here a man may dream and live his dreams.'

She was beautiful. Even for these tiny Han types she was quite exceptional, and Axel felt something stir in him despite himself. She wore a bright red satin ch'i p'ao patterned with tiny blue flowers and cranes and varicoloured butterflies, the long, one-piece dress wrapped concealingly about her dainty figure. Her hair had been cut in a swallowtail bang, the two wings swept down over a pale ivory brow that would have graced the daughter of a T'ang, a clasp of imitation pearls holding the dark flow of her black hair in a tight, unbraided queue. Her hands, small as a child's, were unadorned, the nails varnished but unpainted. She was so astonishing, so unexpected, that he could not help but stare at her, his lips parted, his eyes wide.

'What do they call you?'

She bowed her head again, a faint smile playing on her tiny, rosebud lips. 'My name is Crimson Lotus.'

'Well!' said Ebert, laughing. 'I see Haavikko has made his choice.'

Axel broke from the spell. 'No. Not at all. I... I meant what I said. This...' He looked about him again, surprised anew by the tastefulness, the simple luxury of the room and its furnishings. 'This isn't my thing.'

He looked back down at the girl and saw, behind the surface smile, a faint hint of disappointment in her eyes and at the corners of her mouth. At once he felt upset that he had hurt her, even in so small a way, by his inadvertence. 'I'm sorry...' he started to say, but Ebert spoke over him.

'Ladies, please forgive our friend. We thought we might change his mind by bringing him to your most excellent house, but it seems he's adamant.' Ebert looked to Fest and smiled. 'I should explain. My friend is ya, you understand? A yellow eel.'

Haavikko frowned, not understanding. His knowledge of basic Mandarin included neither term. But the girls understood at once.

'My pardon, honourable sir,' said Crimson Lotus, her face clear, her smile suddenly resplendent, showing her pearl-white perfect teeth. 'If you will but wait a moment I shall call back Mother Chua. I am certain she could provide you with a boy.'

Axel turned to face Ebert, furious.

Ebert roared with laughter, enjoying the confusion on the faces of the girls. Ignoring the edge in Axel's voice, he reached out and touched his shoulder. 'Only a joke, my friend. Only a joke.'

The girls were looking from one to the other of the soldiers, their faces momentarily anxious. Then they too joined in with Ebert's laughter, their heads lowered, one hand raised to their mouths, their laughter like the faint, distant laughter of children.

Axel turned away from Ebert and looked at them again, letting his anger drain from him. Then he smiled and gave the slightest bow. No, he thought. *Make nothing of it. It is Ebert's way. He cannot help it if he is ill-bred and ill-mannered. It comes from being who he is: heir to one of the biggest financial empires in Chung Kuo. He does not have to behave as Fest and I. We serve, but he only plays at being a servant. He, after all, is a master.*

Yes, but watch yourself, Hans Ebert. One day you'll make one joke too many, speak out of place once too often, and then your riches will not help you. No, or your connections.

The smallest of the girls rose with a bow and came towards them, head lowered. 'Would the gentlemen like *ch'a?*'

Ebert answered for them. 'Gods, no! Bring us something stronger. Some wine. And something to eat, too. I'm ravenous!'

Embarrassed by Ebert's brash, proprietorial manner and awkward on his own account, Axel watched the others sit on cushions Crimson Lotus brought for them. 'Will you not sit with us?' she asked him, coming much closer than she had before. The sweet delicacy of her scent was intoxicating and her dark eyes were like a lover's, sharing some secret understanding.

'I'd best not,' he said, rather too stiffly. My sister... he had almost added. He looked down, suddenly embarrassed. Yes, that was why. He had promised his sister. Had sworn on his honour that he would keep himself clean. Would not do as other men did.

He shuddered then met the girl's eyes again. 'If you would send for Mu Chua. Perhaps she would find me a room. I'll eat there and take my rest.'

Crimson Lotus smiled, unoffended, nothing behind her smile this time. Her disappointment had been momentary; now she was the perfect hostess once more, all personal thoughts banished. 'If you will wait a moment, I shall summon her.'

But Mu Chua had been watching everything. She appeared in the doorway at once, knowing what to do, what to say in this instance. She had been told beforehand that it might be so.

'Please follow me, *Shih* Haavikko. There is a room prepared. I will take you there.'

Axel bowed, grateful, then looked across at Ebert and Fest. Fest met his eyes and gave the briefest nod, acknowledging his departure, but Ebert ignored him, concentrating on the young girl – she looked barely ten – who sat beside him now.

'What is the young girl's name?' Haavikko asked Mu Chua, keeping his voice low.

Mu Chua smiled. 'That's Golden Heart. She's the baby of the house. A sweet young thing, don't you think?'

He stared at the girl a moment longer, then turned back to Mu Chua. 'If you would take me to my room.'

Mu Chua smiled, all understanding. 'Of course.'

Axel woke to find the room dark, a strange smell in the air. He sat up suddenly, alert, his training taking over, then remembered where he was and forced himself to relax. But still he felt on edge. Something was wrong.

He heard it. Heard the second thread of breathing in the silent darkness. He felt to his left. Nothing. Then to his right. His hand met a soft warmth.

He swallowed, recognizing the musky smell for what it was. What had they done? Drugged him? And what else? He had seen too many covert operations not to feel vulnerable. What if Ebert had set this up? What if he'd had him drugged, then taped what he'd subsequently done? He shivered and slowly edged away from the girl – was it a girl? – who lay there next to him in the bed, then felt behind him for a lighting panel.

His hand met the slight indentation in the wall. At once a soft light lay across the centre of the bed, blurring into darkness.

Axel gasped and his eyes widened, horrified. 'Kuan Yin preserve me!' he whispered.

The girl was *Hung Mao*. A tall, blonde-haired girl with full breasts and an athletic build. She lay there, undisturbed by the light, one hand up at her neck, the fingers laced into her long, thick hair, the other resting on her smoothly muscled stomach, the fingers pointing down to the rich growth of pubic hair.

Axel stared at her, horrified and yet fascinated, his eyes drawn to her ice-white breasts, to the soft, down-covered swell of her sex. Then he looked at her face again and shuddered. So like her. So very like her.

He turned away, then looked back, his eyes drawn once more to those parts of her he'd never seen. Never dreamed he'd see.

It couldn't be. Surely...?

'Vesa...' he whispered, leaning closer. 'Vesa...' It was his sister's name.

The head turned, the eyes opened. Astonishingly blue eyes, like his sister's. But different. Oh, so thankfully different. And yet...

He pushed the thought back sharply. But it came again. Like Vesa. So very like his darling sister Vesa.

The girl smiled up at him and reached out for him, making a small sound of pleasure deep in her throat.

Instinctively he moved back slightly, tensed, but he was betrayed. Slowly his penis filled with blood until, engorged, it stood out stiffly. And when she reached for it and took it he could do nothing but close his eyes, ashamed and yet grateful.

As he entered her he opened his eyes and looked at her again. 'What's your name?'

She laughed softly, and for the briefest moment the movement of her body against his own slowed and became uncertain. 'Don't you remember, Axel? I'm White Orchid. Your little flower.' Then she laughed again, more raucously this time, her body pressing up against his, making him cry out with the pleasure of it. 'And he said you were *ya*...'

'Shall I wake him?'

'No, Mother Chua. Let him sleep a little longer. The fight is not for another two hours yet. There's plenty of time. Did he enjoy himself?'

Mu Chua smiled but did not answer. Some things she would do for money. Others were against her code. Spying on her guests was one of them. She studied Ebert a moment, trying to establish what it was made him so different from the others who came here. Perhaps it was just the sheer rudeness of the man. His ready assumption that he could have anything, buy anything. She didn't like him, but then it wasn't her job to like all of her clients. As it was, he had brought her something valuable – the two *Hung Mao* girls.

'Have you made your mind up yet?'

Ebert did not look at her. There was a faint smile on his lips. 'I can choose anyone?'

'That was our deal.'

'Then I'll take the girl. Golden Heart.'

Mu Chua looked down. It was as she had expected. 'She's untrained,' she said, knowing it was hopeless but trying to persuade him even so.

'I know. That's partly why I chose her. I could train her myself. To my own ways.'

Mu Chua shuddered, wondering what those ways would be. For a moment she considered going back on the deal and returning the two *Hung Mao* girls, but she knew that it made no sense either to throw away such a certain attraction as the barbarian *shen nu* nor to make an enemy of Hans Ebert.

'Are you certain she's not too young?'

Ebert merely laughed.

'Then I'll draw up the contracts. It will be as agreed. The two girls for the one. And this evening's entertainment free.'

'As we agreed,' said Ebert, smiling to himself.

Mu Chua studied him again, wondering what game he was playing with his fellow officer. She had seen the way he bullied and insulted him. Why, then, had he been so insistent that she drug him and send the *Hung Mao* girl to him? There seemed no love lost between the two men, so what was Ebert's design?

She bowed and smiled, for once feeling the hollowness of her smile, then turned and went to bring the contract. But she was thinking of Golden Heart's dream. Ebert was the tiger come out of the West, and last night he had mated with her. Insatiably, so Golden Heart had said: wildly, his passion barely short of violence. And though there was no chance of Golden Heart conceiving, Mu Chua could not help but think of the image in the dream – the image of the grey-white snake. In most cases it was an auspicious symbol – sign that the dreamer would bear a boy child. But the snake in the dream had been cold and dead.

She shuddered. The first part of the dream had proved so right, how could the second not come about in time? And then, what misery for Golden Heart. *Eat your year cakes now*, thought Mu Chua as she took the contract from the drawer in her room and turned to go back. *Celebrate now beneath the rainbow-coloured clouds, for soon Golden Heart will be broken. And I can do nothing. Nothing at all.*

When he woke the second time he knew she would be there, beside him in the bed. He turned and looked at her, all shame, all horror purged from him, only love and a vague desire remaining. For a moment he was still, silent, watching her, a faint smile on his face. Then, as he watched, there was movement at the mouth of her sex. A dark and slender shape seemed to press up between the soft, pale lips of flesh. Slowly it emerged, stretching a thumbnail's length and more into the air, its blind snout moving purposively, as if sniffing the air. Axel stared at it, fascinated and horrified. It was alive – a living thing! He gave a small cry of shock and surprise and the thing vanished, as though it had never been, burrowing back down into the soft, moist folds of flesh.

His cry woke her. She sat up abruptly, her eyes as blue as a northern sea, heavy with sleep. 'Axel... What is it?'

She focused on his face and seemed to come awake suddenly, seeing the horror there.

'Gods, what is it?' She got up and moved towards him, but he backed away, fending her off with his hands. She stopped still, her body tensed, and lowered her head a fraction, staring at him. 'Tell me what it is, Axel. Please. Was it a bad dream?'

He pointed at her. 'Something...'

It was all he could say, but it seemed she understood. She sat back on the bed, folding her hands in her lap. 'Ah... I see.'

She let out a deep breath. 'What you saw...' She shrugged and looked up at him, strangely vulnerable. 'We all have them.' Her look was as much as to say, *Surely you knew about this? Surely you've heard?*

'I...' he swallowed. 'I don't understand.'

She stared at him a moment longer, then reached down into the folds of her sex and gently began to coax something from within. Axel watched, wide-eyed, as she lifted the thing with her fingers and placed it gently in the palm of her right hand, extending it towards him so that he could see it clearly.

'Look. It's all right. It won't hurt you. It's perfectly harmless.'

It was an insect of some kind. Or so it first appeared. A dark, slender, worm-like shape half the length of a finger. It was smooth and perfectly black. Unsegmented. Unmarked. It seemed blind; devoid, in fact, of all sensory equipment. And yet it had reacted swiftly to his cry.

'What is it?' he asked, coming closer, unable to conceal a shudder.

'As I said, we all have them. All of the girls, that is. They keep us clean, you see. GenSyn developed them. They live off bacteria – special kinds of bacteria. Aids, herpes, venereal diseases of all kinds.'

He wrinkled up his nose. 'Gods,' he said. 'And it's been there all the time. While we were...?'

'All the time. But it never gets in the way. It lives in a special sack in my womb. It only comes out when it senses I'm asleep or perfectly relaxed. It's a parasite, you see. A benevolent one.' She smiled and petted the thing in her hand, then gently put it back.

There was a knock on the door. Axel looked about him.

'Here,' said the girl, handing him a robe, but taking nothing for herself.

He wrapped the er-silk *pau* about him, then turned to face the door. 'Come in!'

It was Mu Chua. 'I heard a noise,' she said. 'Is everything all right?'

'Yes. Yes, it's fine.' He glanced at the girl, who sat there on the bed, looking away from him, then turned back to face Mu Chua. 'It was nothing. Really. Nothing at all.'

Mu Chua met his eyes and held them just a moment longer than was natural, making him wonder what she was thinking as she looked at him; re-awakening, for the briefest moment, his fears of being taped and betrayed. But then she smiled – a warm, candid smile that held no subterfuge. 'Good,' she said. 'Then dress and come through. I've prepared a breakfast for you.'

Her smile warmed him, cleared away the shadows in his head. 'Thank you, Mother Chua. You run a good house. A very good house.'

The Pit was a riot of noise and activity, its tiered benches packed to overflowing. On all sides men yelled and waved their arms frantically, placing bets, dark, faceless figures in the dim red light, while down below, in the intense white light of the combat circle, the two men crouched on their haunches, in the *wa shih* stance, facing each other silently.

Axel Haavikko, sitting on the front bench between Fest and Ebert, narrowed his eyes, studying the two combatants. They seemed an ill-matched pair; one *Hung Mao*, the other Han; one a giant, the other so compact and yet so perfectly formed he looked as though he had been made in a GenSyn vat. But there was a stillness, an undisguised sense of authority about the smaller man that impressed at once. He seemed immovable, as if grown about a central point of calm.

'The Han's name is Hwa. I'm told he's champion here,' said Fest, leaning forward and speaking into his ear. 'Seventeen bouts, he's had. Two more and it'll be a record.'

Axel turned and yelled back at Fest. 'And the other?'

Fest shrugged and indicated the small Han next to him. He leaned forward again, raising his voice. 'My friend here says that no one knows much about him. He's a local boy, name of Karr, but he hasn't fought before. He's something of a mystery. But worth a bet, maybe. You'll get good odds.'

Axel turned to look at the other combatant. Crouched, Karr was taller than most men. Seven *ch'i*, perhaps. Maybe more. Standing, he had been close to twice the size of Hwa; broad at the shoulder and heavily muscled, his oiled skin shining slickly in the brilliant whiteness. Such men were usually slow. They depended on sheer strength to win through. Yet Axel remembered how the crowd had gone quiet when the giant entered the arena and realized that Karr was something unusual, even by their standards.

For a moment he studied the tattoos on Karr's chest and arms. On each arm a pair of dragons – one green, one red, their long bodies thick and muscular – coiled about each other sinuously. Their heads were turned inward, face to face, wide, sharp-toothed mouths snarling, huge, golden eyes flashing. On his chest a great bird spread its wings, its powerful, regal head thrown back defiantly, its cruel beak open in a cry of triumph, a terror-stricken horse held fast in each of its steel-like talons.

Axel looked away, feeling suddenly quite awkward. His silks, his braided hair, his necklaces of silver and jade. Such refinements were an impertinence down here. There was no place for such subtleties. Here everything was bared.

It was warm in the Pit and unbearably stuffy, yet he shivered, thinking of what was to come.

'Look at him!' yelled Ebert, leaning close to join their conversation. 'Meat! That's what he is! A huge sack of meat! It's a foregone conclusion, Haavikko! I'd not waste a single yuan on him! It'll be over in seconds!'

'You think so?'

Ebert nodded exaggeratedly. 'See our man here.' He indicated Hwa. 'I'm told he's a perfectionist. An artist. He practises eight hours a day, sometimes doing nothing but repeating one single movement.' Ebert laughed and his blue eyes gleamed red in the dull light. 'Such training pays off. They say he's so fast you daren't even blink while he's fighting!'

Axel shrugged. Maybe it was so. Certainly there was something different, something *obsessive* about the man that was quite chilling. His eyes, for instance, never moved. They stared ahead, as if in trance, boring into his opponent's face, unblinking, merciless in their focus. Whereas the other...

Even as he looked he saw Karr turn his head and look directly at him.

It was a fierce, insolent gaze, almost primitive in its intensity, and yet not wholly unintelligent. There was something about the man. Something he had seen at once. Perhaps it was the casual, almost arrogant way he had looked about the tiers on entering, or the brief, almost dismissive bow he had greeted his opponent with. Whatever, it was enough to make Axel feel uneasy with Ebert's brusque dismissal of the man. On balance, however, he had to agree with Ebert: the small man looked like an adept – a perfect fighting machine. Height, weight and breadth were no concern to him. His strength was of another kind.

'Of course,' continued Ebert, raising his voice so that it carried to the giant, 'brute strength alone can never win. Intelligence and discipline will triumph every time. It's nature's law!'

Axel saw the giant's eyes flare, his muscles tense. He had heard.

He leaned close to Ebert. 'I'll wager a hundred yuan that the big man wins.'

'I'll give you five to one.'

'You're sure?'

Ebert laughed arrogantly. 'Make it two fifty, and I'll give you ten to one!'

Axel met his eyes a moment, conscious of the challenge in them, then gave the barest nod.

Just then, however, the fight marshal stepped out into the combat circle and the crowd hushed expectantly.

Axel felt his stomach tighten, his heart begin to thud against his rib cage. This was it then. To the death.

The two men rose and approached the centre of the circle. There they knelt and bowed to each other – a full *k'o t'ou*, heads almost touching. Then they sat back on their haunches, waiting, while the marshal gave their names and read the rules.

The rules were short and simple. One. No weapons were permitted but their own bodies. Two. So long as the fight continued they were to keep within the combat circle. Three. Once begun the fight could not be called off. It ended only when one of them was dead.

Axel could feel the tension in his bones. All about him rose a buzz of excitement, an awful, illicit excitement that grew and grew as the moments passed and the two men faced each other at the circle's centre, waiting for the signal.

Then, suddenly, it began.

The small man flipped backwards like a tumbler, then stopped, perfectly, almost unnaturally still, half-crouched on his toes, his arms raised to shoulder level, forearms bent inward, his fingers splayed.

Karr had not moved. He was watching Hwa carefully, his eyes half-lidded. Then, very slowly, he eased back off his knees, drawing himself up to his full height, his weight balanced on the balls of his feet.

Hwa feinted to the left, then sprang at Karr, bounding forward then flipping his body up and sideways, one foot kicking out at the big man's groin.

There was a roar from the crowd. For a moment Karr was down. Then he was up again, his feet thudding against the canvas flooring, a hiss of pain escaping through his teeth. Hwa had missed his target. His foot had struck Karr on the upper thigh. The skin there was a vivid red, darkening by the moment, and as Karr circled he rubbed at the spot tenderly, almost absent-mindedly.

'He's too slow!' Ebert hissed in his ear.

'Wait!' Axel answered. He had been watching Hwa's face, had seen the surprise there when the big man had bounced up again. Hwa had thought he had him.

Hwa crouched again, in the classic *ch'i ma shih*, the riding horse stance, moving side to side from the hips, like a snake. Then he moved his feet in a little dance. From the tiers on all sides came a loud, low shuddering as the crowd banged their feet in applause. A moment later Hwa attacked again.

This time he ran at Karr; a strange, weaving run that ended in a leap. At the same time he let out a bloodcurdling scream.

But Karr had moved.

At the instant Hwa leaped, Karr ducked, rolled and turned. It was a move-ment that was so quick and so unexpected from such a big man that a huge gasp of surprise went up from the crowd. As Hwa turned to face him again, Karr was smiling.

Surprise turned to rage. Hwa attacked a third time, whirling his body about, thrusting and kicking, his arms and legs moving in a blur. But each blow was met and countered. For once Hwa's speed was matched. And when he withdrew he was breathing heavily, his face red from exertion.

The crowd roared its appreciation.

'It's luck!' yelled Ebert next to him. 'You see if it isn't! The Han will have him soon enough!'

Axel made to answer, but at that moment Hwa launched himself again, flipping over once, twice, like an acrobat, then feinting to left, right, then left again. He was only an arm's length from Karr when the big man acted. But this time Karr moved a fraction too slowly. When Hwa kicked Karr was off-balance, striking at a place where Hwa had been but was no longer.

The crack of bone could be heard to the back of the tiers.

Karr groaned audibly and went down.

Hwa struck again at once, his foot kicking out once, twice, forcing the broken arm back at an impossible angle.

Axel gasped, feeling sick. Beside him Ebert gave a yell of triumph.

Hwa moved back, getting his breath, a look of satisfaction replacing the frown of concentration he had worn until that moment.

The Pit was tense, silent, waiting for him to end it. 'Shau,' he said softly, looking at Karr. Burn.

Karr was down on one knee, his face a mask of pain. Slowly, very slowly, he got up, supporting his shattered arm with his left hand. For a moment he seemed to look inside himself. His breathing slowed and his face cleared. With a grimace of pure agony, he wrenched his arm back, the click of bone against bone the only sound in the whole arena. For a moment he swayed, then seemed to gain control of himself again and tucked the useless hand into the cloth belt at his waist, securing it.

'Come,' he said, lifting his chin in challenge to the smaller man. 'It isn't over yet.'

The words were like a goad. Hwa exploded, twirling and somersaulting, kicking and punching in a furious rain of blows that went on for minutes. But Karr was up to the challenge. With his good arm and both legs he parried everything Hwa threw at him, weaving and ducking and turning with a speed and agility that surprised everyone. It seemed impossible for a man so big to move his weight so quickly, so subtly.

But Axel, watching, saw how much it cost him – saw, beneath the mask of outward calm, the agony as Karr flipped and jumped and rolled, avoiding the constant flood of blows. Saw it in his eyes, in the faintest movement at the corners of his mouth. Watched until it seemed impossible that Karr could take any more.

And then, just as Hwa was drawing off, Karr counter-attacked for the first time.

Hwa moved back, his full weight resting momentarily – perhaps, for the only time during the contest – on his back foot, in hou shih, the monkey stance. And as he moved back, so Karr rolled forward, pushing up off the floor with his good left arm, his wrist straining and flexing, the whole weight of his huge frame thrust forward into Hwa.

He caught Hwa totally off-balance, his legs wrapping about the small man's neck, his huge weight driving him down into the canvas.

For an instant there was silence. Then, as the big man rolled over there was a groan. Karr sat up, clutching his arm, his face rent with pain. But Hwa was dead. He lay there next to Karr, pale, unmoving, his back, his neck broken, the back of his skull crushed by the impact of his fall.

Axel let out a shivering breath. Beside him Ebert was suddenly very quiet. On all sides the Pit was in uproar.

'Magnificent!' Fest yelled into Axel's ear. 'They were giving odds of thirty-five to one! It's the biggest upset in five years, so my friend here says!' But Axel was barely listening. He was watching Karr, filled with admiration and respect for the big man.

'He was magnificent,' Axel said softly, turning to look at Ebert.

'He was lucky!' For a second or two Ebert glowered back at him. Then he laughed dismissively and dug something out of his tunic pocket and handed it across to Haavikko.

'It's only money, neh?'

Axel looked down at the thick square of plastic in his hand. It was a secure-image holo-chip. A bearer credit for 2500 yuan. Axel looked up, surprised, then remembered the wager. Two fifty at ten to one. It was more than three months' salary, but Ebert had treated it as nothing. But then, why not? To him it was pocket money.

Ebert was leaning across him, yelling at Fest. 'Hey! Let's go back to the dressing room and congratulate him, neh?'

For a moment longer Axel stared at Ebert, then he looked back at the big man. Karr was picking himself up from the floor painfully, no sign of triumph in his face.

Fest took Axel's arm and began to pull him away. 'Let's go. Hans has had enough.'

'Come on,' said Ebert as they stood outside. 'We'll buy the brute dinner. He can be our guest.'

They stood in the corridor outside the dressing room, leaning against the wall, ignoring the comings and goings of the lesser fighters. There were bouts all afternoon – challengers for the new champion. But they had seen enough. Ebert had sent in his card a quarter bell ago, the invitation scribbled on the back. Now they waited.

'There's a problem with such mechanical virtuosity,' Ebert said rather pompously. 'It can so easily switch over into automatonism. A kind of unthinking, machine-like response. Totally inflexible and unable to adapt to approaches more subtle than its own. That's why Hwa lost. He was inflexible. Unable to change.'

Fest laughed. 'Sound stuff, Hans. But what you're really saying is that you knew the big man would win all the time!'

Ebert shook his head. 'You know what I mean.' There was a slight irritation in his voice. Then he relented and laughed. 'Okay, I'm trying to rationalize it, but we were all surprised. Even Axel here. Even he thought his man was going to lose.'

Haavikko smiled. 'That's true. He was good, though, wasn't he?'

Fest nodded. 'Impressive. Not the best I've seen, maybe, but strong. Brave, too.'

Axel looked about him. 'It's another world,' he said. 'Rawer, more basic than ours.'

Ebert laughed, looking at him. 'I do believe our young friend is in love with it all. Imagine, living down here, in the sweat and grime!' He laughed again, more viciously this time. 'You'd soon be disillusioned.'

'Maybe...'

He managed no more. Just then the door opened and the big man's manager came out. He had the same look about him. *You're Karr's elder brother,* Axel thought, looking at him.

'What do you want?'

Ebert smiled. 'I watched your man. He fought well. I'd like to take him out to supper. My treat.'

Axel saw how the man controlled himself; saw how he looked from one of them to the next, recognizing them for what they were, Above aristocrats, and knew at once how it must be to live as this man did – wanting to stay clear of their kind, but at the same time needing them. Yes, he saw it all there in the man's face, all the dreadful compromises he had had to make just to live down here. It rent at Axel's soul; made him want to turn and leave.

'Okay,' the man said after a moment's hesitation. 'But Karr's not feeling well. The contest took a lot out of him. He needs rest...'

Ebert held the man's hands a moment. 'It's all right, friend. We'll not keep him. A celebration meal, and then...' He shrugged and smiled pleasantly, letting the man's hands go. 'We have influence. Understand? We can arrange things for you. Make it easier...'

Axel narrowed his eyes. 'What do you mean, Ebert?'

Ebert turned and looked at him sharply. 'Shut up, Haavikko! Let me deal with this. I know what I'm doing.'

Axel looked down. *Do as you will.*

Ebert had a reputation for being headstrong. For doing what others would never dare to do. But it was understandable. He had been born to rule. His father, Klaus Ebert, was head of Chung Kuo's second largest Company: a Company that had existed since the first days of the City; that provided all the body-servants for the Great Families – sweet, intelligent creatures, scarcely distinguishable from the human; that provided a range of taste-sculpted servants for the richest of the rich, and armies of mindless automatons for the Seven. A company that produced over a third of all the synthesized food eaten in the levels.

Hans Ebert was heir to GenSyn, second only to MedFac on the Hang Seng Index. Rumour was his father could buy the Net twice over. What, then, if he should haggle with the manager of a small-time fighter? Even so, Axel found himself annoyed. Hadn't Ebert *seen*? Hadn't he realized how fine, how powerful the man was?

'We'll go in, then?' Ebert said, his tone insistent, commanding. The manager lowered his head, then bowed to the waist, letting them pass.

So power is, thought Axel, moving past him. *So power acts.*

Karr was sitting at the far end of the room, his right arm strapped to his chest, a bowl of soup balanced in his left hand. He looked up at them sharply, annoyed at their intrusion.

'What do you want?'

Ebert smiled, ignoring the big man's hostility. 'You fought well. We'd like to celebrate your success. To honour you.'

Karr laughed. He set down the soup and stood up, then came across the room until he stood two paces from Ebert.

'You want to *honour* me?'

For the briefest moment Ebert seemed intimidated. Then he recovered, turning to smile at his fellows before looking back up at Karr. 'Why not? It was a great victory.'

'You think so?' Karr smiled, but his voice was sharp and cold. 'You don't think it was the triumph of *meat* over *intelligence*, then?'

Ebert's mouth worked ineffectually for a moment. Then he took a step backwards. But as he did so, Karr spat on the floor between Ebert's feet.

'Fuck off! Understand? I don't *need* you.'

Ebert's face turned ashen. For a moment he struggled to form words. Then he found his voice again. 'How *dare* he!'

The words were high-pitched, almost strangled.

Fest held his arm tightly, whispering urgently in his ear. 'Don't make trouble here, Hans. Please! They suffer us down here. But if we start anything we'll spark a riot.'

'I'll kill him,' Ebert said, under his breath.

Karr heard and smiled mockingly.

'He'd as like break both your arms,' Fest said quietly.

Ebert sneered. 'I think my father would have something to say about that, don't you?'

Fest pulled on Ebert's arm, drawing him back. 'The less said about your father, the better, Hans. These fellows know only too well who manufactures the *Hei* they send in to crush any sign of an uprising. GenSyn and your father are about as popular here as Genghis Khan.'

Karr was watching them hawkishly. At the mention of GenSyn his eyes narrowed. 'So you're *Ebert's* son?'

Ebert threw off Fest's hand and took a step forward, his head raised arrogantly to face out the big man. 'You understand what it means, then?'

Karr smiled tightly. 'Oh, I know what it means *up there*. But you're not up there now, *Shih* Ebert. This isn't your kingdom and you should mind your manners.'

Ebert went to speak again, but Karr lifted his good hand sharply to cut him off. His face was bitter. 'Let me explain it simply for you. Today I killed a man I admired greatly. A man who taught me much about honour and necessity.' He took a step closer to Ebert. 'He was a *man*, Ebert. A *master*.'

'You were lucky,' said Ebert quietly, provocatively.

A faint smile played on Karr's lips briefly, but his eyes were cold and hard. 'Yes. For once you're right. I *was* lucky. Hwa underestimated me. He thought as you think. And because of that he's dead.'

'Is that a threat?'

Karr laughed, then shook his head. He was about to say something more, but at that moment there was a noise in the corridor outside. An instant later the door swung open. Two uniformed officers of the Special Security squad stood there, their standard issue *deng* rifles held against their chests. Behind them came the General.

Tolonen strode into the dressing room, then stopped, looking about him. Fest, Ebert and Haavikko had come sharply to attention. They stood there, heads bowed, awaiting orders, but the General ignored them a moment. He walked up to Karr and looked him up and down before turning his back on him.

'I'm sorry to have to break things up, but we've heard from our Triad contacts. I'd have notified you before but the matter's no longer urgent.'

'Sir?' Fest straightened up, his face expressing his confusion. He had been told this was a matter of the utmost urgency and that he would be notified at once.

Tolonen turned his head and looked at Fest. 'I'm sorry, lieutenant, I should explain. They're dead. Someone got to them before us. The *Kuei Chuan* Triad are sending a man to take us to the place. I've arranged to meet them here in an hour.'

'Is it far?' Fest asked.

'I'm not sure. They don't use grid references down here. But it's a place called Ammersee.'

Behind him, Karr laughed. 'I know it well. It's quite a warren. You'll *need* a guide.'

Tolonen turned and looked at the fighter again. He was a big man himself, but Karr was head and shoulders taller than him. 'Who's this?' he asked.

'His name is Karr, sir. He was the winner of the combat.'

Tolonen stared at Karr, then nodded. 'Yes. He doesn't look like a loser.' Then he addressed the big man directly. 'How far is this place?'

'Ten, maybe twelve li.'

'And how long would it take us to get there?'

Karr shrugged. 'By foot forty minutes. By rickshaw fifteen, maybe twenty.'

'And you'll take us?'

Karr looked at Ebert. 'I'm not sure I'd be welcome.'

Tolonen looked from Karr to Ebert. 'Oh? And why's that, Hans?'

Ebert lowered his head, not looking at Karr. 'Just a small disagreement, sir. Nothing serious.'

'Good,' said the General. 'That's settled then. The sooner we get there the better. I want to sort this out.' He turned back to Karr. 'I'm indebted, *Shih* Karr. I'll make sure you're well paid for your help.'

Karr bowed, then turned to get his cloak.

DeVore met them in the corridor outside Kao Jyan's apartment. 'I came as soon as I heard, sir.'

'Well, Howard?' said Tolonen. 'What have we got?'

'Three men, sir. Low-level criminals. I've checked with our contacts. They weren't members of any of the local Triads. Two of them were *kwai*. Hired knives. The other – Kao Jyan, who owned the apartment – was a small-time racketeer. Drugs, stolen goods, nothing big.'

Tolonen nodded. 'Nothing to connect them with anyone higher up?'

DeVore shook his head. 'Not yet, sir. But we're still investigating. Kao Jyan was known to frequent a place known as Big White's. He'd do some of his business there, it seems. But the place was gutted yesterday. Victim of one of the local gang wars. Big White himself is dead, so that avenue's closed to us, too.'

'It all seems too convenient. Too systematic.'

DeVore gave a brief nod. 'As if someone's tidying up after them.'

'Yes,' said Tolonen, touching his shoulder. 'That's my thought exactly.'

'In this case, sir, it seems genuine enough. Big White was playing off one Triad against another. It looks like he was a victim of his own greed.'

'Hmm.' Tolonen still seemed unhappy with the coincidence. 'Dig deeper, Howard. It might be genuine, but then it might not. Someone high's behind all of this. Someone high enough to pay off Triads as a matter of course.'

DeVore bowed, obedient, then turned towards the guarded doorway. 'Shall we go in, sir?'

Axel, watching from the doorway, saw the General move about the room; saw how he looked at everything, trying to fit it all into place. In the rickshaw coming over, Tolonen had turned to him, explaining.

'Sometimes, Axel, you need to see things for yourself. Sniff them out first-hand. Sometimes it's the only way. You see things that another might have missed. Understand things. Bring things to light that would otherwise have remained hidden.'

He saw now how the General went about that. How he looked from one thing to the next, his eyes sharp, alert for the hidden connections.

'This is odd, Howard. Very odd.'

Tolonen was leaning over the corpse that lay face down on the bed, holding the surgeon's tag between his fingers. DeVore went over to him.

'Sir?'

'Look at this. The time of death. Two hours before the other two. Why's that?'

'I'd guess they were waiting for them in the room. That they picked them off as they came in.'

Tolonen looked up at him grimly. 'Maybe. But that would take some nerve. To sit with a man you'd murdered, for two hours.'

DeVore said nothing.

'Which one was this?'

'We don't have a surname, sir, but he was known as Chen.'

Tolonen nodded, then carefully moved the bloodied head. It lay there, its shattered left profile upward on the sheets. For a while the General stared at it, as if trying to remember something. He touched the smooth skin beneath the ear and frowned, then shrugged and got up.

'This one.' He pointed down at the corpse of Kao Jyan. 'I recognize him from the tape.'

'The tape?' DeVore looked up sharply.

'Oh, I'm sorry, Howard. I should have said. We had a tape of the two men. A copy from the CompCam files.'

'Ah, yes,' DeVore said hurriedly. 'Of course.'

Tolonen had moved on. He stood over the third of the bodies, one hand stroking his smooth-shaven chin. 'So who was this, then? And how did he fit in?' He looked up and across at DeVore. 'Whose side was he on, I wonder? Was he with these two, or did he come to kill them?'

DeVore met his gaze steadily. 'His name was Chu Heng, sir. A local thug. It seems...'

Karr, in the doorway, interrupted him. 'Excuse me, but he was quite well known in these parts, General. A handy man with a blade. Too handy. It's good to see him dead.'

DeVore looked at the big man curiously, then turned to the General. 'Who's this, sir?'

Tolonen indicated that Karr should come in. 'This is Shih Karr, Howard. He's a fighter – what they call a "blood". He's champion, it seems. For the time being.'

DeVore gave the slightest bow, acknowledging the giant. 'You know these parts, then?'

Karr was kneeling over the corpse, looking at the wounds to Chu Heng's neck and chest with a professional interest. After a moment he looked up at DeVore. 'I was born in Ammersee. Until four years ago I lived here. I know its people and its business.'

'So you knew these men?'

'Kao Jyan? Well, I knew of him. Chen I didn't know. He must have taken up with Kao Jyan quite recently. But he was a good man. He had honour.'

'A good man, eh? You can say that, not knowing him?' DeVore laughed, his eyes weighing up the big man. 'But he was kwai, a killer. Do killers have honour?'

Karr met his eyes firmly. 'Some do. You, for instance. Haven't you had to kill in your line of work?'

DeVore smiled. 'Ah, but that's different.'

'Is it?' Karr straightened up, moving to the second of the bodies, giving it the same scrupulous examination as the first. 'Are people so very different below the Net?' He glanced up at DeVore, then back at the body. 'Do you know what kwai is, Major?'

'They kill for profit. What more do I need to know?'

Karr laughed but did not look up. 'I thought you'd be curious, if only professionally. You see, Chu Heng was kwai, too, but he wasn't typical. He was what they call a "twisted blade". Most kwai would have spat on Chu Heng.'

'A knife's a knife.'

Karr shook his head. 'Not so. Some weapons are better made than others. And some are made by masters. So with a good kwai. You see, to become kwai one must study long and hard. It is a discipline. A way of life.'

'Down here? The only way of life I've seen down here is grab what you can and kill to keep it.'

Karr looked up, his grey eyes calm, controlled. 'Tsao Ch'un was Son of Heaven.'

For once the old saying carried rather too much meaning. Tsao Ch'un was the tyrant who had united Chung Kuo and built the great City. He, in

his time, had grabbed and killed to keep what he had taken. Until the Seven
– his chief ministers – had deposed him.

'Kings do as they must,' DeVore said, his eyes suddenly dangerous.

Karr straightened up to his full height, facing DeVore. 'And *kwai*. As I
said, Major, to be a *kwai* here is an honourable calling. Most are not as Chu
Heng was. Nor should you confuse them with the punks and paper tigers
that run with the Triads. A *kwai* has inner strengths. He draws from deeper
wells than greed.'

DeVore laughed scornfully. He was about to answer Karr, but Tolonen
stepped in between the two men. 'Major DeVore, Fest, Ebert, Haavikko.
Leave us a moment. I want a word with Karr.'

DeVore bowed, then went outside, followed by the other three. When they
were gone, the General turned to face the big man.

'You know the ways of this place, Karr. What do you think happened here?'

Karr looked about him. 'It's messy. Hastily arranged and hurriedly carried
out. Yet the killings... Well, they're odd. If I didn't know better I'd say that
Kao Jyan's death was a piece of Chu Heng's work. This slashing and goug-
ing is his trade mark. He was a sadist. He enjoyed inflicting pain.'

'And the others?'

Karr put his head to one side. 'I've not looked at Chen yet. But whoever
killed Chu Heng was good at it. Trained to kill quickly and efficiently.'

'A soldier, maybe?'

Karr laughed. 'I hadn't thought of that, but yes.'

Tolonen smiled, pleased.

'You're a useful man, Karr, and my ensign, Haavikko, tells me you're a
magnificent fighter. Intelligent, too. I could use a man like you.'

Karr set Kao Jyan's head down gently and looked up at the General. 'I'm
under contract, General. Ten fights, if I live that long.'

'I'll buy your contract out.'

Karr smiled. 'Maybe. But why? I don't understand, General. What use
could I be to you?'

At that the General laughed. 'You have a talent. An eye for things. I could
see it at a glance. And you know this place. Know how its people think and
act. At present we have to rely on our contacts down here. On Triad bosses.
And that's not merely costly but unreliable. They'd as soon be in another
man's pay as ours.'

'And I'm different?'

'I'd judge so.'

Karr stood and looked about him. 'What happened here, General? What *really* happened?'

Tolonen moved across the room. He stood at the games machine, toying with its touch pad. 'What do you mean?'

'You, the Major, those three junior officers outside. That's some team to investigate a small time killing like this. So why are you all here? What's important about these men? What did they do? Or should I ask, what did they know?'

Tolonen laughed. 'What they did was kill a Minister. What they knew, however, remains a mystery. But someone knows. The someone who killed them.'

Karr came and stood at his shoulder, looking at the game that had come up on the screen. 'What's this?'

'It looks like the last stored memory. Kao Jyan was a good player, it seems.'

Karr shook his head. 'That's not Kao Jyan. I'd swear it. In fact, I'd say that wasn't anyone from round here. Look at those patterns. And this is an eighth-level game. Whoever was playing this was a master of *Wei Chi*.'

Tolonen laughed strangely. 'Our killer?'

Karr turned his head, meeting his eyes. 'Well, it would be one way of filling two hours.'

It was a big, five-pole sedan, its mauve er-silk banners emblazoned with black, stylized dogs, symbol of the *Kuei Chuan* Triad. The ten shaven-headed pole-men sat against the wall opposite, tucking into bowls of ducksoy soup and noodles, while in a conspicuously separate group, standing beside the sedan, in mauve and black fake-satin uniforms, were the *pen p'ei* – rushing daggers – numbered patches on their chests indicating their standing in the Triad hierarchy.

Ignoring the lowly pole-men, Ebert strode up to the lowest-numbered of the *p'ei*, who immediately bowed low and touched his forehead to the littered floor of the corridor.

'Let's get going,' Ebert said brusquely. He dropped a fifty-yuan coin beside the man's head. 'There'll be another if you get us there in twenty minutes.'

The p'ei's eyes went to the coin, then, widening, looked up at Ebert. He nodded his head exaggeratedly. 'As you wish, Excellency!' He stood and turned to the pole-men, barking orders in a pidgin Mandarin that none of the three young soldiers could follow. Soup bowls were dropped at once as the pole-men hurried to get into position. Six of the p'ei formed up at the front. Daggers drawn, they would clear the way ahead of the sedan. Behind ran the last four of the p'ei, guarding against ambush.

Axel watched Ebert and Fest climb inside, then followed, stopping in the curtained doorway to look back at the bowed, shaven-headed pole-men.

'Come on, Haavikko!' said Fest impatiently. 'You don't want the man to lose his fee, do you?'

Axel ducked inside, taking the seat across from Fest and Ebert. 'Why did you do that, Hans? There's no hurry to get back.'

Ebert smiled. 'You have to keep these types on their toes, Haavikko. It'll do them good to have a nice long run.' He looked at Fest and laughed. 'You should see the buggers' faces! It's worth a hundred yuan just for that!'

Axel looked at him for a moment, then shrugged. He didn't like it, but they were probably used to it down here. This was how they expected the Above to behave.

The sedan lifted at once and they were away, the carriage swaying rhythmically about them, the shouts of the senior p'ei encouraging the men to run.

'What do you think of that, Hans?' Fest asked, leaning forward to draw the curtain back and look out at the runners. 'It seems the General has bought the fighter's contract.'

Ebert laughed dismissively. 'The man's a brute! A primitive! I tell you, he'll prove nothing but trouble!'

Axel looked down. He had said nothing earlier when Ebert had insulted Karr, but now he had had a belly full of Ebert's arrogance. 'You only say that because he stood up to you.'

Ebert glowered. 'I'll break him! See if I don't!'

Axel laughed and looked up, meeting Ebert's eyes. 'And how will you do that, Hans? Is the General yours to command?'

Ebert bit back the reply, then looked away, a dangerous expression in his eyes. 'No, but there are others who feel as I do.'

It was clear he meant DeVore. Surprisingly, the Major seemed to have been as much put out by the big man as Ebert. In the corridor outside the murdered Han's apartment he had muttered angrily about upstarts and big sacks of wind. It was clear he had not appreciated the big man correcting him about the *kwai*.

'Karr will be the General's man,' Axel insisted. 'Answerable only to him.' He paused, then, rubbing it in, added, 'It seems he has need of such men.'

Ebert laughed mockingly, but Haavikko's words had offended him. He turned aside angrily and, beneath his breath, muttered, 'Gods, but what fools they give us in command!'

Fest leaned forward. 'Hush up, Hans! Have a care what you say!'

But Axel had heard and was furious. This was too much. 'I take it you refer to General Tolonen?'

Ebert turned on him squarely, his right fist bunched, his face dark with anger. 'And what if I do? What's it to you what I say?'

Axel drew himself up in his seat. 'It is discourteous, to say the least. You forget where your duty lies, and to whom. Retract your words, Hans Ebert, or I'll be forced to make you retract them!'

For a while neither spoke, but faced each other out, the sedan swaying about them. Slowly Ebert calmed, his breathing normalizing. Then, turning his face away, he laughed. 'Go fuck yourself, Haavikko.'

At once Axel swung a punch, but Fest, anticipating trouble, had moved between them. He blocked the blow with his arm, then pushed Ebert away to the far side of the carriage.

'For gods' sake, Hans, shut up! As for you, Axel Haavikko, listen carefully. I don't condone what Ebert said just now, but you had best just forget it. *Understand?*'

'Forget it? How can I forget it? It undermines all we are. If I...'

Fest put his hand roughly over Haavikko's mouth, glaring at him.

'*Forget* it! Is that clear? Hans meant nothing by it. His temper was up, that's all. Understandably, I'd say. The barbarian insulted him! Spat at his feet! Would you have stood as much?'

'It doesn't excuse...' Axel began, but Fest silenced him with a look.

'Enough! Do you understand? No one's honour has been besmirched. What passed here... it was only words. Nothing to get fired up about.'

Axel looked across at Ebert, his face gone cold. *Only words*, he thought.

Only words! He turned his head away, disgusted with them, aching to make Ebert eat the words he had uttered and annoyed with Fest for interfering. And understanding now the restraint the big man had shown back in his dressing room.

'Well, Haavikko, some good came of the day after all.'

Tolonen leaned forward across his desk, steepling his big hands together. Karr had just left the office, escorted by two elite guards. His contract had been purchased and he had sworn the oath of allegiance to the T'ang and to General Tolonen. All three junior officers had been witnesses. But now the others had gone and Axel was alone with the General for the first time since the business in the carriage.

Axel hesitated, looking down at the old man. Tolonen had treated him like a son since he had become his duty aide. Had honoured him with advice and explanations. He had learned much in serving the General, but now things had changed.

'Sir, there's something I wish to speak to you about.'

Tolonen smiled good-naturedly. 'Go on, boy.'

'I'd... Well, I'd like a new posting.'

Tolonen sat back slowly, the surprise in his face quite marked. 'What's this?' He drew his hands apart and set them down on the edge of his desk. 'I don't understand you, Haavikko. Aren't you happy here? Don't you like the job?'

Axel lowered his head. 'I was, sir. And I did. But...'

Tolonen was looking at him strangely. 'What is it? What's happened?'

He kept silent. Kept his head lowered.

Tolonen stood up and came round the desk. 'Tell me, boy. What's up?'

He looked up and met Tolonen's eyes openly. 'I'd rather not, sir. It's just that I feel I can't work here any more.'

Tolonen's disbelief surfaced as a laugh. 'What am I supposed to make of that? Can't work here. Don't *feel* like it. Tell me what happened.'

Axel took a breath. 'Sir, I'd rather not.'

The General's bark of anger took him by surprise. 'Rather not? It's not good enough. I'll have no secrets here. You'll tell me what happened. *Why* you want a new posting. I *order* you to tell me.'

Axel swallowed. He had hoped to avoid this. He had wanted to settle his score with Ebert directly, personally. 'It's Ebert, sir.'

Tolonen laughed uncomfortably. 'Ebert, eh? And what's wrong with young Ebert? Has he insulted you?'

'No, sir. Not directly.'

'Well, then, what was it? Don't keep me guessing, boy. Spit it out.'

'He was disrespectful, sir.'

'Disrespectful, eh? To whom?'

Axel felt Tolonen's eyes boring into his own. 'To you, sir.'

Tolonen huffed. He was quiet for a moment, then shook his head. 'I don't believe it. His father is my oldest friend. He's like a son to me, that boy. Disrespect?' There was an ugly movement of the General's mouth. 'What did he say?'

'I'd rather...' Axel began, but Tolonen cut him off angrily.

'Gods, boy! Don't "rather not" me any more! Spit it out – if you're accusing Ebert of disrespect I want to know the full details. And you had better have a witness. I'll have no unsupported hearsay.'

Axel bowed his head dutifully. This was not how he had imagined it. He had thought the General would let him go – reluctantly, but without a fuss. This business of accusations and witnesses had come out of the blue.

'It was earlier today, sir. In the sedan coming back. Fest was present, sir. He heard everything.'

Tolonen turned abruptly and leaned over his desk. Touching the intercom pad, he spoke to his secretary. 'Have Cadet Officers Fest and Ebert brought back here, please. At once.'

He turned back, looking at Haavikko sharply. 'So what did he say?'

Axel hesitated, the import of what he was doing suddenly striking him. There was much he disliked about Ebert – his arrogance and assumed superiority being the chief of them – but he had never intended to get the man thrown out of the service. If the charge of disrespect was proven he could be summarily dismissed from the force. For the first time since their exchange, Axel wished he had taken Fest's advice and forgotten the whole business.

'Well?' The General's roar brought him back to himself with a start. He looked up. Tolonen's face was red with anger. 'Do I have to drag it from you word for word?'

Axel shook his head. In a quiet voice he repeated Ebert's words. Then what he had added afterwards.

Tolonen had gone quiet. He looked away, then back at Haavikko. 'That's it?' he asked, his voice suddenly much softer. 'Those are his precise words?'

Axel nodded curtly, a shiver running down his back. It was done. The accusation made.

The General shook his head slowly and turned away, moving towards the window. He gazed outward distractedly, then looked back at Haavikko. 'You'll be silent until I order otherwise. All right?'

'Sir.'

There was a knock at the door.

Tolonen cleared his throat, then turned to face the door. 'Come in!'

Fest and Ebert entered. They marched to the centre of the room and came to attention.

Tolonen came and stood directly before them, Fest to his left, Ebert to his right. Haavikko stood to the side, near the desk. From there he could see his two fellow cadets' faces. General Tolonen was in profile.

'Do you know why I've summoned you, Ebert?'

Ebert's eyes went to Haavikko, then back to Tolonen. 'I think I can guess, sir.'

Tolonen frowned. 'Really?'

'It's Haavikko, sir. He insulted me. I had to slap him down.'

Tolonen turned to look at Axel, astonished, then looked back at Fest. 'Is this true, Fest?'

Fest bowed slightly. 'It is, sir. It was coming back here from the Net. The two had an argument. Haavikko was very offensive about Ebert's father. Hans... I mean Ebert, had no option but to strike him.'

'I see,' said Tolonen. 'And there was nothing else?'

'Nothing, sir,' answered Fest. 'It was all very unpleasant, but we hoped it would be forgotten. Ebert feels his honour has been upheld.'

'You're certain of this, Fest? You'd swear to it under oath?'

Fest looked straight ahead. His reply was instantaneous, unflinching. 'I would, sir.'

Tolonen considered a moment. Then he moved across until he was directly in front of Ebert. 'Your father and I have been friends for more than fifty years, Hans. I held you as a baby. Played with you as a child. And I've always been proud of you as a soldier under my command. But a serious accusation has been levelled against you. One you must either admit to or deny completely.'

'Sir?' Ebert looked puzzled.

Haavikko started forward, then stepped back. *The liars! The barefaced liars!*

Tolonen turned, looking across at Haavikko. Then, in a cold, quiet voice, he repeated what Haavikko had said to him, all the while keeping his eyes on him. Finished, he half turned, looking at Ebert. 'Well, Cadet Ebert? What have you to say?'

Ebert looked totally nonplussed. He said nothing, merely shook his head. It was Fest who answered for him, his face filled with indignation and anger.

'But this is outrageous, sir! Ebert said nothing of the kind! This is just malicious claptrap, sir! Pure bile! An attempt to get back at Ebert underhandedly!'

Ebert had lowered his head. When he looked up there was a tear on his left cheek. 'General Tolonen...' he began.

'Enough!' Tolonen drew himself up to his full height. 'Fest, Ebert, be kind enough to leave the room. I've heard enough.'

Axel, unable to believe what had happened, watched them leave, and saw, as the General turned to face him, Ebert smile triumphantly at Fest. Then the door closed and he was alone with the General.

'You heard what they said, Haavikko. Explain yourself!'

Axel shuddered. 'They were lying, sir. Both of them. Fest was covering for Ebert...'

Tolonen watched him coldly, then shook his head. 'Take care, Haavikko. Don't compound your error. You realize I could have you court-martialled for what you've done. Dismissed from the service. The only thing that stops me is the promise I made your dead father.'

The old man gritted his teeth, then looked away. His disappointment with Haavikko was written starkly in his face. 'I thought better of you.' He laughed – a sharp, bitter laugh – then turned away. 'Get out of my sight, Haavikko. Right now. You have your posting.'

Three hours later Axel sat at the Security Desk at the lowest level of the Bremen Fortress, waiting for his new orders to come through. His kit – the sum total of his belongings in the world – was packed and stored in a back room down the hallway. To kill the time he had relieved the duty officer while he went to get *ch'a* for them both. The ninth of the evening bells had just sounded and it was quiet.

Outwardly he appeared calm as he sat there in the reception area. Inside, however, he seethed. Anger and bitterness at the General's actions filled him to bursting. The General had done what he had had to do, and, in his place, he might well have done the same. At least, so the logical, reasonable part of him argued. But seeing it that way didn't help. A gross injustice had been done him and his very soul felt bruised and raw. It was not justice he wanted but revenge. He felt like killing them. Slowly, painfully. Fest first, and then Ebert.

Impossible, he thought bitterly. And even if he did, they would come and take all those he loved in retribution. Sister and aunts and all. To the third generation, as the law demanded.

He looked down, momentarily overcome, then looked up again, hearing a noise in front of him.

The Han bowed low before the desk, then met Axel's eyes. He seemed close to exhaustion and his clothes stank.

'I need protection,' he said. 'There are men trying to kill me.'

Axel stared back at him, feeling empty. 'It's an evil world,' he said, indicating a seat at the back of the reception area. 'Sit down. The duty officer will see you in a while.'

He watched the Han turn and go to the seat, then looked away, paying no more attention to the man.

A minute later the duty officer was back. 'You're in luck, Haavikko,' he said, handing him a bowl of *ch'a* from the tray, then taking a sealed packet from his jacket pocket and putting it on the desk in front of him. 'It's just come through. Your new posting.'

Axel stared at it a moment, then took it and broke the seal. He read it then looked down, his face momentarily registering his disgust. England! They were sending him to England, of all the godsforsaken places!

He tucked the orders away in his tunic pocket, masking his bitter disappointment, then drained his bowl at a go. 'Thanks,' he said, letting the other take his seat again. 'I'll get my kit and go.'

'Yes, you'd better.' The duty officer smiled sadly at him; an understanding smile. 'Hey! And good luck!'

After he'd gone, the Han rose slowly from his seat and went across to the desk. The duty officer looked up, then set his *ch'a* down.

'Yes?'

'I need protection,' the Han said tiredly, conscious he had used these same words earlier. 'There are men trying to kill me.'

The officer nodded, then reached for his lap terminal, ready to take details. 'Okay. What's your name?'

'Pi Ch'ien,' the Han answered. 'My name is Pi Ch'ien.'

CHAPTER 29

THE MOON DRAGON

Well, what are we to do?'

Lehmann turned away, looking out at the calm of the lotus-strewn lake; watching as one of the three GenSyn cranes he had bought only the day before lifted its long, elegant wings, then settled again, dipping its bill into the water. Behind him DeVore was pacing restlessly, slapping his gloves against his thigh. Lehmann had never seen him so agitated. Who would have believed that Yang Lai's message carrier, his Third Secretary, Pi Ch'ien, would turn up again, like an envoy from the dead?

'What do you suggest?'

DeVore came and stood by him at the open window. 'You know what we must do. It's what we planned for. In case this happened.'

'You think it's necessary? I mean...Yang Lai is dead. And Cho Hsiang and the two assassins. There's nothing more to connect us. So what if the General has Pi Ch'ien? Pi Ch'ien knows nothing.'

'Not so, I'm afraid. Pi Ch'ien has named Heng Chi-Po as his contact.'

Lehmann turned abruptly. 'Minister Heng? Gods! And he has proof of this?'

'No. But it isn't a question of proof anymore. The General plans to go to the T'ang with what he knows, proof or not. And the T'ang will tell him to investigate. We have to act now. To pre-empt the investigation.' He paused, taking breath. 'We have to sacrifice him, Pietr. We have to give them Wyatt.'

Lehmann turned back, facing DeVore. 'You're certain it's the only way?'

'It's... necessary.'

Lehmann was silent. 'All right. Do what you must.'

DeVore touched his arm. 'Keep heart, Pietr. It's a hard road, I know, but we'll triumph.'

Lehmann looked down. 'I didn't think it would be like this. I thought...'

'You thought you could keep your hands clean, neh?'

'No. Not that. Just... he's a good man. If there's any other way... ?'

He looked up, meeting DeVore's eyes, but the latter shook his head.

'Don't blame yourself, Pietr. Our hands are tied. Chung Kuo is to blame. This world of ours... it's incestuous. You have only to scratch your arse and your enemy sighs with relief.'

'True enough.'

DeVore pressed on. 'Do you think I'd not be open if I could? Do you think I like all this deceit and double-dealing?' He spat neatly onto the water below. 'If I was open for a moment I'd be dead. And you. And all of us. So think of that, Pietr, before you get sentimental over Edmund Wyatt. He was a good man. But he also wanted what we want. Change. A break with the old order. Keep that in mind, Pietr. Don't waver from it. Because if you doubt it for a moment you're dead. You and all of us.'

Lehmann shivered, hearing how DeVore spoke of Wyatt in the past tense. But he could not argue. Their course was set now.

'Then I must seem his friend?'

'And I your mortal enemy.'

'Yes.' Lehmann looked out, watching one of the cranes glide slowly to the bank, then lift itself up onto the pale white rocks, ruffling its feathers as it settled.

The General waited on the central dais, holding himself stiffly upright in the tall-backed Summons Chair. To either side of the dais stood an honour guard of the T'ang's own bodyguard, resplendent in their crimson combat silks, big men with shaven heads and naked feet, while all around him the T'ang's servants moved silently through the great hall, going about their business.

Only six hours ago he had contemplated this meeting with some misgivings, but now he felt confident, almost elated, the frustrations of the past three days behind him. He held DeVore's file tightly in his lap, smiling inwardly. *I've got you now*, he thought. *Both of you. You won't wriggle out of this one.*

He gazed ahead fixedly. Facing him, some fifty paces distant, was the entrance to the Hall of Eternal Truth, where the T'ang held audience.

The double doors were massive, twice as tall as they were broad. In silver across the black, leather surface, its circumference five times the height of a man, was drawn a great circle of seven dragons. At its centre the snouts of the regal beasts met, forming a rose-like hub, huge rubies burning fiercely in each eye. Their lithe, powerful bodies curved outward like the spokes of a giant wheel while at the edge their tails were intertwined to form the rim. It was the *Ywe Lung*, the Moon Dragon, symbol of the Seven. Tolonen could never look at it without a feeling of great pride – glad beyond words that it had fallen to him to play so large a part in defending that great and powerful circle, that his T'ang honoured him so.

Two bells sounded, the first sweet and clear, the second deep and resonant. Slowly, noiselessly, the great doors swung back.

The General stood, then stepped down from the dais, the file and the other papers held tightly against his breast. He turned to his left, then to his right, bowing his head stiffly to the two lieutenants, then marched forward ten paces and stopped, letting the honour guard form up behind him.

The doors were fully open now. He could see the T'ang at the far end of the Hall, seated on the high throne, atop the Presence Dais.

The T'ang's Chancellor, Chung Hu-Yan came forward, greeting him.

'General Tolonen,' he said, smiling and bowing low. 'You are most welcome. The T'ang is expecting you.'

'It is good to see you, Hu-Yan,' the General said quietly, returning both smile and bow. 'I hope you're well. And all your family.'

'And yours, Knut,' he answered softly, straightening up. 'But come. You've waited far too long already.'

Chung Hu-Yan turned, facing the T'ang again. He bowed low, going down onto his knees and pressing his forehead briefly against the tiled floor. Then he stood and walked slowly into the Hall. The General moved forward, following him. Beneath the great lintel he halted and made his own obeisance to the T'ang, the whole of the honour guard behind him making the gesture at the same moment, then rising when he rose. But when he moved forward again they stayed where they were. No one – not even a member of the honour guard – was allowed into the Hall without the T'ang's express permission.

At the foot of the steps Tolonen paused, the Chancellor to the left of him, others of the T'ang's retinue gathered to the right of the Dais.

'*Chieh Hsia*,' he said, making his *k'o t'ou* a second time.

The literal translation of the Mandarin was 'below the steps', but the phrase had long acquired a second, more important meaning – 'Your Majesty'. It dated from those ancient days when ministers, summoned to an audience with the Emperor, were not permitted to address the Son of Heaven directly, but spoke through those officials gathered 'below the steps' of the high-raised throne.

The T'ang rose from his throne and started down the broad steps of the Presence Dais.

'Knut. I'm sorry I kept you waiting.'

Li Shai Tung was wearing his official robes; long, flowing silks of pale gold, trimmed with black, and honey-coloured boots of soft kid. His fine grey hair was pulled back severely from his forehead and bound tightly at the back of his head. He wore a simple necklet of gold, and, on the fingers of his right hand, two rings; the first a simple band of thin white gold, his dead wife's wedding gift; the other a heavier, thicker ring of black iron, bearing on its face a silvered miniature of the *Ywe Lung*, the seal of power.

Li Shai Tung was a tall man; as tall as his General, but willowy. He came down the twelve steps briskly, his movements lighter, more energetic than one might have expected from a man of sixty years. It was often said that the T'ang moved like a dancer, elegantly, powerfully – and it was so; his athletic grace a result of the rigorous training he put himself through each morning. But there was also a dignity to his bearing – an authority – that only those born to rule seem to possess.

Facing his General, he reached out to touch Tolonen's arm, his pale, lined face breaking into a smile. Then the hand fell back; moved to touch, then stroke, his long but neatly trimmed beard. 'I've been kept busy, Knut. This matter of the vacancy. Four families have petitioned me for the appointment. I have been seeing the candidates this very morning.'

'Then what I have to say will be of interest, *Chieh Hsia*.'

Li Shai Tung nodded, then looked about him. Beside the Chancellor there were a dozen others in the Hall, members of his private staff. 'How confidential is this matter?'

The General smiled, understanding. 'It would not do for all to know it yet.'

The T'ang smiled back at him. 'I understand. We'll speak alone. In my grandfather's room.' He motioned to his Chancellor. 'Hu-Yan. You will stand at the door and make certain no one disturbs us until we are done.'

They went through, into one of the smaller rooms at the back of the Hall. The T'ang pulled the doors closed behind him, then turned, looking at Tolonen, his expression unreadable. He crossed the room and sat beneath the twin portraits of his grandfather and Wen Ti, motioning for his General to come to him.

'Sit there, Knut. Facing me.'

Tolonen did as he was bid, yet he felt awkward, being seated in his T'ang's presence. He looked at the nearby fire and unconsciously put out one hand towards its warmth.

The T'ang smiled, seeing the gesture. 'You have something new, then? Something more than when we last spoke?'

'Yes, *Chieh Hsia*. I know who ordered Lwo Kang killed.'

The T'ang considered. 'Enough to prove this thing in law?'

The General nodded. 'And maybe cause the fall of a Great Family.'

'Ah...' Li Shai Tung looked down, into his lap. 'Then the Minister is involved in this?'

Tolonen leaned forward and passed across the file, leaving the other papers in his lap. 'It is all in there, *Chieh Hsia*. All the evidence. Trading connections. Payments and names. Who was used and when. Yang Lai, Fu Lung Ti, Hong Cao, Cho Hsiang – a whole network of names and dates, connecting all the levels of the thing. It was well orchestrated. Too well, perhaps. But we would never have made these connections unless my man DeVore had followed his nose. Wyatt was the hub – the centre of this web of dealings.'

The T'ang nodded, then looked down at the document.

For the next fifteen minutes he was silent, reading. Then, finished, he closed the file and looked up. 'Yes,' he said softly, almost tiredly. 'This is good, Knut. This is what I wanted. You have done very well.'

The General bowed his head. 'Thank you, *Chieh Hsia*. But as I said, the praise is not mine. This is Major DeVore's work.'

'I see.' The T'ang looked back down at the document.

'Then I shall see that the Major is rewarded.'

'Thank you. And the Minister?'

Li Shai Tung gave a short, humourless laugh. 'Heng Chi-Po is a careful man, as this document bears out. Though the finger points at him, at no point does it touch.' He shook his head. 'No matter the weight of circumstantial evidence, we have nothing substantial.'

'Yet it was he who warned Yang Lai. Who sent the message.'

'Maybe so. But it would not hold. Assumptions, that's all we have when it comes down to it, Knut. Junior Minister Yang Lai is missing and the message card Pi Ch'ien held onto was blank. It is not strong evidence.'

The General was quiet a moment. It was true. The message card that Pi Ch'ien had carried from Minister Heng to Yang Lai was worthless as evidence, the message it held having decayed within thirty seconds of Yang Lai activating it with his thumbprint.

'Then you will do nothing against him?'

The T'ang nodded. When he spoke again he was more reserved, more formal than before. 'You must understand me in this, Knut. If I had a single item of evidence against him – however small – I would break the man, and do it gladly. But as it is...' He spread his hands expressively. 'It would not do to accuse one of my own Ministers without irreproachable evidence.'

'I understand.'

'Good.' The T'ang leaned forward, his dark eyes staring intently at his General. 'For now, we'll take Wyatt, and any others that can be traced through him. Lehmann, perhaps, and that foul creature, Berdichev. But before we do, make sure there's not a possibility of doubt. We must act from certainty. Chung Kuo must see us to be correct – to be perfectly justified in our actions. I want no trouble in the House because of this.'

The General bowed his head, keeping his thoughts to himself. In this the T'ang was right. Things had changed subtly in the last ten years. More power than ever before lay in the hands of men like Lehmann. They had money and influence and a vote in the House at Weimar. And though the House was subject to the will of the Seven, it did not do to exercise such power too frequently. The illusion of cooperation – of an independent House, working hand-in-glove with the Council of the Seven – needed to be preserved. In that illusion lay the basis of lasting peace.

Was that, then, the truth behind all this? Tolonen asked himself. The real reason for Lwo Kang's death? Was it all an attempt to force the hand of the Seven? To make it show its true power openly and without veils before the world? To set House against Seven and force the people to a choice? If so, he understood the T'ang's caution.

He looked up again, meeting the T'ang's eyes. 'It is a loathsome business, ours, *Chieh Hsia*. We must deal fairly, honestly, with cheats and scoundrels.' He sighed bitterly. 'Those cockroaches are all bows and fair words to our faces, yet beneath that outward show they seethe with subterfuge. They smile but they want us dead.'

The T'ang smiled sadly. 'Yes, Knut. Yet such is the way of this world. So men are. So they act. And that itself is reason enough for the Seven, neh? Without us where would be the peace our father's fathers worked for? What would happen to the City of Ten Thousand Years they built? We know, you and I. The barbarians would tear it down, level by level, and build some cruder, darker thing in its place.'

Tolonen tilted his head, agreeing, but he was thinking of the giant, Karr, and of the Pit below the Net where life was fought for openly, beneath the acid glare of brilliant lights. He was a cleaner kind of beast. Much cleaner than Lehmann and his like. For once the Major had been wrong – he had seen that instantly. There *was* honour in how a man behaved, even beneath the Net. Karr and the dead man, Chen, they were killers, certainly, but weren't all soldiers killers when it came to it? How you killed, that was the important thing. Whether you faced your adversary, man to man, letting the contest be decided on strength of arm and skill, or whether you skulked through shadows like a thief to slip a poisoned blade into a sleeping back.

Yes, he thought, in truth I should hate the indirectness of all this; the masks and the tricks and the unending layers of intermediaries. Yet I've been trained to indirectness – to be as cunning as the men I fight.

'As far as Wyatt is concerned, I'll have the warrant signed before you leave. Is there anything else, Knut?'

'There are two further matters, *Chieh Hsia*.'

'Well?'

'The first is a request.' The General handed his T'ang one of the papers. 'In a week Han Ch'in, your eldest son, is sixteen and becomes a man. It is my wish to give him something appropriate.'

Tolonen fell silent, watching as Li Shai Tung unfolded the silk-paper deed of ownership. After a moment the T'ang looked up, a surprised smile lighting his features. 'But this is too much, Knut, surely?'

The General bowed his head. 'Han Ch'in will be T'ang one day. And though he has the freedom of your stables, *Chieh Hsia*, I felt it time he had his own horse. Through horsemanship one learns command.'

The T'ang was still smiling. A horse was a princely gift. There were two thousand thoroughbreds at most in the whole of Chung Kuo. To purchase one would have cost even a fabulously rich man like the General more than he could easily afford. Li Shai Tung looked at Tolonen a moment longer, then did what he rarely did and bent his head. 'Then it shall be so, old friend. My family is honoured by your gift. And Han Ch'in will be delighted.'

The General lowered his head, his face burning with pride and pleasure. Across from him the T'ang folded the paper again. 'And the second matter?'

'Ah... That is a gift to myself.' He hesitated, then handed the second of the papers over. 'There is a man I want to use. His name is Karr.'

That evening, Under Secretary Lehmann summoned all those delegates and representatives sympathetic to his cause to a suite of rooms in the penthouse of the House of a Thousand Freedoms in Weimar. There was a brooding silence in the long, packed room. Lehmann sat in his chair, one hand tugging distractedly at his pigtail, a copy of the warrant open on the desk before him, an expression of sheer disbelief and outrage building slowly in his face.

'I don't believe it,' he said finally, his voice soft, controlled. Then he picked the paper up and held it out to the rest of them. 'Does *anyone* here believe this?'

There was a deep murmur of denial and a shaking of heads.

'But there must be some kind of evidence, Pietr. Even the T'ang would not dare to act without clear evidence.'

Lehmann laughed sourly, then turned slightly in his seat and looked across at the delegate who had spoken, a tall, heavily built *Hung Mao* in a pale green *pau*. 'You think so, Barrow Chao? You think the small matter of evidence will stop a T'ang from acting?'

There was an indrawing of breath in some quarters. A T'ang was a T'ang, after all. Lehmann saw this and made a mental note of those who had seemed outraged by his words, then pressed on. He stood up slowly and came round the table, facing Barrow.

'I've known Edmund Wyatt all my life, Chao. I knew him as a child and I've been honoured to know him as a man. I can vouch there's no more honest man in the Above, nor one with less malice in him. For Edmund to have done what this says he did... Well, it's laughable!'

He was facing Barrow now, only an arm's length from him. Barrow shrugged. 'So you say, Pietr. And before today I would have said the same. But I repeat, the T'ang *must* have evidence. And not just any evidence, but proof positive. He would be mad to act without it.'

'Maybe,' Lehmann said, turning aside. 'But maybe not. Just think about it. In the last five years this House has won more freedoms than in the whole of the previous century. We managed to extend the boundaries of trade and win huge concessions in respect of legitimate research and development. In doing so we brought a refreshing and much-needed breath of change to Chung Kuo.'

There were murmurs of agreement from the delegates. Lehmann turned back, facing them.

'Change. That's what the Seven hate above all else. Change. And in the last three years we have seen them act to kill those freedoms we so rightly fought for. At first covertly, with whispered words and meaningful glances. Then with "gifts" for those who would be their friends. Finally, through the alternatives of patronage or the turned back.'

There were nods of angry agreement, the agitated whisper of silks as the delegates turned to talk amongst themselves. There was not one here who hadn't suffered from the backlash. Not one who, as an advocate of change, however limited, had not found himself 'out of favour' and thus out of pocket.

Lehmann waited for things to quieten, then smiled tightly. 'But that was only the start of it, wasn't it? Having failed to check things by covert means, they decided to be more direct. Ministerial appointments, previously and rightly determined by family connections and the common-sense measure of financial power, were suddenly made on some nebulous sense of New Confucian worthiness.'

There were guffaws of laughter at the look of utter disgust on Lehmann's face.

'Worthiness... Well, we all know what that really means, don't we? It means a new breed of Minister, as efficient as a GenSyn domestic and every bit as limited when it comes to making a real decision. But we knew what they were from the first, didn't we? Dams set up against the natural flow. Mouthpieces for the Seven, programmed only to say no to change.'

Again there was a murmur of agreement; but louder this time, more aggressive. Lehmann raised his hands, palms outward, begging their silence, then nodded his head slowly.

'We know their game, neh? We understand what they are trying to do. And we all know what has been happening in the House this last year. We've seen to what lengths they'll go to oppose change.'

It could not be said openly, but all there knew what Lehmann was implying. From the first days of the House the Seven had always maintained a small but influential faction there – men whom the T'ang 'kept' for their votes. Such men were known as tai – 'pockets' – and, historically, had served a double function in the House, counterbalancing the strong mercantile tendencies of the House and serving as a conduit for the views of the Seven. In the past the Seven had chosen well: their tai had been elderly, well-respected men, charismatic and persuasive – their tongues worth a dozen, sometimes as many as fifty votes. As agents of consensus they had proved a strong, stabilizing influence on the House. But with the new liberalization things had slowly changed and their influence had waned. For a long while the Seven had done nothing, but in the past twelve months they had bought their way heavily and indiscriminately into the House, trading influence for the direct power of votes.

Now there was a new breed of 'pocket': brash young men who owed their wealth and power not to trade or family but to their sudden elevation by the Seven. Rival candidates had been paid off or threatened. Elections had been rigged. Campaign money had flowed like the Yangtze flood. Of the 180 delegates elected to the House in the last six months alone, more than two-thirds had been tai.

The effect had been to crystallize the factions in the House, and to radicalize the demands for changes to the Edict of Technological Control – that keystone in the great wall of State or, as some saw it, the dam restraining the gathering waters of change.

'Change will come,' Lehmann said softly, 'whether they wish it or not.

Change must come. It is the natural order of things. They cannot build a wall high enough to contain it.'

Lehmann paused. There was a noise at the doorway as some of the men gathered there moved aside. Edmund Wyatt pushed through.

'I heard you wanted me, Pietr,' he said, then looked around, seeing how everyone was suddenly watching him. He dropped his voice. 'What is it?'

Lehmann took his arm, then led him across to the chair and sat him down.

'General Tolonen was here. He brought a copy of a warrant.'

Wyatt looked blankly back at Lehmann. 'So?'

There was a strong murmuring from the men in the room. Lehmann looked back at them triumphantly, then turned to Barrow. 'There! There's your proof, surely, Barrow Chao? Was that the reaction of a guilty man?'

Behind him Wyatt laughed. His cheeks were pink with embarrassment. 'What is it, Pietr? What am I supposed to be guilty of?'

Lehmann looked down at the paper in his hand, hesitating, then handed it across. For a moment Wyatt was silent, his right hand holding down the paper as he read. Then he looked up, a startled expression in his eyes. 'I... I don't believe it.'

Lehmann had gone round the back of him. Now he stood there, leaning over Wyatt but looking up at the other men in the room as he spoke.

'It's what it appears to be. A warrant. Signed by the T'ang himself. For your arrest, Edmund. For the murder of Lwo Kang.'

Wyatt turned and stared up into his face. His bewilderment, his total incomprehension were there for everyone in the room to see. 'But it can't be, Pietr. I mean, I never...'

His voice gave out again and he looked down sharply, shuddering.

'Then this is real.'

There was a tense silence in the room, then Lehmann spoke again. 'Well, Barrow Chao? What do you reckon?'

Barrow dropped his head and nodded.

Lehmann straightened. 'The question is – how do we fight this?'

Wyatt looked up at him. 'Fight it?'

Lehmann was quiet a moment, concentrating, then gave the slightest nod. 'Yes,' he said. 'We'll hide you. All of us. We could do it. We could keep Tolonen from serving the warrant.'

Lehmann gazed about him defiantly, looking from face to face, challenging anyone to gainsay him, but the mood was in his favour now.

Wyatt got up, then came round and stood there, facing Lehmann. 'No, Pietr. I won't hide. That's what he wants. That's why he came here first, don't you see? He wanted that. Wanted me to run. That way he could put another warrant out. Have me killed without trial. No, let him serve his warrant. I've nothing to fear. I've done nothing.'

Lehmann laughed sourly. 'And what does that mean, Edmund? The T'ang wants payment for his Minister's life. Retribution. Right or wrong is an irrelevance in this instance. It doesn't matter that you're innocent. He wants you. Don't you see that?' His voice was stern now, unyielding. 'And he'll find all the evidence he needs to get you.'

There was a loud murmuring, but no disagreement.

Wyatt turned away. 'When does he plan to serve the warrant?'

Lehmann looked about him, seeing how open each man's face now was; how starkly etched their anger and resentment, their concern and indignation. Then he turned back.

'Midday tomorrow,' he said. 'At your apartment.'

'I see.' Wyatt looked down. 'Then I'll be there. T'ang or not, he's wrong, Pietr. I'm innocent. You know I am.'

Lehmann turned, looking back at him, then reached out and touched his shoulder. 'I know.'

'Minister Heng.'

The T'ang's Chancellor, Chung Hu-Yan, bowed stiffly, his face expressionless, then turned, inviting the Minister to follow him.

Astonished, Heng returned the Chancellor's bow. He had barely arrived a minute before, and here was Chung trying to rush him into audience. Was there to be no ritual of preparation? No honour guard? He stood there a moment, as if he had not heard the words, looking about him, surprised by the emptiness of the great entrance hall. It was strangely disconcerting, as if the T'ang's servants had been sent elsewhere. But why? And why the unseemly haste?

'Please...' Chung Hu-Yan bowed a second time, then repeated the gesture of invitation, making it clear that it had been no mistake.

'Forgive me,' Heng said, bowing again, his composure slipping. 'Of course...'

He followed the Chancellor through, under the great lintel and into the Hall of Eternal Truth. But he had taken only three steps into the great hall when he stopped, taken aback. There, alone beneath the empty Presence Throne, stood General Tolonen; tall, white-haired and elegant in his peacock blue dress uniform. Heng Chi-Po frowned then walked on, conscious for once of the unfavourable contrast he made to the haughty Hung Mao, his hand momentarily straying to the crane patch on the chest of his dark blue pau, symbol of his status as an official of the first rank.

Facing the General, Minister Heng stopped and bowed, but Tolonen stared through him coldly, not even the smallest flicker of recognition in his eyes.

The T'ang's Chancellor waited, watching the exchange carefully. Then, rather stiffly, he bowed. 'Forgive me, Minister Heng, but the T'ang awaits you. Please... if you would follow me.'

Heng turned angrily and followed Chung Hu-Yan into a room to the right of the throne. The T'ang was waiting for him there, standing amongst the tall-leafed plants at the edge of a small, decorative carp pond.

'Chieh Hsia,' he said, bowing deeply, 'I hope you are in good health.'

Li Shai Tung turned from his contemplation of the fish. 'Come in, Minister Heng. Please, take a seat. We've business to discuss.'

Heng sat, his back to the unlit fire, looking about him, noting with pleasure the simple luxuries of the room. There was a tall screen across the centre of the room, a delightful thing of brightly coloured silk, and next to it a low, squat vase, rounded like the belly of a wrestler, its glaze the sweetest, softest lavender he'd ever seen.

'This is a beautiful room, Chieh Hsia.'

'Yes,' said the T'ang, smiling. 'It was my grandfather's favourite room. His picture hangs behind you.'

Heng turned and looked up, first at Wen Ti, then at the painting beside it, conscious at once of the strength, the raw vitality of the man portrayed. 'Ah yes. He has your eyes, Chieh Hsia.'

'My eyes?' The T'ang looked down, thoughtful. 'They say he had perfect vision all his life. That at seventy he could see what type of bird was nesting in a tree more than two li distant. But there's seeing and seeing, neh, Heng?'

He met the Minister's eyes again, a wry yet challenging look in his own.

Heng bowed, conscious of the exaggeration and suddenly wary of its meaning. 'As you say, *Chieh Hsia*.'

'Yes... As I say.' The T'ang looked past him, up at the painting of his ancestor. 'And if I say Heng Yu is not appointed in Lwo Kang's place?'

Heng Chi-Po stiffened in his seat, then forced himself to relax. 'Then that too is as you say. One does not question the word of a T'ang.'

Li Shai Tung sat back. 'No,' he said, watching his Minister closely. 'But that is what you came for, is it not?'

Heng looked up again. 'It was, *Chieh Hsia*. But as you've made your decision...'

The T'ang raised his chin slightly. 'There was nothing else, then? No other matter you wished to speak to me about?'

Heng kept his face a blank. 'Nothing that cannot wait for the next meeting of the Council of Ministers. I thought to plead on my nephew's behalf. To put his qualities before you. He is a good man, a capable man, *Chieh Hsia*.'

Strangely, the T'ang laughed. 'You are quite right, Minister Heng. He is a good man. Which is why I saw him this very morning.'

The look of surprise on Heng's face was unfeigned.

'*Chieh Hsia*?'

'And appointed him.'

Heng's mouth fell open. 'But you said...'

The T'ang clicked his fingers. Two guards came in and stood there at either end of the screen. Heng looked across at them, frowning, not understanding, then looked back at the T'ang.

'Yes. I spoke to him at length. I questioned him about the five classics. Then, finally, I set him a riddle.'

'A riddle, *Chieh Hsia*?'

Li Shai Tung stood up and went over to the screen. 'I put this problem to him. If one knows a man is guilty yet has no proof, how can one act and yet be considered just?'

Heng lowered his eyes.

'You see my drift, Minister Heng? You understand me?'

The T'ang's voice was suddenly harsher, colder.

Heng glanced up; saw how closely the T'ang was watching him now. *No proof*, he thought. *You have no proof!*

The T'ang continued. 'Your nephew considered a moment, then asked me how it was I knew and yet could not prove the matter? Was I, then, not witness to the guilty act? No, I had to answer. What then? he asked. Was there another, perhaps, whose word meant less in the eyes of the world than that of the guilty man? Were the scales of accusation and denial tipped unevenly in the latter's favour? I smiled and nodded. But so it ever is. How to balance them?'

Heng had gone cold.

'And do you know what he said?'

The Minister looked up. He hesitated, then found his voice. 'No, *Chieh Hsia*.'

The T'ang laughed sourly. 'No, you wouldn't, would you, Heng?'

He snapped his fingers again, then moved aside as the guards lifted and carried the screen away.

Heng gasped. His face blanched. Then he looked down sharply, swallowing loudly.

The T'ang came closer and stood over him. 'You're a clever man, Heng Chi-Po. Too clever to leave your print on things. But I know you for what you are. I've seen it here, with my own eyes. Your guilt is as clear on you as the glaze on this vase.'

He turned and looked across to where Pi Ch'ien sat, hands in his lap, silently watching, then looked back down at his Minister.

'Over there, in the corner, is a desk. On the desk you will find an ink block, brushes, writing paper and your seal of office. I want you to write a letter to me explaining that you have been suffering from ill-health these last few months. So much so that you must, with great sadness naturally, resign your post.'

There was the smallest movement of Heng's head as if to protest, then he nodded.

'Good. In which case there will be no loss of pension, no public loss of face. As for your Family, they will gain a better man as Minister. Heng Yu will be appointed in your place.'

Heng Chi-Po looked up mutely, miserably, then bowed his head again and went to do as he was bid.

★

Heng Kou waved the servant away, then leaned across to lock and seal the carriage.

'What is it, first brother? What has happened?'

For a moment Heng Chi-Po was unable to speak. His face was mottled with fury and his hands pulled convulsively at each other. Then he leaned forward across the gap between them until his face was almost touching Kou's.

'This is Tolonen's doing.' Heng Chi-Po blinked angrily, then leaned back again. For a moment he was silent, staring away into the distance, his whole face fixed in a mask of purest hatred. Then he turned and faced his brother again.

'I saw it in his eyes. That man has never liked me, Kou. And now he has poisoned the T'ang against me.'

Kou frowned. 'Poisoned... How?'

'The insect tricked me. Trapped me...' Heng Chi-Po's chest rose and fell violently now. Sweat beads stood out at his forehead.

Heng Kou began to understand. Gods! Heng Chi-Po was out. That was it, wasn't it? For some reason he was out. Nothing else could have brought him to this state. But was this a tragedy for Chi-Po alone or for the whole family? Was all lost? Or could the damage be contained? He had to know.

Heng Kou calmed himself and leaned forward, forcing his brother to look at him. 'Tell me what happened, eldest brother. What misfortune has befallen our great family?'

Heng Chi-Po tried to meet his eyes, then looked down sharply, his voice suddenly bitter with shame. He was close to tears.

'I am no longer Minister. Li Shai Tung has stripped me of my office.'

'Stripped you...' Heng Kou feigned speechlessness. Then he found his voice again. 'He forced you to resign, you mean?'

Heng Chi-po nodded, the first tears rolling down his cheeks. 'But there's more, Kou. He has appointed nephew Yu in my place. Can you believe that? The humiliation of it! We shall be laughing stocks!'

Heng Kou's mind reeled. Nephew Yu! After the first shock of it he wanted to laugh aloud, but he hid both his delight and his relief. 'That's outrageous!' he said. 'It is an insult, elder brother. A slur upon us all.' But he was already considering how to act to minimize the damage to the family.

Heng Chi-Po leaned forward again, his red-rimmed eyes suddenly angry again. 'I'll have him, Kou! I'll have the carrion dead, understand?'

For a moment Heng Kou was too shocked for words, but then he saw that his brother didn't mean the T'ang.

'Leave it, brother. Please. It's done. You can't undo it thus.'

Heng Chi-Po shook his head violently. 'No, Kou. I want Tolonen dead. By tomorrow evening. Understand me? I want that bastard obliterated. I want him non-existent. I want...'

Heng Kou shivered, then bowed his head. 'As you wish, my brother.'

'Do you think they'll incarcerate me, Pietr? Do you think they've proof to hold me until the trial?'

Lehmann smiled and touched Wyatt's shoulder. 'We've the best advocates in the seven cities, Edmund. I'm sure they'll keep you from the cells. But even if they can't, it won't be so dreadful. Privilege is privilege, even behind bars. You'll not lack for comforts.'

Wyatt smiled, but shadows gathered beneath the firm and pleasant line of his mouth, clouding the attractive sparkle of his eyes. Many old friends had come to visit him this morning. More friends than he'd thought he had. For a time he had let himself be buoyed by their good wishes, but now they were gone and he was alone with Lehmann.

'You know, this frightens me, Pietr. I couldn't sleep last night thinking of it. Wondering how I would handle myself. How I would bear up before all these lies and smears. Wondering what kind of man I would be at the end of it.'

'You'll be your father's son, Edmund. You're like him. You have his strength.'

Wyatt looked down. 'Maybe.'

He said no more, but Lehmann, who knew him as well as any man, could sense what he was thinking. Wyatt's father had been strong but inconsiderate, his mother weak and conciliatory. She had died when Edmund was only five, leaving him almost defenceless against his hectoring father. That he had grown up such a sane and balanced individual was testimony to the influence of his sisters and aunts.

Lehmann glanced down at the ornate timepiece inset at his wrist. 'The General will be here soon, Edmund. We should get ready for him.'

Wyatt nodded abstractedly, then turned to face him. 'It's not myself I'm afraid for, it's them.' He shivered, then wrapped his arms about himself. 'It's why I couldn't bear to have them here with me today. If I lose this – if, inexplicably, they find me guilty of Lwo Kang's murder...' He looked down, all colour gone from his cheeks. 'Well, their lives would be forfeit, too, wouldn't they? It's the law. A traitor and all his family...'

Lehmann breathed shallowly, forcing himself to meet Wyatt's eyes. 'That's so. To the third generation.'

'Still...' Wyatt forced a smile, then came across and held Lehmann to him tightly. 'I'm grateful, Pietr,' he said more quietly. 'Truly I am. However this turns out, I...'

Lehmann felt Wyatt's body shudder in his arms and steeled himself against all feeling. Even so, he answered Wyatt gently.

'You would have helped me, wouldn't you?'

Wyatt moved slightly back from him. There were tears in his eyes. 'I'd kill for you, Pietr. You know I would.'

Necessary. He heard DeVore's voice saying it and felt a shiver run down his spine. *It's easy for you, Howard,* he thought; *you never liked him.*

Lehmann smiled. 'Let's talk of living, neh?'

There was a pounding on the mansion's huge front doors.

Wyatt looked up, past him. 'They're early. I didn't think they'd be early.'

They went through, out into the marbled hallway. Wyatt's chamberlain, a stout, middle-aged Han, greeted them with a bow.

'Shall I open the door, master?'

Wyatt shook his head. 'No. Let them wait, Fu Hsien.'

There were footsteps on the stairs overhead and a murmur of talk.

'Ch'un tzu!' Lehmann went to the foot of the stairs and greeted the three elderly Han as they came down to him. It had cost him over a million yuan simply to bring them here this morning. If the case went on for months, as it was likely to do, it would cost his faction somewhere between thirty and fifty million. Wyatt had been told nothing of this, but his sisters and aunts had been briefed already. In time they were certain to let Wyatt know whose money it was that was paying for his defence.

Lehmann turned, smiling, and watched the three greybeards greet Wyatt once again. At the introduction, earlier, all three advocates had seemed impressed by Wyatt's protestations of innocence. As indeed they ought.

Edmund didn't merely seem innocent, he *was*. The full force of his self-belief had carried any remaining doubts the three had had. They had agreed to take the case.

But things were not as simple as they seemed. On paper Wyatt's case seemed good. In court he would make a fine impression. Public sympathy was sure to be in his favour. But Wyatt had to lose. He had to be made to seem a victim of conspiracy and power-broking.

New evidence would be introduced as and when necessary, for his good friend, Edmund Wyatt, was to be a martyr.

The hammering came again. A voice shouted from behind the door. 'Open up! We come on the T'ang's business!'

Again the chamberlain looked at Wyatt. This time he nodded.

Tolonen came through first, in full dress uniform, the *chi ling* or unicorn patch of a first-rank officer resplendent on his chest. Behind him strode two officers and an elite squad of eight armed soldiers.

'General Tolonen,' said Wyatt, with cold politeness, offering his hand. But Tolonen walked past him, ignoring him.

'Who represents the prisoner?' he demanded brusquely.

One of the three Han stepped forward. 'I am Advocate Fou, General. I act for *Shih* Wyatt in this matter. And I'll remind you that my client is not a prisoner but should be addressed as the accused.'

Tolonen snorted and turned away. One of the officers at once handed him a long, silvered tube. He hefted it a moment, then passed it to the advocate.

'Please read the document. All three of you, if necessary. Copies will be provided at your offices.'

Advocate Fou tipped the scroll out into his hand, passed the tube to one of his colleagues, then unfurled the document. Wyatt moved past Tolonen and stood at the advocate's side, trying to make sense of the sheet of blood-red pictograms.

'It's in Mandarin,' he said. 'That's illegal, isn't it?'

Advocate Fou shook his head, then muttered something in Han to his colleagues and rolled the document up again.

'What is it?' Lehmann asked, coming up beside Wyatt.

The advocate looked across at Tolonen, then back at Lehmann. 'I am afraid we cannot help you, Under Secretary. I am most sorry. This matter has been taken out of the jurisdiction of the Courts. Please...' He handed the document across to Wyatt. 'Our apologies, *Shih* Wyatt. We wish you luck. If innocence has weight in law you will triumph yet.'

As one the three Han bowed and took their leave.

Wyatt stood there a moment, dumbfounded, watching them go. Then he turned to Lehmann. 'What in the gods' names is happening, Pietr?' He thrust the document into Lehmann's hand. 'What is this?'

Lehmann looked away. *Gods!* he thought. *This changes everything.*

He turned back. 'It's an Edict, Edmund. The Seven have passed a special Edict.' He unfurled the white, silken roll.

'See here.' He pointed out the rigid line of hardened wax.

'These are their seals. The *Ywe Lung*, symbol of their power. All seven of them. They must have met in an emergency session and agreed to this.'

Wyatt had gone very quiet, watching him, a new kind of fear in his face.

'An Edict?'

'Yes. You are to be tried in camera, by a council of the T'ang's Ministers.' Lehmann swallowed then looked across at Tolonen, an unfeigned anger in his eyes. 'This changes things, Edmund. It changes everything. It means they want you dead.'

Heng Kou paused in the doorway, then knelt down and touched his brow to the cold floor.

'Nephew Yu. I am most sorry to disturb your afternoon sleep. I would not have come, but it is a matter of the utmost urgency.'

Heng Yu tied the sash to his sleeping robe and came across the room quickly. 'Uncle Kou, please, get up at once. In private you are still my uncle.'

Heng Kou let himself be drawn to his feet, then stood there, embarrassed, as Heng Yu bowed to him in the old way.

All that has changed, he thought. *The T'ang gave you years when he gave you power. Now you are our head and the family must bow before you. So it is. So it must be. Or Chung Kuo itself would fall.*

Heng Yu straightened. 'But tell me, what brings you here, uncle?'

'I'm sorry, Yu, but I bring bad news. Your uncle Chi-Po is unwell.'

Heng Yu started. 'Unwell?'

'Please...' Heng Kou bowed and moved aside. 'I felt you should come yourself. At once. My own doctors are seeing to him even now. But...'

Heng Yu gave the slightest nod. 'I understand. Please, lead me to him.'

Heng Chi-Po's bedroom was dimly lit. The four doctors stood at one end of the room, beside the only light source. Seeing the two men in the doorway, they came across.

'How is my uncle?' asked Heng Yu at once, concerned.

The most senior of them bowed low, then answered him. Like all four of them he had been briefed beforehand concerning Heng Yu's new status in the household.

'I regret to say that your uncle passed away five minutes ago. His heart failed him.'

Heng Kou, watching, saw Heng Yu's mouth fall open, his eyes widen in surprise; saw the real pain he felt at the news and knew he had been right not to involve him in the scheme. *Let him believe things are as they are. That disappointment killed my brother. Only I and these four men know otherwise.*

Heng Yu had a servant bring them a lamp, then they went over to where Heng Chi-Po lay on his oversized bed. His eyes had been closed and his face now was at peace. The flesh of his arms and chest and face was pale and misted with a fine sheen of sweat.

'Did he suffer much?' Heng Yu asked.

Heng Kou saw how the doctors looked at him, then looked away.

'Not at all,' he lied, remembering how it had taken all five of them to hold him down while the poison had taken effect. 'Of course, there was pain at first, but then, thankfully, it passed and he lapsed into sleep.'

Heng Yu nodded then turned away with a tiny shudder.

Heng Kou remained a moment longer, looking down at the brother he had always loathed; the brother who, since he had been old enough to walk, had bullied him and treated him like the basest servant. He smiled. *You would have had us kill Tolonen, eh? You would have brought us all down with your foolishness?*

Yes, but you forgot who held the power.

He turned, indicating to the doctors that they should leave. Then, when they were gone, he went to where Heng Yu was standing. He was about to speak when Heng Yu surprised him, raising a hand to silence him.

Heng Yu's whole manner had changed. His voice was low but powerful. 'Don't think me blind, Uncle Kou. Or dull-witted. I know what happened here.'

'And?'

Kou held his breath. If Heng Yu insisted, all would be undone.

'And nothing, uncle. Understand me?'

Heng Kou hesitated, studying the smooth lines of his nephew's face, seeing him for the first time as the T'ang must have seen him.

He smiled, then bowed low. 'I understand, Minister Heng.'

The door slammed shut. DeVore turned and looked back across the cell at Wyatt. They were alone now. Just the two of them.

'Shouldn't there be others?' Wyatt said, watching him warily. 'I thought it was usual for there to be several officers at an interrogation.'

DeVore laughed. 'You don't understand, do you? You still think you're safe. In spite of all that's happened.'

Wyatt turned away. 'If you mistreat me...'

DeVore interrupted him. 'You really *don't* understand, do you?'

He moved closer, coming round the side of Wyatt until he stood there, face to face with the slightly taller man.

'Let me explain.'

Wyatt had turned his face slightly, so as not to have to meet DeVore's eyes, but the suddenness of the slap took him by complete surprise. He staggered backwards, holding his cheek, staring at DeVore, his eyes wide with astonishment.

'Strip off!' DeVore barked, his face suddenly mean, uncompromising. 'Everything. Top clothes. Underclothes. Jewellery. We'll remove your electronic implants later.'

Wyatt shook his head uncertainly. 'But you can't do this...'

'Do what?' DeVore laughed. 'You're a murderer. Understand? You killed the T'ang's Minister. You'll be tried and found guilty. And then we'll execute you.'

DeVore took a step closer, seeing how Wyatt flinched, expecting another blow. His cheek was bright red, the weal the shape of DeVore's hand, each finger clearly delineated. 'That's the truth of this, Edmund Wyatt. You're a dead man. When you killed Lwo Kang you stepped outside the game. You broke all the rules. So now there are no rules. At least, none that you would recognize.'

He reached out and took Wyatt's wrists, savagely pulling him closer, until Wyatt's face was pressed against his own.

'Are you beginning to understand?'

Wyatt shivered and made an awkward nod.

'Good.' He thrust Wyatt back brutally, making him fall. 'Then strip off.'

He turned his back. The cell was bare. He could almost see Wyatt look about him, hesitating. Then he heard the jingle of his thin gold bracelets as he set them down on the floor, and smiled. *I have you now, my proud false Chinaman. I'll strip the Han from you, pigtail, pau and all. Yes, and we'll see how proud you are when I'm done with you.*

When he turned back. Wyatt was naked, his clothes neatly bundled on the floor beside him. His white, soft body seemed so frail, so ill-suited to the trial that lay ahead: already it seemed to cower, to shrink back into itself, as if aware of what was to come. Yet when DeVore looked up past the narrow, hairless chest and met Wyatt's eyes he was surprised to find defiance there.

So, he thought. *That first. They say the Han are strong because they resign themselves to fate. In thirty centuries they have never fought fate, but have been its agents. Flood, famine and revolution have all been as one to them. They have bowed before the inevitability of death and so survived, stronger for their long and patient suffering. So it will be with you, Edmund Wyatt. I'll make a true Han of you yet – stripped bare of all you were, resigned and patient in your suffering.*

He smiled. 'You knew Yang Lai? Lwo Kang's Junior Minister?'

Wyatt looked up sharply, real hatred in his eyes. 'He's dead. You know he's dead. He died with Lwo Kang in the solarium.'

'That's not what I asked. Did you know him well?'

'He was a friend. A good friend. I was at college with him.'

DeVore laughed coldly. 'How good a friend, would you say?'

Wyatt swallowed, then lowered his head. 'He was my lover.'

'You admit it?'

Angered, Wyatt yelled back at him. 'Why not? I expect you knew already! Anyway, what has Yang Lai to do with this?'

DeVore smiled and turned away. 'Yang Lai was murdered. Three days after the assassination. The only thing we found on the body was a small hologram of you.'

Wyatt had gone very still. When DeVore next looked at him he was surprised to find tears in his eyes.

'There,' said Wyatt softly. 'Surely that says something to you? Would I kill a man I loved then leave my holo on him?'

DeVore shook his head. 'You don't understand.'

Wyatt frowned. 'What do you mean?'

'He had it up his arse.'

Wyatt looked away. A shuddering breath racked his body.

'Oh, and there's more. Much more. Kao Jyan's tape. Your trading connections with Hong Cao and Cho Hsiang. The internal flight schedules that coincide perfectly with our reconstruction of the attack on the solarium. Your company's experiments with harmonic triggers. And, of course, your secretary Lung Ti's evidence.'

Wyatt looked back at DeVore blankly. 'Lung Ti?'

This was DeVore's master stroke, the thing that had cemented it all in place. Lung Ti had been with Wyatt from his tenth year. He was his most trusted servant. But eight years ago DeVore had found Lung Ti's weakness and bought him. Now Lung Ti was his creature, reading from his script.

DeVore let the silence extend a moment longer, then lowered his head. 'Lung Ti has confessed to his part in everything. He is to give evidence under the T'ang's pardon.'

Wyatt's mouth worked loosely, but no sound came out.

'Yes,' DeVore said softly, moving closer. 'And now you do understand, neh?' He reached out and put his fingers gently to the weal on Wyatt's cheek. 'We'll find the truth of this, you and I. We've time, you know. Plenty of time.'

And in the end, he thought, *even you will believe you ordered Lwo Kang's death.*

From high above it seemed insignificant, a tiny, circular blemish in the vast field of whiteness, yet as the craft dropped the circle grew and grew until it seemed to fill the whole of the viewing window with its blackness.

The big transporter set down on the roof of the City, close to the circle's edge. Only paces from its struts the surface of the roof was warped, the ice dented and buckled by the vast heat of the explosion. Seen from this close the huge dark circle revealed another dimension. It was a dish – an enormous concave dish, like some gigantic alchemist's crucible; the dark and sticky sludge of its residue already sifted and searched for clues.

They climbed down from the transporter, looking about them; sixty men from the lower levels, white-cloaked and hooded. Others handed down tools from inside the big, insectile machine: shovels and brushes; sacks and other containers. Old-fashioned tools. Nothing modern was needed now. This was the simplest part of all. The final stage before rebuilding.

They got to work at once, forming three chains of twenty men, three from each chain filling sacks at the edge of the sludge-pool and handing them back to the others in the line. And at the top two anchor men moved backward and forward between the human chain and the big machine, passing the sacks up into the interior.

A wind was blowing from the mountains. At the top of the right-hand workchain one of the men – a big, shaven-headed Han – turned and looked back at the distant peaks. For a moment he could relax, knowing no sack was on its way. Taking off a glove, he pulled down his goggles and wiped at his brow. How cool it was. How pleasant to feel the wind brushing against the skin. For a moment his blunt, nondescript face searched the distance, trying to place something, then he shrugged.

Looking down, he noticed something against the dark surface. Something small and green and fragile-looking. He bent down and picked it up, holding it in his bare palm. It was a budding seed.

He looked up, hearing the cry of birds overhead, and understood. It was from the mountainside. A bird must have picked it up and dropped it here. Here on the lifeless surface of the City's roof.

He stared at it a moment longer, noting the shape of its twin leaves, the hardness of its central pip. Then he crushed it between his fingers and let it drop.

Kao Chen, *kwai*, one-time assassin, looked up. Clouds, mountains, even the flat, open surface of the City's roof – all seemed so different in the daylight. He sniffed in the warm air and smiled. Then, hearing the grunts of the men below him, he pulled up his goggles, eased on his glove and turned back.

PART SEVEN   **Beneath the Yellow Springs**

SPRING 2198

'When I was alive, I wandered in the streets of
    the Capital;
Now that I am dead, I am left to lie in the fields.
In the morning I drove out from the High Hall;
In the evening I lodged beneath the yellow springs.
When the white sun had sunk in the Western Chasm
I hung up my chariot and rested my four horses.
Now, even the Maker of All
Could not bring the life back to my limbs.
Shape and substance day by day will vanish:
Hair and teeth will gradually fall away.
For ever from of old men have been so:
And none born can escape this thing.'

—Miu Hsi, Bearer's Song (from Han Burial Songs)

CHAPTER 30

BROTHERS

It was spring in Sichuan province and the trees of the orchard at Tongjiang were ablaze with blossom beneath a clear blue sky. The air was clear, like a polished lens. In the distance the mountains thrust into the heavens, knife-edged shapes of green and blue.

At the orchard's edge four servants waited silently, their heads bowed, heavily laden silver trays held out before them.

Beneath the trees at the lake's edge, the two princes were playing, their laughter echoing across the water. The eldest, Li Han Ch'in, evaded his little brother's outstretched arm and, with a swift, athletic movement, grasped an overhead branch and swung up into the crown of the apple tree. Li Yuan rushed at the tree, making trial jumps, but the branch was too high for him to reach.

'That isn't fair, Han!' Yuan said breathlessly, laughing, his eyes burning with excitement. In the tree above him Han Ch'in was giggling, his head tilted back to look down at his brother, a sprig of pure white blossom caught in his jet black hair.

'Come up and get me!' he taunted, letting one leg dangle, then pulling it up quickly when his brother jumped for it.

Yuan looked about him a moment, then found what he was looking for. He turned back. 'Come down! Come down or I'll beat you!' he threatened, one hand holding the thin switch, the other on his hip; his expression part stern, part amused.

'I won't!' said Han, pulling himself up closer to the branch, trying to work his way further up the tree.

Laughing excitedly, Yuan stepped forward, flicking the leafy switch gently against his brother's back. The older boy yelled exaggeratedly and kicked out wildly, his foot missing by a breath. The boy on the ground screeched, enjoying the game, and hit out harder with the branch. There was another yell from above and again the foot struck out wildly. But this time it connected, sending the small boy crashing backward.

Han Ch'in dropped down at once and went over to where his brother lay, unmoving, on the earth beside the bole.

'Yuan! Yuan!'

He bent down, listening for his brother's breath, his head dropping down onto the small boy's chest.

Yuan rolled, using his brother's weight, as he'd been taught, and came up on his chest, his knees pinning down Han's arms. For a moment he was on top, his face triumphant. Then Han pushed up, throwing him off sideways. Yuan turned and began to scramble away, but Han reached out and grabbed his leg, slowly dragging him back.

'No, Han... No... Please!' But Yuan's protestations were feeble. He could barely speak for laughing.

'Say it!' Han demanded, pinning the small boy's arms against his sides, his arms wrapped tightly about his chest.

'I order you to say it!'

Yuan shook his head violently, his laughter giving way to hiccups. But as Han's arms squeezed tighter he relented, nodding. The grip slackened but remained firm. Yuan took a breath, then spoke. 'You are my master...' He coughed, then continued, '... and I promise to obey you.'

'Good!'

Han Ch'in released him, then pushed him away. The small boy fell against the earth and lay there a moment, breathing deeply. For a while they were quiet. Birds called in the warm, still air.

'What do you think of her, Yuan?'

Li Yuan rolled over and looked up at his brother. Li Han Ch'in was kneeling, looking out across the lake towards the terrace. The sprig of blossom still clung to the side of his head, pure white against the intense blackness of his hair. There was a faint smile on his lips. His dark eyes looked far off into the distance. 'Do you think she's pretty?'

The question brought a colour to Yuan's cheeks. He nodded and looked down. *Yes,* he thought. *More than pretty.* Fei Yen was beautiful. He had known that from the first moment he had seen her. Fei Yen. How well the name fitted her. *Flying Swallow...*

He looked up to find Han Ch'in staring at him, his brow furrowed.

'I was thinking, Yuan. Wondering what it would be like to have several wives. A different woman, perhaps, for every night of the week.' He laughed strangely, a tense, high-pitched sound, then looked down, pulling at the grass. 'I'm sorry. I forget sometimes. You seem so old, so full of wisdom. Like father.' Han fell silent, then looked up again, smiling. 'I guess it doesn't touch you yet. Never mind. You'll understand it when you're older.'

Li Yuan watched his brother a moment longer, then looked down. Sunlight through the branches dappled the earth beside his hand. Leaf shadow lay across his flesh like a discolouration of the skin. He shivered and closed his eyes. Sometimes he felt he understood too well. If he were in Han's place, Fei Yen would have been enough for him; he would have needed no other. He looked back at his brother, keeping his thoughts to himself, knowing that Han would only tease him if he knew. 'You're only six,' he would say. 'What could you possibly know of love?'

'Even so,' Han said, looking at him again, 'Fei Yen will be special. My first wife. And her sons shall inherit.' He nodded, satisfied with the justice of the words. Li Yuan saw how his brother was watching him – smiling, a deep love in his eyes – and looked down, warmed by it.

'They'll be fine sons, Yuan. Good, strong sons. And the first of them will have your name.'

Han Ch'in reached out and held his brother's ankle.

'He'll be strong, like me. But I hope he'll also be wise, like you.'

'And pretty, like Fei Yen,' Yuan said, looking up at his brother through his long dark eyelashes.

Han looked away into the distance, a faint smile on his lips, then nodded. 'Yes... like Fei Yen.'

'Do you mind if I sit here?'

Wang Ti blushed and looked down, cradling the child to her and rocking it gently. All four tiers of Chang's Restaurant were packed, few spaces remaining at the tables. Her table, on the second tier, overlooking the bell tower, was one of the few not fully occupied.

'No. Please do.'

She had seen the man much earlier, moving between the crowded market stalls at the end of Main. Like the others in the crowd, she had watched him momentarily, then turned back to her shopping, impressed by the sheer size of him. Now, as he sat across from her, she realized just how big he was; not just tall but broad at the shoulder and the chest. A real giant of a man.

'What's good here?'

She looked up and met his eyes. Blue, *Hung Mao* eyes.

'It's all good. Chang's is the best here on Twenty-Six. But you might try his green jade soup.'

The big man nodded and half turned in his seat, summoning the nearest girl.

'Master?'

'I'm told the green jade soup is good. Bring me a large bowl. Oh, and some chicken drumsticks and noodles.'

The girl bowed, then turned and went back inside to the kitchens.

'Do you eat here often?'

He was facing her again, a faint, polite smile on his lips.

She looked down at the sleeping child, safe in the harness at her chest. 'When I can afford to,' she answered quietly. 'Which is not often, I'm afraid.'

The man followed her gaze, smiling. 'He's a good child. How old is he?'

She stroked the child's brow, and looked up, her smile broadening momentarily. 'Ten months.'

He leaned forward, looking into the child's sleeping face. 'I bet he's his father's darling.'

She laughed. 'Yes! He's like a child himself when he's with Jyan.'

'Jyan? A pretty name for a child.'

She smiled. 'And you? You speak like a man who has sons.'

The big man sat back and laughed. 'Me? No... One day, perhaps. But for now... well, my job keeps me on the move. It would not do to have ties.'

She looked at him sympathetically a moment, noticing his features properly for the first time. He had a big, open face, the long nose blunted at its tip, his jaw pronounced and his lips full. His dark hair was cut brutally short, making her wonder for a moment what it was he did. But it was not an unkind face. When he smiled it softened. She decided she liked him.

'And that's what brings you here?'

'My job? No, not this time. I'm looking for someone. A relative.'

She laughed again; softly, so as not to wake the child. 'I think I'd have seen any relative of yours.'

His smile broadened. 'Oh, don't judge all my clan by me. This –' He put one hand to his chest, '– they say I inherited from my grandfather. My father's father. My mother was a small woman, you see. Small in size, I should say, for she was a giant to her sons.'

She looked down, pleased by his filial piety. 'And your father?'

For a moment the big man looked away. 'I never knew my father. He left before I was two years old.'

'Ah... like my Chen.'

The giant looked back at her, his eyes narrowed slightly. 'You understand, then?'

She bowed her head slightly. 'It's sad...'

'Yes, well...' He turned. The serving girl was standing at his side, a tray of steaming food balanced on one hand. He moved back from the table, letting her set out the bowls in front of him. 'You've eaten?' He looked at the woman facing him, concerned. 'If not, might I buy you lunch?'

She shook her head hastily. 'Please... I thank you kindly, but my Chen would not permit it.'

He raised a hand. 'I understand. Forgive me...'

She looked up, smiling. 'Thank you. But we have eaten. And now...'

The big man was already spooning his soup down vigorously. 'Hmm. This is delicious. As good as anything I've tasted.'

She smiled, watching him, enjoying his enjoyment. 'As I said. Chang's is the best.'

He looked across at her, then set down his spoon and stood, seeing she was getting up. 'Can I help you?'

She shook her head. 'No. I can manage. I'm quite used to it, I assure you.'

He gave a slight bow with his head. 'Then take care. It was a pleasure talking with you.'

'And you.'

Karr sat there a moment, watching her go. Then, nodding to himself, he looked down at the soup and began to eat again. Reaching for one of the drumsticks, he paused, laughing softly to himself. Jyan! He'd named the boy Jyan! Then, more thoughtfully, he gazed back across the broad corridor, remembering the woman's face, her smile, but mostly remembering what she had said.

There's time, he thought. *Time enough for all things. Even sons.*

Han Ch'in approached the fence at a gallop, the Arab flying beneath him, its sleek neck pushing forward with each stride, its jet black flanks moving powerfully, effortlessly across the hillside, its tail streaming behind it in the wind.

Yuan, watching from the pavilion half a *li* away, held his breath. It was the biggest of the fences, almost the size of the horse; a construction of stone and wood, with the ground dropping away beyond. Han had fallen here before, the last time he'd attempted it. Fallen and bruised his ribs badly. Now, fearlessly, he tried the fence again.

Without checking his pace, Han spurred the Arab on, yelling wildly as it stretched and leapt. For the briefest moment it seemed he had misjudged. The horse rose mightily, its forelegs climbing the air, but, at its highest point, its pasterns seemed to brush the fence. As it hit the ground on the far side it stumbled and threatened to go down.

Yuan cried out, putting his knuckles to his mouth. The horse seemed to stagger, its momentum threatening to topple it dock over poll. In the saddle, Han Ch'in hung on grimly, pulling tightly at the reins, straining to keep the Arab's head up, drawing the horse to the right, into the gradient. The Arab fought back, fear making its movements desperate. Its nostrils flared and it whinnied noisily, contesting with Han's sharp yells of command. Slowly its rump came round, its long, dished face flicking to the left as if in pain. As Han Ch'in eased off, its head came up sharply and it seemed to dance, then settle, slowing to a canter.

Yuan turned, looking up at his father. 'He's done it! Han's done it!'

'Yes...' Li Shai Tung was smiling, but his eyes revealed just how worried he had been.

Han Ch'in turned the horse again, reaching down to pat its neck, then spurred it on towards them. Drawing up in front of them, he threw his head back proudly, then reached up to comb the hair back from his eyes, looking to his father for approval.

'Well done, Han. You proved yourself the master of the beast!'

Han laughed, then looked down at the Arab's face.

'Maybe. But she's a fine horse, father. Any of the others from our stables would have fallen back there. A rider is sometimes only as good as his horse.'

'Or the horse his rider.' The T'ang was looking seriously at his son now. 'I don't say this lightly, Han Ch'in. I was worried for you. But you showed great character. You did not let the beast have her own way. You controlled her.' He nodded and momentarily looked at his younger son. 'Control. That's the key. To beasts and men.'

For a moment longer Han Ch'in stared down at his horse's face, petting the animal, calming her. Then he looked up again and met his father's eyes. 'I didn't think you would be here, father. I thought you would be arranging things. The reception...'

The T'ang smiled faintly at his son, then grew more serious. 'That's all in hand. No, I came because I need you both, two hours from now, in the Hall of the Seven Ancestors. It will be formal, so dress accordingly.'

Han frowned. 'What is it, father?'

Li Shai Tung studied his eldest son a moment, his eyes drinking in the sight of him proudly. 'Later, Han. I'll explain things when you're there.'

Han Ch'in bowed in the saddle, answering for them both. 'As you wish, father. We shall be there.'

'Good. But before then you've a visitor.' He smiled. 'Fei Yen has arrived. She's waiting for you in the Palace.'

Yuan looked across at his brother, watching him. Han bowed to his father, then, unable to hide the grin that had settled on his face, turned his horse and began to move away across the hillside towards the river and the bridge. Halfway down he turned in his saddle and called back.

'I'll see you there, Yuan! Bring Hsueh Chai and old Chou. In the meadow by the lake. We'll have a picnic.'

Fei Yen was standing on the bridge, her maids surrounding her. One stood behind her, shading her mistress with a huge silk umbrella. Another stood at her side, languidly waving a large fan. A third and fourth, their pastel greens and blues matching the colours of the day, waited nearby. Thirty paces off, in the shade of a great willow, stood her aunts and great-aunts in their dark silks and satins, watchful, talking quietly among themselves.

Fei Yen herself was looking out across the lake; watching the warm, spring breeze ruffle the water and bend the reeds at the shoreline. Her face, in the sunlight filtered through the umbrella, seemed like a silken screen of pinks and oranges, her dainty features hidden from Li Yuan, who stood on the bank below, looking up at her.

She was beautiful. He had no need to see her clearly to know that. He had only to remember the last time she had come here to the orchard. Had only to recall the way she smiled, the way her bright pink tongue poked out from between those pearled and perfect teeth. How dark her eyes were, how delicate the contours of her face.

He looked across at Han and saw how his brother looked at her. Saw both the awe and the love there in his face. And understood.

Servants had set up a small, rounded tent in the middle of the water meadow. The Arab was tethered just beyond it, its head down, grazing. In front of the tent they had set down stools and a low table, on which was placed a wine kettle and three small, glazed tumblers. Further off, conspicuous in the centre of the meadow, stood an archery target.

Han Ch'in came forward, striding purposefully across the short grass, like some strange, upright, elegant animal. He had changed from his riding clothes into looser silks of peach and vermilion. Hsueh Chai had braided his hair with golden thread and he wore a simple gold necklet of interwoven dragons. Watching him, Yuan felt all his love for his brother swell up in him. How fine Han was; in his own way, how beautiful. How his dark eyes flashed as he came to the stone flags of the narrow bridge. Eyes that never for a moment left his future bride.

Fei Yen turned, facing Han Ch'in, and came out from beneath the shade.

Again Yuan caught his breath. She was like china. Like perfect porcelain. Her skin so pale, so perfectly white; her nose, her lips, her delicate ears so finely moulded that, for a moment, she seemed like a sculpture come to sudden life. Such diminutive perfection. Then, as she met Han on the gentle downslope of the bridge, he saw her smile, saw how her dark eyes filled with fire and knew, with all the certainty his young soul could muster, that he was lost to her. She was Han's. But he would love her even so. As he loved Han.

Over tea their talk was of court matters. Yuan, silent, looked up at Fei Yen through his lashes, strangely, overpoweringly abashed by her proximity. When she leaned forward, the pale cream of her sleeve brushed against his knees, and he shivered, the faint sweet scent of jasmine wafting to him from her.

'They say Wang Sau-leyan has been up to mischief,' she said softly, looking up past her fan at Han Ch'in. 'Ten years old! Can you imagine it! His eldest brother caught him...'

She hesitated, giving a soft, delicious laugh.

'Go on...' said Han, leaning forward on his seat, his booted feet spread, like two young saplings planted in the earth, his hands placed firmly on his knees.

'Well...' she said, conspiratorially. 'It's said that he was found with a girl. Stark naked in his father's bed!'

'No!' said Han, delighted. 'His father's bed!'

Wang Sau's father was Wang Hsien, T'ang of City Africa. Wang Sau-leyan was his fourth son and his youngest.

'Yes!' Fei Yen clapped her hands together. 'And listen... the girl was only a child. And *Hung Mao*, too!'

Han Ch'in sat back, astonished, then, slowly, he began to laugh.

Yuan, meanwhile, was watching her. Her voice was so sweet, so pure in its tones, it sent a shiver down his spine. He was oblivious to the sense of her words; to him her voice seemed divorced from all human meaning. It had that same, sweet lyrical sound as the *erhu*; the same rich yet plaintive contralto of that ancient instrument. And as she talked he found himself fascinated by the movement, by the very shape of her hands. By the strange pearled opalescence of her nails, the delicacy of her tiny, ice-pale fingers, no bigger than his own. He looked up into her face and saw the fine, cosmetic glaze of her cheeks and brow, the silken darkness of her hair, threads of fine silver catching the afternoon's sunlight.

Han Ch'in leaned forward, still laughing. 'So what happened?'

Fei Yen sat back demurely. Thirty paces off the group of aunts, waited on by servants from their own household, were fanning themselves vigorously and straining to hear what was making Han Ch'in laugh so lustily.

'His father has banished him for a year. He's to stay in the floating palace. Alone. With only his male servants for company.'

Han Ch'in looked down, sobered by the news. He shook his head, then looked up at Fei Yen again. 'That's rather harsh, don't you think? I mean, he's only a boy. Only a bit older than Yuan here. And after all, it's nothing really. Just a bit of high spirits.'

Fei Yen fanned herself slowly, her eyes briefly looking inward. Then she smiled and tilted her head, looking directly at Han. 'But his father's bed... Surely, Han...?' She raised her eyebrows, making Han guffaw with laughter once again.

'Listen,' he said, getting up. 'I plan to issue a challenge. After the wedding. To all the Families, Major and Minor. To all the sons and cousins.'

He glanced across at Hsueh Chai, who was standing with the maids beside the entrance to the tent. The old servant came across at once, bringing a short hunting bow and a quiver of heavy, steel-tipped arrows. Han Ch'in took them and held them up. 'Twelve arrows. And the highest score shall win the prize.'

Fei Yen looked past him at the target. 'And you think you'll win?'

Han Ch'in laughed and looked at the bow in his hand.

'I don't think I'll win. I know I will.'

Her eyes flashed at him. 'My three brothers are good shots. You must be very good if you're better than them.'

Han Ch'in drew the strap of the quiver over his shoulder, then turned and marched to a point marked out on the grass. Taking an arrow from the quiver, he called back to her. 'Watch!'

He notched the arrow quickly to the bow and raised it. Then, without seeming to take aim, he drew the string taut and let the arrow fly. There was a satisfying thunk as the arrow hit and split the wood, a hand's length from the gold.

'Not bad...' Fei Yen began. Her fan was momentarily forgotten, motionless. Her face was suddenly tense, her whole body attentive to what Han was doing.

Han Ch'in drew a second arrow, notched it and let it fly as casually as before. This time it landed at the edge of the gold. Han turned, laughing. 'Well?'

'Again,' she said simply, lifting her chin in what seemed an encouraging gesture. 'It might have been luck.'

'Luck?' Han Ch'in looked surprised, then laughed and shook his head. 'Luck, you think? Watch this, then!'

He notched the arrow, then turned back to face the target. Raising the bow, he twisted it sideways, as if he was on horseback, and let fly. This time the arrow hit the gold dead centre.

Yuan was on his feet applauding wildly. Behind him, Fei Yen set down her fan and stood up slowly. Then, without a word, she walked up to Han Ch'in and took the bow from him, drawing an arrow from the quiver on his back.

'You want to try?' he said, enjoying the moment. 'I'll wager you my horse that you can't even hit the target from here. It's fifty paces, and that's a heavy bow to draw.'

She smiled at him. 'I've drawn heavier bows than this, Han Ch'in. Bows twice this length. But I'll not take your horse from you, husband-to-be. I've seen how much you love the beast.'

Han Ch'in shrugged. 'Okay. Then go ahead.'

Fei Yen shook her head. 'No, Han. Some other prize. Just between us. To prove who's master here.'

He laughed uncomfortably. 'What do you mean?'

She looked at the bow in her hands, then up at him.

'This, maybe. If I can beat you with my three arrows.'

For a moment he hesitated; then, laughing, he nodded. 'My bow, then. And if you lose?'

She laughed. 'If I lose you can have everything I own.'

Han Ch'in smiled broadly, understanding her joke. In two days they would be wed and he would be master of all she owned anyway.

'That's fair.'

He stepped back, folding his arms, then watched as she notched and raised the bow. For a long time she simply stood there, as if in trance, the bow-string taut, the arrow quivering. Yuan watched her, fascinated, noting how her breathing changed; how her whole body was tensed, different from before. Then, with a tiny cry, she seemed to shudder and release the string.

The arrow flew high, then fell, hitting the wood with a softer sound than Han's.

'A gold!' she said triumphantly, turning to face Han Ch'in.

The arrow lay like a dash across the red. Han's arrows had hit the target almost horizontally, burying themselves into the soft wood, but hers stuck up from the gold like a fresh shoot from a cut tree.

Han Ch'in shook his head, astonished. 'Luck!' he said, turning to her.

'You'll not do that twice.' He laughed, and pointed at the target. 'Look at it! A good wind and it'll fall out of the wood!'

She looked at him fiercely, defiantly. 'It's a gold, though, isn't it?'

Reluctantly he nodded, then handed her the second arrow. 'Again,' he said.

Once more she stood there, the bowstring taut, the arrow quivering, her whole self tensed behind it, concentrating. Then, with the same sharp cry, she let it fly, her body shuddering with the passion of release.

This time the arrow seemed to float in the air above the target before it fell abruptly, knocking against the third of Han's.

It was another gold.

Fei Yen turned to Han Ch'in, her face inexpressive, her hand held out for the third arrow.

Han Ch'in hesitated, his face dark, his eyes wide with anger, then thrust the arrow into her hand. For a moment she stood there, watching him, seeing just how angry he was, then she turned away, facing where Yuan sat watching.

Yuan saw her notch the bow then look across at him, her face more thoughtful than he'd ever seen it. Then, to his surprise, she winked at him and turned back to face the target.

This time she barely seemed to hesitate, but, like Han Ch'in before her, drew the string taut and let the arrow fly.

'No!' Yuan was on his feet. The arrow lay a good five paces from the target, its shaft sticking up from the ground, its feathers pointing towards the bull.

Han Ch'in clapped his hands, laughing. 'I win! I've beaten you!'

Fei Yen turned to him. 'Yes, Han,' she said softly, touching his arm gently, tenderly. 'Which makes you master here...'

Representative Barrow huffed irritably and leaned forward in his seat, straining against the harness. 'What do you think the T'ang wants, Pietr, summoning us here five hours early?'

Lehmann looked down through the window, watching the ground come slowly up to meet them. 'What do you think he wants? To keep us down, that's what. To tie us in knots and keep us docile. That's all they ever want.'

Barrow looked at him sharply. 'You think so? You're certain it has nothing to do with the wedding?'

Lehmann shook his head, remembering the alarm he'd felt on receiving the T'ang's summons. Like Barrow he had been told to present himself at Tongjiang by the third hour of the afternoon at the latest. No reason had been given, but he knew that it had nothing to do with the wedding. If it were they would have been notified a good month beforehand. No, this was something else. Something unrelated.

'It's bloody inconvenient,' Barrow continued. 'I was in the middle of a House committee meeting when his man came. Now I've had to cancel that, and the gods know when I'll get a chance now to get ready for the reception.'

Lehmann looked at him, then looked away. Whatever it was, it was certain to make a small thing like a House committee meeting seem of no consequence whatsoever. The T'ang did not send his personal craft to bring men to him without good reason. Neither did he use the warrant system lightly. Whatever it was, it was of the first importance.

But what? His pulse quickened momentarily. Had something leaked out? Or was it something else? A concession, maybe? A deal? Something to guarantee his son's inheritance?

Lehmann laughed quietly at the thought, then felt the craft touch down beneath him. For a moment the great engines droned on, then they cut out. In the ensuing silence they could hear the great overhead gates sliding back into place, securing the hangar.

He undid his straps, then stood, waiting.

The door opened and they went outside. The T'ang's Chancellor, Chung Hu-Yan, was waiting for them at the foot of the ramp.

'Ch'un tzu.' The Chancellor bowed deeply. 'The T'ang is waiting for you. The others are here already. Please...' He turned, indicating they should go through.

Lehmann hesitated. 'Forgive me, but what is all this about?'

Chung Hu-Yan looked back at him, his expression unreadable. 'In time, Under Secretary. The T'ang alone can tell you what his business is.'

'Of course.' Lehmann smiled sourly, moving past him.

The Hall of the Seven Ancestors was a massive, high-ceilinged place, its walls strewn with huge, opulent tapestries, its floor a giant mosaic of carved marble. Thick pillars coiled with dragons lined each side. Beneath them stood the T'ang's private guards, big, vicious-looking brutes with shaven heads and crude Han faces. The small group of Hung Mao had gathered to the left of the great throne, silent, visibly awed by the unexpected grandeur of their surroundings. Across from them, to the right of the throne and some fifteen paces distant, was a cage. Inside the cage was a man.

'Under Secretary Lehmann. Representative Barrow. Welcome. Perhaps now we can begin.'

The T'ang got to his feet, then came down the steps of his throne, followed by his sons. Five paces from the nearest of the Hung Mao, he stopped and looked about him imperiously. Slowly, hesitantly, taking each other's example, they bowed, some fully, some with their heads only, none knowing quite what etiquette was demanded by this moment. They were not at Weimar now, or in the great halls of their own Companies. Here, in the T'ang's own Palace, they had no idea what was demanded of them, neither had the T'ang's Chancellor been instructed to brief them.

Li Shai Tung stared at them contemptuously, seeing the ill-ordered manner of their obeisance. It was as he had thought; these Hung Mao had fallen into bad habits. Such respect as they owed their T'ang was not an automatic thing with them. It was shallow rooted. The first strong wind would carry it away.

Slowly, deliberately, he looked from face to face, seeing how few of them dared meet his eyes, and how quickly those who did looked away. Hsiao jen, he thought. Little men. You're all such little men. Not a king among you. Not one of you fit to be my chamberlain, let alone my equal. He ran his hand through his ice-white, plaited beard, then turned away, as if dismissing them, facing the man in the cage.

The man was naked, his head shaven. His hands were tied behind him with a crude piece of rope. There was something ancient and brutal about that small detail, something that the two boys at the old man's side took note of. They stood there silently, their faces masks of dispassionate observation. 'This now is a lesson,' their father had explained beforehand. 'And the name of the lesson is punishment.'

The trial had lasted nineteen months. But now all evidence was heard and the man's confession – thrice given as the law demanded – had placed things beyond doubt.

Li Shai Tung walked round the cage and stood there on the far side of it, an arm's length from its thick, rounded bars. The cage was deliberately too small for the man, forcing him to kneel or bend his back. He was red-eyed, his skin a sickly white. Flesh was spare on him and his limbs were badly emaciated. The first two months of incarceration had broken his spirit and he was no longer proud. His haughty, aquiline profile now seemed merely bird-like and ludicrous – the face of an injured gull. All defiance had long departed from him. Now he cowered before the T'ang's approach.

The old man pointed to the symbol burned into the caged man's upper arm. It was the stylized double helix of heredity, symbol of the Dispersion faction.

'Under Secretary Lehmann. You know this man?'

Lehmann came forward and stood there on the other side of the cage, looking in.

'*Chieh Hsia?*'

There was the blankness of non-recognition in Lehmann's eyes. *Good*, thought the T'ang. *He is not expecting this. All the better. It will make the shock of it far sharper.*

'He was your friend.'

Lehmann looked again, then gasped. 'Edmund...'

'Yes.' The T'ang came round the cage again and stood there, between Lehmann and the throne. 'This prisoner was once a man, like you. His name was Edmund Wyatt. But now he has no name. He has been found guilty of the murder of a Minister and has forfeited all his rights. His family, such as it was, is no more, and his ancestors are cut adrift. His place and purpose in this world are annulled.'

He let the significance of his speech sink in, then spoke again.

'You disown him? Your faction disowns his actions?'

Lehmann looked up, startled.

'Do you *disown* him, Under Secretary?'

It was a tense moment. At the trial Lehmann had been Wyatt's chief advocate. But now it was different. If Lehmann said yes he sanctioned the T'ang's actions. If no...

The silence grew. Lehmann's face moved anxiously, but he could not bring himself to speak. Across from him the T'ang held steady, his arm outstretched, his head turned, staring at the House Deputy. When the silence had stretched too thin, he broke it. He repeated his words, then added. 'Or do you condone murder as a political option, Under Secretary?'

Li Shai Tung raised his voice a shade. 'Am I to take it, then, that your silence is the silence of tacit agreement?'

Under the force of the old man's staring eyes, Lehmann began to shake his head. Then, realizing what he was doing, he stopped. But it was too late. He had been betrayed into commitment. He need say nothing now. Li Shai Tung had won.

'This man is mine then? To do with as I wish?'

The T'ang was like a rock. His age, his apparent frailty, were illusions that the hardness of his voice dispelled. There was nothing old, or frail about the power he wielded. At that moment it lay in his power to destroy them all, and they knew it.

Lehmann had clenched his fists. Now he let them relax. He bowed his head slowly, tentatively, in agreement. 'He is yours, *Chieh Hsia*. My... my faction disowns his actions.'

It was a full capitulation. For Li Shai Tung and the Seven it was a victory, an admission of weakness on the part of their opponents. Yet in the old man's face there was no change, neither did his outstretched hand alter its demanding gesture.

The two boys, watching, saw this, and noted it.

At last, Li Shai Tung lowered his arm. Slowly, uncertainly, the *Hung Mao* turned away and began to make their way out of the Hall. It was over. What the T'ang did with the man no longer concerned them. Wyatt was his.

When they were gone, Li Shai Tung turned to his sons. 'Come here,' he said, beckoning them closer to the cage.

Li Han Ch'in was seventeen; tall and handsome like his father, though not yet fully fleshed. His brother, Li Yuan, was only eight, yet his dark, calculating eyes made him seem far older than he was. The two stood close by their father, watching him, their obedience unquestioning.

'This is the man who killed Lwo Kang, my Minister. By the same token he would have killed me – and you and all the Seven and their families. For to attack the limbs of State is to threaten the body, the very heart.'

The man in the cage knelt there silently, his head bowed.

Li Shai Tung paused and turned to his eldest. 'Considering such, what should I do, Han Ch'in? What punishment would be fitting?'

There was no hesitation. 'You must kill him, father! He deserves to die.' There was a fiery loathing in the young man's eyes as he stared at the prisoner. 'Yes, kill him. As he would have killed you!'

Li Shai Tung was silent, his head tilted slightly to one side, as if considering what his eldest son had said. Then he turned, facing his second son. 'And you, Yuan? Do you agree with your brother?'

The boy was silent a moment, concentrating.

Li Yuan was less impetuous than his brother. He was like the current beneath the ocean's swell, his brother the curling, foaming waves – all spray and violent show. Magnificent, but somehow ephemeral. Li Shai Tung, watching his sons, knew this and hoped the younger would prove the voice of reason at the ear of the elder. When it was time. When his own time was done.

Li Yuan had come to a decision. He spoke earnestly, gravely, like an old man himself. 'If you kill him you will bring only further hatred on yourself. And you kill but a single man. You do not cure the illness that he represents.'

'This illness...' The T'ang brought his head straight. The smile had gone from his lips. 'Is there a cure for it?'

Once more the boy was silent, considering. Again he gave an earnest answer. 'Immediately, no. This illness will be with us a long while yet. But in time, yes, I believe there is a way we might control it.'

Li Shai Tung nodded, not in agreement, but in surprise. Yet he did not dismiss his youngest's words. Li Yuan was young, but he was no fool. There were men ten times his age with but a fraction of his sense, and few with a *liang* of his intelligence.

'We must speak more of this...' he waved a hand almost vaguely, '... this means of control. But answer me directly, Yuan. You feel this man should be spared, then, to alleviate the short-term hatred, the resentment?'

The small boy allowed himself the luxury of a brief smile. 'No, father, I suggest nothing of the kind. To spare the prisoner would be to exhibit weakness. As you said to us earlier, it is a lesson, and the name of the lesson is punishment. The man must be killed. Killed like the basest piece of Clay. And all hatred, all resentment, must be faced. There is no other way.'

At his side, Han nodded emphatically.

'Then it is right, as Han Ch'in said, to kill this man?'

'Not right, father. It could never be right. *Necessary.*' The boy's face showed no emotion. His features were formed into a mask of reason. 'Moreover, it should be done in public, for it must be seen to be done. And it must be done dispassionately, without malice and with no thought of revenge – merely as evidence of our power. As a lesson.'

Li Shai Tung nodded, profoundly satisfied with his youngest son, but it was his first son he addressed. 'Then it is as you said, Han Ch'in. We must kill him. As he would have killed us.'

He turned and looked back at the man in the cage, something close to pity in his eyes. 'Yes. But not for revenge. Merely because we must.'

Han Ch'in laughed then clapped his hands, delighted by the gift. 'But, father, they're marvellous! Just look at them! They're so strong, so elegant!'

The four creatures stood in a line before the royal party, their long heads bowed, their broad ox-like bodies neatly clothed in rich silks of carmine and gold. Nearby, their creator, Klaus Stefan Ebert, Head of GenSyn – Genetic Synthetics – beamed, pleased beyond words at the prince's reaction.

'They are the first of their kind,' Ebert said, giving a slight bow. 'And, if the T'ang wishes it, they shall be the last.'

Li Shai Tung looked at his old friend. Ebert had been one of his staunchest supporters over the years and, if fate decided, his son would one day be Han Ch'in's General. He smiled and looked at the ox-men again. 'I would not ask that of you, Klaus. This gift of yours pleases me greatly. No, such marvels should be shared by others. You shall have a patent for them.'

Ebert bowed deeply, conscious of his T'ang's generosity. His gift to Han Ch'in was worth, perhaps, two hundred million yuan, but the T'ang's kindness was inestimable. There was no one in the whole of City Europe's elite who would not now want such a creature. To a more mercenary man that would have been cause for great delight, but Klaus Ebert counted such things of trivial worth. He had pleased his T'ang, and no amount of money could buy the feeling of intense pride and worthiness he felt at that moment.

'I am deeply honoured, *Chieh Hsia*. My great joy at your pleasure reaches up into the heavens.'

Han Ch'in had gone closer to the beasts and now stood there, looking up into one of their long, bovine faces. He turned and looked back at Ebert. 'They're really beautiful, *Shih* Ebert. Strong, like horses, and intelligent, like men. Do they talk?'

Ebert bowed to the T'ang once more, then went across and stood beside Han Ch'in. 'They have a form of language,' he said, his head lowered in deference to the Prince. 'Enough to understand basic commands and to carry trivial messages, but no more than a human three year-old would have.'

Han Ch'in laughed. 'That depends on the three year-old. My brother Yuan could talk a counsellor to a halt at three!'

Ebert laughed. 'So it was! I remember it only too well!'

Li Shai Tung joined their laughter, then turned to General Tolonen who was standing to his left and slightly behind him. 'Well, Knut, are things ready within?'

The General, who had been watching the exchange with real pleasure, turned to his T'ang and was silent a moment, listening to a voice in his head. Then he bowed. 'Major Nocenzi advises me that all the guests are now assembled and that full security measures are in operation. We can go inside.'

The ceiling of the Great Hall was festooned with broad silk banners that hung in elegant sweeps between the dragon-encircled pillars. Huge, man-sized bronze urns were set at intervals along the walls, each filled to overflowing with giant blooms. Beneath the banners and between the blooms, the floor of the Great Hall was filled with guests. Han Ch'in stood at the top of the steps beside his father, looking down on everything. Two colours dominated, red and gold; auspicious colours – red for good fortune, gold for a future emperor.

At their appearance the great buzz of conversation died and, at a signal from the chamberlain, all below the steps knelt to the T'ang and his first son, their heads lowered.

Tolonen, behind them, watched the huge crowd rise again, a low buzz of expectation rising from their midst. Then Li Shai Tung began to descend, his son three steps behind him.

Li Yuan was waiting at the bottom of the steps to greet his father formally with a full k'o t'ou. Behind him stood his uncles – his father's brothers and half-brothers – and with them a dark-haired Hung Mao; a slender, handsome man, unfashionably bearded. An 'Englishman' as he liked to term himself. These were the T'ang's chief advisors. As Li Yuan rose, so the three brothers bowed, bending fully to the waist before they straightened up. Only the Hung Mao remained unbowed, a faint smile on his face. The T'ang smiled, acknowledging all four, then turned to let Han Ch'in come up beside him.

Tolonen, following them, paused halfway down the steps and looked out across the mass of heads. Everyone who was anyone in City Europe was here today. Representatives and Heads of Corporations, Chief Magistrates and Administrators, Ministers and Executives. Men of power and their consorts. Li Yuan was the only child there.

Below the steps all formalities were over for the moment.

'Have you seen them, Yuan?' Han asked eagerly. 'They're huge. Three times your size!'

Li Yuan's eyes lit up. 'Is it true what Hsueh Chai said? Do they smell?'

In answer Han Ch'in bent down and whispered something in his brother's ear. Yuan laughed, then glanced guiltily at the Englishman, who was now deep in conversation with the T'ang. 'Like *Hung Mao*,' Han had whispered. And it was true of most. But some – like the General and Hal Shepherd – refrained from eating milk-based products. They smelt like Han, not beasts.

'What will you do with them?' Yuan asked. 'Will you give them to Fei Yen?'

Han Ch'in looked aghast. 'Gods! I never thought! What will she say?'

'You could always ask her. After all, she'll be here any time now.'

Han Ch'in made a face, then laughed again. Both knew what ritual lay before him. All that bowing and nodding. All that *ch'un tzu* insincerity as he and his future wife accepted the best wishes of almost three thousand loyal subjects.

He was about to make some comment on the matter when all about them the crowd grew quiet again as Fei Yen appeared at the head of the stairs on her father's arm. This time, as she descended, the guests remained standing. Only the T'ang and his eldest son bowed to her, honouring her.

Li Yuan gazed at Fei Yen, stilled by the beauty of her. It was as though a craftsman – a master artisan – had given her some final, subtle touch – one single deft and delicate brushstroke – that made of her perfection. Her hair had been put up, its fine coils of darkness speared by slender combs of ivory shaped like dragonflies. Beneath its silken splendour, her face was like the radiant moon, shining cold and white and brilliant, the fineness of her cheekbones balanced by the soft roundness of her chin and the unmarked perfection of her brow. She wore a simple *erh tang* of red jade and silver in each lobe and a *ying lo* of tiny pearls about her neck, but in truth her face needed no adornment.

He stared at her as she came down the steps towards him, fascinated, drinking in the sight of her.

Her ears were tiny, delicate, her lips like folded petals, softly roseate, as if awaiting the dawn's moist kiss, while her nose was so small, so fine, the roundness of the tip so perfect, it seemed unreal, like porcelain. All this he saw and noted, pierced by the beauty of it, yet all the while his gaze was drawn to her eyes – to those dark, sweet, almond eyes that were unearthly in their beauty. Eyes that seemed to stare out at him from the other side of the heavens themselves, fierce and strong and proud. Eyes that seemed to burn within the cold and fragile mask of her face, making him catch his breath.

He shivered then looked down, noting the pale lilac silks she wore, the fine layers of material specked with tiny phoenixes in a delicate dark blue lace. He studied her tiny, perfect hands and noticed how she held the ceremonial fan, her fingers gently curled about the red jade handle, each one so fine and white and delicate. Again he shivered, overcome by her. She was magnificent. So small and fine and perfect. So unutterably beautiful.

The crowd's dull murmur rose again. Li Yuan felt a touch on his arm and turned to see who it was.

'Hal...'

Hal Shepherd smiled and inclined his head slightly, as if amused by something. 'Come, Yuan,' he said, taking the boy's hand. 'Let's seek our entertainment over there.'

Yuan looked, then mouthed the word. 'Berdichev?'

Shepherd nodded, then leaned forward slightly, speaking in a whisper. 'Your father wants me to sound the man out. I think it could be fun.'

Yuan smiled. Shepherd had been his father's chief advisor for almost twenty years, and though he was some years the T'ang's junior, Li Shai Tung would not act on any major issue without first consulting him. Shepherd's great-great-great grandfather, Amos, had been the architect of City Earth and had been granted certain rights by the tyrant, Tsao Ch'un, amongst them the freedom from bowing to his lord. When the Seven had deposed the tyrant they had honoured those rights to the last generation of Shepherds. They alone could not be ordered. They alone could talk back to the T'ang as equal. 'Only they, of all of them, are free,' Li Shai Tung had once said to his sons. 'The rest do not own the bones in their own skins.'

Yuan glanced at Fei Yen momentarily, then looked back at Shepherd. 'What does my father want?'

Shepherd smiled, his dark eyes twinkling. 'Just listen,' he said softly. 'That's all. I'll say all that needs to be said.'

Yuan nodded, understanding without needing to be told that this was what his father wanted. For the past four months he had worked hard, studying thousands of personal files, learning their details by heart until, now, he could put a name to every face in the Great Hall. A name and a history.

Berdichev was with his wife, Ylva, a tall, rather severe-looking woman some ten years younger than him. Beside them was one of the Eastern Sector Administrators, a covert Dispersionist sympathizer named Duchek. Making up the group was Under Secretary Lehmann.

'Shepherd,' said Berdichev, on his guard at once. 'Li Yuan,' he added quickly, noticing the Prince behind Shepherd and bowing deeply, a gesture that was copied immediately by all in the immediate circle.

'We're not interrupting anything, I hope?' said Shepherd lightly, disingenuously.

'Nothing but idle talk,' Lehmann answered, smiling coldly, his manner matching Shepherd's.

'Idle talk? Oh, surely not, Under Secretary. I thought such important men as you rarely wasted a word.'

'It was nothing,' said Berdichev touchily. 'But if it interests you so much, why not ask us? We have nothing to hide.'

Shepherd laughed warmly. 'Did I say you had? Why no, Soren, I meant nothing by my words. Nothing at all. This is a social occasion, after all. I meant merely to be sociable.'

Yuan looked down, keeping the smile from his face. He had seen how Berdichev had bridled when Shepherd used his first name; how his eyes had lit with anger behind those tiny, rounded glasses he so affectedly wore.

'We were talking of the world,' said Lehmann, meeting Shepherd's eyes challengingly. 'Of how much smaller it seems these days.'

Shepherd hesitated as if considering the matter, then nodded. 'I would have to agree with you, Under Secretary. In fact, I'd go further and argue that we've actually lost touch with the world. Consider. What is City Earth, after all, but a giant box on stilts? A huge hive filled to the brim with humanity. Oh, it's comfortable enough, we'd all agree, but it's also quite unreal – a place where the vast majority of people have little or no contact with the earth, the elements.'

Shepherd looked about the circle, half-smiling, meeting each of their eyes in turn. 'Isn't that how it is? Well, then, it's understandable, don't you think, that feeling of smallness? Of being contained? You see, there's nothing real in their lives. No heaven above, no earth below, just walls on every side. All they see – all they are – is an illusion.'

Lehmann blinked, not certain he had heard Shepherd right. What had been said was unorthodox to say the least. It was not what one expected to hear from someone who had the T'ang's ear. Lehmann looked across and saw how Berdichev was looking down, as if insulted. His company, SimFic – Simulation Fictions – provided many of the 'illusions' Shepherd was clearly denigrating.

'Men have always had illusions,' Berdichev said fiercely, looking up again, his eyes cold behind their glasses. 'They have always made fictions. Always had a desire for stories. Illusion is necessary for good health. Without it…'

'Yes, yes, of course,' Shepherd interrupted. 'I'm sure I worry far too much. However, it does seem to me that this world of ours is nothing but illusion. One giant, complex hologram.' He smiled and looked away from Berdichev, focusing on Lehmann once again. 'It's all *yin* and no *yang*. All male and no female. We've lost contact with the Mother, don't you agree, Under Secretary?'

It was Duchek who answered him, his eyes flaring with passionate indignation. 'It's all right for you, *Shih* Shepherd. You have the Domain. You *have* your Mother!'

For a moment there was a tense, almost shocked silence in their circle. It was a fact, and all of them knew it, but it was rarely mentioned in polite company. The Domain, where Shepherd lived, like the estates of the Seven, was an exception. Barring plantation workers, no one of any stature was allowed to live outside the City. There was, of course, good reason for this, for most of the land outside the City was under intense cultivation, organized into huge 10,000 *mou* fields planted with super-hybrids, not a *mou* wasted. Even so, a great deal of jealousy existed in the Above. There were many, Berdichev and Lehmann amongst them, who would have given half their wealth to live outside, under the sun.

'Well, it's true!' said Duchek after a moment, embarrassed by his slip, but unapologetic. 'It's easy for him to criticize. He can get out!'

Lehmann studied Duchek a moment, then turned back to Shepherd, still intrigued by what he had heard him say. 'I'm surprised to hear you talk this way, *Shih* Shepherd. You sound...' he laughed, '... almost dissatisfied.'

Shepherd glanced briefly at Li Yuan, noting how intently the young boy was following things, then smiled and answered Lehmann. 'Should I be satisfied? Should I, as a man, just accept what is without question?' He laughed softly. 'Why, we would still be in the caves, or in the woods if that were so. There would be no civilization. No Chung Kuo.'

Yuan, whose eyes caught everything, saw how Lehmann made to answer, then checked himself, as if he had suddenly realized what was happening. Hal Shepherd's words, whilst passionately spoken, were suspiciously close to Dispersionist orthodoxy and their creed of 'Change and Expand'. Lehmann hesitated, then laughed casually and turned to take a fresh tumbler of wine from a passing servant.

'So you advocate change?'

Shepherd's face changed subtly; the smile, the patina of charm remained, but behind it now lay something much harder and more ruthless. 'You mistake me, Pietr. I do not like change, neither do I welcome it. But if I could change one thing, I would change that. I would give men back their contact with the earth.' His smile hardened, and a trace of sadness and regret lingered momentarily in his eyes. 'However, the world is as it is, not as it ought to be. There are too many of us now. The earth could not support us in the old way.'

Again it was a fact. Even though every cultivable piece of land outside the City was in use, still only sixty per cent of Chung Kuo's demand was met that way. The rest was synthesized within the City or grown in the giant orbital farms. And as the population grew the problem grew with it. How to feed the many mouths of Chung Kuo?

Yuan felt himself tense, knowing that Shepherd was coming to the nub of it. Through Shepherd, his father was fishing for something; some concession, maybe. Some way of healing the anticipated breach, of keeping Chung Kuo from war.

'But there are other ways, neh?'

Lehmann let the words lie there between himself and Shepherd. He sipped at his wine and looked across at Berdichev, a faint smile on his lips.

Shepherd tilted his head slightly, as if considering Lehmann's words. Then he sighed and shook his head. 'The T'ang himself has tried to make changes. For three years now he has tried to persuade the Council to take certain measures. But they are reluctant. They do not feel the House would give its full support to such changes.'

Yuan had seen how Lehmann's eyes had widened at Shepherd's use of the word 'changes' in the context of his father and the Council; had seen how surprised both Berdichev and Duchek also were.

Lehmann spoke for them. 'Changes? I don't understand you, Shih Shepherd. What changes?'

'Controls. Concessions. A deal, you might call it.'

'A deal?' Lehmann's mouth twisted almost scornfully. 'I thought the Seven were above deals. What could they possibly want from the House?'

Shepherd looked at each of the men in turn, then smiled. 'Population controls. Perhaps even reductions?'

Lehmann's laughter made heads turn nearby. He leaned towards Shepherd and almost spat the word back at him. 'Impossible!'

'So you say, but what if...'

But Shepherd never got to finish his sentence. Yuan felt a touch on his shoulder and knew at once it was Han Ch'in. No one else would have dared lay a hand on him.

'Ha! Ha! Have you seen them? Have you seen my ox-men? They're marvellous!'

Shepherd drew back from the edge. Calmly he turned to Han Ch'in and smiled. 'So that's what they were, Han. I did wonder. I thought perhaps you had invited a few brutes up from the Clay!'

The rest of the circle had bowed at Han Ch'in's sudden entry into their ranks. Now Shepherd's comment drew their laughter. But Han Ch'in himself was more thoughtful.

'It must be awful, Hal, being born down there.'

Berdichev, who, with Lehmann and Wyatt, had been beneath the City's floor into the Clay and seen it for himself, bowed again, then answered Han.

'It would be, were they really conscious of their misery. But it's all they know. In any case, they're really little more than animals. They don't live long enough to consider how awful their lives truly are.'

'We should gas them,' said Duchek. 'We should pump the Clay full of gas and clean it up.'

Han Ch'in looked sharply at the Administrator but said nothing.

'It would, perhaps, be best,' said Lehmann, coming to Duchek's aid. 'After all, it would ease their suffering. And we could use the land down there for other things.'

'So I understand,' Han Ch'in answered, his distaste for Lehmann quite open. 'You have argued for it in the House often enough.'

Lehmann bowed his head then looked at Shepherd, his frustration at being interrupted at such a crucial moment threatening, for an instant, to goad him into an impropriety. Then he relaxed again and smiled at the T'ang's eldest son.

'I am honoured that the Prince pays such attention to my humble affairs. You may be sure I am no less your own admirer.'

Han Ch'in stared back at him a moment, nothing but coldness in his eyes, then he turned to Shepherd and laughed.

'You know, Hal, I can't get over how marvellous my ox-men are. They even talk. Baby talk, admittedly, but it's talk of a kind, eh? And you should smell them. Rich, they are! Ripe!' He looked meaningfully around the circle, then back at Shepherd. 'Perhaps I should have uncle Klaus make more of them for me. Then I could form my own House and watch the beasts debate.'

Tolonen's eyes took in everything about him. He had a sense of where each person was within ten paces of the T'ang; how far away the nearest of them were; how casually or otherwise each stood. As for himself, he stood there, seemingly at ease, a drink in his left hand, his right hand resting against his thigh. Casual. Listening, or so it seemed, to every word that was being said. Indeed, at any moment he might have repeated anything that had just been said by the T'ang and his party, yet his attention was split. He watched, attentive to every sign, knowing that this, the safest place, was also the most dangerous. They could never take Li Shai Tung by force. But surprise?

Earlier that afternoon he had checked out the servants for himself, trusting no one. He had had every servo-mechanism checked for programme quirks, every GenSyn neuter for behavioural deviancy. And then, at the last moment, he had brought in his own guards. It was they who now went amongst the guests, serving drinks and offering spiced delicacies. At any moment Tolonen could tune in to any conversation and hear whatever was being said through the direct relay in his head. His guards picked up all talk, positioning themselves so that not a word in the Great Hall would be missed. It would all be replayed and investigated for significance later. For now, however, only one thing mattered. He had to keep Li Shai Tung alive.

For years now he had learned to outguess his enemies, to anticipate their next move. But now things were changing, the situation escalating, and in his heart of hearts he knew that the tenuous peace that had existed for more than a century was about to be broken. The Dispersionists, a covert, loosely knit organization before the arrest of Edmund Wyatt, were now an open faction in the House, not merely respected but heavily supported. Their strength had upset the traditional balance. In the last two years they had radicalized the House and brought the clamour for Change to a head.

It was time to come to an agreement. To make concessions. But first they would have justice. For Lwo Kang's death and the insult to the Seven.

Tolonen breathed deeply, hearing Lehmann's voice sound clearly in his head. In two hours the smile would be wiped off that bastard's face.

He had been listening to the conversation between Shepherd and the others, amused by the way Shepherd ran them, like fish upon a line, only to reel them slowly in. But Han Ch'in's sudden interjection had snapped the fragile line. Tolonen looked across and saw the young prince leaning forward, one hand on his younger brother's shoulder, and heard his voice clearly, transmitted to him by the waiter at Berdichev's side.

'It must be awful, Hal. Being born down there.'

'Knut!'

He turned at the T'ang's summons and went across to him, the fingers of his right hand surreptitiously moving across the control panel beneath the cloth of his uniform trousers, shutting off the voices in his head.

'*Chieh Hsia?*'

The circle about the T'ang made room for the General.

'Klaus was asking me about Major DeVore. He's back tomorrow, isn't he?'

'He was due then, *Chieh Hsia*, but the flight from Mars was delayed. He docks the morning of the wedding.'

'Good. Klaus was saying how much his son would like to serve the Major again. I hope he'll be granted the opportunity.'

Tolonen bowed his head. What the T'ang 'hoped' for was tantamount to a command. 'I shall see to it personally, *Chieh Hsia*.'

'He has done well out there, I understand.'

Again the T'ang was being diplomatic. He knew perfectly well how DeVore had performed as Chief Security Officer to the Martian Colony. He had seen all the reports and discussed them at length with Tolonen.

'Indeed he has, *Chieh Hsia*. And I have put his name before the Marshal to fill the next vacancy for General.'

'Your own?' Li Shai Tung smiled.

'If the T'ang no longer feels he needs me.'

'Oh, that will be some time yet, Knut. A good long time, I hope.'

Tolonen bowed deeply, profoundly pleased.

Just then Major Nocenzi appeared at the edge of the group, his head bowed, awaiting permission to speak.

The T'ang looked at him. 'What is it, Major?'

Nocenzi kept his head lowered. 'There is a message, *Chieh Hsia*. For the General.'

Tolonen turned to the T'ang. 'You'll excuse me, *Chieh Hsia*?'

'Of course.'

He bowed and turned away, then followed Nocenzi across to an anteroom they were using as coordination centre for Security. When the door was closed behind them, Tolonen faced his Major.

'What is it, Vittorio?'

'Karr has been on, sir. He says he's traced his man.'

'What?'

'He's waiting to talk to you, sir. On the switching channel.'

At once Tolonen reached down and touched the relevant button on the panel inset into his thigh. 'Well, Karr?' he said, knowing Karr would hear him, wherever he was in the City. Karr's voice came back to him at once, as clear in his head as if he stood in the same room.

'Forgive me for disturbing you, General. But I'm certain I've found him. He fits the profile perfectly, right down to the scar. I'm following him right now.'

Tolonen listened carefully, making Karr repeat the coordinates three times before he cut connection. Then he turned to Nocenzi.

'I must go, Vittorio. Take charge here. Ensure by your life that nothing happens.'

Nocenzi looked down. 'Are you sure you should go personally, sir? It could be dangerous. The man's a killer.'

Tolonen smiled. 'I'll be all right, Vittorio. Anyway, Karr will be with me.'

'Even so, sir...'

Tolonen laughed. 'If it makes you easier, Vittorio, I order you to take charge here. All right? In this instance I have to go. Personally. It's too important to leave to anyone else. Too much has slipped through my hands as it is, and this man's the key to it all. I know he is. I feel it in my bones.'

Nocenzi smiled. 'Then take care, Knut. I'll make certain all's well here.'

Tolonen reached out and held Nocenzi's shoulder briefly, returning his smile. 'Good. Then I'll report what's happening to the T'ang.'

'Well, Chen? Would you like a beer?'

Chen looked up at the brightly pulsing sign over the door. Fu Yang's Bar, it read. His mouth was dry and the thought of a beer was good. It was some while since he'd allowed himself the luxury. Even so he looked down and shook his head. 'Thank you, *Pan Chang* Lo, but I should be getting back. It's late and Wang Ti will have to cook.'

Supervisor Lo took his arm. 'All the better. You can get a meal at the bar. Call her. Tell her you'll be a bit late, and that you've eaten. She'll not mind. Not this once. Come on, I'll treat you. You've helped me out and I appreciate that.'

Chen hesitated, then nodded. Lo was right: it wasn't as if he made a habit of this. No, Wang Ti could hardly complain if he had a few beers for once; not after he had worked a double shift. Anyway, he had bought her something. He traced the shape of the necklace in his overall pocket and smiled to himself, then followed Lo Ying into the crowded bar, squeezing in beside him at one of the tiny double booths.

Lo Ying turned to him, his deeply lined, wispily bearded face only a hand's breadth away. 'What'll you have? The soychicken with ginger and pineapple's good. So's the red-cooked soypork with chestnuts.'

Chen laughed. 'They both sound excellent. We'll have a large dish of each, neh? And I'll share the cost with you.'

Lo Ying put his long, thin hand over Chen's. 'Not at all, my friend. As I said, you did me a good turn tonight. It was good of you to work the shift at short notice. I was in a hole and you helped me out of it. It's the least I can do to buy you a meal and a few beers.'

Chen smiled, then looked down, rubbing at the red marks at the back of his head and on his forehead where he had been wearing the wraparound. Lo Ying was a good man. A bit dull, maybe, but fair and reliable, unlike most of the pan chang he'd encountered up here. 'Okay,' he said. 'But I was glad of the extra shift. We've not much, Wang Ti, baby Jyan and I, but I've ambitions. I want better for my son.'

Lo Ying looked at him a moment, then nodded his head. 'I've watched you often, Chen. Seen how hard you work. And I've wondered to myself. Why is Chen where he is? Why is he not higher up the levels? He is a good man; a good, strong worker; reliable, intelligent. Why is he here, working for me? Why am I not working for him?'

Chen laughed shortly, then looked up, meeting Lo Ying's eyes. 'I was not always so, Lo Ying. I was a wild youth. A waster of my talents. And then... well, a wife, a son – they change a man.'

'Ah yes. So it is.'

A girl came and took their order, then returned a moment later with two bulbs of Yao Fan Te beer. Lo Ying handed one to Chen, then toasted him.

'To your family!'

'And yours, Lo Ying!'

He had told no one of his past. No one. Not even Wang Ti. For in this, he knew, he was vulnerable. One careless word said to the wrong person and he would be back there, below the Net. Back in that nightmare place where every man was for himself and men like Lo Ying were as rare as phoenix eggs.

Lo Ying put his beer down and wiped the froth from his wispy moustache. 'Talking of work, I've been meaning to ask you...' He looked sideways at Chen. 'As you know, Feng Shi-lun is up for a pan chang's job. I happen to know he'll get it. Which means there's a vacancy as my assistant.'

Lo Ying fell silent, leaving unstated the meaning of his words. Chen took a deep draught of his beer, studying the old Han beggar on the label a moment. Then he wiped his mouth and looked up again. 'You're offering me the job?'

Lo Ying shrugged. 'It's not up to me, Chen, but... Well, I could put a word in higher up.'

Chen considered a moment, then looked directly at him. 'How much would it cost?'

'Two hundred yuan.'

Chen laughed. 'I haven't twenty! Where would I find such money?'

'No, you don't understand me, Chen. I'd lend you it. Interest free. I'd...' He hesitated, then smiled. 'I'd like to see you get on, Chen. You're worth a dozen of those useless shits. And maybe someday...'

Again, it was left unsaid. But Chen had grown used to the ways of these levels. Favours and bribes – they were the lubricants of this world. You scratch my back, I scratch yours. You pay squeeze, you move up. Refuse and you stay where you are. It was the way of the world. But Lo Ying was better than most. He offered his help interest free and with only the vaguest of strings. Chen looked at him and nodded. 'Okay, but how would I repay you? My rent's eight yuan. Food's another six. That leaves eleven from my weekly pay to see to clothing, heating, light. I'm lucky if I save five yuan a month!'

Lo Ying nodded. 'That's why you must take this opportunity. *Pan chang*'s assistant pays thirty a week. You could pay me the difference until the debt is cleared. You say you've twenty?'

Chen nodded.

'Good. Then that's one hundred and eighty you'll need from me. Thirty six weeks and you're free of obligation. Free... and five yuan better off a week.'

Chen looked at him, knowing how great a favour Lo Ying was doing him. If he went to a shark for the money it would be two years, maybe four, before he'd be clear. But thirty-six weeks. Nine months, give or take. It was nothing. And he would be one step higher.

He put out his hand. 'Okay, Lo Ying. I'm grateful. If ever...'

'Yes, yes...' Lo Ying smiled, then turned. 'Look, here's our food.'

They tucked in, looking at each other from time to time and smiling.

'It's good, neh?' said Lo Ying, turning to order two more beers. Then he frowned. 'Hey, Chen, look...'

Chen turned, his mouth full of chicken, and looked. On the big screen over the serving counter the *Ywe Lung* had appeared. All over the bar people were turning to look and falling silent.

'It's nothing,' Chen said. 'Just another announcement about the wedding.'

'No... Look. The background's white. Someone's dead. One of the Seven.' A low murmur went around the packed bar. A few got up from their seats and went to stand at the bar, looking up at the screen.

Chen looked at Lo Ying's face and saw the concern there. There was still a strong feeling for the Seven at this level, whatever was happening Above or far below. Here they identified with the Seven and were fiercely loyal. 'Trouble for the Seven is trouble for us all' – how often he'd heard that said in the last year and a half. And something of that had rubbed off on him, he realized as he sat there, his pulse raised by the ominous white background to the imperial symbol.

Martial music played. Then, abruptly, the image changed.

'What's that?' said Lo Ying softly.

There was a buzz of noise, then quiet. On the screen was a plain, red-carpeted room. In the middle of the room was a very solid-looking block; a big thing, an arm's length to a side. Its top was strangely smooth, as if melted or worn flat by the passage of feet or water over it, and cut into its dull grey side was the *Ywe Lung*, the wheel of dragons.

For a moment the screen was silent. Then came the voice.

It was the same voice he had heard numerous times before, making official announcements, but now it seemed more sombre, more threatening than he had ever heard it. And the shadow voice, softer, more sing-song, that spoke in native Mandarin, seemed to contain the same dark threat.

Chen put the bulb to his lips and emptied it. 'Listen,' said Lo Ying, reaching out to take his arm again. 'There's been a trial.'

The voice spoke slowly, carefully, outlining what had happened. There had been an assassination. The T'ang's Minister, Lwo Kang...

Chen felt himself go cold. Lwo Kang. He looked down.

A man named Edmund Wyatt had confessed to the killing. He had organized it. Had been the hand behind the knife.

Chen stiffened. Wyatt? Who in hell's name was Wyatt? Why not Berdichev? That was the name Kao Jyan had mentioned on his tape. Berdichev, not Wyatt. He shook his head, not understanding.

The image changed again, and there, before them, was Wyatt himself, speaking into camera, admitting his part in everything. A worn yet handsome man. An aristocrat. Every inch an aristocrat.

From the watching men came a sharp hissing. 'Scum!' shouted someone. 'Arrogant First Level bastards!'

Chen looked down, then looked up again. So Kao Jyan had been wrong. A pity. But then, why had they killed him? Why kill him if he was wrong about Berdichev?

Or *had* he been wrong?

Wyatt's face faded, leaving the image of the empty room and the block. Again there was silence, both on the screen and below it in the bar. Then, suddenly, there was movement to the right of the screen. Two big, hugely muscled men brought a tall, very angular man into the centre of the room and secured him over the block, his chest pressed against the upper surface, his bowed head jutting out towards the watching billions.

The man was naked. His hands had been secured tightly behind his back and his feet shackled with manacles. He looked very ill. Feebly he raised his head, his lips drawing back from his teeth in a rictus of fear, then let it fall again. His shaven head was like a skull, its paleness dotted with red blotches, while his bones seemed to poke through at shoulder and elbow.

'Gods...' whispered Lo Ying. 'He looks half-dead already, poor bastard!'

Chen nodded, unable to look away. One of the guards had gone off screen. The other leaned over the prisoner and brought his knee down firmly, brutally onto his back, pressing him down against the block. Then the first guard came back.

From the men in the bar came a single gasp. Of surprise. And fear.

In the guard's hands was a sword, a huge, long, two-edged weapon with an exaggeratedly broad, flat blade and a long, iron-black handle. It was cruel and brutal, like something out of a museum, but it had been polished until it shone like new. The edges winked viciously in the brightness of the room as the guard turned it in his hands, accustoming himself to its weight and balance.

Lo Ying swallowed noisily, then made a small whimpering sound in his throat. 'Gods...' he said again, barely audibly. But Chen could not look away. It seemed alive. Hideously alive. As if some awful power animated the weapon. Its heaviness, its very awkwardness, spoke volumes. It was a brutal, pagan thing, and its ugly, unsophisticated strength struck dread into him.

Beside him Lo Ying groaned. Chen looked about him, his eyes searching from face to face, seeing his own horrified fascination mirrored everywhere.

Lo Ying's voice shook. 'They're going to execute him!'

'Yes,' said Chen softly, looking back at the screen. 'They are.'

The guard had raised the sword high. For a moment he held it there, his muscles quivering with the strain. Then, as if at some unspoken command, he brought it down onto the block.

The sword met little resistance. The head seemed to jump up on its own, a comet's trail of blood gouting behind it. It came down to the far left of the screen, rolled over once and lay still, eerily upright, the eyes staring out sightlessly at the watching billions. The headless corpse spasmed and was still. Blood pumped from the severed neck, dribbling down the sides of the block to merge with the deep red of the carpet.

There was a fearful, awful silence. The guards had gone. Now there was only the block, the body and the head. Those and the blood.

Chen sat there, like the rest, frozen into immobility, unable to believe it had been real. Despite himself, he felt shocked. It couldn't have happened, could it? He saw the surprise, the sudden pain in the dead man's staring eyes and still could not believe it had been real. But all round him grown men were on their feet, shuddering, groaning, laughing with shock or crying openly as they stood there, unable to look away from the screen and the severed head. Then Chen unfroze himself and stood up.

'Come on,' he said, taking Lo Ying's arm firmly. 'Let's get out of here.'

Above them the screen went dark. Chen turned and pushed his way through the crowd, pulling Lo Ying along behind him, anxious to get outside. But out in the corridor he stopped, breathing deeply, feeling giddy suddenly. *Why?* he asked himself. *I've killed men before now. With these very hands I've taken their lives. Why, then, was that so awful?*

But he knew why. Because it was different. Because it had been witnessed by them all.

It was a sign. A sign of things to come.

'Gods... Gods...' Lo Ying was shaking violently. He was barely in control of himself. 'I didn't think...'

He turned away, was sick against the wall.

Yes, thought Chen. *A sign. Times are changing. And this, the first public execution in more than a century, is the beginning of it.*

He turned and looked at Lo Ying, suddenly pitying him. It had shocked him; what then had it done to such as Lo Ying? He took his arms and turned him around. 'Listen,' he said. 'You'll come back with me. Stay with us tonight. We'll make space.'

Lo Ying went to shake his head, then saw how Chen was looking at him and nodded.

'Good. Come on, then. We can send a message to your family. They'll understand.'

Lo Ying let himself be led along, wiping distractedly at his mouth and beard and mumbling to himself. But at the junction of Chen's corridor he stiffened and pulled back.

Chen turned, looking at him. 'What is it?'

'There...' Lo Ying bent his head slightly, indicating something off to Chen's right. 'Those men. I saw them earlier. Back at the bar.'

Chen stared at him. 'You're sure?'

Lo Ying hesitated, then nodded. 'The big one... he was sitting across from us. I noticed him. Before it happened...' He shuddered and looked down.

Chen turned slowly and glanced at the men as casually as he could, then looked back at Lo Ying, speaking as softly as he could. 'Lo Ying? Have you your knife on you?'

Lo Ying nodded. As *pan chang* he was permitted to carry a knife for his duties.

'Good. Pass it to me. Don't let them see.'

Lo Ying did as he was told, then clutched at Chen's shirt. 'Who are they, Chen?'

Chen took a deep breath. 'I don't know. I don't think I've seen them before. Perhaps it's just a coincidence.'

But he knew it wasn't. He knew it was all tied in somehow. It was no coincidence that Wyatt had been executed tonight. And now they had come for him. Tidying up. He wondered vaguely how they'd traced him.

'Stay here. I'll go down towards home. If they follow me, whistle.'

Lo Ying nodded once, then watched as Chen turned away from him and, seeming not to notice the two men waiting twenty paces off, made for his home corridor.

Chen had only gone three or four paces when the men pushed away from the wall and began to follow him. Lo Ying let them turn into the corridor, making sure they were following, then put his fingers to his lips and whistled.

Chen turned abruptly, facing the men.

'What do you want?'

They were both big men, but the younger of them was a real brute, a giant of a man, more than a head taller than Chen and much broader at the shoulders. Like a machine made of flesh and muscle. The other was much older, his close-cropped hair a silver grey, but he still looked fit and dangerous. They were *Hung Mao*, both of them. But who were they working for? Berdichev? Or the T'ang?

'Kao Chen,' said the older of them, taking two paces nearer. 'So we meet at last. We thought you were dead.'

Chen grunted. 'Who are you?'

The old man smiled. 'I should have realized at once. Karr here had to point it out to me. That stooge you used to play yourself. The man who died in Jyan's. You should have marked him.' He pointed to the thick ridge of scar tissue beneath Chen's right ear. 'Karr noticed it on the film.'

Chen laughed. 'So. But what can you prove?'

'We don't have to prove anything, Chen.' The old man laughed and seemed to relax. 'You know, you're a tricky bastard, aren't you? Your brother, Jyan, underestimated you. He thought you dull-witted. But don't go making the same mistake with me. Don't underestimate me, Chen. I'm not some low-level punk. I am the T'ang's General, and I command more *kwai* than you'd ever dream existed. You can die now, if you want. Or you can live. The choice is yours.'

A ripple of fear went through Chen. The T'ang's General! But he had made his choice already, moments before, and the old man was only two paces off now. If he could keep him talking a moment longer.

'You're mistaken, General,' he said, raising a hand to keep the General off. 'Jyan was not my brother. We only shared the same surname. Anyway, I...' He broke off, smiling, then let out a scream. 'Lo Ying!'

The big man began to turn just as Lo Ying jumped up onto his back. At the same moment Chen lunged forward, the knife flashing out from his pocket. Grasping the old man's arm he turned him and brought the knife up to his throat.

Karr threw his attacker off and felled him with a single punch, then turned back, angry at being tricked. He came forward two paces then stopped abruptly, seeing how things were.

'You're a fool, Chen,' the General hissed, feeling Chen's arm tighten about his chest, the knife's point prick the skin beneath his chin. 'Harm me and you'll all be dead. Chen, Wang Ti and baby Jyan. As if you'd never been.'

Chen shuddered, but kept his grip on the old man. 'Your life... It must be worth something.'

The General laughed coldly. 'To my T'ang.'

'Well, then?'

Tolonen swallowed painfully. 'You know things. Know what Jyan knew. You can connect things for us. Incriminate others.'

'Maybe.'

'In return we'll give you an amnesty. Legitimize your citizenship. Make sure you can't be sent back to the Net.'

'And that's all? A measly amnesty. For what I know?'

The General was silent a moment, breathing shallowly, conscious of the knife pressed harder against his throat. 'And what *do* you know, Kao Chen?'

'I watched him. Both times. Saw him go in there that first time. He and the Han. Then watched him come out two hours later, alone, after he'd killed Kao Jyan. Then, later, I saw him go back in again. I stood at the junction and saw him, with my own eyes. You were there too. Both of you. I recognize you now. Yes. He was one of yours. One of you bastards.'

The General shuddered. 'Who, Chen? Who do you mean?'

Chen laughed coldly. 'The Major. That's who. Major DeVore.'

CHAPTER 31

THE LIGHT IN THE DARKNESS

The first thing to see was darkness. Darkness coloured the Clay like a dye. It melted forms and re-cast them with a deadly animation. It lay within and without; was both alive and yet the deadest thing of all. It breathed, and yet it stifled.

For many it was all they knew. All they would ever know.

The settlement was on the crest of a low hill, a sprawl of ugly, jagged shapes, littering the steep slope. Old, crumbling ruins squatted amongst the debris, black against black, their very shapes eroded by the darkness. The walls of houses stood no taller than a man's height, the brickwork soft, moist to the touch. There were no roofs, no ceilings, but none were needed here. No rain fell in the darkness of the Clay.

The darkness seemed intense and absolute. It was a cloth, smothering the vast, primaeval landscape. Yet there was light of a kind.

Above the shadowed plain the ceiling ran to all horizons, perched on huge columns of silver that glowed softly, faintly, like something living. Dim studs of light criss-crossed the artificial sky; neutered, ordered stars, following the tracks of broad conduits and cables, for the ceiling was a floor, and overhead was the vastness of the City; another world, sealed off from the foetid darkness underneath.

The Clay. It was a place inimical to life. And yet life thrived there in the dark; hideous, malformed shapes spawning in obscene profusion. The dark plain crawled with vulgar life.

Kim woke from a bad dream, a tight band of fear about his chest. Instinct made him freeze, then turn slowly, stealthily, towards the sound, lifting the oilcloth he lay under. He had the scent at once – the thing that had warned him on waking. *Strangers...* Strangers at the heart of the camp.

Something was wrong. Badly wrong.

He moved to the lip of the brickwork he had been lying behind and peered over the top. What he saw made him bristle with fear. Two of his tribe lay on the ground nearby, their skulls smashed open, the brains taken. Further away, three men – strangers, intruders – crouched over another body. They were carving flesh from arm and thigh and softly laughing as they ate. Kim's mouth watered, but the fear he felt was far stronger.

One of the strangers turned and looked directly at the place where Kim was hiding. He lidded his eyes and kept perfectly still, knowing that unless he moved the man would not see him. So it proved. The man made a cursory inspection of the settlement then returned to his food, his face twitching furtively as he gnawed at the raw meat.

For a moment Kim was blank, a shell of unthinking bone. Then something woke in him, filling the emptiness. He turned away, moving with a painful slowness, his muscles aching with the strain of it as he climbed the rotten sill, each moment begging that it wouldn't crumble beneath his weight and betray him. But it held. Then, slowly, very slowly, he eased himself down the cold, broad steps. Down into the cellar of Baxi's house.

In the far corner of the cellar he stopped, lifting rocks, scrabbling silently with his fingers in the intense darkness, looking for something. There! His fingers found the edge of the cloth and gently pulled the package up out of the soft dust. Kim shivered, knowing already what was inside. These were Baxi's. His treasures. He was not meant to know of them. Baxi would have killed him had he known.

Kim tugged at the knot and freed it, then unwrapped the cloth, ignoring the fear he felt. Another Kim – another self – had taken over.

Straightening up, he knelt there, staring down sightlessly at the items hidden in the cloth, a feeling of strangeness rippling through him like a sickness. For a moment he closed his eyes against the sudden, unexpected giddiness, then felt it ebb from him and opened them again, feeling somehow different – somehow... changed.

Spreading the objects out with his fingers, he picked up each object in turn, feeling and smelling them, letting the newly woken part of him consider each thing before he set it down again.

A tarnished mirror, bigger than his hand, cracked from top to bottom. A narrow tube that contained a strange sweet-smelling liquid. Another tube, but this of wood, long as his lower arm, small holes punctuating its length. One end was open, hollow, the other tapered, split.

There was a small globe of glass, heavy and cold in his palm. Beside that was a glove, too large for his hand, its fingers heavily padded at the back, as if each joint had swollen up.

Two strings of polished beads lay tangled in a heap. Kim's clever fingers untangled them and laid them out flat on the threadbare cloth.

There were other things, but those he set aside. His other self already saw. Saw as if the thing had already happened and he had been outside himself, looking on. The thought made him feel strange again; made his head swim, his body feel light, almost feverish. Then, once more, it passed.

Quickly, as if he had done all this before, he laid the things out around him, then placed the cloth over his head. Unsighted, he worked as if he saw himself from above, letting some other part of him manipulate his hands, his body, moving quickly, surely, until the thing was done. Then, ready, he turned towards the doorway and, by touch and scent, made his way out into the open.

He heard a gasp and then a shout, high-pitched and nervous. Three voices babbled and then fell silent. That silence was his signal. Lifting the globe high, he squeezed the button on the side of the tube.

Some gift, unguessed until that moment, made him see himself as they saw him. He seemed split, one self standing there before them, the cloth shrouding his face and neck, the cracked mirror tied in a loop before his face, the other stood beyond the men, looking back past them at the awesome, hideous figure who had appeared so suddenly, flames leaping from one hand, fire glinting in the centre of the other, giant fist, flickering in the hollow where his face should have been, while from the neck of the figure a long tongue of wood hung stiffly down.

The figure hopped and sang – a strange, high-pitched wail that seemed to come in broken, anguished breaths. And all the while the fire flickered in the centre of the empty face.

As one, the strangers screamed and ran.

Kim let the pipe fall from his lips. His finger released the button on the tube. It was done. He had seen them off. But from the darkness of the slopes came an intense, ape-like chattering. Others had seen the sudden, astonishing brightness.

He set down the glass sphere, unfastened the mirror and laid it down, then sat there on the broken ground, wondering at himself. It had worked. He had seen it in his head, and then... He laughed softly, strangely. And then he'd done it!

And it had worked.

He tore the cloth from his head and bared his sharp teeth in a feral grin of triumph. Tilting his head back, he let out a howl; a double whoop of delight at his own cleverness. Then, so suddenly that the sound still echoed from the ceiling high above, he shuddered, gripped by a paralysing fear, a black, still coldness flooding his limbs.

It was not triumph, merely reprieve. He was still here, trapped, smothered by the darkness. He coughed, then felt the warm corruption of the dark fill his lungs, like a liquid, choking him. He stood up, gulping at the foetid air as if for something sweeter, cleaner. But there was nothing – only this.

He whimpered, then, glancing furtively about him, began to wrap the treasures as he'd found them. Only when they were safely stored did he stop, his jaw aching from fear, his muscles trembling violently. Then, like some mad thing, he rushed about the settlement on all fours, growling furiously, partly to keep up his faded courage, partly to keep away the prowlers on the hillside below.

It was then that he found the knife. It had fallen on its edge, the handle jutting up at an angle where one of the strangers had dropped it. The handle was cold and smooth and did not give to Kim's sharp teeth when he tested it. Not wood, or flint, but something far better than those. Something *made*. He drew it slowly from the tiny crevice in which it had lodged and marvelled at its length, its perfect shape. It was as long as his arm and its blade was so sharp it made his testicles contract in fear. A *wartha*, it was. *From Above*.

When they came back he was squatting on the sill of Baxi's house, the long, two-edged blade laid carefully across his knees, the handle clenched firmly in his left hand.

Baxi looked about him, his body tensed, alarm twitching in his face. The stockade was down, the women gone. A few of the bodies lay where they had fallen. Some – those on the edges of the settlement – had been carried off. Behind Baxi his two lieutenants, Rotfoot and Ebor, made low, grunting noises of fear. He turned and silenced them, then faced Kim again.

'Pandra vyth gwres?' *What is this?*

Baxi glared at Kim, then saw the knife. His eyes widened, filled with fear and a greedy desire to own the weapon. There was a fierce, almost sexual urgency in his broad, squat face as he hopped from foot to foot, making small noises, as if in pain.

Kim knew he would kill to have the knife.

'Lagasek!' Baxi barked angrily, edging closer. 'Pandra vyth gwres?' His hands made small grasping movements.

Lagasek. It was the name they had given him. *Starer.*

Kim stood then raised the knife high over his head. There was a gasp from the other members of the hunting party as they saw the weapon, then an excited chattering. Kim saw Baxi crouch, his muscles tensing, as if he suspected treachery.

Slowly, careful not to alarm Baxi, Kim lowered the blade and placed it on the ground between them. Then he crouched, making himself smaller than he was, and made a gesture with his hands, the palms open, denoting a gift.

Baxi stared at him a moment longer, the hairs bristling on his arms and at the back of his neck. Then he too crouched, a broad, toothless grin settling on his face. The Chief was pleased. He reached out, taking Kim's gift gingerly by the handle, respecting the obvious sharpness of the blade.

Baxi lifted the weapon and held it high above his head. He glanced briefly at Kim, smiling broadly, generous now, then turned, looking back at his hunters, thrusting the knife time and again into the air, tilting his head back with each thrust and baying at the ceiling high above.

All about him in the almost-dark the hunters bayed and yelled. And from the hillsides and the valley below other groups took up the unearthly sound and echoed it back.

Kim squatted at Ebor's side in the inner circle of the hunters, chewing a long, pale-fleshed lugworm and listening to the grunts, the moist, slopping sounds the men made as they ate, realizing he had never really noticed them before. He glanced about him, his eyes moving swiftly from face to face around the circle, looking for some outward sign of the change that had come to him, but there was nothing. Rotfoot had lost his woman in the raid, but now he sat there, on the low stone wall, contentedly chewing part of her thighbone, stripping it bare with his sharply pointed teeth. Others too were gnawing at the meat that Baxi had provided. A small heap of it lay there in the centre of the circle, hacked into manageable pieces. Hands and feet were recognizable in the pile, but little else. The sharp knife had worked its magic of disguise. Besides, meat was meat, whatever the source.

Kim finished the worm. He leaned forward, looking about him timidly. Then, seeing the smiles on the hunters' faces, he reached out and grasped a small hunk of the meat. A hand. He was tearing at the hard, tough flesh when Baxi settled by his side and placed an arm about his narrow shoulders. Reflex made him tense and look up into the Chief's face, fear blazing in his eyes, but the warrior merely grunted and told him to come.

He followed Baxi through, aware that the circle of heads turned to follow him. Afraid, he clutched the severed hand to himself, finding a strange comfort in its touch. His fingers sought its rough, bony knuckles, recognized the chipped, spoonlike nails. It was Rotfoot's woman's hand.

At the entrance to Baxi's house they stopped. The Chief turned, facing the boy, and pointed down to a small parcel of cloth that lay on the ground beside the sill.

Kim froze in fear, thinking he'd been discovered. He closed his eyes, petrified, expecting the knife's sharp blow. Where would it strike? In his back? His side? Against his neck? He made a small sound of fear, then opened his eyes again and looked up at Baxi.

Baxi was looking strangely at him. Then he shrugged and pointed at the parcel again. Kim swallowed and set down the hand, then picked up the cloth bundle and, at Baxi's encouragement, began to unwrap it.

He saw what it was at once and looked up, surprised, only to find Baxi smiling down at him. 'Ro,' said the Chief. 'Ro.' A gift.

The tarnished mirror was just as he remembered it, the crack running down the silvered glass from top to bottom. There was no need to feign surprise or delight. He grinned up at Baxi, giving a silent whoop of joy, almost forgetting that they thought him dumb. Baxi too seemed pleased. He reached out to touch Kim, caressing his upper arms and nodding his head vigorously. 'Ro,' he said again, then laughed manically. And from the watching circle came an answering roar of savage laughter.

Kim stared down at the mirror in his hand and saw his face reflected in the darkness. How strange and alien that face. Not like his hands. He knew his hands. But his face... He shivered, then smiled, taken by the strangeness of his reflected features. Lagasek, he thought, seeing how the stranger smiled back at him. *Such eyes you have. Such big, wide staring eyes.*

Kim was scavenging, looking for food in a place where nothing grew. The air all about him was rich with the stink of decay, the ground beneath him soft and damp and treacherous. Here, at the edge of the great dump, the dangers multiplied. There were many more like him, hidden shadows scattered across the vastness of the wasteland, wary of each other as they climbed the huge, rotting mounds, picking at the waste. All of them looking for something to eat or trade. Anything. Good or rotten.

The darkness was almost perfect, but the boy saw clearly. His wide, round eyes flicked from side to side, his small, ill-formed head moved quickly, furtively, like the head of some wild creature. When another came too close he would scuttle away on all fours, then rest there, at a distance, his teeth bared in challenge, growling at the back of his throat.

He moved in deeper, taking risks now, jumping between what looked like firm footholds. Some sank slowly beneath his weight, others held. He moved on quickly, not trusting anything too long, until he reached one certain resting place, the tower of an old church, jutting up above the vast mound of sewage from the City overhead.

Kim glanced up. The ceiling was far above him, its nearest supporting pillar only a stone's throw from where he squatted. From his vantage point he looked about him, noting where others were, checking which paths were clear for his escape. Then he settled, reaching deep inside his ragged, dirty shirt to take out the object he had found. He sniffed at it and licked it, then grimaced. It smelled like old skins and had a stale, unappetizing taste. He turned it in his hands, looking for a way inside the blackened casing, then picked at the metal clasp until it opened.

He looked up sharply, suddenly very still, watchful, the hairs rising on the back of his thin neck, his rope-like muscles stretched as if to spring. Seeing nothing, he relaxed and looked back down at the open wallet in his hand.

Deftly he probed into each slender compartment, removing the contents and studying them closely before replacing them. There was nothing he recognized. Nothing edible. There were several long, thin cards of a flexible, shiny material. From one of them a faded face stared up at him, coming to vivid life when he pressed his thumb against it. Startled, he dropped the card, then steeled himself and retrieved it from the moss-covered slate on which it had fallen, deciding he would keep it.

There was only one other thing worth keeping. In a zippered compartment of the wallet was a small circle of shining metal on a chain. A kind of pendant. He lifted it gently, fascinated by its delicate perfection, his breath catching in his throat. It was beautiful. He held it up and touched the dangling circle with one finger, making it spin. It slowed, then twisted back, spinning backward and forward. Kim sat back on his haunches and laughed softly, delighted with his find.

The laughter died in his throat. He turned, hearing how close the others had come while he had been preoccupied, smelling the tartness of their sweat as they jumped up onto the tower.

Kim yelped, closing his fist about the pendant, and edged back away from them. There were three of them, one no older than himself, the others taller, better muscled than he. Their round eyes gleamed with greed and they smiled at one another with their crooked, feral teeth. They thought they had him.

He snarled and the hair on his body rose, as if for fight, but all the while he was thinking, calculating, knowing he had to run. He looked from one to the other, discounting the smallest of them, concentrating on the two eldest, seeing who led, who followed. Then, so quick that they had no chance to stop him, he threw the wallet down, nearest the one who was quite clearly the follower. For a moment their attention went from him to the wallet. The leader snarled and made a lunge across the other, trying to get at the wallet.

Kim saw his opportunity and took it, flipping backward over the parapet, hoping that no one had disturbed the mound that lay below. His luck held and the soft ooze broke his fall wetly, stickily. Pulling himself up, he saw them leaning over the parapet, looking down. In a second or two they would be on him. He pulled his arm free and rolled, then scrambled onto all fours and began to run.

He heard their cries, the soft squelch of the sticky mound as they jumped down onto it. Then they were after him, through the nightmare landscape, hopping between dark, slimy pools. Desperation made him take chances, choose paths he would normally ignore. And slowly, very slowly, he drew away from them, until, when he looked back over his shoulder, he found they were no longer pursuing him.

He turned and stood up, looking back across the choked mouth of the river. He could not make out the tower against the background of the rising land. Neither were any of the other familiar landmarks evident.

For the second time that day he felt afraid. He had come a long way. This was a side of the dump he didn't know. Here he was doubly vulnerable.

He was breathing deeply, his narrow chest heaving with exertion. If they attacked him now he was done for. He crouched down, looking all about him, his face twitching with anxiety. This side seemed deserted, but he knew he couldn't trust his eyes. He glanced down at the pendant in his hand, wondering if it had been worth the finding, then dismissed the question. First he had to get home.

Slowly, painstakingly, he made his way about the edge of the waste, his eyes straining for the least sign of movement, his sharp ears registering the least sound. And again his luck held. There, far to his left, was the broad pillar that they called the Gate, and beyond it, in the midst of the waste itself, the church tower. Kim grinned, allowing himself to savour hope for the first time since they had surprised him on the tower. He went on, clambering over the uneven surface, making a beeline for the Gate.

He was only a few paces from it when the ground gave way beneath his feet and he fell.

For a time he lay there, on his back, winded. It had not been much of a fall and he seemed not to have broken anything, but he could see from the smooth sides of the pit that it would be difficult to climb out. The earth was soft but dry beneath him. Tiny insects scuttled away from his probing hands, and the air seemed warm and strangely close. He sat up, groaning, feeling a stiffness in his back. His neck ached and his arms were sore, but he could move.

He looked up. Above him the opening formed a circle against the greater darkness, like two shades of the same non-colour. The circle had jagged edges, as if something had once lain across it. Kim's mind pieced things together nimbly. The pit had had some kind of lid on it. A wooden lid, maybe. And it had rotted over the years. It had taken only his own small weight to bring it down.

He felt about him in the darkness and found confirmation of his thoughts. There were splinters of soft, rotten wood everywhere about him. Then, with delight, he found the chain to the pendant with his fingers and drew it up to his face, pleased to find it unbroken. But then his pleasure died. He was still trapped. Unless he got out soon someone would come along and find him. And then he would be dead.

He looked about him, momentarily at a loss, then went to the side of the pit and began to poke and prise at it. The curved walls of the pit were made of a kind of brickwork. Kim worked at the joints, finding the joining material soft and crumbly to the touch. He dug away at it, loosening and then freeing one of the bricks. Throwing it down behind him, he reached up a bit higher and began to free another.

It took him a long time and at the end of it his fingertips were sore and bleeding, but he did it. Kneeling on the edge of the pit he looked back down and shivered, knowing that he could easily have died down there. He rested a while, then staggered across to the Gate, close to exhaustion. There, almost beside the broad, hexagonally sided shaft, was a pool. He knelt beside it, bathing his fingers and splashing the tepid water in his face.

And then it happened.

The darkness of the pool was split. A shaft of intense brightness formed in the midst of its dark mirror. Slowly it widened, until the pool was filled with a light so intense that Kim sat back on his heels, shielding his eyes. A flight of broad, stone steps, inverted by the lens of the water, led down into the dark heart of the earth.

Kim glanced up, his mouth wide open. The Gate was open. Light spilt like fire into the air.

Trembling, he looked down again. The surface of the pool shimmered, rippled. Then, suddenly, its brightness was split by bands of darkness. There were figures in the Gateway! Tall shapes of darkness, straight as spears!

He looked up, astonished, staring through his latticed hands. Jagged shadows traced a hard-edged shape upon the steps. Kim knelt there, transfixed, staring up into the portal.

He gasped. What *were* they? Light flashed from the darkness of their vast, domed heads – from the winking, glittering, brilliant darkness of their heads. Heads of glass. And, beneath those heads, bodies of silver. Flexing, unflexing silver.

Slowly his hands came down from his face. Light lay in the caves of his eyes, a bright wet point of brilliance at the centre of each pupil. He knelt there, in the darkness at the edge of the pool, watching them come down. Three kings of glass and silver, passing so close to him he could hear the soft sigh and moan of their breathing.

He screamed, a raw, high-pitched sound, the noise dragged up from deep inside him, then huddled into himself, knowing that death was near. The pendant fell from his hand, unnoticed, flashing in the air before the water swallowed it.

One of the giant figures turned and looked down at the huddled boy, barely recognizing him as a creature of his own species, seeing only a tiny, malformed shape. A shuddering, thin-boned thing. Some kind of ill-groomed beast, long-maned and filthy.

'Clay...' he said beneath his breath, the word heavy with nuances – contempt, disgust, the vaguest trace of guilt. Then he turned away, glad that his face mask filtered out the stench of the place. Through the infrared of his visor he could see other shapes in movement, some close, some far away. Splashes of warmth against the cold, black backdrop.

He walked on, joining the other, suited men. Behind him, cowering beside the man-sized pool of light, the boy turned and followed him with his eyes, watching him go down into the darkness.

Then they were gone.

Kim stretched, pushing his hands against the soft, wet earth, steadying himself. The trembling passed from him, but still his mouth lay open, his fear transformed to wonder.

He turned, looking up at the Gate, a shiver running down his spine.

A wartha! The Above! The words formed in his head, framed in awe, like an incantation. He cupped water in one hand and wet his lips, then said the words aloud, whispering them, in an accent as malformed as himself.

'A wartha...'

Again he shivered, awed by what he had seen. And in his head he pictured a whole world of such creatures, a world of liquid, brilliant light. A world above the darkness and the Clay.

His mouth formed a tiny O, round as his eyes.

Above him the Gate began to close, the pillar of brilliant silver fading into black, the broad steps swallowed slowly by the dark. And afterwards the blackness seemed more intense, more horrible than it had ever been. Like a giant hand it pressed down on him, crushing him, making him gasp for each breath. Again he screamed, a new, unbearable pain, born of that moment, gripping his insides, tugging at him.

The Light...

His fingers groped wildly in the mud, then flailed at the water, looking for fragments of the pearled light. But he was blind. At first his fingers found nothing. Then, for the third time, his fingers closed upon a slender length of chain, sought out the tiny metal pendant and drew it up from out of the liquid, holding it to his face, pressing it hard against his lips, not understanding why, yet feeling its presence soothe him, calm him. Like a promise.

It was a web. A giant web. Alive, quiveringly alive, expanding, filling the darkness with its pearls of light. Moist beads of brilliance strung on translucent fibres of light. It grew, at the same time both frail and strong – incredibly strong. The light could not be broken. He stared up at it, open-mouthed, and felt himself lifted, filled with joy. Incredible, brilliant joy, born of the growing light.

Kim lifted his hands to the light, aching to join with it. If only he could reach it; only lift his head and break the surface membrane of the darkness in which he was embedded, breathing fresh air. He stretched towards it, and felt the joy tighten like a metal band about his chest, crushing him.

And woke, tears in his eyes, hunger in his belly.

He shuddered, horrified. It lay all about him like a glue. He rested on it and it pressed its vast weight down on top of him. Each pore of his was permeated by its sticky warmth. It was darkness. Darkness, the very stuff of the Clay.

The dream made him grit his teeth and sit there, rocking back and forth in pain, moaning softly to himself. For the last few days it had been as if he were awake while all about him slept. As if it was their nightmare he inhabited, not his own. Yet there was no waking from their dream of darkness. Their dream outweighed his hope.

He straightened up, shuddering, hearing the movement in the darkness all about him. It was time. The tribe was preparing to move.

He got up quickly and went to the corner of the square of brick and stone in which he slept and relieved himself. Then he came back and packed up his few possessions: a blanket, a flint shard, the small bundles containing his treasures, lastly a square of cloth – a scarf of sorts – that had been his mother's.

The one he had known as mother was long dead. He had been taken with her from the carriage and had watched while they held her down by the roadside, feeling a vague disquiet at their actions, not understanding the naked jutting of their buttocks, the squeals from the woman beneath them. But then they had begun to beat her and he had cried out and tried to get to her, desperate to save her from them. And that was all he knew, for one of them had turned and struck him hard with the back of his hand, sending him crashing into the stone of a low wall.

So he had joined the tribe.

Most days he did as they did, thoughtlessly. Yet sometimes a strange, dissociated pain would grip him – something not of the body, more like his glimpse of the light: something intangible yet real. Disturbingly real. And he would know it had to do with her. With a vague sense of comfort and safety. The only comfort, the only safety he had ever known. But mainly he shut it out. He needed his wits to survive, not to remember.

Kim stood at the edge of the group while Baxi spoke. They were going to raid a small settlement further down the valley, counting upon surprise to win the encounter. They would kill all the men and boys. Women, girls and babies they would capture and bring back alive.

Kim listened, then nodded with the rest. It would be his first raid. He clutched his flint anxiously, excitement and fear alternating in him; hot and cold currents in his blood. There would be killing. And afterwards there would be meat. Meat and women. The hunters laughed and grunted among themselves. Kim felt his mouth water, thinking of the meat.

They left eight men behind to guard the settlement. The rest followed Baxi down the stream in single file, keeping low and moving silently. Four hands of men, running swiftly, lithely down the stream path, their bare feet washed by the greasy, sluggish flow. Kim was last of them and smallest. He ran behind them like a monkey, hands touching the ground for balance as he crouched forward, the flint shard between his teeth.

There was a tumble of rocks, a small stretch of flat, exposed land, and then the other settlement. There was no chance of subtlety, only of surprise.

Baxi sprang from the rocks and sprinted silently across the open space, the knife raised high. Rotfoot and Ebor were after him at once, running as fast as their legs could carry them, followed a moment later by others of the tribe.

It nearly worked. Baxi was almost on the guard when he turned and called out. His cry rose, then changed in tone. He went down, the knife buried to the hilt in his chest, its tip jutting from a point low in his back.

Kim squatted on the highest of the rocks, watching as the fight developed. He saw Baxi scream and curse as he tried to free the knife from the dead man's rib cage, then turn to fend off a defender's blow. Others of the tribe were struggling with the strangers, some of them rolling on the ground, some exchanging vicious swinging blows with flints and cudgels. The air was alive with grunts and screams. Kim could smell the stink of fear and excitement in the darkness.

He watched, afraid to go down, repulsion battling with the fascination he felt. His tribe was winning. Slowly the defenders left off trying to fight their attackers and, one by one, began to run away. Already his side were dragging away the unconscious women and girls and squabbling over the corpses. But still small pockets of the fight went on. Kim saw and realized where he was, what he had been doing. Quickly he scrambled across the rocks and dropped down onto the ground, fearing what Baxi would do if he saw.

He had held back. Shown fear. He had let the tribe down.

Kim hurried across the uneven ground, stumbling, then hurled himself onto the back of one of the escaping defenders. His weight brought the man down, but the stranger was twice Kim's size and in an instant Kim found himself on his back, pinned down, the scarred, one-eyed stranger staring down at him. That single eye held death. The stranger's right hand clutched a rock.

He raised the rock.

Kim had only an instant in which to act. As if he saw someone beyond and above the stranger, he called out anxiously, looking past the stranger's face.

'Nyns!' he screamed. No! 'Ny mynnes ef yn-few!' *We want him alive!*

It was enough to make the stranger hesitate and shift his weight, half-turning to see who it was behind him. It was also enough to allow Kim to turn sideways and tip the stranger from him.

One-eye rolled and turned, facing Kim, angry at being tricked, but conscious that each moment's delay brought his own death closer. He swung wildly with the rock and misjudged. Kim lunged in with his sharply pointed flint, aiming for the softest, most vulnerable place, and felt his whole arm judder as he connected. There was a moment of sickening contact, then Kim saw the man's face change into a mask of naked pain. One-eye had been castrated, his testicles crushed.

One-eye fell at Kim's side, vomiting, his hands clutching at his ruined manhood. Kim jerked his hand away, leaving the flint embedded where it was, then looked about anxiously.

Baxi was watching him, smiling ferociously.

Kim looked back, appalled, hearing the wretch heaving up each painful breath. Then, as he watched, Baxi came close, the knife in his hand, and pushed its point deep into the base of One-eye's neck.

One-eye spasmed then lay still.

'Da,' said the chief and turned away. *Good.* Kim watched him strut, triumphant, self-satisfied, then throw back his head and whoop.

A web... A web of sticky darkness. Kim felt a warmth, a kind of numbness, spread outward from the core of him, a hand of eight fingers closing on him slowly like a cage, drawing him down beneath the surface of the dark. Darkness congealed above him like a lid, tar in his open mouth. And then he fainted.

They had never heard him say a word. Baxi thought him dumb or just simple, and others took their lead from that. They called him 'Lagasek', or Starer, for his habit of looking so intently at an object. That, too, they saw as a sign of his simplicity.

For an age, it seemed, he had been as if asleep among them. Their hideous shapes and forms had become as familiar as the darkness. He had watched them without understanding, seeing their scars and deformities as natural things, not departures from some given norm. But now he was awake. He stared at them through newly opened eyes, a bright thread of thought connecting what he saw to the sharp-lit centre of awareness at the back of his skull.

He looked about the flickering fire at their missing hands and eyes, their weeping sores and infected scabs; saw them cough and wheeze for breath, aged well beyond their years, and wondered what he was doing there among them.

Sitting there in the dust, the thick and greasy soup warm in his belly, he felt like weeping. As he looked about the small circle of men and boys he saw, for the first time, their gauntness, their strange furtiveness. They twitched and scratched. They stretched and stood to urinate, their eyes never still, never settling for long, like the blind white flies that were everywhere in the Clay.

Yes, he understood it now. It had begun there with that glimpse of otherness – that vision of glass and silver, of kings and brightness. He felt like speaking out – telling them what he had seen at the Gate, what he had done to scare off the intruders – but habit stilled his tongue. He looked down at his tiny, narrow hands, his long thin arms. There were no scars but there were sores at the elbows and the bone could be seen clear beneath the flesh.

He looked away, shuddering, his face filled with pain and a strange, hitherto untasted shame, then looked back again. They were talking among themselves now, their crude, half-savage speech suddenly foreign to his ear. It made him feel uneasy, as if he had knowledge of something better, some long-buried memory of things before the tribe. Across from him Tek and Rotfoot exchanged half-hearted blows in savage-gentle play, their broken faces filled with light and shadows. He lifted his head, sniffing at them in instinct, then settled, realizing what he was doing, filled with a sudden, intense sense of self-disgust.

For a moment he closed his eyes, feeling the warmth on his face and arms and chest. That too was strange. It was rare to have a fire. Rare to sit as they sat now, the circle of the dark behind, the circle of the light in front. But this was a special time.

Baxi sat in his place, on a huge, rounded stone above the others. A stack of wood – itself a kind of treasure – lay at his side. From time to time he would reach down and throw a piece upon the blaze, growling with pleasure.

They had found the sacks of firewood in a store room in the conquered settlement; three of them, hidden beneath a pile of other things scavenged from the dump. Baxi had brought them back and built the fire himself with a care that made Kim think he had seen it done before. Then he had gone down to his cellar, returning moments later with the fire-stick.

Kim had watched them all gasp and fall back as the flame leapt from his hand and spread amongst the gathered wood, muttering darkly between themselves, their eyes filled with fear and fascination. But Kim had known. He had crouched there, still and silent, watching as the fire kindled, like some strange, living creature jumping from one dark surface to another, consuming all it touched. Like the unspoken thoughts in his head, he realized. Yet this had a voice, a crackling, popping, sputtering voice, its breath strangely thick and dark, curled like a beard, yet evanescent – vanishing into the dark above the blaze.

For a brief moment it seemed he understood; held in his head a key to the pattern of all things. Then it too was gone, drawn up into the darkness overhead.

He felt misplaced. Torn from the light and cast down into darkness. But if misplaced, what then? How could he change things?

Run away, a small voice inside him called out. *Run far away. To a place where the darkness ends.*

He looked out beyond the fire, blinded by its brilliance, seeing nothing but the after-image of the flames. The darkness was unending and eternal. There was nothing but the darkness...

No, he reminded himself. *Not true. There is a place of brightness. Up there. A wartha.*

Among the gods.

Not only that, but there was a way. A single door into the brightness. A one-way door that often led to death, or so the men said. A door that only the youngest and the bravest took.

Kim looked down at his hands again. He was young, but was he brave enough? Was he prepared to risk everything on a single gamble?

He thought of the escapade with the mirror and the fire-stick and his spirits rose. Then the image of himself, scared and cowering on the rocks, came back to him. His stomach knotted. He wanted it. Wanted the brightness like he wanted life itself. But he was afraid. Dreadfully, awfully, numbingly afraid. He felt he could not do it – would die before he took the first step.

Better to stay here a thousand years...

A cold shiver passed through him, ice beneath the firelight on his face and chest and limbs. No, not that. Death was preferable to that.

He looked up. On the far side of the fire, beyond Rotfoot, stood Baxi, watching him. For a moment their eyes met and locked and some kind of raw understanding passed between them. And, in the moment before he looked away, Kim saw a crude kind of affection there in the older man's eyes: a strange, almost wistful tenderness that he found unsettling.

Far away, said the voice inside. *To a place where the darkness ends.*

Kim rose and turned to face the darkness. The heat lay on his naked back, like the promise of comfort, but now his face was cold and the tension in him was worse than it had ever been. For a moment longer he hesitated, need and fear at war within him. Then, with a violent shudder, he nodded to himself and jerked away from the fire, his decision made.

He would go. Now. Before the darkness took him back.

The sign was ancient. Time had turned the whiteness of its paint a mottled grey, had faded the dark, heavy lettering. Where the bolts held it to the wall a red-gold rust had formed two weeping eyes.

Kim looked up at it, struggling to understand. Like so much else it was a mystery; a symbol of all the things denied him. He studied the strange yet familiar shapes of the letters, wondering what they meant, filling the gap, the darkness of incomprehension, with his own meanings. The first letter was easy. It was an arrow, facing to the left. There was a gap and then the second, its double curves facing away from the arrow like a straight-backed woman's breasts. The third was a ring. The fourth a drawn bow. The fifth? Two steep hills, perhaps, linked by a valley. The sixth again was easy. It was an upright column, like the column beyond the wall. The seventh? He felt the seventh was like the fifth, yet its difference – its lack of an upright strut – was significant. A gate, maybe. Or two interlocking flints – perhaps the sign for war. Then, after another gap, came the last of them; an eye with a dark, curled eyebrow overhead, linked at the eye's left corner.

But what did it mean in total? What message had it once conveyed?

He looked about him, then ducked beneath the rotten lintel, pushing through the gap in the wall. There, like some vast subterranean serpent breaching the far wall of the ruined building, stood the column, its silvered surface gleaming in the half-light.

Kim stumbled forward and stood before it, his eyes drawn upward to where it met the ceiling of the Clay far overhead. There were many such pillars spread regularly throughout the Clay, but this one, Kim knew, was different from the others. It was a gate. An entrance into the Above.

Long ago they had chased a boy from another tribe across the nearby hills and trapped him here, between the walls of this old, ruined building. Faced with certain death, the boy had turned, gone to the pillar and pressed his hands against it.

Miraculously, the pillar had opened. A narrow aperture had formed in its perfect roundness, a dim, fierce light burning out from the space within. Fearfully, with a backward glance at them, the boy had gone inside. At once the opening had closed, throwing the space between the walls into an intense and sudden darkness.

They had camped there some while, waiting for the boy to come out, but he never had. And when one of the older boys grew brave enough to approach the pillar and press against it, they could all see that the space inside was empty.

It had eaten the boy.

For a time he had believed this version of events, and in truth part of him still believed it, making him cower there, terrified to enter. But the newly woken part of him reasoned otherwise. What if the boy had not been killed? What if he had been taken up into the Above?

They were huge assumptions. Hunches, not certainty. And the boy had gone inside only because he had had no option. But what of himself? There were no knives awaiting him should he turn away. Only the darkness. Only the foetid Clay.

He grimaced and closed his eyes, tormented by indecision. He didn't want to die. He didn't want to be wrong.

Is death any worse than this?

The thought came like a voice in his head, and with the voice came the realization that he was no longer a single creature. There were two of him, sharing a single skull, a single body. One dark, one light. One kept him here, the other craved escape. Here, at the gate to the Above, they would have to fight it out between them.

For a time the darkness had him and he stood there, thoughtless, his animal self shuddering uncontrollably, a gobbet of spittle dribbling down his chin. Then, with an abruptness that caught the animal unaware, Kim threw himself at the column and scratched at its surface, trying to find an opening.

He could hear himself gibbering with fear, and in another moment he would have backed away, defeated, but suddenly the aperture slid open with an outbreath of air and he tumbled in, onto the smooth, uncluttered floor, his hands going up to cover his eyes against the brilliance.

The brightness hurt him. It cut into his head like a flint. Then the door hissed shut behind him, trapping him. He whimpered in fear then lay there, shivering, his legs drawn up beneath him, waiting to die.

What happened next seemed worse than death. The light in the room pulsed gently and a deep voice boomed out, filling the narrow space.

'Kewsel agas hanow, map!' *Speak your name, boy!* 'Agas hanow!'

Kim gagged, then shat himself. His muscles went into spasm. For a while he could do nothing to control them. Again he was an unthinking animal, there on the floor inside the alien column. A stinking piece of quivering meat and bone. Then the bright thing in him bobbed up again and floated on the surface of his awareness. His name? What *was* his name?

'Laga...' He could not say it. He'd had too little practice. In any case, it was wrong. Lagasek – Starer – was not his name; or, if his name, then his name only in the darkness. It was not the name his mother had given him. Not the name he wished to take with him into the light.

He tried again. 'Kim,' he said, the word strange, more awkward in his mouth than in his head. His voice barely sounded the K and the rest of it was inaudible.

'Kewsel arta,' said the voice. *Speak again.* It seemed warmer than before, more soothing.

'Kim,' he said more clearly, then lay there, perfectly still, wondering what would happen.

'Da, Kim,' said the voice. *Good.* 'Praga bos why omma?' *Why be you here?* 'Praga prak why entradhe hemma pylla?' *Why did you enter this pillar?* 'Gul nebonen sewya why?' *Does someone pursue you?*

'Nyns,' he answered. *No.*

'Nyns,' the voice repeated and then chuckled to itself. What it said next was difficult to follow. The words were alien to Kim, like the nonsense utterances of his nightmares. 'We've a fluent one here.' This last seemed not to be directed at Kim.

Kim sat up, looking around him. Then he stood and went to the curve of the wall across from where the opening had been. No, he hadn't been mistaken: there was a shape in the wall's otherwise unblemished face. A pattern of light, almost too faint to see. He stood beside it, trying to figure it out.

'Ah,' said the voice. 'My gweles why cafos an matrix.' *I see you've found the...* But the last word was new. It was like the other words – alien.

Kim twitched and turned about sharply. The creature with the voice was watching him, then. Was close by. He stared up into the dimly lit tunnel overhead and tried to make out something in the darkness, but it seemed empty.

'Matrix?' Kim asked, pronouncing the word carefully, as if feeling the shape of it in his mouth.

There was laughter – soft, warm laughter – then the voice came back. 'My bos ken tyller,' it said, as if that explained everything. *I be somewhere else.* 'Ha an tra a-dherak why bos un matrix.' *And that thing before you be a matrix.* 'Ef gul pycturs ha patron.' *He make pictures and patterns.*

Kim struggled to understand, but could grasp nothing of what the voice was saying. Pictures? Patterns? How did it make these things?

'Gasa-vy dysquehs why.' *Let me show you.*

The faint area glowed, then seemed to explode with colour.

Kim shrieked and leaped backward, scrambling away until his back was against the far curve of the wall.

'Ef ny a-wra pystyk why. Golyas. Kensa un fas.' *He won't harm you. Watch. First a face.*

The screen formed a face. A typical face from the Clay, seen in partial darkness, its scars and deformities nothing unusual. Kim nodded, his eyes watching the matrix closely.

'Nessa, un patron. Un semple patron. Tyby kettep myn bos un men.' *Next, a pattern. A simple pattern. Imagine each point be a stone.* 'My muvya an meyn formya un form. Un patron.' *I move the stones to form a shape. A pattern.*

When the image on the screen reformed it showed three lines of three points. A square.

'Den lufyow, le un bys,' said Kim. *Two hands, less a finger.* It was the most he had said until then.

'Ahah,' said the voice, and this time Kim could hear a second voice speak softly in the background. 'Numerate, this one. That's rare.' The hair on his neck stood up, hearing that foreign tongue again, and his lips peeled back, his dark self hostile to it, knowing it for the language of the light.

Unknown to him, however, he had taken his first step into the Above. And when the voice sounded again its tone was slightly different: less cosy, much more businesslike.

'Dos ogas an matrix, Kim. Dos ogas ha my deryvas why fatel muvya an meyn a drodhe.'

Come near the matrix, Kim. Come near and I'll tell you how to move the stones about.

CHAPTER 32

MACHINES OF FLESH

Klaus Ebert, Head of GenSyn, Chung Kuo's second largest company, looked down at the corpse on the dissecting table and slowly shook his head.

'No, Knut. I've never seen its like.'

He pointed out its internal structure: the lack of a spleen; the simplification of the respiratory system; the artificial latticework of the rib cage; the replacement of the stomach and intestinal system by a single sack, sealed off and unconnected to the anus. Most obvious of all was the flat, compact battery, like a black lacquered hipflask, placed where the human liver should have been.

'I'll have my experts look at this, but it's not GenSyn, that's certain. It isn't even organic. It's just a machine; too simple to function longer than a few months. It can't digest. It can't even process blood. Whoever built it designed it for rapid redundancy.'

Ebert turned, facing the General, his face ashen.

'Gods, Knut, but it's so like me, isn't it? Looking at it there, it feels like part of me has died.'

The General studied his old friend a moment, then looked back at the part-dissected corpse. It was a perfect copy. Too good in some respects. He had seen the films of it before his men had neutralized it – saw how cleverly it had mimicked Ebert's voice and mannerisms. And if there had been something unnatural about it, something just a bit too animated about its speech, its gestures, that was only noticeable in retrospect. It had been good enough to fool Ebert's personal staff. But the eyes... When the thing had been cornered in Ebert's private suite, those eyes had burned, like the eyes of an addict.

'Who could have built this, Klaus? Who has the know-how?'

Ebert laughed uncomfortably. 'GenSyn. MedFac, maybe. No one else. At least, no one on-planet.'

The General looked up sharply. 'You think it's from outside, then? From one of the colonies?'

Ebert dragged his eyes away from the dead thing on the table, then turned his back on it. 'I don't know, Knut. Six months back I'd have said no, but I've seen a few strange things since then. Controls are less tight out there. The Edict has less force...' He shook his head. 'The Seven should do something, Knut. Now. Before it's too late.'

'I know,' the General said simply. But he was thinking of DeVore. If what the *kwai*, Kao Chen, had said were true, it would explain much.

And Wyatt? He pushed the thought away. Wyatt was guilty. There was the evidence. Even so...

Ebert was looking at him, fear in his eyes. 'What does this mean, Knut? Why would they want to copy me? I don't understand.'

The General shuddered. *Nor I*, he thought, *not fully, anyway, but now I'm forearmed. We can rig up checkpoints. Scan for copies. Make sure nothing like this gets into the Forbidden City.*

There would be more than a hundred thousand guests at the wedding. And not one of them could be allowed to pass through without being tested. For if just one of these... *things* got through, it might prove disastrous.

He reached out and took his old friend's arm. 'I'm sorry, Klaus, but I think they meant to substitute this thing for you at the wedding. It was their way of getting at the T'ang.'

'You mean they meant to kill me, Knut?'

Tolonen met his eyes. 'I think so. They know how close you are to Li Shai Tung, and this...' He hesitated, then looked away, shaking his head. 'Look, I don't know who's behind this, Klaus, but it couldn't have come at a worse time.'

'Or more fortunate?'

Tolonen turned back. 'What do you mean?'

Ebert was looking down at the replicant's left hand; at the ring on the second finger with its insignia of two separated strands of DNA – an exact copy of his own. He looked back at Tolonen. 'It just seems odd, Knut, that's all. Odd how easily we caught this one. And yet I can't believe they would want us to know about this. This...' He pointed at the corpse-like thing on the table. 'It must have cost... what... eighty, maybe a hundred million yuan to build. And that's without the initial R&D costs. Why, there's memory technology involved here that we haven't even begun to explore at GenSyn. That alone would have cost them two or three hundred million yuan minimum. And maybe three, four times that. They wouldn't throw that away casually, would they?'

'No. I suppose they wouldn't.'

But Tolonen was already thinking things through – aware of the huge administrative nightmare this would create. They would have to set up a network of gates in front of the Forbidden City. Secure rooms. Thousands of them, specially equipped to check for fakes. And they would need to rehearse more than twenty thousand stewards in the subtle questions of etiquette and 'face' involved.

The General sighed, then tugged his uniform gloves tighter, aware that his craft had been waiting twenty minutes now. He would have to leave soon if he was to meet DeVore off the Mars shuttle. 'This will cause a great deal of bad feeling, Klaus. But you're right, it was fortunate. Now we know these things exist we can't afford to take chances. The lives of the Seven are at risk, and I'd offend every last man and woman in the Above to protect the Seven.'

Ebert laughed. 'I do believe you would, Knut.' He grew serious. 'But why now? Things are good, aren't they? We've built a good world, haven't we? Why do they want to tear it down, eh? Why?'

Tolonen looked up and saw how Ebert was watching him. Saw how, in this, he was looking to him for answers.

'Because the cycle's ending, Klaus. I feel it in my bones. Change is coming.'

Yes, he thought. *And things we thought true are no longer so.* He looked at the dead thing on the table and thought of DeVore. At least this fake was honest to itself. Was built a fake. But men? Who was to say what moulded them for ill or good?

★

It was just after four in the morning and Nanking Port lay in darkness, a loose-spaced ring of lights, five li from the central hub, tracing the periphery of the vast apron.

Tolonen stood in the topmost office of the towering Port Authority Building, the duty captain at attention before him.

'Gone? What do you mean, he's gone?'

The young captain bowed deeply to the visiting General, his cheeks red with embarrassment.

'He's not aboard the ship, sir. When our men went to arrest him, he simply wasn't there. And no one could say where he'd gone.'

Tolonen shook his head in disbelief.

'That's impossible! How could he get off the ship? It's moored at the orbital station, isn't it?'

'Yes, sir.'

'Well? He was aboard only eight hours ago, wasn't he?'

'Yes, sir.'

'So he's either still aboard or on that station, no?'

'No, sir. We've searched both ship and station thoroughly.'

Tolonen's anger exploded. 'Incompetents! How could you let him get away?' He snorted. 'Where could he be, eh? Out there? In the vacuum? No! Think, boy! He *must* be here. On Chung Kuo. But how did he get here? Who brought him down?'

'Sir?' The captain was totally flustered now.

'What service craft have visited the station in the past four hours? What ships, beside your own, have left the station since the Colony Ship docked?'

'None, sir.'

'None? Surely...'

'We put a *cordon sanitaire* about the station as soon as you instructed us, General. No service craft has docked at or left the station in the past thirteen hours.'

The General shivered. 'Who was aboard your craft?' he asked softly.

'Sir?' The captain stared back at him blank-faced, not understanding.

'I want them brought here. Now. Everyone who was aboard your patrol craft.'

'Sir!' The captain bowed, then turned away.

Tolonen went to the window and looked up into the circle of darkness overhead, his thoughts in turmoil.

Then it was true what the *kwai*, Kao Chen, had said. DeVore was the traitor. Tolonen shuddered. It was hard to believe. DeVore... The man had been such an excellent soldier. Such a fine, efficient officer. More than that, he had been a friend. A good friend. Had been a guest in the General's home many a time. Had held Tolonen's baby daughter, Jelka, in his arms.

Tolonen turned, facing the doorway. *If DeVore were to come into the room right now and swear he'd had no part in things, would I believe him? Yes! Even now I find the whole idea of DeVore as a traitor unbelievable. I would have known. Surely I would have known?*

And yet his absence...

The captain returned, followed by a dozen others. They formed up, awaiting the General's pleasure.

'This is all?'

The captain bowed his head deeply, then went down onto his knees. 'Sir, I... I don't know how this happened.' He kept his head bent low, his eyes averted. His shame seemed to radiate from him.

'They're gone, too, eh?'

The captain continued to kneel. 'Yes, sir.'

'How many?'

'Two officers. Eight men.'

Tolonen shook his head in disbelief. Ten men! Was DeVore's influence that strong, then? Or was it something else? He turned away, deeply agitated. Of course. Dispersionist money. Vast sums of it. Enough to buy out two Security officers and eight underlings.

'Gods!' he said softly. How much would it have cost them? A million yuan? Ten million? Fifty? He shivered, then turned and looked down again at the kneeling officer. 'Get up, captain.'

The captain remained as he was. 'I have failed you, sir. I ask permission to seek an honourable death.'

Angered now, Tolonen reached down and pulled the man to his feet.

'I'll not have good officers killing themselves for nothing. It is not your fault. Do you understand me, Captain? DeVore was too clever for you. Too clever for all of us.'

No, he thought, meeting the captain's eyes. *It's really not your fault at all. But now DeVore's at large. What mischief will he do?*

The captain backed away, white-faced, bowing. Then, at Tolonen's curt, angry command, he turned and led his men away.

Alone again, Tolonen let his anger drain from him. He went to the window and stood there once more, looking out over the still, dark forms of a hundred different craft, grounded at his order.

The certainty of DeVore's treachery sickened him. More than that, it undermined him, because it contradicted all he had thought he knew about men. His thoughts ran back over the last few years, trying to make sense of things. Could he have known? Was there any way he could have known?

No. DeVore had been the perfect officer. The perfect copy.

Tolonen tapped at the control blisters inset into his wrist and made connection with Major Nocenzi, half the globe away.

'General?' Nocenzi's voice came through clear in his head. His image appeared ghostly on the General's palm.

'Vittorio. I want you to do something for me.'

He spoke quickly but clearly, itemizing the things he wanted done. Then, finished, he cut connection, knowing time was against him.

So it was here at last, the war Li Shai Tung had long ago said would come. A secretive, dirty war, fought in the darkness between levels. A guerilla war, where friend and enemy had the same face. A war of money and technology and, at the last, sheer cunning. And who would win?

Tolonen smiled.

Karr, he thought. *I'll use Karr. He found Chen. Maybe he can find DeVore.*

Wang Ti opened the door slowly, surprised to see the big man standing there, but even more surprised when her husband called out from behind her, telling her to let him in.

Karr bowed his head respectfully and drew off his boots. Barefoot, he followed Wang Ti through into the back of the apartment, ducking under partitioning curtains.

Chen was sitting on the floor by the back wall, his legs folded under him, the baby asleep in his lap. There was little furniture in the cramped room. A double bedroll was folded neatly against the wall to Chen's right and a low table had been set up next to the *kang*. Wang Ti had been cooking, and the smell of it still hung in the air. From the far side of the long, dividing curtain on Chen's left came the sound of their neighbours' two young sons playing boisterously.

Karr smiled and bowed again, then squatted across from Chen.

'How's the child?'

Chen looked down at his infant son and gently stroked his brow.

'He's well.'

'Good.'

Wang Ti stood at his side dutifully, head bowed, eyes averted.

'You'll share ch'a with us, Shih...?'

'Karr...' The big man turned slightly and bowed his head, acknowledging her. 'I thank you for your kind offer, Wang Ti, but no. I have business to discuss with your husband.'

She nodded, then took the baby from Chen's lap and backed away. Karr waited until she had ducked out under the curtaining before speaking again. She would hear all he said, but the illusion of privacy was necessary. It was all the face a man had at these levels.

'You were right, Chen. It was DeVore.'

Chen grunted, his blunt peasant face inexpressive. 'So what now?'

Karr reached into the inner pocket of his overshirt and pulled out a thin tab of ice. 'Here,' he said, offering it.

Chen hesitated, remembering Jyan. He too had made deals with the Above. And where was he now? With his ancestors. Dead, his spirit untended, with no sons to burn offerings for his soul.

'What is it?'

Karr laughed. 'Still suspicious, eh? You've no need to be, Chen. You gave us more than we could have asked for. This...' He placed the tab between them on the floor. 'This is in settlement. A blanket amnesty. Your citizenship papers. A ten-deck security pass. And a bonus. A thousand yuan...'

Chen started. Then he was not to follow Wyatt to the block? He stared at the big man open-mouthed.

'You are kwai, Chen. A tool. And a good tool. The General was surprised how good,' he laughed. 'We Net types, we can teach them a thing or two, neh?'

Still Chen hesitated. Was this all some kind of elaborate ruse? Some awful taunting of him? But why should they bother?

'Then I'm free?'

Karr looked away, conscious of the woman listening beyond one curtain, the neighbours beyond another. 'Not exactly. You'll have to leave this place.

After what happened...'

'I see.'

Karr met his eyes. 'We'll resettle you. Retrain you.'

'Retrain me?'

'Yes. You've a new job, Chen. You've joined Security. As my adjutant.'

Chen stared, then looked down. 'And if I say no?'

Karr shrugged, watching the Han closely. 'You are *kwai*, Chen, not a warehouseman. Leave such jobs to good men like Lo Ying.'

Chen looked up, suddenly angry. 'And how is Lo Ying?'

Karr laughed, remembering how Lo Ying had jumped him. 'A brave man, but no fighter. Oh, he's happy now, Chen. He too has his bonus.'

Chen looked down at the tab. 'You plan to buy me, then?'

Karr hesitated, then shook his head. 'I would not insult you so, Kao Chen. We both know that you cannot buy a man's loyalty. However, you can try to earn it.' He sat back, then shrugged his great shoulders. 'All right. I ask you openly, Kao Chen. Will you become the T'ang's man? Or will you rot here at this level?'

Chen looked down. He had a life here. A good life. There was his wife, his son now to consider. But to be *kwai* again... He felt himself torn in two by the offer.

There was a whisper of cloth. Chen looked up past Karr. Wang Ti had come out from behind the curtains and was standing there, staring imploringly at him. Then, abruptly, she came round and threw herself down in front of Karr in a full *k'o t'ou*.

'Wang Ti! What are you doing?'

She lifted her head and glanced at Chen anxiously, then returned her forehead to the floor before the big man.

'My husband accepts your kind offer, *Shih* Karr. He will be honoured to work with you.'

Han Ch'in stood there silently in the darkened room, his back to the doorway. Outside the two assassins waited. He breathed deeply, calming himself, remembering what he'd been taught. The still man has advantages. He hears better. He has choice of action. The moving man is committed. His strength, his very movement can be used against him.

Let them come to you, then. Feign unawareness. But let your body be as the dragon's, alive, alert to every movement of the air behind your back.

Outside they hesitated. Then the first of them came through.

Han turned when the man was only an arm's length away, ducking low, sweeping his leg out, his left arm straight-punching upwards. As the man went down Han rolled backwards and flipped up onto his feet, facing the second assassin.

The dark, masked figure feinted, kicking to Han's left, making shapes with his hands in the air, each movement accompanied by a sharp hiss of expelled breath.

Han shadowed the assassin's movements, knowing he could not afford to do otherwise. He was alone now. Death awaited him if he made the smallest mistake. He had only winded the man on the floor, so time now was precious. He would have to dispense with the man before him, then deal finally with the other.

He saw his chance. The assassin had put his full weight on his right foot. It anchored him. Han feinted further to the right, then leapt, turning in the air and kicking high, aiming for the man's chin.

His foot brushed air. Then he was falling.

The assassin was on him in an instant, his forearm locked about Han's neck. Han cried out.

The lights flicked on at once. The two assassins backed away, bowing deeply, respectfully. Han turned over and sat up, gasping for breath. Shiao Shi-we was standing in the doorway, looking in at him, his expression hard to read.

'Again!' he barked finally. 'How many times, Han? Have you learned nothing from me?'

Han knelt and bowed to his instructor. Shi-we was right. He had been impatient.

'I am sorry, Master Shiao. I was worried about the second man.'

Shiao Shi-we made a small sound in his throat, then lifted his chin. Han Ch'in got to his feet at once.

'You are a good fighter, Han Ch'in. Your reflexes are as good as any man's. Your body knows how to move. How to kick and punch. How to block and fall and roll. You have real courage. A rare thing. Yet for all these qualities you lack one vital thing. You have not learned to think as your opponent thinks.'

Han bowed again, chastened.

'What then should I have done, Master Shiao? Should I have waited for him to attack?'

Shiao Shi-we was a small man, almost a head shorter than his seventeen-year-old pupil. His head was shaved and oiled and he was naked but for a small, dark red loincloth. His chest and forearms and legs were heavily muscled, yet as he crossed the room he moved with the grace of a dancer. He was sixty-five years old, but looked forty.

He stood in front of Han Ch'in, looking up at the T'ang's heir, but there was no deference in his posture. In this room Shiao Shi-we was as a father to Han Ch'in. Once, ten years before, he had put the young boy across his knee and spanked him for his impertinence. When Han Ch'in had gone before his father to complain, the T'ang had merely laughed, then growing stern, had ordered the punishment repeated, so that the lesson should be learned. Since that time Han Ch'in had known better than to argue with his tutor.

'Three things,' began Shi-we. 'Discipline, patience and control. Without them even a good fighter is certain to lose. With them...' the tutor lifted his head proudly, the muscles of his neck standing out like ridges of rock, '...the good becomes the supreme.'

There was a noise in the doorway. Without turning, Shiao Shi-we lifted a hand. 'Please wait there a moment, Yuan. I must finish talking to your brother.'

Li Yuan made a tiny bow to the instructor's back, amazed, as ever, that the old man could tell, without looking, who it was behind him. Each man has his own sounds, Shi-we once said. How he moves, who he is – these things can be distinguished as distinctively as the grain of a man's skin, the identifying pigmentation of the retina. Still yourself, listen, learn to tell the sound of your friend from that of your enemy, and such skills might one day save your life.

So it might be, but try as he had, Li Yuan had found he could not distinguish the sound of his brother from that of one of his servants. If it's a skill, he thought, it's one few men possess. Better to have a good man at one's back.

Li Yuan looked past Shiao Shi-we at his brother. Han Ch'in had his head lowered and there was a slight colour in his cheeks. What has Han done now? he wondered, knowing how impulsive his brother was. Has he 'died' again?

Master Shiao sniffed loudly, then pointed to Han's left. 'Position.'

Han moved at once, standing where he had been only a minute or so before, facing the assassin. Shiao Shi-we gave a slight nod then positioned himself in front of his pupil. 'Discipline,' he said, crouching down and rubbing at his thighs, warming himself up. 'Patience.' He straightened, then twisted at the waist to left and right, relaxing the muscles there. 'And control.'

Without warning, Shiao Shi-we launched himself at Han Ch'in.

Li Yuan gasped, startled by the abruptness of Shiao Shi-we's attack. But Han had moved back and away, and Shi-we's fist merely glanced the side of his face. Had it connected it would have broken his nose.

Han Ch'in moved quickly, breathing heavily, clearly shaken by the violence of the attack. Yet he made no complaint. Crouching, flexing his body, he prepared himself for the next attack, calming his breathing, repeating the triad in his mind. *Discipline. Patience. Control.*

The next assault was like nothing either boy had ever seen before. Shiao Shi-we ran at Han in a zig-zag, almost lunatic manner, his movements like those of an automaton. And as he ran a strange, unsettling scream came from his widely opened mouth.

Through half-lidded eyes Han Ch'in watched him come and, at the last moment, ducked and came up under the older man, tossing him into the air, then turned to face him again.

'Excellent!' Shiao Shi-we was on his feet, unharmed. He smiled momentarily, then grimaced as he threw himself at Han again.

So it went on, Shiao Shi-we attacking wildly, Han Ch'in defending, until, with a suddenness that was as surprising as the first attack, the old man backed off, bowing deeply.

'Good!' he said, looking at his pupil with pride. 'Now go and bathe. Young Yuan must have his hour.'

Han bowed and did as he was bid. Li Yuan turned, watching him go, then turned back, facing Master Shiao.

'You could have killed him,' he said softly, still shocked by what he had seen.

Shiao Shi-we looked away, more thoughtful than Li Yuan had ever seen him before. 'Yes,' he said finally. 'I could have, had he not fought so well.'

*

'Well, Chen, will you come to bed?'

Wang Ti pulled back the cover and patted the space beside her on the bed. Chen had been silent all day, angry with her for her intervention. She had understood and had gone about her business patiently, but now it was evening and Jyan was asleep. Now he would have to talk to her. She would not have him lie beside her still angry with her, his innermost thoughts unpurged.

'Well, husband?'

He turned, looking across at her in the faint light of the single lamp, then looked down, shaking his head.

So. She would have to be the one to talk.

'You're angry with me still?'

He did not look at her, merely nodded. His whole body was stiff and awkward, shaped by the words he was holding back. She sat up, unfastening her hair, letting the covers fall from her breasts.

'You would have said no.'

He looked at her mutely, looked away, then looked back again, his eyes drawn to her breasts, her shoulders. Meeting her eyes, he sighed and shrugged.

'You would have said no. And then you would have felt trapped. Bitter. With me. With Jyan. I would have had to watch your joy in us turn to sourness.'

He began to shake his head but she was insistent, her voice soft yet firm.

'It is so, Kao Chen. I know it is so. You think I could live with you this long and not know it?'

He looked at her uncomprehendingly.

'I knew. Understand? Knew you were kwai.'

Chen's eyes were wide. 'You knew? When? How?'

She patted the bed beside her. 'When I first met you. I knew at once. Even before my father told me.'

Chen crossed the room and sat beside her. 'Your father? He knew as well?'

'Oh, Chen. You think we didn't know immediately? One look at you was enough. You were like a bird let out of its cage. We knew from the first that you weren't born in these levels. And as for your papers...'

Chen looked down at her hand where it lay above the bedclothes and covered it with his own. 'And yet you married me. Why, if you knew?'

She hesitated, then took his other hand. 'You met Grandfather Ling?'

Chen nodded, remembering the wizened, grey-haired old man who had sat silently at the back of the room when he had negotiated for Wang Ti's hand. He recalled how the old man's eyes had followed his every movement.

'Yes. I remember Wang Ling. What of him?'

Wang Ti smiled. 'He was *kwai*. Like you. And, like you, he came up from the Net.'

Chen laughed, astonished. 'And you say your father knew?'

'He made... enquiries.'

Chen shook his head, astonished. 'Enquiries... And none of you minded? You, Wang Ti... you knew and yet you didn't mind what I was or where I'd come from?'

She drew him closer, her face only a hand's width from his own, her dark eyes looking deeply into his. 'You are a good man, Kao Chen. I knew that from the first moment I set eyes on you. But this last year I've seen you suffer, seen you put bit and bridle on, and my heart has bled for you.'

She shook her head, her teeth momentarily clenched between parted lips. 'No, Chen, the big man was right. You are not a warehouseman.'

He shivered, then, slowly, nodded to himself. 'Then it is as you said, Wang Ti. I will be *kwai* again.'

Wang Ti laughed softly, then drew Chen down beside her, drawing the sheet back to expose her nakedness. 'Ah, you foolish man. Don't you understand me yet? To me you have always been *kwai*.'

She reached down, freeing his penis from the folds of the cloth and taking it firmly in her hand. 'Here, give me your knife, I'll sheath it for you.'

The General leaned across the huge scale model of the *Tzu Chin Ch'eng*, the Purple Forbidden City, indicating the group of buildings gathered about the *Yu Hua Yuan*, the Imperial Gardens.

'We could close the *Shen Wu* Gate and the *Shun Ch'en* Gate and cut off the six Eastern palaces and the six Western palaces, here and here. That would make things easier.'

Shepherd came round him and looked at the two huge gates at the rear of the Imperial City for a moment, then nodded.

'Yes. But why stop at that? Why not seal the whole of that area off? That way we could concentrate on a much smaller area. In fact, why not seal off everything we're not going to use? Close the *Hung I Ko* and the *T'i Jen Ko*, too. Confine the lesser guests to the space between the Meridian Gate and the Hall of Supreme Harmony. Likewise, confine those special guests who will attend the second ceremony to the Inner City and the Imperial Gardens.'

Tolonen shook his head. 'Not possible, I'm afraid. Li Shai Tung has prepared a banquet for the lesser guests outside the Arrow Pavilion. He would lose face if he had to cancel that.'

Shepherd put his hand to his neck, rubbing away the tiredness. He had barely slept these last three days. And now this. He looked at the model, realizing once again how difficult Tolonen's task was. The *Ku Kung*, the Imperial Palace, was composed of almost nine thousand buildings and measured more than two *li* in length, one and a half in width. It covered fifteen hundred *mou* – almost two hundred and fifty acres in the old measure. Even if they sealed off everything he had suggested, it still meant policing over five hundred *mou*.

He looked up from the glass-covered model to the original. They had set the table up in the centre of the courtyard in front of the *Ta'i Ho Tien*, the Hall of Supreme Harmony. In less than twelve hours the whole of this huge open space would be packed with courtiers and guests, servants and Security. He turned, looking back towards the Gate of Supreme Harmony and, beyond it, the five white bridges crossing the Golden Water. Would something happen here today? Would their enemies succeed? Or could they stop them?

They had talked late into the night, he, Li Shai Tung and Tolonen, knowing that the thing they had found – the 'copy' of Klaus Ebert – signified something hugely important. Copies of living individuals – it was something the Seven had long feared would happen, ban or no, and whilst the Edict carried the strictest penalties for straying from its guidelines in respect of human genetic technology, there had been numerous cases over the years where scientific curiosity had overcome the fear of punishment. Now those harsh measures were vindicated. With such copies in the world who could feel safe in their own body? Who could be trusted?

It was only two days since Wyatt's execution and the shock of that still reverberated around the world. It might be that the Dispersionists planned to answer that. But it was more likely that they had set things in motion long before, hoping to maximize the impact of their scheme by striking when the whole of Chung Kuo was watching.

'The gods be thanked we found the thing in time,' Tolonen had said, showing the T'ang the holo of the copy Ebert. 'At least we know what we're looking for now.' But Shepherd had had his doubts. What if it was a blind? What if all of this were some huge diversionary tactic, designed to make them look elsewhere while the real attack took place? 'Would they waste two hundred million yuan on a decoy?' Tolonen had asked him, and he had answered yes. A thousand million. Two thousand. Whatever it took to make them look elsewhere. But the T'ang had agreed with his General. It was a fortunate accident, Ebert returning to his office when he did, and anyway, the thing was too good a likeness to throw away so casually. It was clear that they had meant to kill Ebert and then penetrate the inner sanctum of the Imperial City. There would be others; Li Shai Tung was certain of it. They would set up the gates and check each guest as he entered. And not only guests, but Family and Seven too. For the good of all.

'We'll see,' Shepherd had said, accepting his T'ang's final word. But he had been thinking, *And what if there are no further copies? What if they plan to strike some other way?*

Tolonen had been considering his suggestion about sealing off parts of the Imperial City; now he broke into his thoughts. 'Maybe you're right, Hal. It would be no great task to seal off the whole of the western side of the City, likewise this part here in the north-east. There's enough room here by the Southern Kitchens to take the overspill and it won't interfere with the banquet.'

Shepherd yawned, then laughed. 'Best do it quick, Knut, before we all nod off.'

The General stared at him a moment, then laughed. 'Yes. Of course. I'm sorry, Hal. Would you like something to pep you up? My adjutant could fetch you something.'

Shepherd shook his head. 'Thank you, but no. I don't believe in tablets. They bugger my system. No, I'll sleep when it's all over.'

'As you will.' The General hesitated, then reached out and took Shepherd's arm. 'Are you feeling real?'

Shepherd laughed. 'Real enough. Why's that?'

'The gates are ready. I wanted to test one of them. Will you come through with me?'

'Of course. Lead on.'

At the Gate of Heavenly Peace, Shepherd stopped and let his eyes stray upward. Only one li away the blank, pearled walls of City Asia began, climbing two li into the heavens like the sheer face of a huge glacier, surrounding the ancient capital on every side. This, he reminded himself, was the centre of it all – the very heart of Chung Kuo. Where it had all begun more than a century ago. These had been the first stacks to be built, constructed to his great-great-great grandfather, Amos's design. They towered over the old Imperial City. Yet, turning, looking back, he could not decide which was the greater. The new City was a magnificent achievement, yet did it have even a fragment of the grandeur, the sheer, breathtaking splendour of the Forbidden City?

Not the least part.

The gates had been set up in the space between the two Cities. Six lines of them, linked by a maze-like series of corridors, open to the air. It was a hasty, crude-looking arrangement. At various intersections between corridors watchtowers had been set up on stilts overhead, from which both manual and computer-controlled guns pointed downwards.

'They'll not like that,' Shepherd said, turning to Tolonen.

'No. I'm afraid they won't. But for once they'll have to put up with it.'

Shepherd shook his head sadly. It was bad. Particularly after the execution. It would give the impression that they were entering a new, more brutal era. What ought to be a day of celebration would, for many, take on far more ominous overtones.

But whose fault was that?

'You really think you'll catch some of these copies?'

The General smiled bleakly. 'I'm certain of it, Hal. You think I'm wrong, I know. Well, it's possible I am. Anything's possible. Which is why I've prepared for a hundred other unpleasant eventualities. An assault from the air. Bombs. Assassins amongst my own elite guards. Poison in the food. Snipers. Treachery in a hundred different guises. I've read my history. I know how many ways a king can be killed.'

Tolonen's granite face showed a momentary tiredness. 'I've done dreadful things to safeguard my T'ang, Hal. Awful, necessary things.'

Yes, Tolonen thought. *Like the killing of the fifteen men who designed these security gates. Fifteen more to add to the vast tally against my name. Good men, too. But their deaths were necessary. To safeguard the Seven. Because without the Seven...*

He shuddered and pushed the thought away, then began to walk towards the gates. Shepherd fell in beside him, silent now, deep in thought. As they approached the nearest of the gates the elite guards came to attention, shouldering their arms.

'Where's the duty officer?'

'Here, General.' The elite squad captain hurried up, then came to attention, bowing formally to both men. 'We're almost done, sir. Only another twenty or so to test.'

'Good. Then you'll show us to one of the Secure Rooms. I want to show the T'ang's chief advisor what we've prepared.'

The captain hesitated, about to say something, then bowed again. 'Of course, sir. Please, follow me.'

They went to one of the larger gates. Steps led up inside. Behind a curtain was a richly upholstered chair. Surrounding the chair was a whole array of the most up-to-date medical equipment.

'I'm impressed,' said Shepherd, looking about him and touching various instruments familiarly. 'It all seems very thorough.'

The General nodded to the medical technician who had hastily joined them and, without ceremony, began to strip off. 'I'll go first. Then you.'

Shepherd smiled. 'Of course.'

There was a slight hiss from behind the curtain, then the sound of a wheel being spun.

'Now we're sealed in. If I'm not who I claim to be – if I'm a fake – then this whole cabin will be filled with a highly toxic gas.'

Shepherd laughed. 'Then I'll pray you are who you say you are.'

Tolonen nodded, then dropped his trousers and stepped out of his webbed pants.

'You've some interesting scars, Knut.'

Tolonen looked down, then laughed. 'Ah, yes. Believe it or not I got that from a woman. A she-cat she was.' He smiled and met Shepherd's eyes. 'Ah, but that was long ago. Forty years now.'

He sat in the armchair and let himself be wired up. The technician busied himself about him, visibly nervous that he should be called upon to test the T'ang's General.

The first tests were simple body scans. Then he was fingerprinted, his retinal patterns checked and his genotype taken.

The General looked up at Shepherd calmly. 'If they're like the Ebert copy then these first few tests should catch them. But I'm taking no chances. Anyway, while we're testing for fakes, we can test for other things – psychological indoctrination and drugs.'

'It must have been hard for Klaus.'

'He took it very badly.'

Shepherd looked away momentarily. 'It must be disturbing to see yourself like that. Dead. Opened up like a sack of meat. Your own face white and cold.'

Tolonen said nothing for a moment, then nodded solemnly.

The technician had been waiting, listening to their talk. Now he pulled a large, dome-shaped machine down from above the General's head.

Tolonen explained. 'It's basically a HeadStim. But it's been rewired to monitor bodily responses. It flashes images at me – holograms of senior Family members – and monitors my pulse rate and heartbeat. Any abnormalities register on the telltale screen that side.'

He reached round the machine as the technician fastened it about his head, and tapped the tiny black screen there.

'It also provides a full brain-scan.'

Shepherd looked at it thoughtfully. 'As I said. Very thorough. If any more of these things exist, you ought to get them.'

The General made no answer. The test had begun. The technician glanced nervously at Shepherd, then busied himself again. Shepherd understood at once. If they found even one of these copies it would be neutralized immediately. That was good. But the unlucky technician who was in the secure room with it would be neutralized too.

'I shouldn't worry,' Shepherd said reassuringly. 'I doubt if any more of them exist.'

Outside, beyond the great walls of the City, the sun was rising over Pei Ching. The new day – the day of Han Ch'in's wedding – had begun.

Maria stood in the doorway, looking in at her husband. Josef Krenek was dressing, his back to her. She watched him pull the new silk *pau* about him and fasten it with the cord. Then, and only then, did he turn to her.

'What is it, Maria? Can't you see I'm getting ready?'

She had dressed an hour back and had been waiting ever since for him to wake and dress so that she might talk with him.

'It's your brother, Josef. I think he's ill. He hasn't eaten for days, and when I went to wake him there was no answer from his room. He's locked himself in and there's no reply, either from him or from Irina.'

Krenek groaned. His brother, Henryk, and his wife had arrived three days ago from Mars and were due to leave tomorrow, after the Wedding. All four were guests of the T'ang, with seats at table before the great Arrow Pavilion. But if Henryk was ill...

Krenek pushed past his wife irritably and strode purposefully down the corridor. Stopping before one of the doors, he hesitated, then knocked hard.

'Henryk! Are you all right?'

Almost at once the door slid open. His brother stood there, dressed, his midnight blue velvet *ma k'ua*, or ceremonial jacket, tightly buttoned, his dark hair combed back severely from his brow.

'Josef... What do you want?'

Krenek bowed slightly, acknowledging his elder brother's status. He had returned from Mars only three weeks ago, newly promoted to Senior Representative of the Colony.

'Maria was worried for you. She...'

Henryk Krenek smiled, returning to a lesser degree his brother's bow. His tall, regal-looking wife, Irina, had come across and now stood behind him. Henryk looked past his brother at his brother's wife.

'I'm sorry, Maria, but it was a secret. I have a gift for my young brother, you see. For being such a good host to us these last three days.'

Josef beamed with delight. 'A gift? It is you who honour *me*, brother.'

Henryk half turned, glancing at his wife, then turned back again. 'Perhaps you'd like to come in, Josef? Maria, you'll excuse us a moment?'

Maria bowed low. 'I've still much to do, Henryk. I'm sorry I disturbed you with my foolish fears.' Her cheeks red, she backed away, then turned and fled down the corridor.

Henryk watched her a moment, then turned and went inside, locking the door behind him.

'Well, brother...' he said, turning to face Josef. And even as he said the words he saw Irina come up behind the man and pull the cord tight about his neck, dragging him down with a strange, inhuman strength.

★

Servants made their k'o t'ou as Han Ch'in entered the Chien Ching Kung, the Palace of Heavenly Purity. Rows of tables had been set up the length and breadth of the great hall. Thousands filled the space between the pillars. Cloths of imperial yellow covered every table and on each was piled a great heap of wedding gifts.

Han Ch'in looked about him, then ventured into the dimness of the hall. At once two of the servants hastened to accompany the prince, one going before him, the other just behind, each carrying a simple oil lantern on a long pole. It was a tradition that these halls remained unlit by modern power sources: a tradition no one sought to change.

Han Ch'in strode about, examining things, then turned, his face and shoulders lit from above, his dark eyes shining wetly. His shadows stretched away from him on either side, like ghostly dancers, dark and long and thin, flickering in the uneven light. 'Yuan! Come! Look at this!'

Li Yuan had paused in the tall doorway, staring up at the richly decorated ceiling. This was his first visit to the Imperial City and he was astonished by its sheer opulence. Their own palaces were so small by comparison, so mean, despite their luxury. This was grandeur on an unimaginable scale. Was beauty almost to excess. He sighed and shook his head. Beauty, yes, and yet this beauty had its darker side. He knew his history: had learned how the Ch'ing – the Manchus – who ruled from here for two centuries and more, had fallen, weighed down by their own venality, pride and ignorance. This palace – indeed, this city of palaces – had been built on suffering. On injustice and exploitation.

The history of Chung Kuo – it was a succession of dreams and disappointments, vast cycles of grandeur followed by decadence. It was as if a great wheel turned through Time itself, ineluctable, raising men up, then hurling them down, to be crushed, together with their dreams of peace or further conquest. So it had been, for three thousand years and more. But it was to end such excess that the City had been built. To end the great wheel's brutal turn and bring about the dream of ten thousand peaceful years.

But was the great wheel turning once again, imperceptible beneath the ice? Or had it already come full circle? Were they the new Ch'ing, destined in their turn to fall?

'Yuan!' Han stood there beside one of the tables, looking back at him. 'Stop daydreaming and come here! Look at this!'

Li Yuan looked across, then, smiling, went over to him, a servant lighting his way.

Han Ch'in handed him the model of the horse. 'It's beautiful, isn't it? All the gifts from the more important guests have been put on display at this end. The horse is from the Pei family.'

Li Yuan turned it in his hands then handed it back. It was solid gold. 'It's very heavy, isn't it?'

Han laughed. 'Not as heavy as the silver phoenix the House of Representatives has sent as its gift. You should see it! It's enormous! It took eight men to carry it in here!'

Li Yuan looked around him, staring into the shadows on every side. The tables seemed to stretch away forever, each piled with a small fortune of wedding gifts. 'There's no end to it, is there?'

Han shook his head, a strange expression in his eyes. 'No.' He laughed uneasily. 'It's astonishing. There are more than eight million items. Did you know that, Yuan? They've been cataloguing them for weeks now. And still more are arriving all the time. The secretarial department are working all hours just sending out letters to thank people. In fact, it's got so bad they've had to take on an extra ten thousand men in the department!'

Han was silent a moment, looking out into the shadowed body of the hall, the torchlight flickering in his dark hair. Then he turned, looking directly at Yuan. 'You know, I was thinking, *ti ti*...'

Li Yuan smiled at the familiar term. 'Young brother', it meant. Yet between them it was like a special name. A term of love.

'You, thinking?'

Han Ch'in smiled, then looked away again, a more thoughtful expression on his face than usual. 'Look at it all. It fills this hall and five others. Fills them to overflowing. And yet if I were to spend from now until the end of my days simply looking at these things, picking them up and touching them...' He shook his head, then looked down. 'It seems such a waste, somehow. I'd never get to look at half of it, would I?'

He was silent a moment, then put the horse back. 'There are so many things here.'

Li Yuan studied his brother a moment. *So it affects you too, this place. You*

*look about you and you think, how like the Ai Hsin Chiao Lo – the Manchu – we are,
and yet how different. But then you ask, in what way different? And you worry, lest
your excesses be like theirs.* He smiled, a faint shiver running down his spine. *Oh,
Han Ch'in, how I love you for that part of you that worries. That part of you that
would be a good T'ang – that feels its responsibilities so sharply. Don't change, dear elder
brother. Don't ever forget the worries that plague you, for they are you – are all that's
truly good in you.*

Han Ch'in had moved on. Now he was studying one of the big tapestries
that were hung against the side wall. Li Yuan came and stood beside him. For
a moment they were both silent, looking up through the uneven, wavering
lamplight at the brightly coloured landscape, then Han knelt and put his
arm about Yuan's shoulders.

'You know, Yuan, there are times when I wish I wasn't heir.' His voice was
a whisper now. 'Sometimes all I want is to give it all away and be normal. Do
you understand?'

Li Yuan nodded. 'I understand well enough. You are like all men, Han.
You want most that which you cannot have.'

Han was quiet a moment, then he shook his head. 'No. You don't understand. I want it because I want it. Not because I can't have it.'

'And Fei Yen? What about Fei Yen? Would you give her up? Would you give
up your horse? Your fine clothes? The palaces outside the City? You would
really give up all of that?'

Han stared straight ahead, his face set. 'Yes. Sometimes I think I would.'

Li Yuan turned, looking into his brother's face. 'And sometimes I think
you're mad, elder brother. The world's too complex. It would not be so
simple for you. Anyway, no man ever gets what he truly wants.'

Han turned his head and looked at him closely. 'And what do you want,
ti ti?'

Li Yuan looked down, a slight colour in his cheeks. 'We ought to be going.
Father will be looking for us.'

Han Ch'in stood, then watched Li Yuan move back between the tables
towards the great doorway, the servant following with his lantern. *No, he
thought, you don't understand me at all, little brother. For once you don't see the drift
of my words.*

The thought had grown in him this last year. At first it had been a fancy
– something to amuse himself with. But now, today, it seemed quite clear to

him. He would refuse it. Would stand down. Would kneel before his younger brother.

Why not? he thought. *Why does it have to be me?*

Li Yuan, then. Han smiled and nodded to himself. Yes. So it would be. Li Yuan would be T'ang, not Li Han Ch'in. And he would be a great T'ang. Perhaps the greatest of all. And he, Li Han Ch'in, would be proud of him. Yes. So it would be. So he would insist it was.

Maria Krenek bowed abjectly, conscious that her husband, Josef, had already moved on. 'I am deeply sorry, Madam Yu. My husband is not himself today. I am certain he meant nothing by it.'

Madam Yu raised her fan stiffly, her face dark with fury, dismissing the smaller woman. She turned to the two men at her side.

'How *dare* he stare through me like that, as if he didn't know me! I'll see that haughty bastard barred from decent company! That'll take him down a few levels! Now his brother is Representative for Mars he thinks he can snub who he likes. Well! We'll see, eh?'

Maria backed away, appalled by what she had heard. Madam Yu was not a woman to make an enemy of. She had entry to the Minor Families. Her gatherings were an essential part of life in the Above – and she herself the means by which one man came to meet another to their mutual benefit. She had destroyed bigger men than Josef Krenek, and now she would destroy him.

'Josef!' she said, softly but urgently, catching up with her husband and taking his arm. 'What were you thinking? Go back and kneel before her. For all our sakes, please, go and kneel to her. Say you're sorry. Please, Josef!'

He looked down at her hand on his arm, then across to his brother and his wife. Then, astonishingly, he threw her arm off.

'Go home, Maria. Now! This moment!'

Her mouth gaped. Then, blushing deeply, humiliated beyond anything she had ever known before, Maria turned and ran.

Nocenzi's voice sounded urgently in the General's head. 'Knut! I've got something!'

The General was standing beside the back entrance to one of the Secure Rooms. They had just unsealed it and brought out the thing that had tried to get through their screen. Like the others it was disturbingly human – better than the Ebert copy. Different. Far more complex. As if the Ebert copy had been an attempt to throw them off the trail.

'What is it, Vittorio?'

'I've checked the incomings at Nanking against the guest list. And guess what?'

'They're coming in from Mars.'

'That's right.'

'All of them?'

They had caught eight of the copies so far. Eight! It frightened him to think what might have happened if they had not discovered the fake Ebert. But unlike the 'Ebert' these were armed. They were walking arsenals, their weaponry concealed inside their flesh. Just two of them could have caused havoc if they had got through. But eight...

Nocenzi hesitated, getting confirmation, then, 'Every one of them so far.'

Tolonen knelt over the dead thing, then drew his knife and cut the silks open, revealing its torso. This one was a young woman of seventeen, the daughter of a leading businessman from the Brache settlement. He was waiting inside the Forbidden City, unaware that his daughter had been murdered months ago and replaced by this thing. Tolonen shuddered, trying not to let his emotions cloud his thinking. This was a bad day. A very bad day. But it could have been far worse.

He hesitated, then cut into one of the breasts. Blood welled and ran down the smooth flank of the thing. Tolonen steeled himself and cut again, pulling the flesh apart to reveal the hard, protective case beneath. Yes, it was like the other ones. They all had this protective casing over their essential organs and beneath the facial flesh. As if whoever had made them had designed them to withstand heavy fire: to last long enough to do maximum damage.

'Listen, Vittorio. I want you to get files on all the Mars Colonists we haven't checked yet and get an elite squad to pick them out before they get to the gates. I want one of them alive, understand?'

Alive... His flesh crawled. *Functional, I mean. These things were never alive. Not in any real way.*

He got up, signalling to the technicians to take the thing away.

'And, Vittorio. Warn your men these things are dangerous. Perhaps the most dangerous thing they've ever had to face.'

As soon as he stepped out into the space between the Cities, Josef Krenek knew something was wrong. Guests were queuing to pass through what seemed like checkpoints. Checkpoints which shouldn't have been there. Beside him Henryk and Irina were unaware that anything was amiss. But then they wouldn't be: their programming was far simpler than his own.

He looked about him, trying to gauge the situation. Three-man elite squads were moving slowly down the lines of people, checking IDs. Further off, above what seemed like some kind of rat run, they had set up guard towers.

They know we're here, he thought at once. *Those gates are screens.*

Casually he drew Henryk and Irina back, away from the queue, as if they had left something in the reception hall. Then, in an urgent whisper, he told them what he thought was happening.

'What shall we do?' Henryk's cold, clear eyes searched Josef's for an answer. 'We've no instructions for this.'

Josef answered him immediately. 'I want you to go out there, Henryk. I want you to go up to one of those squads and ask them why you have to queue. I want you to find out what they're looking for. Okay?'

'What if they're looking for me? What if they try to arrest me?'

Josef smiled coldly. 'Then you'll bring them over here.'

He watched Henryk walk out and greet them and saw at once how the soldiers reacted. He heard their shouted questions, then saw Henryk turn and point back to where he stood beside Irina.

Ah, well, the part of him that was DeVore thought, *it could have worked. Could have worked beautifully. Imagine it! The twelve of them climbing the marble steps, death at their fingertips, the Families falling like leaves before them!*

He smiled and turned to Irina. 'Do nothing until I say. I'm going to try to get through that lot.' He indicated the rat run of screens and corridors and guard-towers. 'But not directly. With any luck they'll take me through. If not...'

Henryk came up and stood before them, one of the elite Security guards holding his arm loosely. Other squads were hurrying from elsewhere, heading towards them.

'What seems to be the problem, Captain?' Josef said, facing the officer calmly.

'For you, sir, nothing. But I'm afraid your brother and his wife must accompany me. I've orders to detain all Mars Colonists.'

Josef hid his surprise. *Why not me?* he wondered. Then he understood. *They've seen the Mars connection. But I wasn't brought in that way. I was here already. The first to come. The lynchpin of the scheme.*

'Oh, dear,' he said, looking at Henryk, concerned. 'Still, I'm sure it's all a misunderstanding, elder brother. We had best do as these men say, yes? Until we can sort things out.'

The captain shook his head. 'I'm sorry, sir, but my orders are to take Mars Colonists only.'

'But surely, Captain.' For a moment he was Josef Krenek at his most unctuous, as if persuading a client to buy a new product range. 'You must allow me to accompany my elder brother and his wife. There are laws about unjust detention and the right of representation. Or have they been repealed?'

The captain hesitated, listening to orders in his head, then gave a curt nod. 'I'm told you can come along, *Shih* Krenek. But, please, don't interfere. This is an important matter. I'm certain we can settle it quite quickly.'

Krenek smiled and followed them silently. *Yes, I'm certain we can. But not here. Not yet.*

The General looked through the one-way glass at the men and women crowded into the small room.

'Well?' he asked. 'Is that all of the Colonists?'

Nocenzi nodded. 'Every last one. Sixty-two in all.'

Tolonen stroked his chin thoughtfully, then turned and looked directly at his Major. 'Can we set up a gate here? I want to trace any remaining copy-humans. But I don't want them terminated. Understand?'

Nocenzi nodded. 'My men are working on it already.'

'Good.' His first instinct had been to gas all the copies, but they needed one in functional order. To trace it back. To find out where these things came from and get to the men behind them.

'What percentage of the Colonists have proved to be these things?'

Nocenzi looked at his lieutenant, who bowed and answered for him.

'Nine from three hundred and eighteen. So just under three per cent.'

Tolonen looked back into the room. So if the percentage was constant that meant there was at least one, maybe two of the things in there. But how did you tell? They were indistinguishable to the naked eye.

'At least they're not booby-trapped,' Nocenzi said, coming closer and standing beside him at the glass. 'Think of the damage they could have done if they had been. If I'd built them I'd have made them tamper-proof. More than that, I'd have made them a bit less docile. Not one of them queried going into the secure rooms. It's as if they weren't programmed for it. Yet they must have had pretty complex programming for them to keep up appearances, let alone come here. They must have had a plan of some kind.'

Tolonen started, then turned to face his Major. 'Of course! Why didn't I see it before?' He laughed shortly, then shivered. 'Don't you see, Vittorio? Twelve of them. One of them the lynchpin, the strategist, holding it all in his head, the others with the bare outlines of what they have to do, but no sense of the larger strategy.'

Nocenzi understood at once. 'An elite attack squad. Like our own Security squads. Functioning in the same way.'

'Yes!' Tolonen said, elated. 'That explains why they were so docile. They only needed a certain amount of programming. They were just following orders. But one of them – one of the "people" in that room – is the leader. The thinker.'

DeVore. It all led back to DeVore. His hand behind all of this. His thinking. His elite training.

'There'll be three of them, I warrant you. Two soldiers and a strategist. It's the last I want. The leader. The others will know nothing. But that one...'

But even as he said the words he saw it. Saw the two of them meet in the centre of the room and touch and spark, blue veins of electric current forming in the air about them.

'Down!' he yelled, throwing himself to the floor as the room beyond the mirror filled with blinding light.

And then the ceiling fell on them.

Krenek knelt and bowed his head, his empty hands placed palms down on his thighs, fingers pointed inward, his whole stance mimicking the tens of thousands surrounding him. Then he straightened, studying the group of people gathered at the top of the steps directly in front of the Hall of Supreme Harmony. Yin Tsu and his family were to the left, Li Shai Tung and his to the right. Beneath them, on the steps themselves, the seven New Confucian officials bowed and chanted the ancient, ceremonial words.

He looked right, then left, then bowed his head again, as others did surrounding him. Guards were everywhere, armed and watchful. GenSyn many of them, no doubt. Unquestioning, obedient creatures. Reliable. Predictable.

Krenek smiled. *So different from me*, he thought. *They made me better than that. More devious. More human.*

But there was still a problem. He was too far back. Had even two of the others been here it might still have worked. But now?

He looked about him, calculating distances, gauging where they were weak, where strong, running high-probability scenarios through his head until he saw it clearly. Then, and only then, did he establish his plan. *I'll have fifteen seconds. Eighteen at most. I can make it halfway there by then. They'll protect the T'ang and the T'ang's sons. Or try to. But they'll also try to protect Yin Tsu and his daughter Fei Yen. That will split their attention.*

Yes, but they'd expect him to try to take the T'ang. That's where they would concentrate their defences. Again he smiled, the DeVore part of him remembering his elite training. He could see how they'd do it, forming a screen of bodies in front of him, two guards dragging him back, making the smallest possible target of him. And if seriously threatened they'd open fire, killing anything that came at them, innocent or otherwise.

But he would not attack the T'ang. Or Han Ch'in. He'd strike where they least expected. Li Yuan would be his target. As he'd always been.

DeVore's words rang clearly in his head. 'Kill the brain and the beast will fall. Li Shai Tung is old, Han Ch'in incompetent. Only Li Yuan, the youngest, is a threat to us. Get Han Ch'in if you can. Kill the T'ang if you must. But make sure Li Yuan is dead. With him gone the House of Li will not last long.'

He waited, knowing the time was fast approaching. Any moment now the saffron-robed officials would turn, facing them, and the vast crowd would rise as one to roar their approval of the marriage. It was then that he'd move forward, using their packed bodies as a screen. He would have five seconds, and then they would kneel again.

Yes, he thought, visualizing it clearly now. He could see himself running, fire blazing from his ruined hands. Could smell the crowd's blind panic, hear the ear-shattering stutter of the crossfire. And then, before his eyes closed finally, he would see the T'ang's son sprawled out on the marble, face down, blood streaming from a dozen separate wounds.

Yes. Seconds from now.

There was a sudden lapse in the sing-song incantation. As one the officials turned and faced the crowd. As one the vast crowd rose to its feet.

He made to move forward and felt himself jarred to a halt, then lifted from his feet. Two great hands tore at his chest, two hugely muscled arms pinned his own arms to his sides, slowly crushing him.

'Going somewhere, Mister Krenek?'

Karr threw down the lifeless carcass of the thing, then came to attention before Tolonen.

'I don't know what happened, sir. One moment it was fine. The next it was like this.'

Tolonen got up unsteadily from his chair and came over to where the thing lay. His chest and arm had been strapped tightly and, despite the pain-killing drugs, he was finding it difficult to breathe easily. He had cracked two ribs and dislocated his shoulder. Otherwise he'd been very lucky. Luckier than Nocenzi. The Major was even now in intensive care, fighting for his life.

Now, cleaned up and in new dress uniform, the empty left sleeve pinned loosely to the tunic, Tolonen was back in charge. Looking at the copy, he felt all his anger rise to the surface again.

'Who let this through? Who authorized the closure of the gates?'

Karr lowered his head slightly. 'It was Marshal Kirov, sir. He assumed the explosion in the room killed the last of the copies. It was getting late, and there were still thousands of guests to be processed...'

'Damn it!' Tolonen's chest rose and fell sharply and a flicker of pain crossed his face. How could Kirov be so foolish? How could he risk the T'ang's life so idiotically? So a few thousand guests were inconvenienced – what was that beside the survival of a T'ang?

Kirov was nominally his superior. He had been elected Marshal by the Council of Generals only six months back and in the emergency had been right to step in and take command, but what he had done was inexcusable.

Tolonen shuddered. 'Thank you, Karr. I'll deal with things from here.'

He watched the big man go, aware that, on his own initiative, Karr had probably saved the T'ang. He alone had thought to get the copy of the tape showing what had happened in the room. He alone had identified from the files the two who had 'joined' to such devastating effect. Then he alone had traced the brother, Josef Krenek, understanding what he was and what he planned.

Thank the gods, Tolonen thought. *This time we've beaten them.*

Tolonen lifted the dead thing's face with the toe of his boot, then let it fall again. A perfect likeness, this one. The best of them all, perhaps. It was a pity. Now they would never know.

He turned from the body and signalled to his adjutant. At once the young man came across and helped him back to his chair.

'Tell Major Kroger to take over,' he said, putting the chair into gear. 'I must see Li Shai Tung at once.'

It was evening. The sun's last rays had climbed the eastern wall and left the *Yu Hua Yuan*, transforming the garden of the Imperial City into a huge, square dish of shadows. Brightly coloured paper lanterns lit the bamboo grove and hung from lines above the lotus-strewn pools and in the eaves of the tea houses. Caged birds sang their sweet, drug-induced songs in the gnarled and ancient branches of the junipers. Below, servants went amongst the guests with wine and cordials and trays of delicacies, while *shao lin* guards stood back against the walls and amongst the rocks like ghosts.

Li Yuan, looking down on it all from the height of the marble terrace, smiled. All ceremony was done with now. Below him, to his right, the wedding party moved among the guests informally, Han Ch'in talking excitedly, Fei Yen silent, demurely bowing at his side.

He saw his father laugh and reach out to pick a single white blossom from Han's dark hair, then turn to whisper something to his uncle, Li Yun-Ti. There was a gay, almost light-hearted atmosphere to things; a feeling of relief that things had turned out as they had. Yet only an hour earlier things had been very different. Li Yuan had been there at his father's interview with the General.

He had never seen the General so angry. It had taken all his father's skill to calm Tolonen down and persuade him not to confront Kirov himself. But he had seen how shaken his father was to have been proved so conclusively right about the 'copies', how outraged at Kirov's stupidity. His face had been rigidly controlled as he had faced his General.

'I ask you to do nothing, Knut. Leave this to me. Kirov is Wei Feng's man. I shall speak with Wei Feng at once.'

He had been as good as his word. Yuan leaned out and looked down. Tolonen sat there now in his chair, directly below him, subdued, talking to his fellow Generals. Kirov was not amongst them.

Wei Feng, T'ang of East Asia, had been distraught. The thought that his General had almost cost the lives of a fellow T'ang and his family was more than he could bear. He had turned angrily on Kirov and torn the chi ling patch, symbol of the Marshal's status as a military officer of the first rank, from his chest, before taking the ceremonial dagger from Kirov's belt and throwing it down.

'You are nothing,' he had said to the now prostrate Marshal, tears of anger in his eyes. 'And your family is nothing. You have shamed me, Kirov. Now go. Get out of my sight.'

News had come only minutes later that Kirov had committed suicide; his son, a Major under his command, seconding him before he too had killed himself.

Han Ch'in, meanwhile, knew nothing of these things. No shadows were to fall upon his nuptial bed.

'Let them be innocent of this,' his father had said, taking Li Yuan's arm as they made their way back to the Yu Hua Yuan. 'For if the seed is strong it will take root and grow a son.'

A son... Yuan looked back at them. They were closer – almost below where he stood. He could see them clearly now. Fei Yen was breathtaking. Her dark hair had been plaited with golden threads and bows and tiny orchids, then curled into a tight bun on the top of her head, revealing a pale gold, swan-like neck. She was so delicate. Her ears, her nose, the lines of her cheekbones; all these were exquisite. And yet there was fire in her bright, hazel eyes, strength in her chin and mouth. She stood there at Han's side in an attitude of obedience, yet she seemed to wear the cloth of crimson and gold as if born to it. Though her head was tilted forward in the ritual stance of passive acceptance, there was a power to her still form that contradicted it. This bird, this flying swallow, was a proud one. She would need her wings clipped before she settled.

He looked from Fei Yen to his brother, seeing how flushed Han was. How his eyes would take small sips of her; each time surprised by her, each time astonished she was his. In this, as in so many things, Han was his junior. So much surprised him. So much evaded his grasp. 'It's easy for you, ti Yuan,' he had once said. 'You were born old. It all comes new to me.'

It would be an interesting match, he thought. A love match. The strongest kind of power and the hardest to control. She would be Fire to his Earth, Earth to his Fire.

Li Yuan laughed, then turned and went down quickly, his hard-soled ceremonial shoes clattering on the wooden slats, his long-sleeved silks billowing out behind him as he ran. Down, down, and straight into the arms of his cousin, Pei Chao Yang.

Chao Yang, eldest son and heir to the Pei family, one of the Twenty-Nine, the Minor Families, was standing at the edge of the decorative rock pile, beside the pavilion. His father, Pei Ro-hen, who stood nearby, was a bondsman of Li Shai Tung and a childhood friend of the T'ang. Almost fifty years ago they had shared a tutor.

'Here, Yuan! Slow down, boy!'

Chao Yang held onto Li Yuan's arm a moment, getting down onto his haunches and smiling good-naturedly at him, teasing him.

'What is it, little Yuan? Is your bladder troubling you again? Or has one of the little maids made you a promise?'

He winked and let Li Yuan go, watching him run off down the narrow, tree-lined path and through the small gate that led down to the Lodge of Nature-Nourishment. Then, realizing the newly-weds were almost on him, he straightened up, turning towards them.

Chao Yang was a tall, handsome man in his mid-thirties, the product of his father's first marriage. Easy-going, intelligent and with a reputation for knowing how to enliven a dull occasion, he was welcomed in all the palaces and had had Above tongues wagging many times with his reputed intrigues. His own wives, three in number, stood behind him now as he was introduced to the newly-weds. With smiles and bows he summoned each forward in turn, his senior wife, Ye Chun, first to be presented. That duty done, he was free to make less formal conversation.

'It's good to see you again, Chao Yang,' said Han Ch'in, shaking his hands vigorously. 'You should come visit us once we've settled in. I hear you like to ride.'

Chao Yang bowed deeply. 'I am honoured, Li Han Ch'in. I'd like to ride with you.' Then, leaning closer, he lowered his voice. 'Tonight, however, you ride alone, neh?'

Han Ch'in roared with laughter. 'Trust you, Chao Yang! You would lower the tone at a funeral.'

Chao Yang laughed. 'That depends on what was being buried, neh, my young friend?'

He saw Fei Yen lower her eyes to hide her amusement and smiled inwardly as he bowed to her. But as he straightened he experienced a slight giddiness and had to take a step backward, steadying himself. He had been feeling strange all day. Earlier, dressing himself, he had reached out to take a hair-brush from the table next to him, but his hand had closed on nothing. He had frowned and turned his head away, surprised, but when he had looked again, he had seen that there really was nothing on the table. He had imag-ined the brush. At the time he had shaken his head and laughed, in self-mockery, but he had been disturbed as well as amused.

Chao Yang bowed once more to the couple then watched them move away, conscious of Han Ch'in's nervousness, of Fei Yen's beauty. The latter stirred him greatly – he could taste her perfume on his tongue, imagine the olive pallor of her flesh beneath the gold and crimson cloth. Again he smiled. No. Best not even think what he was thinking, lest in wine such thoughts betrayed him.

Han had stopped a few paces on. For a moment Chao Yang studied the side of his face in the lantern light, noticing how similar the shapes of Han's ear, chin and neck were to those of his wife, Ye Chun. Then some-thing peculiar began to happen. Slowly the flesh about the ear began to flow, the ear itself to melt and change, the skin shrivelling up like a heated film of plastic, curling back to reveal, beneath, a hard, silvered thing of wires and metal.

Chao Yang staggered back, horrified.

'Han Ch'in...' he gasped, his voice a whisper. 'Han Ch'in!'

But it wasn't Han Ch'in.

Chao Yang cried out, his senses tormented by the smell of burning plastic, the odour of machine oils and heated wiring. For the briefest moment he hesitated, appalled by what he saw, then he lurched forward and threw himself at the thing, grasping it from behind, tugging hard at the place where the false flesh had peeled back. He faltered momentarily as Fei Yen leapt at him, clawing at his eyes, but he kicked out at her brutally, maintaining his grip on the machine, dragging it down, his knee in its back. Then something gave and he was rewarded with the sweet burning smell of mechanical malfunction.

The thing gave a single, oddly human cry. Then nothing.

Now, as it lay in his arms, it felt strangely soft, curiously warm. Such a perfect illusion. No wonder it had fooled everyone.

He let the thing slide from him and looked about, seeing the expression of horror on the faces surrounding him. So they had seen it too. He smiled reassurance but the oddness, that strange feeling of forgetfulness, was returning to him. He tried to smile but a curious warmth budded, then blossomed in his skull.

Pei Chao Yang knelt there a moment longer, his eyes glazed, then fell forward onto his face, dead.

Tolonen had moved away, towards the steps, when it began. The first scream made him turn the chair, his heart pounding, and look back to where the sound had come from, his view obscured by trees and bushes. Then he was up out of the chair and running, ignoring the pain in his side, the life-link stuttering, faltering in his head. The screams and shouting had risen to a crescendo now. *Shao lin* were running from every side, their swords drawn and raised, looking about them urgently. With one arm Tolonen pushed through the crowd, grimacing against the pain in his chest and shoulder each time someone banged against him.

Abruptly, the life-link cut out. He tapped the connection in his head, appalled, then stumbled on, his mind in turmoil. What had happened? What in the gods' names had happened? His heart raced painfully in his chest. Let it all be a mistake, he pleaded silently, pushing through the last few people at the front. Let it all be a malfunction in the relay. But he knew it wasn't.

He looked around him, wide-eyed, trying to take in what had happened. Fei Yen lay off to one side, clutching her side and gasping, in extreme pain, one of her maids tending to her. A few paces from her lay Han Ch'in.

'Medics!' Tolonen yelled, horrified by the sight of Han lying there so life-lessly. 'In the gods' names get some medics here! Now!'

Almost at once, two uniformed men appeared and knelt either side of Han Ch'in. One ripped Han's tunic open and began to press down urgently on his chest with both hands while the other felt for a pulse.

Tolonen stood over them, his despair almost tearing him apart. He had seen enough dead men to know how hopeless things were. Han lay there in an unnatural pose, his spine snapped, his neck broken.

After a moment one of them looked up, his face ashen.

'The Lord Han is dead, General. There is nothing we can do for him.'

Tolonen shuddered violently. 'Get a life preservation unit here. Now! I want him taken to the special unit. The T'ang's own surgeons will see to him at once!'

He turned and looked down at the other body, knowing at once who it was. *Gods!* he thought, pained by the sight of his godson, Pei Chao Yang. *Is there no end to this?* He looked about him anxiously, searching the faces of the onlookers.

'Who did this? Who saw what happened?'

There was a babble of contesting voices. Then one came clear to him. Fei Yen's. 'It was Chao Yang,' she said, struggling to get the words out. 'Chao Yang was the killer.'

Tolonen whirled about, confused. Pei Chao Yang! No! It couldn't be! It was impossible!

Or was it?

Quickly he summoned two of the *shao lin* and had them turn Chao Yang over. Then he took a knife from one of them and knelt over the body, slitting open Chao Yang's tunic. For a second or two he hesitated, then he plunged the knife into the chest and drew it to left and right.

His knife met only flesh and bone. Blood welled out over his hands. He dropped the knife, horrified, then looked across at Fei Yen.

'You're certain?'

She lowered her head. 'I am.'

There was a commotion just behind her as the crowd parted. Li Shai Tung stood there, his horror-filled eyes taking in the scene. Those near to him fell back slowly, their heads bowed.

'*Chieh Hsia*,' Tolonen began, getting up. 'I beg you to return to your place of safety. We don't know...'

The T'ang raised a hand to silence him.

'He's dead?'

Li Shai Tung's face was awful to see. He had lifted his chin in that familiar way he had when giving orders, but now he was barely in command, even of himself. A faint tremor in the muscles at his neck betrayed the inner struggle. His lips were pinched with pain, and his eyes...

Tolonen shuddered and looked down. 'I am afraid so, *Chieh Hsia*.'

'And the killer?'

The General swallowed. 'I don't know, *Chieh Hsia*. It seems...'

Fei Yen interrupted him. 'It was... Pei Chao Yang.'

The T'ang's mouth opened slightly and he nodded.

'Ah... I see.' He made to say something more, then seemed to forget.

Tolonen looked up again. He could hardly bear to meet the T'ang's eyes. For the first time in his life he knew he had let his master down. He knelt, his head bowed low, and drew his ceremonial dagger, offering its handle to the T'ang in a gesture that said quite clearly, My life is yours.

There was silence for a moment, then the T'ang came forward and put his hand on Tolonen's shoulder. 'Stand up, Knut. Please, stand up.'

There was anguish in Li Shai Tung's voice, a deep pain that cut right through Tolonen and made him tremble. He had caused this pain. His failure had caused it. He stood slowly, feeling his years, his head still bowed, the dagger still offered.

'Put it away, old friend. Put it away.'

He met the T'ang's eyes again. Yes, there was grief there – an awful, heavy grief. But behind it was something else. An acceptance of events. As if Li Shai Tung had expected this. As if he had gambled and lost, knowing all the while that he might lose.

'The fault is mine,' Li Shai Tung said, anticipating the General. 'I knew the risks.' He shivered, then looked down. 'There has been death enough today. And I need you, Knut. I need your knowledge, your ability, your fierce loyalty to me.'

He was silent a moment, struggling to keep control, then he looked up again, meeting Tolonen's eyes. 'After all, Knut, I have another son. He'll need you, too.'

More medics came, wheeling a trolley. General and T'ang stood there a moment in silence, watching as they placed Han Ch'in in the unit and sealed the lid. Both knew the futility of the gesture. Nothing would bring Han back now. When Li Shai Tung turned to face Tolonen again, his fists were clenched at his sides. His face was a mask of pain and patience.

'Find out who did this. Find out *how* they did it. Then come to me. Do not act without my order, Knut. Do not take it on yourself to avenge me.' He shivered, watching the medics wheel the trolley past. 'Han must not die in vain. His death must mean something.'

Tolonen saw that the T'ang could say no more. He was at his limit now. His face showed signs of crumbling and there was a fierce movement about the eyes and beneath the mouth that revealed the true depths of what he was feeling. He made a brief, dismissive gesture of his hand, then turned away.

The General sheathed his dagger and turned to face the guests. Already the news of Han Ch'in's death would be spreading through the levels of Chung Kuo. And somewhere, he was certain, a group of men would be celebrating: smiling cruelly and raising their glasses to each other.

Somewhere... Tolonen shuddered, grief giving way to anger in him. He would find the bastards. Find them and kill them. Every last one of them.

CHAPTER 33

KIM'S GAME

They had sedated the boy and moved him to the observation centre on the island of Corsica, three thousand *li* distant. There they cleaned and inoculated him, and put him in a cell.

It was a bare, unfurnished cell, a cube fifteen *ch'i* to a side. The ceiling was lost in the darkness overhead and there was no door, though a small window high up in one of the smooth, dark walls suggested that there was at least a way outside. From the ceiling and window came a faint glow, barely enough to warrant the name of light, while from the centre of the ceiling hung a six-eyed camera on a long, flexible neck.

The boy huddled against the wall beneath the window, staring up at the camera, his face both curious and hostile. He did not move, for when he did the camera would turn to follow him, like something living, two of its eyes focused constantly on him. He knew this because he had experimented with it; just as he had tried to climb the wall beneath the window.

In an adjacent room a man sat at a control desk, watching the boy on a screen. Behind him stood another. Both men were dressed in identical, tight-fitting suits of black. A fine gauze mesh of white was stretched across each of their faces like masks, showing only the eyes with their ebony lenses.

For a time there was nothing. Then the boy spoke.

'Bos agas pen gweder? Bos eno enawy py plas why dos mes?'

The seated man translated for the benefit of the other.

'Is your head made of glass? Is there light where you come from?'

T'ai Cho laughed. He was growing to like the boy. He was so quick, so bright. It was almost a pleasure to be his partner in these sessions. He half turned, looking up at the standing man, who grunted non-committally.

'I need to see more, T'ai Cho. Some clear sign of what he's capable of.'

T'ai Cho nodded, then turned back to the screen. 'Ef bos enawy,' he answered pleasantly. *He be light*, it meant, translated literally, though its sense was *It is light*. 'Pur enawy,' he went on. *Very light*. 'Re rak why gordhaf whath, edrek.' *Too much for you to endure, I'm sorry*. 'Mes bos hebask. A-brys why mynnes gweles py plas my dos mes.' *But be patient. In good time you will see where I come from.*

The boy considered, then nodded, as if satisfied.

'Da,' he said. *Good*.

'What is that language?' asked the standing man. His name was Andersen and he was Director of the Project. It was T'ai Cho's job to convince him that his candidate was worth spending time and money on, for this was a department of the T'ang's government, and even government departments had to show a profit.

'Old Cornish,' said T'ai Cho, half turning in his seat, but still watching the screen. 'It's a bastardized, pidgin version, almost devoid of tenses. Its grammatical structure is copycat English.'

He knew much more but held his tongue, knowing his superior's habitual impatience. They had been brave men, those few thousand who had formed the kingdom of Kernow back in the first years of the City. Brave, intelligent men. But they had not known how awful life would be in the Clay. They had not conceived what vast transforming pressures would be brought to bear on them. Intelligence had knelt before necessity and the weight of all that life stacked up above them, out of reach. They had reverted. Regressed ten thousand years in as many days. Back to the days of flint and bone. Back to the age of stone. Now only the ragged tatters of their chosen language remained, its sounds as twisted as the bodies of their children's children's children.

Andersen leaned forward and tapped the screen with his long fingernails. 'I want something conclusive. Something I can show to our sponsors. Something we can sell.'

T'ai Cho's eyes left the screen a moment, meeting Andersen's eyes. He had a gut instinct about this one. Something told him that this one was different from the rest: was, perhaps, what the Project had been set up to find. But 'something conclusive' – could he get that? The Director's eyes were inexpressive.

'I'll try,' T'ai Cho said after a moment. 'Tomorrow, first thing.'

Andersen nodded curtly and turned away. 'Tomorrow, then.'

Tomorrow began early. T'ai Cho was up at fifth bell and at his post, watching the sleeping boy. Slowly, almost imperceptibly, he increased the lighting in the cell. It was the boy's fourth day here, but, like all those brought up from the Clay, he had no real conception of time. Day and night were as one down there, equally dark.

Slowly he would be taught otherwise. Would learn the patterns of the world above.

When he had first arrived they had placed food and drink in his cell. On waking he had seen it at once, but had merely sniffed, then left the two bowls untouched. On the second day, however, hunger and thirst had overcome his fear and he had eaten wolfishly.

T'ai Cho had seen this many times before. He had logged eight years in Recruitment and seen more than a dozen of his candidates through Assessment into Socialization. But never, until now, had he felt such conviction about a candidate. There was something about this one, a charisma, if that were possible in such a scraggy, scrawny creature; a powerful, almost tangible sense of potentiality.

They were pitiful to watch in the first few days. Most were like trapped animals gnawing at their bonds. Some went mad and tried to kill themselves. Some went into coma. In either case there was a simple procedure to be followed. A matter of policy. At the touch of a button on the control desk, the cell would be filled with a deadly, fast-acting gas. It would be over in seconds.

Kim, however, had quickly overcome his initial fear. When nothing had happened to him, he had begun to explore his cell methodically, growing in confidence as each hour passed and he remained unharmed. Curiosity had begun to have the upper hand in his nature. The material of the walls, the watching camera, the waste vent, the manufacture of the bowls – each had been subjected to an intense scrutiny; to an investigation that was, T'ai Cho thought, almost scientific in its thoroughness. Yet when T'ai Cho spoke to the boy he saw at once just how fragile that confidence was. The boy froze in mid-action, the hair rising from his flesh, then scurried back to his corner and crouched there, shaking, his big, round eyes wide with terror.

T'ai Cho had seen cleverness before, and cunning was second nature to these children from the Clay, but there was something more than cleverness or cunning here. It was not simply that the boy was bright, numerate and curious – there were clear signs of something more.

Many factors seemed to militate against the development of real intelligence in the Clay, malnutrition chief amongst them. When existence was stripped down to its bare bones the first thing lost was the civilizing aspect of abstract thought. And yet, in some, it surfaced even so.

In the last year, however, the Project had been under scrutiny from factions in the House who wanted to close it down. Their arguments were familiar ones. The Project was expensive. Twice in the last five years it had failed to show a profit. Neither did the fact that they had extended their network beneath the whole of City Europe mollify their critics. Why did they need the Project in the first place? At most it had produced five thousand useful men in twenty years, and what was that in the context of the greater scientific community? Nothing. Or as good as nothing.

In his darker moments T'ai Cho had to agree with them. After a day in which he had had to flood the cell with gas, he would return uplevel to his apartment and wonder why they bothered. There was so much inbreeding, so much physical suffering, such a vast break in the chain of knowledge down there. At times these seemed insurmountable barriers to the development of intelligence. The Clay was a nightmare made real. Was ti yu, the 'earth-prison' – the world beneath the earth; the place of demons. Down there intelligence had devolved into a killer's cunning, blunted by a barbarous language that had no room for broader concepts. If he thought of it in those terms, what he did seemed little more than a game. A salving of conscience, maybe, but no more than that.

So they all felt, at times. But that feeling didn't last. T'ai Cho had killed maybe a hundred boys like Kim, knowing it was best – pitying them for the poor trapped creatures they were; knowing they had no future, above or below. And yet he had seen the light of intelligence flash in their eyes: eyes that, by rights, should have been simply dull or feral. And each time it had seemed a miracle of sorts, beyond simple understanding. Each time it gave the lie to those who said the Clay bred true: that environment and genetics were all there was. There was more than that.

It was a thing none of them mentioned; almost a kind of heresy. Yet there was not one of them who didn't feel it. Not one who didn't know exactly what it was that informed and inspired their work here.

Man was more than the plastic of his flesh and the keyboard of his senses. More than a carrier of genetic codes. To Mankind alone was the diffuse and evasive spark of individuality given. It seemed a paradox, yet it was so. Each time they 'saved' one from the Clay it reaffirmed their faith in this. Man was more than *po*; more than the animal soul, the flesh that rotted in the ground at death. There was a spirit soul, a *hun*.

There, that was it. The unuttered thought they shared. A *hun*.

And so they did their work, trawling the dark depths for those special souls whose eyes flashed with the spark of life itself. Each one miraculous. Each one an affirmation. 'We make a profit; provide a service for the Companies,' they would argue, when put to it. But the real reason they hid from others. It was their dark, vocational secret.

He began. At his order a uniformed Mech entered the room and set a tray down on the floor beside the sleeping boy. On the tray were a number of different objects, covered by a thin black cloth.

The room was sealed again. T'ai Cho waited. An hour passed.

When Kim woke he saw the tray at once. He paused, abruptly alert, fully awake, the hairs on his neck bristling. He lifted his head, sniffing the air, then circled the tray slowly. With his back against the wall he stopped and looked up at the camera, a definite question in his dark eyes.

'Pyn an jawl us wharfedhys?' *What now?*

T'ai Cho, watching, smiled, then leaned forward and tapped out a code on the intercom in front of him.

There was a pause, then Andersen's voice came back to him. 'What is it, T'ai Cho?'

'I think this will interest you, sir. I'm with the boy. I think you should see this for yourself.'

Andersen hesitated, then agreed. He cut the connection.

T'ai Cho sat back in his chair, watching.

The boy's gaze went between the camera and the tray, then settled on the tray. Slowly, almost timidly, he moved closer. He looked up, his brow deeply furrowed, his big, round eyes filled with suspicion. Then, with a quick, sudden movement, he flicked the cloth aside.

It was a standard test and T'ai Cho had witnessed this moment fifty, maybe a hundred times. He had seen boys sniff and paw and try to taste the objects, then ignore them or play with them in a totally uncomprehending manner, but this time it was different – totally different from anything he had seen before. He watched in silence, aware all the while of the Director watching at his side.

'This is wrong, surely? This is supposed to be a memory game, isn't it?'

The Director reached out to switch on the intercom, but T'ai Cho put his hand in the way, turning to look up at him.

'Please. Not yet. Watch what he does.'

The Director hesitated, then nodded. 'But what exactly is he doing?'

T'ai Cho turned back to the screen and smiled to himself.

'He's doing what he does all the time. He's changing the rules.'

At first the boy did not lift any of the objects but moved them about on the tray as if to get a better idea of what they were. Then, working with what seemed like purpose, he began to combine several of the objects. A small hand mirror, a length of plastic tubing and a twine of string. His hands moved quickly, cleverly, and in a moment he had what looked like a child's toy. He took it to the wall beneath the window and raised it to his eye, trying to see outward. Failing, he sat down with the thing he had made and patiently took it apart.

The two men watched the screen, fascinated, seeing how the boy positioned his hand before the mirror and tilted it slowly, studying what effect it had on the image. Then, as if satisfied, he returned to the tray and took a heavier object in one hand. He hefted it a moment, thoughtfully, then reached for a second object and placed them at his side.

Scurrying across the floor, he retrieved the discarded cloth and laid it out on the floor of the cell. Then he placed the mirror face down on top of it. He laid the carved block halfway across the mirror, taking care with its positioning, then struck the back of the block firmly with the torch.

He picked the two halves of the hand mirror up carefully, checking the sharpness of their edges with his thumb. T'ai Cho, watching, moved his hand instinctively towards the touchpad, ready to fill the cell with gas should the boy do anything rash. But Kim was not out to harm himself. Using the edge of the mirror, he cut the twine into four pieces, then began to reconstruct his toy, placing a piece of glass at each end of the tube. He tested the angles of the glass five times before he was satisfied, then tightened the twine and went to the window again. This time he should be able to see out.

Andersen leaned forward. 'Do you think he's seen this done before?'

'Where? In the Clay?' T'ai Cho laughed, then turned to look up at Andersen. 'No. This is all first time for him. An experiment. Just think of how we learn things. How, as children, we watch others and copy them. How we have to be taught even the most basic of skills. But Kim's not like that. He has no one to copy. He's never had anyone to copy. It's all had to come from within his own mind. That's why it's so astonishing, what he does. Can't you see it? He treats the world like something new. Something yet to be put together.'

The boy took the makeshift periscope from his eyes and sat down slowly, clearly disappointed by what he had seen. Then he tilted back his head and spoke into the darkness overhead.

'Pandra vyth gwres?' *Where am I?*

He waited, but when no answer came he threw the viewing tube away from him and let his head fall onto his chest, as if exhausted.

T'ai Cho turned and looked up at the Director. 'Well?'

Andersen stood there a moment longer, staring down into the screen, then looked back at T'ai Cho. 'All right. I'll get a six-month contract drawn up this afternoon.'

Beneath his white gauze mask, T'ai Cho smiled. 'Then I'll start at once?'

The Director hesitated, then nodded curtly. His eyes, usually so lifeless, seemed thoughtful, even, perhaps, surprised.

'Yes,' he said finally. 'Begin at once. But let me know immediately if anything of interest happens.'

An hour later Andersen was at his desk. The directive he had been warned was on its way had now arrived. It lay there on the desk before him. Two months he had. Two months to turn things round. And the new financial targets they had given him were four times the size of the old ones.

He laughed bitterly. It would need a miracle. He hadn't a chance of meeting the old targets, let alone these new figures. No – someone higher up had decided to pull the plug on the Project, he was certain of it. This was political.

Andersen leaned forward and spoke into his intercom. 'Send through a standard contract. Six months' term. For the new boy, Kim.'

He sat back again. A miracle... Well, maybe T'ai Cho was right. Maybe the boy *was* special. But would his specialty translate into cash? Anyway, he didn't pin his hopes too greatly on it. Six months? If the Project folded Kim would be dead in two. He and a hundred others like him.

'Politics!' he muttered, wondering who was behind this latest directive and what he could do to get the deadline extended – who he could speak to to get things changed. Then, as the contract slid from the desktop printer he leaned forward and took his brush from the ink block, signing the Mandarin form of his name with a flourish at the bottom of the page.

The viewing-tube lay where Kim had thrown it, the lower mirror dislodged from the shaft, the twine hanging loose. Kim sat there, perfectly still, his arms wrapped about his knees, his head tucked down between his legs, waiting.

He heard it first. Sensed a vague movement in the air.

He scuttled back, then crouched beneath the wall, wide-eyed, the hair rising on the back of his neck. Then, as the facing wall began to peel back from the centre, he cried out.

What had been the wall was now an open space. Beyond the opening was a room the same as the one in which he sat. Inside, behind a narrow barrier of wood, sat a giant. A giant with a face of bone-white glass.

The giant stood, then began to come around the wall. Kim cried out again and tried to back away, but there was nowhere to run. He looked about him desperately, yelping, urine streaming down his legs.

And then the giant spoke.

'Ow hanow bos T'ai Cho. My bos an den kewsel yn why.' *My name be T'ai Cho. I be the man talk to you.*

The giant fell silent, then came into the room and stood there, his hands out at his sides, empty. It was a gesture designed to say, Look, I am no threat to you, but the man was almost twice as tall as the tallest man Kim had ever seen. He was like the gods Kim had seen in the Clay that time, yet his limbs and body were as black as the earth, his eyes like dark jewels in the pure, glassy whiteness of his face.

It was a cruel face. A face that seemed curiously at odds with the soft reassurance of the voice.

Kim drew back his teeth and snarled.

And then the giant did something unexpected. It knelt down. It was still taller than Kim, but it was less threatening now. Keeping its arms out at its sides, it spoke again.

'My golyas why, Kim.' *I watch you, Kim.* 'My gweles pandra why canna obery.' *I see what you can do.* 'Why a-vyn bewa a-ughof?' *Do you want to live up above?*

Slowly the darkness deep within him ebbed away. He took a breath, then answered. 'My a-vyn.' *I want to.*

The giant nodded. 'Da. Ena why gweres-vy.' *Good. Then you help me.* 'Bysy yu dheugh obery pandra my kewsel.' *You must do what I say.*

The giant reached up and removed the flesh from his face. Beneath it he wore a second face, the mouth of which smiled redly, showing perfect teeth. His inner mouth. So he was not made of glass at all.

Kim thought about what the giant had said. It seemed too all-inclusive. He shook his head. 'Ny puptra.' *Not everything.*

The giant nodded. This time the words came from his inner mouth. The other flesh hung loose about his chin.

'Ny puptra. Mes moyha taclow.' *Not everything. But most things.* 'May of gul styr.' *When it makes meaning.*

He considered that. It did not commit him too much. 'Da,' he said softly.

'Flowr,' said the giant, smiling again. *Perfect.* 'Ena bysy yu dheugh gortheby onen tra a-dherak pup ken.' *Then you must answer me one thing before all else.* 'Pyu dysky why fatel nyvera?' *Who teach you how to count?*

Andersen sat behind his desk, studying T'ai Cho's report. It was the end of the first week of Assessment. Normally there would have been a further seventeen weeks of patient observation, but T'ai Cho had asked for matters to be expedited. Andersen had agreed readily. Only that morning he had spoken to the First Secretary of one of the Junior Ministers and been told that his request for a referral hearing had been turned down. Which meant that the directive was final. Yet things were not all bad. He had been busy this last week.

He looked up. 'Good,' he said simply, then pushed the file aside. 'I'll countersign my recommendation. The board sits tomorrow. I'll put it before them then.'

T'ai Cho smiled and nodded his gratitude.

'Off the record,' Andersen continued, leaning forward over the desk-top, 'how high do you rate his potential? You say here that you think he's a genius. That can mean many things. I want something I can sell. Something that will impress a top Executive.'

'It's all in there,' said T'ai Cho, indicating the file. 'He has an eidetic memory. Near perfect recall. And the ability to comprehend and use complex concepts within moments of first encountering them. Add to that a profound, almost frightening grasp of mathematics and linguistics.'

The Director nodded. 'All excellent, T'ai Cho, but that's not quite what I mean. They can build machines that can do all that. *What can he do that a machine can't?*'

It was an odd thing to ask. The question had never arisen before. But then there had never been a candidate quite like Kim. He was already fluent in basic English and had assimilated the beginnings of algebra and logic as if they were chunks of meat to be swallowed down and digested.

The Director sat back and turned slightly in his chair, looking away from T'ai Cho. 'Let me explain the situation. Then you might understand why I'm asking.'

He glanced at the operative and smiled. 'You're good at your job, T'ai Cho, and I respect your evaluation. But my viewpoint is different from yours. It has to be. I have to justify the continuation of this whole operation. I have to report to a board that reports back to the House itself. And the House is concerned with two things only. One – does the Recruitment Project make a profit? Two – is it recruiting the right material for the market place?'

He held up a hand, as if to counter some argument T'ai Cho was about to put forward. 'Now I know that might sound harsh and unidealistic, but it's how things are.'

T'ai Cho nodded but said nothing.

'Anyway, things are like this. At present I have firm approaches from five major Companies. Three have signed contracts for auction options when the time comes. I expect the other two to sign shortly.'

T'ai Cho's eyes widened with surprise. 'An auction?'

Andersen raised one hand. 'However... if he *is* what you say he is, then we could fund the whole of this programme for a year, maybe more. That's if we can get the right deal. If we can get one of the big companies to sign an exclusive rights contract.'

T'ai Cho shook his head, astonished now. An exclusive rights contract! Then the Director wasn't talking of a normal sponsorship but about something huge. Something between two and five million yuan! No wonder he wanted something more than was in the report. But what could he, T'ai Cho, offer in that vein?

'I don't know...' he began, then stopped. There *was* something Kim could do that a machine couldn't. He could invent. He could take two things and make a third of them.

'Well?' said Andersen. 'Say I'm Head of SimFic. How would you convince me to hand over twenty million yuan in exchange for a small boy, genius or not?'

T'ai Cho swallowed. *Twenty million yuan!* He frowned, concentrating on the problem he had been set, 'Well, he connects things... Things we'd normally consider unconnected.' He looked down, trying to capture in words just what it was that made Kim so special. 'But it's more than that. Much more. He doesn't just learn and remember and calculate, he *creates.* New ideas. Wholly new ideas. He looks at things in ways we've never thought of looking at them before.'

'Such as?'

T'ai Cho shrugged. It was so hard to define, to pinpoint, but he knew this was what made Kim so different. It wasn't just his ability to memorize or his quickness, it was something beyond those. And because it was happening all the time it was hard to extract and say 'he does this'. It was his very mode of thought. He was *constantly* inventive.

T'ai Cho laughed. 'Do you know anything about astronomy?'

'A little.' Andersen stared at him strangely. 'Is this relevant, T'ai Cho?'

T'ai Cho nodded. 'You know what a nova is?'

Andersen shrugged. 'Refresh my memory.'

'A nova is an old star that collapses into itself and in doing so explodes and throws out vast quantities of energy and light. Well, Kim's a kind of nova. I'm tempted to say a supernova. It's like there's some dense darkness at the very centre of him, sucking all knowledge down into itself, then throwing it all back out as light. Brilliant, blinding light.'

Andersen shook his head. 'Old stars... Is there nothing more practical?'

T'ai Cho leaned forward, earnest now. 'Why don't you bring him here, your Head of SimFic? Show him the boy. Let him bring his own experts, make his own assessments – set his own tests. He'll be astonished, I guarantee you.'

'Maybe,' Andersen muttered, then repeated the word more strongly. 'Maybe... You know, that's not a bad idea at all.'

T'ai Cho put his request in the next day, expecting it to be turned down out of hand. Within the hour, however, he had received notification, under the Director's hand, with full board approval. He was to be transferred from Assessment to S & I – Socialization and Indoctrination – for an eighteen-month tour of duty. And he was to be directly responsible for the new candidate, Kim Ward.

Normally personal involvement was frowned upon. It was seen as necessary to make a clean break between each section, but the Director had convinced the board that this was a special case. And they had agreed, recognizing the importance of nurturing the boy's abilities, though perhaps the thought of twenty million yuan – a figure mentioned unofficially and wholly off the record – had proved an additional incentive to break with tradition just this once. Thus it was that T'ai Cho took Kim up the five levels to Socialization and helped him settle into his new rooms.

A week later T'ai Cho found himself at the lectern in a small hexagonal lecture room. The room was lit only at its centre, and then by the dimmest of lamps. Three boys sat at a distance from each other, forming a triangle at the heart of which was the spiderish shape of a trivee. T'ai Cho stood in the shadows behind the smallest of the boys, operating the image control.

It was a lecture about Chung Kuo and City Earth. Images of the vast hive-like structure appeared and then vanished. Exteriors, cutaways, sections. The first glimpse these children had ever had of the environment built above the Clay.

As T'ai Cho talked his way through the sequence of images he wondered whether they ever dreamed themselves back there, beneath the vast, over-towering pile of the City. How strange that would be. How would they feel? Like bugs beneath a house, perhaps. Yes, looking at these images even he felt awed. How, then, did it strike them? For this was their first sight of it – their first glimpse of how insignificant they were: how small the individual, how vast the species. A City covering the Earth like a glacier, broken only by ocean and mountain and plantations. A species almost forty billion strong.

Yes, he could see the awe in the faces of the two boys seated across from him. Their mouths were open wide in wonder and their eyes were screwed up, trying to take it all in. Then he glanced down at the small, dark-haired head just below his lectern and wondered what Kim was thinking.

'It's too big,' Kim said suddenly.

T'ai Cho laughed. 'It's exactly as big as it is. How can that be too big?'

'No.' Kim turned and looked up at him, his dark eyes burning with inten-sity. The other boys were watching him carefully. 'I didn't mean that. Just that it's too vast, too heavy a thing to stand on its pillars without either collapsing or sinking into the earth.'

'Go on,' said T'ai Cho, aware that something important was happening. It was like the construction of the viewing-tube, but this time Kim was using concepts as his building blocks.

'Well, there are three hundred levels in most places, right?'

T'ai Cho nodded, careful not to interrupt.

'Well, on each of those levels there must be thousands, perhaps millions of people. With all their necessities. Food, clothing, transportation, water, machines. Lots of machines.' Kim laughed softly. 'It's ridiculous. It just can't be. It's too heavy. Too big. I've seen for myself how small the pillars are on which it all rests.'

'And yet it is,' said T'ai Cho, surprised by that single word 'small' and what it implied. Kim had grasped at once what the others had failed even to see: the true perspectives of the City. His imagination had embraced the scale of things at once. As if he'd always known. But this next was the crucial stage. Would Kim make the next leap of understanding?

T'ai Cho glanced across at the other boys. They were lost already. They hadn't even seen there was a problem.

'It exists?' Kim asked, puzzled. 'Just as you've shown us?'

'Exactly. And you might also consider that there are vast factories and foundries and masses of other industrial machinery distributed amongst its many levels. At least one level in twenty is used for warehousing. And there are whole levels which are used to store water or process waste matter.'

Kim's face creased into a frown of intense concentration. He seemed to stare at something directly in front of him, his brow puckering, his eyes suddenly sharply focused.

'Well?' T'ai Cho prompted when the silence had extended uncomfortably.

Kim laughed. 'You'll think I'm mad...'

'No. Try me.'

'Well... It must be something to do with its structure. But that can't be the whole of it.' Kim seemed almost in pain now. His hands were clenched tightly and his eyes were wide and staring.

T'ai Cho held his breath. One step further. One small but vital step.

'Then it must be built of air. Or something as light as air but... but as tough as steel.'

As light as air and as tough as steel. A substance as strong as the bonding between the atoms and so light that three hundred levels of it weighed a fraction of a single layer of clay bricks. A substance so essential to the existence of City Earth that its chemical name was rarely used. It was known simply as ice. Ice because, in its undecorated state, it looked as cold and fragile as the thinnest layer of frozen water. 'Corrugated' layers of ice – only a few hundred molecules thick – formed the levels and walls of City Earth. Moulded sheets of ice formed the basic materials of lifts and bolts, furniture and pipework, clothing and conduits, toys and tools. Its flexibility and versatility, its cheapness and durability had meant that it had replaced most traditional materials.

City Earth was a vast palace of ice. A giant house of cards, each card so unbelievably thin that if folded down the whole thing would be no thicker than a single sheet of paper.

Slowly, piece by piece, T'ai Cho told Kim all of this, watching as the boy's face lit with an inner pleasure. Not air but ice! It made the boy laugh with delight.

'Then the pillars hold it down!' he said. 'They keep it from flying away!'

*

Soren Berdichev glanced up from the pile of papers he was signing.

'Well, Blake? You've seen the boy?'

His Head of Personnel hesitated long enough to make Berdichev look up again. Blake was clearly unhappy about something.

'He's no use to us, then?'

'Oh, quite the contrary, sir. He's everything the report made him out to be. Exceptional, sir. Quite exceptional.'

Berdichev set the brush down on the inkstone and sat back, dismissing the secretary who had been hovering at his side.

'Then you've done as we agreed and purchased the boy's contract?'

Blake shook his head. 'I'm afraid not, sir.'

'I don't understand you, Blake. Have you let one of our rivals buy the boy?'

'No, sir. Director Andersen offered us an exclusive rights contract.'

'Then what's the problem? You offered him the sum I authorized? Five million yuan?'

'I did...' Blake swallowed. 'In fact, I raised the offer to eight million.'

Berdichev smiled coldly. 'I see. And you want me to sanction the increase?'

'No, sir. That's it, you see. Andersen turned me down flat.'

'What?!' Berdichev sat forward, his eyes, behind the tiny pebble glasses, wide with anger. 'Eight million and he turned us down?'

'Yes, sir. He said he wanted twenty million minimum, or no contract.'

Berdichev shook his head slowly, astonished. 'And you walked away, I hope?'

Blake lowered his head. There was a definite colour in his cheeks now. Berdichev leaned forward and yelled at him.

'Come on, man! Out with it! What's all this about?'

Blake looked up again, his whole manner hesitant now. 'I... I promised Andersen I'd come back to you, sir. I said I'd ask you to agree the deal.'

'You *what*?' Berdichev laughed incredulously. 'Twenty million yuan for a six-year-old boy? Are you mad, Blake?'

Blake met his eyes determinedly. 'I believe he's worth it, sir. Every last *jen* of it. I would not have dared come back to you unless I believed that.'

Berdichev shook his head. 'No... Twenty million. It's out of the question.'

Blake came forward and leaned over the desk, pleading with his superior. 'If only you saw him, sir – saw him for yourself – you'd understand. He's like nothing I've ever come across before. Voracious, he is – just hungry to learn things. Really, sir, if you'd only see him!'

Berdichev looked down at where Blake's hands rested on the edge of the desk. Blake removed them at once and took a step back, straightening up.

'Is that all, Blake?'

'Please, sir. If you'd reconsider. If you'd take the time...'

'You know that I haven't the time,' he snapped back, irritated now by Blake's persistence. He picked up the brush angrily. 'The murder of the T'ang's son has thrown everything into flux. The market's nervous and I have meetings all this week to calm things down. People need reassuring, and that takes time.' He looked up at his Personnel Manager again, his face hard and angry. 'No, Blake, I really haven't the time.'

'Forgive me, sir, but I think you should make time in this instance.'

Berdichev stared at Blake a moment, wondering whether he should dismiss him on the spot. But something cautioned him. Blake had never stepped out of line before – had never dared to contradict him in this manner. There must be good reason. He looked down at the pile of papers that awaited his signature, barely seeing them, calming himself, trying to see the thing clearly. Then he looked up again.

'You think he's worth it, then? Twenty million yuan? But what if he gets some childhood illness and dies? What if he has an accident? What if he proves to be one of these child prodigies who burns up before he's out of his adolescence? Twenty million yuan. It's a huge sum, even by our thinking.'

Blake bowed his head, all humility now that he had got Berdichev to listen. 'I agree, sir. But I've provisionally agreed a six-stage payment. Twenty per cent on signature, four two-yearly payments of ten per cent and forty per cent on delivery of the boy to us at sixteen. There would also be provisions for clawback in the case of death or accident. Our risk would be reduced substantially.'

Berdichev considered a moment. This was more like the Blake he knew and valued.

'Would you take a gamble, Blake?'

'How do you mean, sir?'

'Would you back up your hunch? Would you stake your job on me being impressed by the boy?'

Blake looked down, a smile slowly spreading across his face. 'I think I already have.'

*

'Kim! What in hell's name are you doing?'

Kim turned from the half-deconstructed trivee and smiled. T'ai Cho, horrified, rushed across the room and pulled him away from the machine.

'Kuan Yin! Don't you realize that that could kill you? There's enough power in that thing to fry you to a cinder!'

Kim shook his head. 'Not now there isn't.' He took T'ai Cho's hand, prised open the palm and dropped something into it. T'ai Cho stared at the small, matt black rectangular tube for a moment, then, realizing what it was, dropped it as if it were red hot. It was the power core.

He knelt down and took Kim's upper arms in his hands, glaring at him, for the first time genuinely angry at the boy. 'I forbid you to tinker with things this way! These machines can be lethal if mishandled. You're lucky to be alive!'

Again Kim shook his head. 'No,' he answered softly, clearly shaken by T'ai Cho's anger. 'Not if you know what you are doing.'

'And you know what you are doing, eh?'

'Yes...' The small boy shivered and looked away.

T'ai Cho, whose anger had been fuelled by his fear for Kim, found himself relenting, yet it was important to keep the boy from harming himself. He kept his voice stern, unyielding. 'How did you know?'

Kim looked back at him, his wide, dark eyes piercing him with their strange intensity. 'I asked the man – the maintenance engineer. He explained it all to me. He showed me how to take it all apart and put it back together. How it all functioned. What the principles were behind it.'

T'ai Cho was silent for a moment. 'When was this?'

Kim looked down. 'This morning. Before the call.'

T'ai Cho laughed. 'Before the call?' The call was at six bells. Before then Kim's cell, like all the others, had been locked. 'He came and saw you, then, this man? And had a trivee with him, conveniently?'

Kim shook his head but said nothing.

'Tell me the truth, Kim. You were just tinkering, weren't you? Experimenting.'

'Experimenting, yes. But not tinkering. I knew what I was doing. And I was telling you the truth, T'ai Cho. I'd never lie to you.'

T'ai Cho sat back on his heels. 'Then I don't understand you, Kim.'

'I...' Kim looked up. The snow-pale flesh of his neck was strangely flushed. 'I let myself out of the cell and came down here. The man was working here – servicing the machine.'

T'ai Cho was quiet. He stared at Kim for a long while, then stood up. 'You know that isn't possible, Kim. The locks are all electronically coded.'

'I know,' said Kim simply. 'And a random factor generator changes the combination every day.'

'Then you realize why I can't believe you.'

'Yes. But I took the lock out.'

T'ai Cho shook his head, exasperated now. 'But you can't have, Kim! It would have registered as a malfunction. The alarm would have gone off over the door.'

Kim was shaking his head. 'No. That's not what I mean. I took the lock out. The electronics are still there. I rigged them so that it would still register as locked when the door was pulled closed.'

Still T'ai Cho was not convinced. 'And what did you do all this with? The locking mechanism is delicate. Anyway, there's a maintenance plate covering the whole thing.'

'Yes,' said Kim, the colour gone now from his neck. 'That was the hardest part. Getting hold of these.' He took a slender packet from his tunic pocket and handed it to T'ai Cho. It was a set of scalpel-fine tools.

'They're duplicates,' said Kim. 'The service engineer probably hasn't even missed them yet.'

T'ai Cho stared at the tools a moment longer then looked back at Kim. 'Heavens...' he said softly. 'So it's true?'

Kim nodded, the smile returned to his face. 'It's as I said, T'ai Cho. I'd never lie to you.'

Director Andersen bowed deeply as Berdichev came into his office. He had spent the morning reading the file on SimFic's owner and had been impressed by what he'd read. Here was a man who had taken his Company from nowhere to the number eighteen slot on the Hang Seng Index in the short space of ten years. Now he was worth a reputed eighteen *billion* yuan. It was not a T'ang's ransom by any means, but it was enough to have satisfied any Emperor of old.

'Your presence here honours us,' he said, offering his chair.

Berdichev ignored his offer. 'Where's the boy?' he said impatiently. 'I'd like to see him. At once.'

'Of course,' said Andersen, looking to T'ai Cho, who was standing just outside the doorway next to Blake. T'ai Cho bowed, then turned away to prepare things.

Berdichev stared coldly at the Director. 'You'll ensure he doesn't know he's being watched?'

'Of course. It's how we always work here. There's a viewing room. My assistants will bring you refreshments...'

Berdichev cut him off sharply, the light glinting on his spectacles. 'We'll not be taking refreshments. Just show me the boy, Director Andersen. I want to see why you feel you can insult me.'

Andersen blanched. 'I...' He bowed again, fear making his mouth dry. 'I'll take you there at once.'

The two machines had been left on the worktop, as the boy had asked. One was the MedFac trivee he had been working on earlier, the other a standard SimFic ArtMould IV. Between them lay a full technician's kit.

'What's this?' Berdichev asked, taking his seat at the observation window only an arm's length from the worktop's edge.

'They're what the boy asked for.'

Andersen swallowed, praying that T'ai Cho was right about this. He alone knew just how much depended on it. 'I understand he wants to try something out.'

Berdichev half turned in his seat and looked coldly up at Andersen. 'I don't understand you, Director. Try what out?'

Andersen began to shake his head, then stopped and smiled, knowing he had to make the best of things. 'That's just it. We're never quite certain what Kim's about to do. That's why he's so valuable. He's so unpredictable. So inventive.'

Berdichev stared through Andersen a moment, then turned back. He seemed totally unconvinced. It seemed as if the only reason he was there at all was the ridiculously high sum he had been asked to pay for the boy's contract. Andersen leaned against the back of the empty chair next to Berdichev's, feeling weak. The boy was going to ruin it all. He just knew he was. Things would go wrong and he would be humiliated, in front of Berdichev. Worse than that, it would be the end of things: the closure of the Project and early retirement for himself. He shuddered, then took the fan from his belt and flicked it open, fanning himself.

'I suppose he's going to do something with those two machines?'

Andersen's fan stopped in mid-motion. 'I believe so.'

'And how long has he been in your charge?'

'Twenty-three days.'

Berdichev laughed. 'It isn't possible. It takes our best engineers months to learn how to operate those things.'

'Four months' intensive training,' said Blake from the back of the viewing room.

'And he's taught himself?'

Andersen licked his lips to wet them. 'In two days.'

Berdichev sat back, laughing again. 'I do believe you're making fun of me, Director Andersen. Wasting my valuable time. If that's so...'

Andersen bowed deeply. 'Believe me, *Shih* Berdichev, I would never dream of such a thing. Please, be patient. I'm certain the boy will not disappoint you.'

The door at the far end of the lecture room opened and T'ai Cho entered with the boy. Andersen, watching Berdichev, saw him frown, then a strange expression cross his face.

'Where did you find the boy?'

Blake answered before Andersen could find his tongue. 'In the Western Island, sir. He comes from the Canton of Cornwall.'

Berdichev nodded. A strange sobriety seemed to have gripped him. 'Ah, yes. I know it well. I went there once. With friends.'

T'ai Cho knelt down, talking to the boy a moment, then he let him go. Kim ran across the room, a naked eagerness in his face. Climbing up onto a stool, he set to work at once, dismantling the insides of the trivee, then dragging the heavy ArtMould machine closer to him.

Berdichev, watching the boy, felt himself go cold inside. The resemblance was uncanny; a grotesque distortion of the original, admittedly, yet in some ways so like him that simply to look at the boy was to bring all those feelings back. All the love and guilt and hurt.

Edmund, he thought; *you're Edmund Wyatt's son. I'd swear it.*

He watched, barely conscious of what the boy was doing; aware only of that strange and unexpected likeness. He should have looked at the holo Blake had given him. Should have found time to look at it. But he had been too busy. Otherwise he would have come here before now, he was certain of it.

Normally he would have dismissed it at once as one of those strange tricks life played on men, but in this case it all fitted. Fitted perfectly. The boy was not only the right age but he came from the right location.

Edmund was with me. Down there in the Clay. Eight years ago. Edmund, Pietr and I. Down there in the darkness below the City. Yes... he was there that first time, when we went to see the King Under the City, the Myghtern, in his castle in ancient Bodmin. Was there when we visited the Myghtern's sing-song house. And now his seed has returned.

Back from the dark.

Berdichev shivered then stood up. 'I've seen enough.'

Andersen, flustered, bowed deeply. The colour had gone from his face and his eyes were wide with sudden panic. 'I beg you, Excellency, wait. Please, wait just a little longer. He's only just begun.'

Berdichev turned to Blake, ignoring him. 'Have you the contract?'

Blake pulled the contract from his carry-pouch and handed it across.

For a moment Berdichev hesitated, looking down at the contract, wondering what was best. His first instinct had been to tear it to shreds, but now he didn't know. He looked back at the boy. If he was Edmund Wyatt's son – and there was a quick way of proving that he was, by genotyping – he was not worth a single *jen*, let alone twenty million yuan, for his life was forfeit under the law that said all the family of a traitor shared his fate, to three generations ascending and descending.

He looked at Andersen. The man was almost shitting himself. 'Ten million,' he said.

He would delay. Perhaps he would even get the genotype done and make certain. But then? He shivered. Then he would do nothing.

'Fifteen,' Andersen answered, his voice betraying how intimidated he felt.

'Ten, or I ask my friends in the House to close you down in two weeks, not eight.'

He saw Andersen blink with surprise, then swallow. Seeing how things were, the Director bowed his head.

'Good. Then we'll finalize at once.' But he was thinking, Who else would see the resemblance? Who else would know about our visit to the Myghtern? Who now but Lehmann and I?

Maybe it would be all right, then. And perhaps, after all, he could help his dead friend. Perhaps now he could ease the guilt he had suffered from since Edmund's death.

Berdichev shivered then looked back at the boy. *Yes, and maybe I can do myself a favour at the same time.*

When it was all over T'ai Cho came back into the lecture room. He was carrying a tray and in his pocket was something the Director had given him to return to Kim. He set the tray down on the desk, beside the ArtMould, then sat on the stool next to Kim.

'Things went well this morning,' he said, reaching out to ruffle Kim's dark, fine hair. 'The Director was very pleased with you.'

'Why should he be pleased?'

T'ai Cho looked down. 'He was watching what you did. And with him was someone very important. Someone who has decided to... adopt you.'

'Adopt me?'

'Oh, don't worry, Kim. You'll be here until you're sixteen. But then you'll join one of the Companies. The one that makes this, as a matter of fact.'

He reached out and touched the modified ArtMould, still surprised by what Kim had done.

'Berdichev,' said Kim.

T'ai Cho laughed, surprised. 'Yes. How did you know?'

'It was on a newscast two days back. They said he owns SimFic.'

'That's right.' *And now he owns you.* The thought disturbed T'ai Cho, though why it should be different with Kim than with all the others he didn't know. It was what happened to all his charges in time. They were saved, but they were also owned. He shivered, then reached out and took the cup from the tray and offered it to Kim, then watched as he gulped the drink down savagely.

'I've something for you, too,' he said, filling the cup once more from the jug. 'We don't usually let our boys keep anything from their time in the Clay, but Director Andersen thought we should make an exception in your case.'

T'ai Cho took it from his pocket and put it into Kim's hand, closing his fingers over it.

Kim opened his hand, then gave a small laugh. He held the pendant up and touched the dangling circle with one finger, making it spin. It slowed, then twisted back, spinning backward and forward. He seemed delighted with the gift, yet when he looked up at T'ai Cho again his eyes were dark with hurt.

'What is it?' T'ai Cho asked.

'Bodmin.'

T'ai Cho shook his head. 'What? I don't follow you, Kim.'

'The place I came from. It was called Bodmin, wasn't it?'

T'ai Cho laughed, surprised. 'Why, yes, now I come to think of it. But how did you find out?'

Kim leaned forward and dipped his finger in the mug, then drew on the worktop, dipping his finger each time he formed a letter.

'An arrow. A space. A woman's breasts. A ring. A drawn bow. Two steep hills. An upright column. A gate. An eye with a curled eyebrow. It was a sign, close by the Gate. Six li.'

'Miles,' said T'ai Cho. 'But it doesn't matter. I'm surprised.'

'Why?'

T'ai Cho was silent a moment. 'Do you remember everything?'

Kim shook his head, the hurt back in his eyes, stronger now than before. 'No. Not everything. I was asleep, you see. For a long time I was asleep. And then I woke. The light woke me.'

CHAPTER 34

WUWEI

Darkness lay on the water like oil. It was almost dawn, but day would be a month coming this far north. They lay there silently in the flat boats, half a li from the shore of the island, waiting for the signal in their heads. At ten minutes past five it came and they began to move in, their faces and hands blacked up, their wet suits blending with the darkness.

Hans Ebert, commanding the raiding party, was first ashore. He crouched on the slick stone steps, waiting, listening for sounds above the steady slapping of the water on the rocks below.

Nothing. All was well. A few seconds later the second signal sounded in his head and he moved on quickly, his body acting almost without thought, doing what it had rehearsed a hundred times in the last few days.

He could sense his men moving in the darkness all about him; two hundred and sixty-four of them, elite-trained. The best in City Europe.

At the top of the steps Ebert stopped. While his sergeant, Auden, set the charge on the solid metal door he looked back through the darkness at the mainland. Hammerfest lay six li to the east, like a vast slab of glacial ice, thrusting out into the cold northern sea. To north and south of it the great wall of the City's edge ran into the distance like a jagged ribbon, its pale whiteness lit from within, tracing the shoreline of the ancient Finnmark of Norway. He shivered and turned back, conscious of the unseen presence of the old fortress walls towering above him in the moonless dark. It was a bugger of a place. Just the kind of site one would expect SimFic to build a special research unit in.

Auden came back to him. Together they crouched behind the blast shield, lowering their infrared lenses over their eyes. The charges would be fired automatically by the third signal. They waited. Without warning the night was rent by a whole series of detonations, some near, some further off. They let the shield fall forward and, not waiting for the smoke to clear, charged through the gaping doorway, followed by a dozen other men. At fifteen other points about the island the same thing was happening. Even as he entered the empty corridor he could hear the first bursts of small-arms fire.

The first intersection was exactly where it should have been. Ebert stood at the corner, looking to his left, his gun held against his shoulder, searching out targets in the darkness up ahead. He waited until his squad was formed up behind him, then counted them through, Auden first. Up ahead was the first of the guard posts, if the plans were accurate, and beyond that the first of the laboratories.

Ebert touched the last man's arm as he went through, then glanced back the way he'd come. For a moment he thought he saw movement and hesitated, but there was nothing in the infrared. He turned back quickly, then set off, running hard after his squad, hearing their boots echoing on the floor up ahead of him. But he had gone only ten or so strides when the floor seemed to give in front of him and he was tumbling forward down a slope.

He spread his legs behind him to slow himself and tried to dig his gun into the glassy surface of the floor. He slowed marginally, slewing to the left, then, abruptly, thumped into the wall. For a moment he was disoriented, his body twisted about violently. He felt his gun clatter away from him, then he was sliding again, head first this time, the yells closer now, mixed with a harsh muttering. A moment later he thumped bruisingly into a pile of bodies.

Ebert groaned, then looked up and saw Auden above him, the heated recognition patch at his neck identifying him.

'Is anyone hurt?' Ebert said softly, almost breathlessly, letting Auden help him to his feet.

Auden leant close and whispered in his ear. 'I think Leiter's dead, sir. A broken neck. He was just behind me when it went. And there seem to be a few other minor injuries. But otherwise...'

'Gods...' Ebert looked about him. 'Where are we?'

'I don't know, sir. This isn't on the plans.'

To three sides of them the walls went up vertically for forty, maybe fifty ch'i. It felt like they were at the bottom of a big, square-bottomed well. Ebert stepped back and stared up into the darkness overhead, trying to make something out. 'There,' he said, after a moment, pointing upward. 'If we can fire a rope up there we can get out.'

'If they don't pick us off first.'

'Right.' Ebert took a breath, then nodded. 'You break up the surface about six or eight ch'i up the slope. Meanwhile, let's keep the bastards' heads down, eh?'

The sergeant gave a slight bow and turned to bark an order at one of his men. Meanwhile Ebert took two grenades from his belt. It was hard to make out just how far up the entrance to the corridor was. Thirty ch'i, perhaps. Maybe more. There was only the slightest change in the heat emission pattern – the vaguest hint of an outline. He hefted one of the grenades, released the pin, then leaned back and hurled it up into the darkness. If he missed...

He heard it rattle on the surface overhead. Heard shouts of surprise and panic. Then the darkness was filled with sudden, brilliant light. As it faded he threw the second grenade, more confident this time, aiming it at the smouldering red mouth of the tunnel. Someone was screaming up there – an awful, unnatural, high-pitched scream that chilled his blood – then the second explosion shuddered the air and the screaming stopped abruptly.

Ebert turned. Auden had chipped footholds into the slippery surface of the slope. Now he stood there, the big ascent gun at his hip, waiting for his Captain's order.

'Okay,' Ebert said. 'Try and fix it into the roof of the tunnel. As soon as it's there I'll start up. Once I'm at the top I want a man to follow me every ten seconds. Got that?'

'Sir!'

Auden looked up, judging the distance, then raised the heavy rifle to his shoulder and fired. The bolt flew up, trailing its thin, strong cord. They heard it thud into the ceiling of the tunnel, then two of the men were hauling on the slack of the cord, testing that the bolt was securely fixed overhead.

One of them turned, facing Ebert, his head bowed. 'Rope secure, sir.'

'Good.' He stepped forward and took the gun from the soldier's shoulder. 'Take Leiter's gun, Spitz. Or mine if you can find it.'

'Sir!'

Ebert slipped the gun over his right shoulder, then took the rope firmly and began to climb, hauling himself up quickly, hands and feet working thoughtlessly. Three-quarters of the way up he slowed and shrugged the gun from his shoulder into his right hand, then began to climb again, pulling himself up one-handedly towards the lip.

They would be waiting. The grenades had done some damage, but they wouldn't have finished them off. There would be backups.

He stopped just beneath the lip and looked back down, signalling to Auden that he should begin. At once he felt the rope tighten beneath him as it took the weight of the first of the soldiers. Turning back, Ebert freed the safety with his thumb, then poked the barrel over the edge and squeezed the trigger. Almost at once the air was filled with the noise of return fire. Three, maybe four of them, he estimated.

Beneath him the rope swayed, then steadied again as the men below took the slack. Ebert took a long, shuddering breath, then heaved himself up, staring over the lip into the tunnel beyond.

He ducked down quickly, just as they opened up again. But he knew where they were now. Knew what cover he had up there. Quickly, his fingers fumbling at the catch, he freed the smoke bomb from his belt, twisted the neck of it sharply, then hurled it into the tunnel above him. He heard the shout of warning and knew they thought it was another grenade. Taking another long breath, he pulled the mask up over his mouth and nose, then heaved himself up over the lip and threw himself flat on the floor, covering his eyes.

There was a faint pop, then a brilliant glare of light. A moment later the tunnel was filled with billowing smoke.

Ebert crawled forward quickly, taking cover behind two badly mutilated bodies that lay one atop the other against the left-hand wall. It was not a moment too soon. Bullets raked the tunnel wall only a hand's width above his head. He waited a second, then, taking the first of his targets from memory, fired through the dense smoke.

There was a short scream, then the firing started up again. But only two of them this time.

He felt the bullets thump into the corpse he was leaning on and rolled aside quickly, moving to his right. There was a moment's silence. Or almost silence. Behind him he heard sounds – strangely familiar sounds. A soft rustling that seemed somehow out of context here. He lifted his gun, about to open fire again, when he heard a faint click and the clatter of something small but heavy rolling towards him.

A grenade.

He scrabbled with his left hand, trying to intercept it and throw it back, but it was past him, rolling towards the lip.

'Shit!'

There was nothing for it now. He threw himself forward, his gun held chest-high, firing into the dense smoke up ahead. Then the explosion pushed him off his feet and he was lying amongst sandbags at the far end of the tunnel, stunned, his ears ringing.

'Light!' someone was saying. 'Get a fucking light here!'

Auden. It was Auden's voice.

'Here!' he said weakly and tried to roll over, but there was something heavy across the back of his legs. Then, more strongly. 'I'm here, sergeant!'

Auden came across quickly and reached down, pulling the body from him. 'Thank the gods, sir! I was worried we'd lost you.' He leaned forward and hauled Ebert to his feet, supporting him.

Ebert laughed, then slowly sat back down, his legs suddenly weak. 'Me too.' He looked up again as one of the soldiers brought an arc lamp across to them.

'Shit!' he said, looking about him. 'What happened?'

'You must have blacked out, sir. But not before you did some damage here.' Ebert shuddered, then half turned, putting his hand up to his neck. There were two bodies sprawled nearby, face down beside the sandbags. He looked up at Auden again.

'What are our losses?'

'Six men, sir. Including Leiter. And Grant has a bad head wound. We may have to leave him here for now.'

'Six men? Fuck it!' He swallowed, then sat forward. 'Do we know how the other squads are doing?'

Auden looked down. 'That's another problem, sir. We've lost contact. All the channels are full of static.'

Ebert laughed sourly. 'Static? What the fuck's going on?'

Auden shook his head. 'I don't know. I really don't know, sir. But it's odd. There's an intersection up ahead that isn't on the map. And when you went up...' Auden hesitated, then went on. 'Well, it seems they must have had a sluice or something at the bottom of the slope. One moment I was standing there, helping get the men on the rope, the next I was knee-deep in icy water.'

Ebert looked down. So that was the strange sound he had heard. He shivered, then looked back up at Auden. 'I wondered. You know that? As I was climbing the rope I was asking myself why they hadn't finished us off at once. Just a couple of grenades. That's all it would have taken. But that explains it, doesn't it? They meant to drown us. But why? What difference would it make?'

Auden smiled grimly back at him. 'I don't know, sir, but if you're feeling all right we'd best press on. I don't like this quiet. I have the feeling they're watching us all the while, getting ready to hit us again.'

Ebert smiled and reached out to touch his sergeant's shoulder briefly. 'Okay. Then let's get moving, eh?'

Auden hesitated a moment longer. 'One last thing, sir. Something you ought to know.'

Ebert saw how Auden's eyes went to one of the corpses and felt himself go cold inside. 'Don't tell me. They're like the copies at the wedding. Is that it?'

Auden shook his head, then went across and turned over one of the corpses, tugging off its helmet.

'Gods!' Ebert got up slowly and went across, then crouched above the body and, taking his knife from his belt, slit the jacket open, exposing the naked chest beneath.

He looked up at Auden and saw his own surprised bemusement mirrored back at him. 'The gods preserve us!' He looked back down at the soft curves of the corpse's breasts, the soft, brown, blinded eyes of the nipples, and shuddered. 'Are they all like this?'

Auden nodded. 'All the ones I've looked at so far.'

Ebert pulled the jacket back across the dead woman's breasts then stood up, his voice raised angrily. 'What does it all mean? I mean, what in hell's name does it all mean?'

Auden shrugged. 'I don't know, sir. But I know one thing. Someone told them we were coming. Someone set us up.'

★

General Tolonen dismissed the two guards, locked the door, then turned to face the young prince, his head bowed.

'I am sorry I had to bring you here, young master, but I couldn't chance letting our enemies know of this, however small the risk.'

Li Yuan stood there stiffly, his chin raised slightly, a bitter anger in his red-rimmed eyes. He was barely half the General's height and yet his air of command, even in grief, left no doubt as to who was master, who servant there. The prince was wearing the *cheng fu*, the rough, unhemmed sackcloth of traditional mourning clothes, his feet clad in simple, undecorated sandals, his hands and neck bare of all jewellery. It was all so brutally austere – so raw a display of grief – it made Tolonen's heart ache to see him so.

They were in a Secure Room at the heart of the Bremen fortress. A room no more than twenty *ch'i* square, cut off on all six sides from the surrounding structure, a series of supporting struts holding it in place. It was reached by way of a short corridor with two airlocks, each emptied to total vacuum after use. Most found it an uncomfortable, uneasy place to be. Once inside, however, absolute secrecy could be guaranteed. No cameras looked into the room and no communications links went out from there. In view of recent developments, Tolonen welcomed its perfect isolation. Too much had happened for him to take unnecessary risks.

'Have you spoken to him yet?' Li Yuan asked, anger burning in his eyes. 'Did the bastard lie through his teeth?'

The young boy's anger was something to be seen. Tolonen had never dreamed he had it in him. He had always seemed so cold and passionless. Moreover, there was an acid bitterness to the words that struck a chord in Tolonen. Li Yuan had taken his brother's death badly. Only vengeance would satisfy him. In that they were alike.

Tolonen removed his uniform cap and bowed to him. 'You must be patient, young master. These things take time. I want solid evidence before I confront our friend Berdichev.'

The eight-year-old turned away sharply, the abruptness of the gesture revealing his inner turmoil. Then he turned back, his eyes flaring. 'I want them dead, General Tolonen. Every last one of them. And I want their families eradicated. To the third generation.'

Tolonen bowed his head again. *I would,* he thought, *were that my T'ang's command. But Li Shai Tung has said nothing yet. Nothing of what he feels, or wants, or of what was said in Council yesterday. What have the Seven decided? How are they to answer this impertinence?*

Yes, little master, I would gladly do as you say. But my hands are tied.

'We know much more now,' he said, taking Li Yuan's shoulder and steering him across the room to where two chairs had been placed before a screen. He sat, facing Li Yuan, conscious not only of the boy's grief and anger but also of his great dignity. 'We know how it was done.'

He saw how Li Yuan tensed.

'Yes,' Tolonen said. 'The key to it all was simulated vision.' He saw that it meant nothing to Li Yuan and pressed on. 'We discovered it in our raid on the SimFic installation at Punto Natales. They had been conducting illegal experiments with it there for more than eight years, apparently. It seems that the soft-wire they found in Chao Yang's head was part of one of their systems.'

Li Yuan shook his head. 'I don't understand you, General. SimFic have been conducting illegal experiments? Is that it? They've been wilfully flouting the terms of the Edict?'

Tolonen nodded but raised a hand to fend off Li Yuan's query. This was complex ground and he did not want to get into a discussion about how all Companies conducted such experiments, then lobbied to get their supposedly 'theoretical' products accepted by the Ministry.

'Setting that aside a moment,' he said, 'what is of primary importance here is the fact that Pei Chao Yang was not to blame for your brother's murder. It seems he had brain surgery for a blood clot almost five years ago – an operation that his father, Pei Ro-hen, kept from the public record. Chao had a hunting accident, it seems. He fell badly from his horse. But the operation was a success and he had had no further trouble. That is, until the day of the wedding. Now we know why.'

'You mean, they implanted something in his head? Something to control him?'

'Not to control him, exactly. But something that would make him see precisely what they wanted him to see. Something that superimposed a different set of images. Even a different set of smells, it seems. Something that made him see Han Ch'in *differently...*'

'And we know who carried out this... operation?'

Tolonen looked back at the boy. 'Yes. But they're dead. They've been dead for several years, in fact. Whoever arranged this was very thorough. Very thorough indeed.'

'But SimFic are to blame? Berdichev's to blame?'

He saw the ferocity on Li Yuan's face and nodded. 'I believe so. But maybe not enough to make a conclusive case in law. It all depends on what we find at Hammerfest.'

She came at him like a madwoman, screeching, a big, sharp-edged hunting knife in her left hand, a notched bayonet in her right.

Ebert ducked under the vicious swinging blow and thrust his blade between her breasts, using both hands, the force of the thrust carrying her backwards, almost lifting her off her feet.

'Gods...' he said, looking down at the dying woman, shaken by the ferocity of her attack. 'How many more of them?'

It was five minutes to six and he was lost. Eight of his squad were dead now, two left behind in the corridors, badly wounded. They had killed more than twenty of the defending force. All of them women. Madwomen, like the one he had just killed. And still they came at them.

Why women? he kept asking himself. But deeper down he knew why. It gave his enemy a psychological edge. He didn't feel good about killing women. Neither had his men felt good. He'd heard them muttering among themselves. And now they were dead. Or good as.

'Do we go on?' Auden, his sergeant, asked.

Ebert turned and looked back at the remnants of his squad. There were four of them left now, including himself. And not one of them had ever experienced anything like this before. He could see it in their eyes. They were tired and bewildered. The past hour had seemed an eternity, with no knowing where the next attack would come from.

The ground plans they had been working from had proved completely false. Whoever was in charge of this had secretly rebuilt the complex and turned it into a maze: a web of deadly cul-de-sacs and traps. Worse yet, they had flooded the corridors with ghost signals, making it impossible for them to keep in contact with the other attacking groups.

Ebert smiled grimly. 'We go on. It can't be far now.'

At the next junction they came under fire again and lost another man. But this time the expected counter-attack did not materialize. Perhaps we're almost there, thought Ebert as he pressed against the wall, getting his breath. Maybe this is their last line of defence. He looked across the corridor and met Auden's eyes. *Yes*, he thought, *if we get out of this I'll commend you. For you've saved me more than once this last hour.*

'Get ready,' he mouthed. 'I'll go first. You cover.'

Auden nodded and lifted his gun to his chest, tensed, ready to go.

The crossway was just ahead of them. Beyond it, about ten paces down the corridor and to the right, was a doorway.

Ebert flung himself across the open space, firing to his left, his finger jammed down on the trigger of the automatic. Behind him Auden and Spitz opened up noisily. Landing awkwardly, he began to scrabble forward, making for the doorway.

He heard her before he saw her. Turning his head he caught a glimpse of her on the beam overhead, her body crouched, already falling. He brought his gun up sharply, but it was too late. Even as he loosed off the first wild shot, her booted feet crashed into his back heavily, smashing him down into the concrete floor.

The film had ended. Tolonen turned in his seat and looked at the boy.

'There are two more, then we are done here.'

Li Yuan nodded but did not look back at him. He was sitting there rigidly, staring at the screen as if he would burn a hole in it. Tolonen studied him a moment longer, then looked away. This was hard for the boy, but it was what his father wanted. After all, Li Yuan would be T'ang one day and a T'ang needed to be hard.

Tolonen sat back in his chair again, then pressed the handset, activating the screen again.

On the evening of the wedding the walls of the *Yu Hua Yuan* had been lined with discreet security cameras. The logistics of tracking fifteen hundred individuals in such a small, dimly lit space had meant that they had had to use flat-image photography. Even so, because each individual had been in more than one camera's range at any given moment, a kind of three-dimensional effect had been achieved. A computer programmed for full-head recognition of each of the individuals present had analysed each of the one hundred and eighty separate films and produced fifteen hundred new, 'rounded' films of seventeen minutes' duration – timed to bracket the death of Han Ch'in by eight minutes either side. The new films eliminated all those moments when the heads of others intruded, enhancing the image whenever the mouth was seen to move, the lips to form words. What resulted was a series of individual 'response portraits' so vivid one would have thought the lens had been a mere arm's length in front of each face.

They had already watched five of the seventeen minute films. Had seen the unfeigned surprise – the shock – on the faces of men whom they thought might have been involved.

'Does that mean they're innocent?' Li Yuan had asked.

'Not necessarily,' Tolonen had answered. 'The details might have been kept from them deliberately. But they're the money men. I'm sure of it.'

This, the sixth of the films, showed one of Tolonen's own men, a captain in the elite force; the officer responsible for the *shao lin* posted in the garden that evening.

Li Yuan turned and looked up at Tolonen, surprised.

'But that's Captain Erikson.'

The General nodded. 'Watch. Tell me what you think.'

Li Yuan turned back and for a time was silent, concentrating on the screen.

'Well?' prompted Tolonen.

'His reactions seem odd. His eyes... It's almost as if he's steeled himself not to react.'

'Or as if he was drugged, perhaps? Don't you think his face shows symptoms similar to arfidis trance? He's not been known to indulge before now, but who knows? Maybe he's an addict.'

Li Yuan turned and looked up at the General again. Between the words and the tone in which they had been said lay a question mark.

'You don't believe that, do you?' he said after a moment. 'You don't think he would have risked public exposure of his habit.'

Tolonen was silent, watching the boy closely. Li Yuan looked away again, then started, understanding suddenly what the General had really been saying.

'He knew! That's what you mean, isn't it? Erikson knew, but... but he didn't dare show it. Is that right? You think he risked taking arfidis in public?'

'I think so,' said Tolonen quietly. He was pleased with Li Yuan. If one good thing had come out of this rotten business it was this: Li Yuan would be T'ang one day. A great T'ang. If he lived long enough.

'Then that explains why no *shao lin* were close enough to act.'

'Yes.'

'And Erikson?'

'He's dead. He killed himself an hour after the assassination. At first I thought it was because he felt he had failed me. Now I know otherwise.'

Tolonen stared up at Erikson's face, conscious of the misery behind the dull glaze of his eyes. He had suffered for his betrayal.

Li Yuan's voice was strangely gentle. 'What made him do it?'

'We're not certain, but we think he might have been involved in the assassination of Lwo Kang. He was on DeVore's staff at the time, and is known to have been in contact with DeVore in a private capacity while the latter was in charge of Security on Mars.'

'I see.'

The film ended. The next began. Lehmann's face filled the screen.

Something was wrong. That much was clear at once. Lehmann seemed nervous, strangely agitated. He talked fluently but seemed distanced from what he was saying. He held his head stiffly, awkwardly and his eyes made small, erratic movements in their sockets.

'He knows!' whispered Li Yuan, horrified, unable to tear his eyes away from the image on the screen. 'Kuan Yin, sweet Goddess of Mercy, he *knows!*'

There, framed between Lehmann's head and the screen's top edge, he could see his brother standing with his bride, laughing with her, talking, exchanging loving glances...

No, he thought. No-o-o! Sheer dread welled up in him, making his hands tremble, his stomach clench with anguish. Lehmann's face was huge, almost choking the screen. Vast it was, its surface a deathly white, like the springtime moon, bleak and pitted, filling the sky. And beyond it stood his brother, Han, sweet Han, breathing, talking, laughing – alive! – yes, for that frozen, timeless moment still alive – and yet so small, so frail, so hideously vulnerable.

Lehmann turned and looked across to where Han was talking to the Generals. For a moment he simply stared, his hostility unmasked, then he half turned to his right, as if in response to something someone had said, and laughed. That laughter – so in contrast with the coldness in his eyes – was chilling to observe. Li Yuan shivered. There was no doubting it now. Lehmann had known what was about to happen.

Slowly, almost unobtrusively, Lehmann moved back into the circle of his acquaints, until, as the newly-weds stopped before Pei Chao Yang, he was directly facing them. Now there was nothing but his face staring down from the massive screen; a face that had been reconstructed from a dozen separate angles. All that lay between the lens and his face had been erased, the intruding images of murder cleared from the computer's memory.

'No...' Li Yuan moaned softly, the pressure in his chest almost suffocating him, the pain growing with every moment.

Slowly, so slowly the seconds passed, and then Lehmann's whole face seemed to stiffen.

'His eyes,' said Tolonen softly, his voice filled with pain. 'Look at his eyes...'

Li Yuan groaned. Lehmann's features were shaped superficially into a mask of concern, but his eyes were laughing, the pupils wide, aroused. And there, in the dark centre of each eye, was the image of Pei Chao Yang, struggling with Han Ch'in. *There* – doubled, inverted in the swollen darkness.

'No-o-o!' Li Yuan was on his feet, his fists clenched tightly, his face a rictus of pain and longing. 'Han!... Sweet Han!'

When Ebert came to, the woman was lying beside him, dead, most of her head shot away. His sergeant, Auden, was kneeling over him, firing the big automatic into the rafters overhead.

He lifted his head, then let it fall again, a sharp pain accompanying the momentary wave of blackness. There was a soft wetness at the back of his head where the pain was most intense. He touched it gingerly, then closed his eyes again. *It could be worse*, he thought. *I could be dead.*

Auden let off another burst into the overhead, then looked down at him. 'Are you all right, sir?'

Ebert coughed, then gave a forced smile. 'I'm fine. What's happening?'

Auden motioned overhead with his gun, his eyes returning to the web-like structure of beams and rafters that reached up into the darkness.

'There was some movement up there, but there's nothing much going on now.'

Ebert tried to focus, but found he couldn't. Again he closed his eyes, his head pounding, the pain engulfing him. Auden was still talking.

'It's like a rat's nest up there. But it's odd, sir. If I was them I'd drop gas canisters or grenades. I'd have set up a network of automatic weapons.'

'Perhaps they have,' said Ebert weakly. 'Perhaps there's no one left to operate them.'

Auden looked down at him again, concerned. 'Are you sure you're all right, sir?'

Ebert opened his eyes. 'My head. I've done something to my head.'

Auden set his gun down and lifted Ebert's head carefully with one hand and probed gently with the other.

Ebert winced. 'Gods...'

Auden knelt back, shocked by the extent of the damage. He thought for a moment, then took a small aerosol from his tunic pocket and sprayed the back of Ebert's head. Ebert gritted his teeth against the cold, fierce, burning pain of the spray but made no sound. Auden let the spray fall and took an emergency bandage, a hand-sized padded square, from another pocket and applied it to the wound. Then he laid Ebert down again, turning him on his side and loosening the collar of his tunic. 'It's not too bad, sir. The cut's not deep. She was dead before she could do any real damage.'

Ebert looked up into Auden's face. 'I suppose I should thank you.'

Auden had picked up his gun and was staring up into the overhead again. He glanced down quickly and shook his head. 'No need, sir. It was my duty. Anyway, we'd none of us survive long if we didn't help each other out.'

Ebert smiled, strangely warmed by the simplicity of Auden's statement. The pain was subsiding now, the darkness in his head receding. Looking past Auden, he found he could see much more clearly. 'Where's Spitz?'

'Dead, sir. We were attacked from behind as we crossed the intersection.'

'So there's only the two of us now.'

'Yes, sir.' Auden scanned the overhead one last time, looked back and front, then slipped his gun onto his shoulder. 'I'll have to carry you, sir. There's a stairwell at the end of this corridor. If we're lucky we'll find some of our own up top. I've heard voices up above. Male voices. I think they're some of ours.'

Putting his hands under Ebert's armpits, he pulled the wounded man up into a sitting position, then knelt and, putting all his strength into it, heaved his captain up onto his shoulder. For a moment he crouched there, getting his balance, then reached out with his right hand and picked up his gun.

Li Yuan found her in the eastern palace at Sichuan, seated amidst her maids. It was a big, spacious room, opening on one side to a balcony, from which steps led down to a wide, green pool. Outside the day was bright, but in the room it was shadowed. Light, reflected from the pool, washed the ornate ceiling with ever-changing patterns of silver and black, while beneath all lay in darkness.

Fei Yen wore the ts'ui and the *shang*, the coarse hemp cloth unhemmed, as was demanded by the first mourning grade of *chan ts'ui*. Three years of mourning lay before her now – twenty-seven months in reality. All about her her maids wore simple white, and in a white, rounded bowl beside the high-backed chair in which she sat was a dying spray of flowers, their crimson and golden glory faded.

She looked up at him through eyes made dark from days of weeping, and summoned him closer. She seemed far older than he remembered her. Old and bone-tired. Yet it was only four days since the death of Han Ch'in.

He bowed low, then straightened, waiting for her to speak.

Fei Yen turned slowly and whispered something. At once her maids got up and began to leave, bowing to Li Yuan as they passed. Then he was alone with her.

'Why have you come?'

He was silent a moment, daunted by her; by the unexpected hostility in her voice.

'I... I came to see how you were. To see if you were recovering.'

Fei Yen snorted and looked away, her face bitter. Then, relenting, she looked back at him.

'Forgive me, Li Yuan. I'm mending. The doctors say I suffered no real physical harm. Nothing's broken...'

She shuddered and looked down again, a fresh tear forming in the corner of her eye. Li Yuan, watching her, felt his heart go out to her. She had loved his brother deeply. Even as much as he had loved him. Perhaps that was why he had come: to share with her both his grief and the awful denial of that love. But now that he was here with her, he found it impossible to say what he felt – impossible even to begin to speak of it.

For a while she was perfectly still, then she wiped the tear away impatiently and stood up, coming down to him.

'Please forgive me, brother-in-law. I should greet you properly.'

Fei Yen embraced him briefly, then moved away. At the opening to the balcony she stopped and leaned against one of the pillars, staring out across the pool towards the distant mountains.

Li Yuan followed her and stood there, next to her, not knowing what to say or how to act.

She turned and looked at him. Though eight years separated them he was not far from her height. Even so, she always made him feel like a child beside her. Only a child. All that he knew – all that he was – seemed unimportant. Even he, the future T'ang, was made to feel inferior in her presence. Yes, even now, when her beauty was clouded, her eyes filled with resentment and anger. He swallowed and looked away, but still he felt her eyes upon him.

'So now *you* will be T'ang.'

He looked back at her, trying to gauge what she was thinking, for her words had been colourless, a statement. But what did she feel? Bitterness? Jealousy? Anger that no son of hers would one day be T'ang?

'Yes,' he said simply. 'One day.'

Much earlier he had stood there in his father's study, staring up at the giant image of Europe that filled one wall – the same image that could be seen from the viewing circle in the floating palace, 160,000 li above Chung Kuo.

A swirl of cloud, like a figure 3, had obscured much of the ocean to the far left of the circle. Beneath the cloud the land was crudely shaped. To the east vast plains of green stretched outward towards Asia. All the rest was white; white with a central mass of grey-black and another, smaller mass slightly to the east, making the whole thing look like the skull of some fantastic giant beast with horns. The white was City Europe; glacial, in the grip of a second age of ice.

From up there the world seemed small, reduced to a diagram. All that he saw his father owned and ruled. All things, all people there were his. And yet his eldest son was dead, and he could do nothing. What sense did it make?

He moved past her, onto the balcony, then stood there at the stone balustrade, looking down into the pale green water, watching the fish move in the depths. But for once he felt no connection with them, no ease in contemplating them.

'You've taken it all very well,' she said, coming up beside him. 'You've been a brave boy.'

He looked up at her sharply, bitterly; hurt by her insensitivity, strangely stung by her use of the word 'boy'.

'What do you know?' he snapped, pushing away from her. 'How dare you presume that I feel less than you?'

He rounded on her, almost in tears now, his grief, his unassuaged anger making him want to break something; to snap and shatter something fragile. To hurt someone as badly as he'd been hurt.

She looked back at him, bewildered now, all bitterness, all jealousy drained from her by his outburst. 'Oh, Yuan. Little Yuan. I didn't know...' She came to him and held him tight against her, stroking his hair, ignoring the pain where he gripped her sides tightly, hurting the bruises there. 'Oh, Yuan. My poor little Yuan. I'm sorry. I'm so, so sorry. How was I to know, my little one? How was I to know?'

The stairs led up to a wide landing cluttered with crates. Three corridors led off. Two were cul-de-sacs, the third led to another, much longer stairwell. Auden went up again, his gun poked out in front of him, the safety catch off, his trigger finger aching with the tension of preparedness. Ebert was a numbing weight on his left shoulder.

Near the top of the steps he slowed and looked about him, his eyes on the level of the floor, his gun searching for targets. It was a vast, open space, like the floor of a warehouse, broken every now and then by huge, rectangular blockhouses. The ceiling was high overhead and criss-crossed with tracks. Stacks of crates stood here and there and electric trolleys were parked nearby. Otherwise the place seemed empty.

'I don't like it,' Auden said quietly for Ebert's benefit. 'All that back there. And then nothing. We can't have got them all. And where are our men?'

'What is it?'

'Some kind of loading floor. A huge big place. And there are blockhouses of some kind. They look empty, but they might easily be defended.'

Ebert swallowed painfully. His head ached from being carried upside down and he was beginning to feel sick. His voice was weak now. 'Let's find somewhere we can shelter. Somewhere you can set me down.'

Auden hesitated. 'I'm not sure, sir. I think it's a trap.'

Ebert's weariness was momentarily tinged with irritation. 'Maybe. But we've little choice, have we? We can't go back down. And we can't stay here much longer.'

Auden ignored the sharpness in his captain's voice, scanning the apparent emptiness of the loading floor once again. Nothing. He was almost certain there was nothing out there. And yet his instincts told him otherwise. It was what he himself would have done. Hit hard, then hit hard again and again and again. And then, when your enemy expected the very worst, withdraw. Make them think they had won through. Allow them to come at you without resistance. Draw them into the heart of your defences. And then...

Ebert's voice rose, shattering the silence. 'Gods, sergeant, don't just stand there, do something! I'm dying!'

Auden shuddered. 'All right,' he said. 'We'll find shelter. Somewhere to put you down.'

He breathed deeply for a few seconds, then hauled himself up the last few steps, expecting at any moment to be raked with heavy automatic fire or cut in half by one of the big lasers, but there was nothing. He ran as fast as he could, crouching, wheezing now, the weight of Ebert almost too much for him.

He made the space between two stacks of unmarked boxes and turned, looking back at the stairwell. For a moment he could have sworn he saw a head, back there where he had just come from. He took two shuddering breaths, then put his gun down and gently eased Ebert from his shoulder, setting him down on his side.

'We need to get help for you, sir. You've lost a lot of blood.'

Ebert had closed his eyes. 'Yes,' he said painfully, his voice a whisper now. 'Go on. Be quick. I'll be all right.'

Auden nodded and reached behind him for his gun. His hand searched a moment, then closed slowly, forming a fist. Instinct. He should have trusted to instinct. Raising his hands, he stood up and turned slowly, facing the man with the gun who stood there only three paces away.

'That's right, sergeant. Keep your hands raised and don't make any sudden movements. Now come out here, into the open.'

The man backed away as Auden came forward, keeping his gun levelled. He was a tall, gaunt-looking Han with a long, horse-like face and a wide mouth. He wore a pale green uniform with the SimFic double-helix insignia on lapel and cap. His breast-patch showed a bear snatching at a cloud of tiny, silken butterflies, signifying that he was a fifth rank officer – a captain. As Auden came out into the open other guards came from behind the stacks to encircle him.

'Good,' said the captain. Then he signalled to some of his men. 'Quick now! Get the other one to the infirmary. We don't want him to die, now do we?'

Auden's eyes widened in surprise. He half turned, watching them go to Ebert and lift him gently onto a stretcher. 'What's happening here?' he asked, looking back at the SimFic captain. 'What are you playing at?'

The captain watched his fellows carry Ebert away, then turned back to Auden and lowered his gun. 'I'm sorry, sergeant, but we couldn't take risks. I didn't want to lose any more men through a misunderstanding between us.' Unexpectedly, he smiled. 'You're safe now. The base has been liberated. The insurrection has been put down.'

Auden laughed, not believing what he was hearing. 'Insurrection? What do you mean?'

The Han's smile became fixed. 'Yes. Unknown to the Company, the installation was infiltrated and taken over by a terrorist organization. We only learned of it this morning. We came as soon as we could.'

'Quite a coincidence,' said Auden, sickened, realizing at once what had happened. It was like he'd said to Ebert. They had been set up. The whole thing had been a set-up. A charade. And all to get SimFic off the hook.

'Yes. But fortunate too, yes? If we had not come you would all be dead. As it is, more than a dozen of your men have got out alive.'

Auden shivered, thinking of all the good men he'd fought beside. Dead now. Dead, and simply to save some bastard's butt higher up the levels. 'And the terrorists?'

'All dead. They barricaded themselves into the laboratories. We had to gas them, I'm afraid.'

'Convenient, eh?' He glared at the Han, bitter now.

The captain frowned. 'I'm sorry, but I don't understand you, sergeant. This whole business... it was unfortunate, but it could not be helped, neh? I lost more than thirty of my own men in the fighting.'

Auden stared back at him. Yes, he thought, loathing the slick-tongued Han who stood before him; *you lost thirty 'men' – but not to terrorists, that's for certain!*

There was the sound of raised voices in the corridor outside. At the same moment, the light on the desk intercom began to flash urgently. Soren Berdichev, Head of SimFic, looked up past the five men who were seated round the desk with him and straightened his small, round-rimmed glasses, clearing the computer-generated figures that were displayed in duplicate on their inner surfaces.

'What in heaven's name...?'

It was just after eight in the morning and they were two hours into their weekly strategy conference.

The man closest to him on his left stood, then turned and bowed to him. 'Excuse me, sir. Shall I find out what the trouble is?'

Berdichev put his hand over the cancel on the intercom and looked up at his Senior Executive. He spoke coldly, sternly. 'Thank you, Paul. Please do. If it's a member of staff you will dismiss them immediately. I'll not tolerate such behaviour in these offices.'

Moore bowed again and turned to do as he was bid. But he had got barely halfway across the room when the door crashed open.

Tolonen stood there in the doorway, tall and grey-haired, his eyes burning with anger, his whole manner menacing. He was wearing full combat uniform, the helmet loose about his neck, a light automatic in the holster at his waist, as if he had come straight from action. Behind him several members of Berdichev's staff stood with their heads bowed, shamed that they had not been able to prevent the intrusion.

Berdichev got up slowly, his own outrage tightly, deliberately controlled. 'General Tolonen... I hope you have good reason for bursting in on me like this?'

Tolonen ignored the comment. He looked about the room, then came in, striding past Moore without a glance, making straight for Berdichev.

Shoving between two of the seated men, he leaned across and brought his fist down hard on the table.

'You know perfectly well why I'm here, you wall lizard!'

Berdichev sat back composedly and put his hands together. 'Your manners leave much to be desired, General. If you had had the common courtesy to talk to my secretary I would have seen you this afternoon. But now... Well, you can be certain that I'll be reporting your behaviour to the House committee on Security matters. These are private offices, General, and even you cannot enter without permission.'

Angrily, Tolonen straightened up and took the warrant from his tunic pocket, then flung it down on the desk in front of Berdichev. 'Now explain yourself! Or I'll come round and choke the bloody truth from you!'

Berdichev picked up the small, card-like warrant and studied it a moment, then threw it back across the table at Tolonen. 'So you have a right to be here. But legality doesn't excuse your poor manners, General. My complaint still stands. Your behaviour has been atrocious. You have insulted me and openly threatened me before witnesses. I...'

Tolonen cut him short. He leaned across the table and roared at him. '*Hsin fa ts'ai!* What do you know of manners, you *hsiao jen*!'

For the first time Berdichev bristled. The insults had stung him, but inwardly he felt a small satisfaction. His tactic had the General rattled. The fact that he had slipped into Mandarin revealed just how emotionally off-balance Tolonen was.

He leaned forward, undaunted, and met the General's eyes. 'Now that you're here, you'd best tell me what you want of me. I'm a busy man, *social upstart* or not, *little man* or not. I have an empire to run... if you'll excuse the phrase.'

Tolonen glared at him a moment longer, then straightened up again. 'Dismiss these men. I need to talk to you alone.'

Berdichev looked to the nearest of his men and gave a slight nod. Slowly, reluctantly, they began to leave. His Senior Executive, Moore, stood his ground, however, staring concernedly at his superior. Only as he was about to turn and leave did Berdichev look back at him.

'Paul... please stay. I'd like a witness to what is said here.'

'I said...' began Tolonen, but Berdichev interrupted him.

'I assure you, General, I will say nothing without a witness present. You see, there are no cameras in this room, no tapes. Much is said here that is of a secret nature. Things we would not like to get to the ears of our competitors. You understand me, General? Besides which, you have made threats to me. How can I feel safe unless one of my own is here to see that my rights are not violated?'

Tolonen snorted. 'Rights! Fine words from you, who has so little respect for the rights of others!'

Berdichev looked down. 'Again you insult me, General. Might I ask why? What have I done that should make you treat me thus?'

'You know damn well what you've done! And all this acting won't save your arse this time! You're implicated to the hilt, Shih Berdichev! I'm talking about the murder of Li Han Ch'in, not some petty matter of manners. Two of your installations are directly involved. And that means that you're involved. You personally!'

Berdichev took off his glasses and polished the lenses, then looked back at the General. 'I assume you mean the business at Hammerfest.'

Tolonen laughed, astonished by the sheer effrontery of the man. 'The business at Hammerfest... Yes. I mean the matter of your duplicity.'

'My duplicity?' He stared at the General, shaking his head sadly. 'Again, I don't understand you, General. Have I not been totally open? Have I not given you copies of all the documents relating to both our Punto Natales installation and the base at Hammerfest? Indeed, were it not for my men, I understand that you would have lost all of your force to the terrorists, Klaus Ebert's son amongst them.'

'Terrorists! That's just more of your nonsense! You know damned well there were no terrorists!'

'You can prove that, General?'

Tolonen lowered his voice. 'I have no need to prove it. I know it. Here...' he tapped his heart, '...and here,' he tapped his head.

'And what does that mean?' Berdichev leaned forward, his thin face hardening, his glasses glinting in the overhead light. 'You are making serious accusations, General, and I hope you can substantiate them. I regret what happened at Hammerfest, but I am not responsible for it.'

Tolonen shook his head. 'That's where you're wrong, Berdichev. The research undertaken at both installations was illegal and has been directly linked to the assassination of Li Han Ch'in. Such work was undertaken in the name of SimFic, carried out on properties leased by SimFic and even funded by SimFic. As Head of SimFic you are directly responsible.'

'I disagree. Some projects, undertaken in our name, may well have been illegal, as you say. They may – though it remains to be proved conclusively – be linked to Li Han Ch'in's most unfortunate death. But just because something is done under our corporate name, it does not mean to say that we knew about it, or that we sanctioned it. As you know, General, as soon as I found out what was happening I ordered full cooperation with the Security forces and even ordered my own security squads to assist you.'

Tolonen was silent a moment, his face coldly furious. 'You want me to believe that you didn't know what was going on?'

'To be frank with you, General, I don't really care what *you* believe. I care only for the truth of the matter.' He pointed past Tolonen at a huge chart on the right-hand wall. 'See that there, General? That is a chart of my organization. Its structure, if you like. You'll see how it divides and then subdivides. How certain parts of the organization have a degree of autonomy. How others are buried deep in a long chain of sub-structures. A company like SimFic is a complex creation. A living, functional entity, changing and evolving all the time.'

'So?'

Berdichev folded his arms and sat back again. 'How many men do you command, General? Half a million? A million?'

Tolonen stood straighter. 'I command four Banners. Two million men in all.'

'I see.' He turned to his Senior Executive. 'Paul... How many men do we employ in our African operation?'

'Four hundred and eighty thousand.'

'And in North America?'

'Seven hundred and forty thousand.'

'And in the Asian operation?'

'One million, two hundred thousand.'

Berdichev looked back at the General. 'Those three comprise a third of our total operations, the major part of which is based here, in City Europe. So you see, General, my own "command" is three times the size of your own. Now, let me ask you a question. Do you know what all of *your* men are doing all of the time?'

Tolonen huffed. 'Why, that's absurd! Of course I don't!'

Berdichev smiled coldly. 'And yet you expect me to know what all of my managers are up to all of the time! You expect *me* to be responsible for their actions! Aren't you, by the same argument, responsible for DeVore's actions? For his betrayal?'

Tolonen did not answer, merely stared back at Berdichev, an undisguised hatred in his eyes.

'Well?' Berdichev asked after a moment. 'Are you finished here?'

Tolonen shook his head; his whole manner had changed with the mention of DeVore. He was colder now, more distant. 'I have only one more thing to say to you, *Shih* Berdichev. You claim you are not responsible. So you say. Nonetheless, you will find out who was responsible for this. And you will deliver their heads or your own, understand? I give you three days.'

'Three days!' Berdichev sat forward. 'By what authority...?'

Tolonen went to the door, then turned and looked back at Berdichev. 'Three days. And if you don't I shall come for you myself.'

When he was gone, Berdichev leaned forward and placed his hand on the intercom. 'Did you get all of that?'

A voice answered at once. 'Everything. We're checking now, but it looks like all six angles were fine. We'll have the edited tape to you in an hour.'

'Good!' He closed contact and looked up at Moore. 'Well, Paul?'

Moore was still staring at the door. 'You push him too far, Soren. He's a dangerous man. You should be more cautious of him.'

Berdichev laughed. 'Tolonen? Why, he's an impotent old fool! He can't even wipe his own arse without his T'ang's permission, and Li Shai Tung won't give him authority to act against us in a thousand years – not unless he has proof positive. No, we've done enough, Paul. That just now was all bullshit and bluster. Don't fear. Tolonen will do nothing unless it's sanctioned by his T'ang!'

Tolonen's audience with the T'ang was three hours later. Shepherd, the T'ang's advisor, had got there some time before and had updated Li Shai Tung on all relevant matters. As soon as Tolonen arrived, therefore, they got down to more important business.

The T'ang sat there, in a seat placed at the foot of the dais, dressed in the rough, unhemmed hempcloth of mourning, subdued and solemn, a thousand cares on his shoulders. He had not left the Imperial Palace since the murder of his son, neither had he eaten. At his neck was stitched a broad square of white cloth and in his left hand he held a bamboo staff. Both symbolized his grief.

There were only the three of them in the vast, high-ceilinged Throne Room, and the T'ang's voice, when he spoke, echoed back to them.

'Well, Knut? What do you suggest?'

The General bowed, then outlined his plan, arguing in favour of a pre-emptive strike. War, but of a contained nature, attacking specific targets. A swift retribution, then peace with all other factions.

Li Shai Tung listened, then seemed to look deep inside himself. 'I have lost the most precious thing a man has,' he said at last, looking at each of them in turn. 'I have lost my eldest son. To this I cannot be reconciled. Neither can I love my enemies. Indeed, when I look into my heart I find only hatred there for them. A bitter hatred.' He let out a long breath, then stared fixedly at Tolonen. 'I would kill them like animals if it would end there, Knut. But it would not. There would be war, as you say, but not of the kind you have envisaged. It would be a dirty, secretive, incestuous war, and we would come out poorly from it.'

He smiled bleakly at his General, then looked away, the misery in his dark eyes so eloquent that Tolonen found his own eyes misting in response.

'For once, my good General, I think you are wrong. I do not believe we can fight a contained war. Indeed, the Seven have known that for a long time now. Such a contest would spread. Spread until the Families faced the full might of the Above, for they would see it as a challenge; an attack upon their rights – upon their very existence as a class.'

Tolonen looked down, recalling the look in Lehmann's eyes, the foul effrontery of Berdichev, and shuddered. 'What then, Chieh Hsia?' he said bluntly, almost belligerently. 'Shall we do nothing? Surely that's just as bad?'

Li Shai Tung lifted his hand abruptly, silencing him. It was the first time he had done so in the forty-odd years he had known the General and Tolonen looked back at him wide-eyed a moment before he bowed his head.

The T'ang looked at the staff he held. It was the very symbol of dependency; of how grief was supposed to weaken man. Yet the truth was otherwise. Man was strengthened through suffering, hardened by it. He looked back at his General, understanding his anger; his desire to strike back at those who had wounded him. 'Yes, Knut, to do nothing is bad. But not as bad as acting rashly. We must seem weak. We must bend with the wind, sway in the storm's mouth and bide our time. *Wuwei* must be our chosen course for now.'

Wuwei. Non-action. It was an old Taoist concept. *Wuwei* meant keeping harmony with the flow of things – doing nothing to break that flow.

There was a moment's tense silence, then Tolonen shook his head almost angrily. 'Might I say what I feel, *Chieh Hsia*?' The formality of the General's tone spoke volumes. This was the closest the two men had ever come to arguing.

The T'ang stared at his General a moment, then looked away. 'Say what you must.'

Tolonen bowed deeply, then drew himself erect. 'Just this. You are wrong, Li Shai Tung. Execute me for saying so, but hear me out. You are wrong. I know it. I feel it in my bones. This is no time for *wuwei*. No time to be cool-headed and dispassionate. We must be like the tiger now. We must bare our claws and teeth and strike. This or be eaten alive.'

The T'ang considered for a moment, then leaned further forward on his throne. 'You sound like Han Ch'in,' he said, amusement and bitterness in even measure in his voice. 'He too would have counselled war. "They have killed me, father," he would have said, "so now you must kill them back."' He shivered and looked away, his expression suddenly distraught. 'Gods, Knut, I have considered this matter long and hard. But Han's advice was always brash, always hasty. He thought with his heart. But I must consider my other son now. I must give him life, stability, continuity. If we fight a war he will die. Of that I am absolutely certain. They will find a way – just as they found a way to get to Han Ch'in. And in the end they will destroy the Families.'

Li Shai Tung turned to Shepherd, who had been silent throughout their exchange. 'I do this for the sake of the living. You understand that, Hal, surely?'

Shepherd smiled sadly. 'I understand, Shai Tung.'

'And the Seven?' Tolonen stood there stiffly, at attention, his whole frame trembling from the frustration he was feeling. 'Will you not say to them what you feel in your heart? Will you counsel them to *wuwei*?'

The T'ang faced his General again. 'The Seven will make its own decision. But, yes, I shall counsel *wuwei*. For the good of all.'

'And what did Li Yuan say?'

Tolonen's question was unexpected, was close to impertinence, but Li Shai Tung let it pass. He looked down, remembering the audience with his son earlier that day. 'For your sake I do this,' he had said. 'You see the sense in it, surely, Yuan?' But Li Yuan had hesitated and the T'ang had seen in his eyes the conflict between what he felt and his duty to his father.

'Li Yuan agreed with me. As I knew he would.'

He saw the surprise in his General's eyes; then noted how Tolonen stood there, stiffly, waiting to be dismissed.

'I am sorry we are not of a mind in this matter, Knut. I would it were otherwise. Nonetheless, I thank you for speaking openly. If it eases your mind, I shall put your view to the Council.'

Tolonen looked up, surprised, then bowed. 'For that I am deeply grateful, *Chieh Hsia*.'

'Good. Then I need keep you no more.'

After Tolonen had gone, Li Shai Tung sat there for a long while, deep in thought. For all he had said, Tolonen's conviction had shaken him. He had not expected it. When, finally, he turned to Shepherd, his dark eyes were pained, his expression troubled. 'Well, Hal. What do you think?'

'Knut feels it personally. And, because he does, that clouds his judgement. You were not wrong. Though your heart bleeds, remember you are T'ang. And a T'ang must see all things clearly. Whilst we owe the dead our deepest respect, we must devote our energies to the living. Your thinking is sound, Li Shai Tung. You must ensure Li Yuan's succession. That is, and must be, foremost in your thinking, whatever your heart cries out for.'

Li Shai Tung, T'ang, senior member of the Council of Seven and ruler of City Europe, stood up and turned away from his advisor, a tear forming in the corner of one bloodshot eye.

'Then it is *wuwei*.'

The small girl turned sharply, her movements fluid as a dancer's. Her left arm came down in a curving movement, catching her attacker on the side. In the same instant her right leg kicked out, the foot pointing and flicking, disarming the assailant. It was a perfect movement and the man, almost twice her height, staggered backward. She was on him in an instant, a shrill cry of battle anger coming from her lips.

'Hold!'

She froze, breathing deeply, then turned her head to face the instructor. Slowly she relaxed her posture and backed away from her prone attacker.

'Excellent. You were into it that time, Jelka. No hesitations.'

Her instructor, a middle-aged giant of a man she knew only as Siang, came up to her and patted her shoulder. On the floor nearby her attacker, a professional fighter brought in for this morning's training session only, got up slowly and dusted himself down, then bowed to her. He was clearly surprised to have been bested by such a slip of a girl, but Siang waved him away without looking at him.

Siang moved apart from the child, circling her. She turned, wary of him, knowing how fond he was of tricks. But before she had time to raise her guard he had placed a red sticker over the place on her body shield where her heart would be. She caught his hand as it snaked back, but it was too late.

'Dead,' he said.

She wanted to laugh but dared not. She knew just how serious this was. In any case, her father was watching and she did not want to disappoint him. 'Dead,' she responded earnestly.

There were games and there were games. This game was deadly. She knew she must learn it well. She had seen with her own eyes the price that could be paid. Poor Han Ch'in. She had wept for days at his death.

At the far end of the training hall the door opened and her father stepped through. He was wearing full dress uniform, but the uniform was a perfect, unblemished white, from boots to cap. White. The Han colour of death.

The General came towards them. Siang bowed deeply and withdrew to a distance. Jelka, still breathing deeply from the exercise, smiled and went to her father, embracing him as he bent to kiss her.

'That was good,' he said. 'You've improved a great deal since I last saw you.'

He had said the words with fierce pride, his hand holding and squeezing hers as he stood there looking down at her. At such moments he felt a curious mixture of emotions – love and apprehension, delight and a small, bitter twinge of memory. She was three months short of her seventh birthday, and each day she seemed to grow more like her dead mother.

'When will you be back?' she asked, looking up at him with eyes that were the same breath-taking ice-blue her mother's had been.

'A day or two. I've business to conclude after the funeral.'

She nodded, used to his enigmatic references to business, then, more thoughtfully. 'What will Li Shai Tung do, Daddy?'

He could not disguise the bitterness in his face when he answered. 'Nothing,' he said. 'He will do nothing.' And as he said it he imagined that it was Jelka's funeral he was about to go to; her death he had seen through others' eyes; her body lying there in the casket, young as spring yet cold as winter.

If it were you, my blossom, I would tear down Chung Kuo itself to get back at them.

But was that a deficiency in him? Were his feelings so unnatural? Or was the lack in Li Shai Tung, putting political necessity before what he felt? To want to destroy those who have hurt your loved ones – was that really so wrong? Was he any less of a man for wanting that?

Tolonen shuddered, the thought of his darling Jelka dead filling him with a strange sense of foreboding. Then, conscious of his daughter watching him, he placed his hands on her shoulders. His hands so large, her bones so small, so fragile beneath his fingers.

'I must go,' he said simply, kneeling to hug her.

'Keep safe,' she answered, smiling at him.

He smiled back at her, but his stomach had tightened at her words. It was what her mother had always said.

A cold wind was blowing from the west, from the high plains of Tibet, singing in the crown of the tree of heaven and rippling the surface of the long pool. Li Shai Tung stood alone beneath the tree, staff in hand, his bared head bowed, his old but handsome face lined with grief. At his feet, set into the dark earth, was the Family tablet, a huge rectangle of pale cream stone, carved with the symbols of his ancestors. More than half the stone – a body's length from where he stood – was marble smooth, untouched by the mortician's chisel. So like the future, he thought, staring at Han Ch'in's name, fresh cut into the stone. The future... that whiteness upon which all our deaths are written.

He looked up. It was a small and private place, enclosed by ancient walls. At the southern end a simple wooden gate led through into the northern palace. Soon they would come that way with the litter.

He spoke, his voice pained and awful; like the sound of the wind in the branches overhead. 'Oh, Han... Oh, my sweet little boy, my darling boy.'

He staggered, then clenched his teeth against the sudden memory of Han's mother, his first wife, Lin Yua, sitting in the sunlight at the edge of the eastern orchard by the lake, her dresses spread about her, Han, only a baby then, crawling contentedly on the grass beside her.

Bring it back, he begged, closing his eyes against the pain; Kuan Yin, sweet Goddess of Mercy, bring it back! But there was no returning. They were dead. All dead. And that day no longer was. Except in his mind.

He shuddered. It was unbearable.

Li Shai Tung drew his cloak about him and began to make his slow way back across the grass, leaning heavily on his staff, his heart a cold, dark stone in his breast.

They were waiting for him in the courtyard beyond the wall; all those he had asked to come. The Sons of Heaven and their sons, his trusted men, his son, his dead son's wife and her father, his brothers, and, finally, his own third wife. All here, he thought. All but Han Ch'in, the one I loved the best.

They greeted him solemnly, their love, their shared grief unfeigned, then turned and waited for the litter.

The litter was borne by thirty men, their shaven heads bowed, their white, full-length silks fluttering in the wind. Behind them came four officials in orange robes and, beyond them, two young boys carrying a tiny litter on which rested an ancient bell and hammer.

Han lay there in the wide rosewood casket, dressed in the clothes he had worn on his wedding day. His fine, dark hair had been brushed and plaited, his face given the appearance of perfect health. Rich furs had been placed beneath him, strewn with white blossom, while about his neck were wedding gifts of jewels and gold and a piece of carmine cloth decorated with the marriage emblems of dragon and phoenix.

At the foot of the coffin lay a length of white cotton cloth, nine ch'i in length, Han Ch'in's own symbolic mourning for his father – for tradition said that the son must always mourn the father before he himself was mourned.

Li Yuan, standing at his father's side, caught his breath. It was the first time he had seen his brother since his death, and, for the briefest moment, he had thought him not dead but only sleeping. He watched the litter pass, his mouth open, his heart torn from him. *Merciful gods,* he thought; *sweet Han, how could they kill you? How could they place you in the earth?*

Numbed, he fell into line behind the silent procession, aware only vaguely of his father beside him, of the great lords of Chung Kuo who walked behind him, their heads bared, their garments simple, unadorned. In his mind he reached out to pluck a sprig of blossom from his brother's hair, the petals a perfect white against the black.

At the far end of the long pool the procession halted. The tomb was open, the great stone door hauled back. Beyond it, steps led down into the cold earth.

Most of the bearers now stood back, leaving only the six strongest to carry the litter down the steps. Slowly they descended, followed by the officials and the two boys.

His father turned to him. 'Come, my son. We must lay your brother to rest.'

Li Yuan held back, for one terrible moment overcome by his fear of the place below the earth. Then, looking up into his father's face, he saw his own fear mirrored and found the strength to bow and answer him.

'I am ready, father.'

They went down, into candlelight and shadows. The bearers had moved away from the litter and now knelt to either side, their foreheads pressed to the earth. Han lay on a raised stone table in the centre of the tomb, his head to the south, his feet to the north. The officials stood at the head of the casket, bowed, awaiting the T'ang, while the two boys knelt at the casket's foot, one holding the bell before him, the other the hammer.

Li Yuan stood there a moment at the foot of the steps, astonished by the size of the tomb. The ceiling was high overhead, supported by long, slender pillars that were embedded in the swept earth floor. Splendidly sculpted tomb figures, their *san-t'sai* glazes in yellow, brown and green, stood in niches halfway up the walls, candles burning in their cupped hands. Below them were the tombs of his ancestors, huge pictograms cut deep into the stone, denoting the name and rank of each. On four of them was cut one further symbol – the *Ywe Lung.* These had been T'ang. His father was fifth of the Li family T'ang. He, when his time came, would be the sixth.

A small table rested off to one side. On it were laid the burial objects. He looked up at his father again, then went over and stood beside the table, waiting for the ritual to begin.

The bell sounded in the silence, its pure, high tone like the sound of heaven itself. As it faded the officials began their chant.

He stood there, watching the flicker of shadows against stone, hearing the words intoned in the ancient tongue, and felt drawn up out of himself.

Man has two souls, the officials chanted. There is the animal soul, the p'o, which comes into being at the moment of conception, and there is the hun, the spirit soul, which comes into being only at the moment of birth. In life the two are mixed, yet in death their destiny is different. The p'o remains below, inhabiting the tomb, while the hun, the higher soul, ascends to heaven.

The officials fell silent. The bell sounded, high and pure in the silence. Li Yuan took the first of the ritual objects from the table and carried it across to his father. It was the pi, symbol of Heaven, a large disc of green jade with a hole in its centre. Yin, it was – positive and light and male. As the officials lifted the corpse, Li Shai Tung placed it beneath Han's back, then stood back, as they lowered him again.

The bell sounded again. Li Yuan returned to the table and brought back the second of the objects. This was the tsung, a hollow, square tube of jade symbolizing Earth. Yang, this was – negative and dark and female. He watched as his father placed it on his brother's abdomen.

Each time the bell rang he took an object from the table and carried it to his father. First the huang, symbol of winter and the north, a black jade half-pi which his father laid at Han's feet. Then the chang, symbol of summer and the south, a narrow tapered tablet of red jade placed above Han's head. The kuei followed, symbol of the east and spring, a broad tapered tablet of green jade, twice the size of the chang, which was laid beside Han's left hand. Finally Li Yuan brought the hu, a white jade tiger, symbol of the west and autumn. He watched his father place this at his dead brother's right hand, then knelt beside him as the bell rang once, twice, and then a third time.

The chant began again. Surrounded by the sacred symbols, the body was protected. Jade, incorruptible in itself, would prevent the body's own decay. The p'o, the animal soul, would thus be saved.

Kneeling there, Li Yuan felt awed by the power, the dignity of the ritual. But did it mean anything? His beloved Han was dead and nothing in heaven or earth could bring him back. The body would decay, jade or no jade. And the souls...? As the chant ended he sat back on his haunches and looked about him, at stone and earth and the candlelit figures of death. When nothing returned to speak of it, who knew if souls existed?

Outside again he stood there, dazed by it all, the chill wind tugging at his hair, the afternoon light hurting his eyes after the flickering shadows of the tomb. One by one the T'ang came forward to pay their respects to his father and once more offer their condolences, the least of them greater in power and wealth than the greatest princes of the Tang or Sung or Ch'ing dynasties. Wang Hsien, a big, moon-faced man, T'ang of Africa. Hou Ti, a slender man in his forties, T'ang of South America. Wei Feng, his father's closest friend among his peers, T'ang of East Asia, his seemingly ever-present smile absent for once. Chi Hu Wei, a tall, awkward man, T'ang of the Australias. Wu Shih, T'ang of North America, a big man, built like a fighter, his broad shoulders bunching as he embraced Li Yuan's father. And last Tsu Tiao, T'ang of West Asia, the old man leaning on his son's arm.

'You should have stayed inside,' Li Shai Tung said, embracing him and kissing his cheeks. 'This wind can be no good for you, Tsu Tiao. I thought it would be sheltered here with these walls.'

Tsu Tiao reached out and held his arm. He seemed frail, yet his grip, like his voice, was strong. 'High walls cannot keep the cold wind from blowing, neh, old friend? I know what it is to lose a son. Nothing would have kept me from paying my respects to Li Han Ch'in.'

Li Shai Tung bowed, his face grim. 'That is true, Tsu Tiao.' He turned to the son. 'Tsu Ma. Thank you for coming. I wish we had met in happier circumstances.'

Tsu Ma bowed. He was a strong, handsome man in his late twenties who had, until recently, led a headstrong, dissolute life. Now, with his father ill, he had been forced to change his ways. It was rumoured Tsu Tiao was grooming him for regent, but this was the first time he had appeared publicly at his father's side.

'I too regret that we should meet like this, *Chieh Hsia*. Perhaps you would let me visit you when things are easier?'

Both Tsu Tiao and Li Shai Tung nodded, pleased by the initiative. 'That would be good, Tsu Ma. I shall arrange things.'

Li Yuan's uncles were next to pay their respects – Li Yun-Ti, Li Feng

Chiang and Li Ch'i Chun. Advisors to Li Shai Tung, they stood in the same relationship to his father as he once had to *his* brother. Their lives were as his own might once have been. But it was different now. For Han Ch'in was dead and now he, Li Yuan, was destined to be T'ang.

He had seen the sudden change in them. Eyes that had once passed through him now checked their course and noted him, as if his brother's death had brought him substance. Now strangers bowed and fawned before him. Men like his uncles. He saw how obsequious they had become; how their distant politeness had changed to fear.

Yes, he saw it even now, the fear behind the smiles.

It amused him in a bitter way. Old men afraid of a boy not yet nine. Would I, he asked himself, have grown like them, twisted from my true shape by fear and envy? Perhaps. But now I'll never know.

Others came and stood before them. Fei Yen and her father, the old man almost as devastated as his daughter, his earnest, kindly eyes ringed with darkness.

Last were his father's men, Hal Shepherd and the General.

'This is an ill day, old friend,' said Shepherd. He embraced the T'ang, then stood back, looking around him. 'I hoped not to see this place in my lifetime.'

'Nor I,' said Tolonen. For a moment he stared outward at the distant mountains of the Ta Pa Shan. And when his eyes fell upon the tomb, it was almost as if *his* son lay there beneath the earth, such broken love lay in his gaze.

Tolonen stared at the tomb a moment longer, then looked back at his T'ang. 'We must act, *Chieh Hsia*. Such bitterness cannot be borne.'

'No, Knut. You're wrong. It must and can be borne. We must find the strength to bear it.'

'The Council has made its decision?'

'Yes. An hour back.'

The General bowed his head, his disappointment clear. 'Then it is *wuwei*?'

'Yes,' the T'ang answered softly. '*Wuwei*. For all our sakes.'

The House was in session and Speaker Zakhar was at the lectern, delivering a speech on expansion funding, when the big double doors at the far end of the chamber burst open. Zakhar turned, astonished.

'General Tolonen! What do you mean by this?'

Then Zakhar saw the armed guards pouring in after the General and fell silent. House security was breached. These were the General's own men – his elite guards. They formed up around the upper level of the chamber, their long snub-nosed rifles pointed down into the heart of the assembly.

The General ignored the storm of protests. He moved swiftly, purposefully towards the bench where the senior representatives were seated, and went straight for Under Secretary Lehmann.

Lehmann was shouting, as vehement as any other in his protest. Tolonen stood there a moment, facing him, as if making certain this was the man he wanted, then reached across the desk and grabbed Lehmann by the upper arms.

There was a moment's shocked silence, then the uproar grew fierce. Tolonen had dragged Lehmann over the desk and was jerking him along by his hair, as if dealing with the lowest cur from the Clay. Lehmann's face was contorted with pain and anger as he struggled to get free, but the General had a firm grip on him. He tugged him out into the space between the benches of the Upper Council and the seats of the General Assembly, then stopped abruptly and pulled Lehmann upright. Lehmann gasped, but before he had time to act, Tolonen turned him and pulled his arm up sharply behind his back. The General had drawn his ceremonial dagger and now held it at Lehmann's throat.

He stood there, waiting for them to be silent, scowling at any who dared come too close. Above him, encircling the chamber, his men stood patiently, their laser rifles raised to their shoulders.

He had only a second or two to wait. The House grew deathly still, the tension in the chamber almost tangible. Tolonen tugged gently at Lehmann's arm to keep him still, the point of his dagger pricking the Under Secretary's skin and drawing a tiny speck of blood.

'I've come for justice,' Tolonen said, staring about him defiantly, looking for those faces he knew would be most interested, most fearful at this moment. *They never imagined I would come here for them.* The thought almost made him smile, but this was not a moment for smiling. His face remained grim, determined. Nothing would stop him now.

A low murmur had greeted his words and a few shouts from nearer the back of the hall. He had stirred up a hornet's nest here and Li Shai Tung would be furious. But that did not matter now. Nothing mattered but one thing. He had come to kill Lehmann.

As he stood there, three of his men brought a portable trivee projector down into the space beside him and set it up. The image of Lehmann's face, ten times its normal size, took form in the air beside the frightened reality.

'I want to show you all something,' Tolonen said, raising his voice. He seemed calm, deceptively benign. 'It is a film we took of our friend here at Li Han Ch'in's wedding. At the private ceremony afterwards, in the Imperial Gardens. I should explain, perhaps. The Under Secretary is looking towards where the T'ang's son was standing with his bride. The rest, I think, you'll understand.'

Tolonen scanned the crowded benches again, noting how tense and expectant they had become, then turned and nodded to his ensign. At once the great face came to life, but Tolonen did not look at it. He had seen it too many times already; had seen for himself the effect it had had on Li Yuan.

For the next few minutes there was silence. Only during the final moments of the film was there a growing murmur of unease. They did not have to be told what was happening. The image in the blown-up eye told the story as clearly as any words.

The image faded from the air. Lehmann, who had turned his head to watch, began to struggle again, but the General held him tightly, drawing his arm as far up his back as it would go without breaking, making Lehmann whimper with pain.

'Now you've seen,' said Tolonen simply. 'But understand. I do this not for Li Shai Tung but for myself. Because this man has shamed me. And because such vileness must be answered.' He raised his chin defiantly. 'This act is mine. Do you understand me, *ch'un tzu*? Mine.'

The words were barely uttered when Tolonen drew his knife slowly across Lehmann's throat, the ice-edged blade tearing through the exposed flesh as if through rice paper.

For what seemed an eternity, the General held the body forward as it gouted blood, staring about him at the shocked faces in the chamber. Then he let the body fall, blood splashing as it hit the floor, and stepped back, the trousers of his white ceremonial uniform spattered dark red.

He made no move to wipe it away, but stood there, defiant, his dagger raised, as if to strike again.

IN TIMES TO COME...

Chung Kuo: The Middle Kingdom, is the third volume of a vast dynastic saga that covers more than half a century of this vividly realized future world. In the seventeen volumes that follow, the Great Wheel of fate turns through a full historical cycle, transforming the social climate of Chung Kuo utterly. Chung Kuo is the portrait of these turbulent – and often apocalyptic – times and the people who lived through them.

The story of the young prince, Li Yuan – his love for the beautiful Fei Yen, his accession to the throne, and his long, relentless struggle against the traitorous DeVore – is interwoven with the tales of many others, among them the brilliant young scientist Kim Ward, whose 'web' will one day make it possible at last for Mankind to reach the stars, and the artist Ben Shepherd, whose development of a completely new art form – the Shell – will revolutionize the culture of Chung Kuo.

This epic tale continues in Book Four, Ice and Fire, as Tsu Ma becomes T'ang of West Asia, struggling, alongside his fellow T'ang who make up the ruling Seven, to maintain stasis and prevent change, even as the 'War That Wasn't A War' is fought within the levels of Chung Kuo's great city: a war fought not with armies but with an inventive evil – using bombs and betrayals, brutal assassinations and sly poisonings.

And even as this is happening, other factors – seemingly unimportant of themselves – are adding to the pressure for change. One of these is Kim's creation of 'The Aristotle File' – a document that charts the true history of the world, not the version invented and policed by the Ministry – the Thousand Eyes – who have, for so long, maintained this great secret – this dark shadow at the very heart of Chung Kuo. Its discovery by the Dispersionists will fuel their ardent desire for change and for an end to Han rule.

Lined up against DeVore and the Dispersionists are a handful of men utterly loyal to the Seven – men like General Tolonen, along with the two men he recruited from the Lowers, Gregor Karr and Kao Chen. Kao Chen's experiences in the plantations convince him of the evil of DeVore and his allies, yet it is the giant, Karr, with his supreme athleticism and fearlessness, whom Tolonen uses, like a hawk, to fly against their enemies. And it is this decision, to act directly against the Dispersionists, that will change Chung Kuo for good in what is, effectively, a declaration of war.

CHARACTER LISTING

MAJOR CHARACTERS

DeVore, Howard

A major in the Security forces of the T'ang, Li Shai Tung, he is also the leading figure in the struggle against the Seven. A highly intelligent and coldly logical man, he is the puppet master behind the scenes as the great 'War of the Two Directions' begins.

Ebert, Hans

Son of Klaus Ebert and heir to the vast GenSyn Corporation, he is a captain in the Security forces, admired and trusted by his superiors. Ebert is a complex young man: a brave and intelligent officer, he also has a selfish, dissolute and rather cruel streak.

Fei Yen

Daughter of Yin Tsu, one of the heads of the 'Twenty-Nine', the minor aristocratic families of Chung Kuo. The classically beautiful 'Flying Swallow' is engaged to Li Han Ch'in, prince and heir to City Europe. Fragile in appearance, she is surprisingly strong-willed and fiery.

Kao Chen

Once an assassin from the Net, the lowest levels of the great City, Chen is to raise himself from his humble beginnings to become a captain in the T'ang's Security forces, and, as friend and helper to Gregor Karr, he is to be one of the foot soldiers in the war against DeVore.

Karr, Gregor

He was recruited by Marshal Tolonen from the Net. In his youth he was an athlete and, later, a 'blood' –

a to-the-death combat fighter. A giant of a man, he is to become the 'hawk' Li Shai Tung will fly against his adversary, DeVore.

Li Shai Tung

T'ang of City Europe and one of the Seven, the ruling Council of Chung Kuo, Li Shai Tung is now in his seventies. For many years he was the fulcrum of the Council and unofficial spokesman for the Seven, representing their strong determination to prevent Change at all costs.

Li Yuan

Second son of Li Shai Tung, he is considered to be old before his time. His cold, thoughtful manner conceals a passionate nature, expressed in his love for his brother's bride, Fei Yen.

Tolonen, Jelka

Daughter of Marshal Tolonen, Jelka has been brought up in a very masculine environment, lacking a mother's influence. However, her genuine interest in martial arts and in weaponry and strategy mask a very different side to her nature; a side which will be brought out by violent circumstances.

Tolonen, Knut

General to Li Shai Tung, Tolonen is a big, granite-jawed man and the staunchest supporter of the values and ideals of the Seven. Possessed of a fiery, fearless nature, he will stop at nothing to protect his masters.

Tsu Ma

T'ang of West Asia and one of the Seven, the ruling Council of Chung Kuo, Tsu Ma has thrown off his former dissolute ways to support his father in Council. A strong, handsome man, he has still, however, a weakness in his nature – one that will almost prove his undoing.

Wang Sau-leyan

Fourth and youngest son of Wang Hsien, T'ang of Africa, the murder of his two eldest brothers has placed him closer to the centre of political events. Thought of as a wastrel, he is, in fact, a shrewd and highly capable political being who is set – through circumstances of his own devising – to become the harbinger of Change inside the Council of Seven.

Ward, Kim

Born in the Clay, that dark wasteland beneath the great City's foundations, Kim has a quick and unusual bent of mind. His vision of a giant web, formulated in the darkness, has driven him into the light of the Above. Rescued from oblivion, he begins to show his true potential as the most promising young scientist in the whole of Chung Kuo.

THE SEVEN AND THE FAMILIES

Li Feng Chiang	brother and advisor to Li Shai Tung
Li Han Ch'in	first son of Li Shai Tung and heir to City Europe
Li Shai Tung	T'ang of City Europe
Li Yuan	second son of Li Shai Tung and brother to Li Han Ch'in
Lin Yua	first wife of Li Shai Tung
Pei Ro-hen	head of the Pei family, one of the 'Twenty-Nine' Minor Families
Tsu Ma	son of Tsu Tiao, T'ang of West Asia
Tsu Tiao	T'ang of West Asia
Wang Hsien	T'ang of Africa
Wang Sau-leyan	fourth son of Wang Hsien
Wei Feng	T'ang of East Asia
Wu Shih	T'ang of North America
Yin Fei Yen	'Flying Swallow', Minor Family princess and daughter of Yin Tsu
Yin Tsu	head of the Yin family, one of the 'Twenty-Nine', the Minor Families

FRIENDS AND RETAINERS OF THE SEVEN

Auden, William	sergeant in Security
Chung Hu-Yan	chancellor to Li Shai Tung
Ebert, Hans	captain in Security and heir to the GenSyn Corporation
Ebert, Klaus Stefan	Head of GenSyn (Genetic Synthetics) and Advisor to Li Shai Tung
Fest, Edgar	lieutenant in Security
Haavikko, Axel	ensign in Security

Haavikko, Vesa	sister of Axel Haavikko
Heng Yu	Minister of Transportation for City Europe
Kao Chen	'Kwai' (knife) and, later, sergeant in Security
Karr, Gregor	'Blood' and, later, major in Security
Lwo Kang	Minister of the Edict under Li Shai Tung
Nocenzi, Vittorio	major in Security, City Europe
Shepherd, Hal	Advisor to Li Shai Tung and head of the Shepherd family
Tolonen, Jelka	daughter of Knut Tolonen
Tolonen, Knut	general in Security
Yang Lai	junior minister under Li Shai Tung

DISPERSIONISTS

Berdichev, Soren	head of SimFic (Simulated Fictions)
DeVore, Howard	major in Li Shai Tung's Security forces
Lehmann, Pietr	leader of the Dispersionists and Senior Representative in the House at Weimar
Wyatt, Edmund	businessman and (unknown to him) father of Kim Ward

OTHER CHARACTERS

Golden Heart	young prostitute purchased by Hans Ebert for his household
Lu Ming-Shao	Whiskers Lu – *Tong* Boss in the Net
Mu Chua	'Madam' of the House of the Ninth Ecstasy, a sing-song house, or brothel
Pi Ch'ien	Third Secretary to Junior Minister Yang Lai
T'ai Cho	tutor and guardian to Kim Ward
Wang Ti	wife of Kao Chen
Ward, Kim	'Clayborn', orphan and scientist

THE DEAD

Alison	Jake Reed's girlfriend at New College; Evaluation Executive at GenSyn
Chang Hsuan	Han painter from the eighth century AD
Chao Ni Tsu	Grand Master of *Wei Chi* and computer genius. Servant of Tsao Ch'un
Croft, Rebecca	'Becky', daughter of Leopold, with a lazy eye
Dick, Philip K.	American science fiction writer
Ebert, Gustav	genetics genius and co-founder of GenSyn, Genetic Synthetics
Ebert, Wolfgang	financial genius and co-founder of GenSyn, Genetic Synthetics
Griffin, James B.	Sixtieth President of the United States of America
Hubbard, Mary	wife of Tom Hubbard and mother of Cathy, Meg and Beth. Second wife of Jake Reed
Hubbard, Tom	Farmer; resident in Church Knowle. Husband of Mary Hubbard and father of Beth, Meg and Cathy. Best friend to Jake Reed
Jiang Lei	general of Tsao Ch'un's Eighteenth Banner Army, also known as Nai Liu
Ludd, Drew	biggest grossing actor in Hollywood and star of *Ubik*
Mao Tse Tung	first Ko Ming emperor (ruled AD 1948 to 1976)
Nai Liu	'Enduring Willow'; pen name of Jiang Lei and the most popular Han poet of his time
Palmer, Joshua	'Old Josh', record collector
Reed, Anne	first wife of Jake Reed; mother of Peter Reed and sister of Mary Hubbard (Jake's second wife)
Reed, Jake	'Login' or 'Webdancer' for Hinton Industries. Father of Peter Reed
Reed, Peter	son of Jake and Anne Reed; GenSyn Executive
Trish	Artificial Intelligence 'filter avatar' for Jake Reed's penthouse apartment
Tsao Ch'un	ex-member of the Chinese Communist Politburo and architect of 'The Collapse'. Mass murderer and tyrant
Wang Yu-lai	Cadre servant of the Ministry, 'the Thousand Eyes'. Instructed to report back on Jiang Lei

GLOSSARY OF MANDARIN TERMS

The transcription of standard Mandarin into a European alphabetical form was first achieved in the seventeenth century by the Italian, Matteo Ricci, who founded and ran the first Jesuit Mission in China from 1583 until his death in 1610. Since then several dozen attempts have been made to reduce the original Chinese sounds, represented by some tens of thousands of separate pictograms, into readily understandable phonetics for Western use. For a long time, however, three systems dominated – those used by the three major Western powers vying for influence in the corrupt and crumbling Chinese Empire of the nineteenth century: Great Britain; France; and Germany. These systems were the Wade-Giles (Great Britain and America – sometimes known as the Wade System), the Ecole francaise d'Extrême-Orient (France) and the Lessing (Germany).

Since 1958, however, the Chinese themselves have sought to create one single phonetic form, based on the German system, which they termed the *hanyu pinyin fang'an* (Scheme for a Chinese Phonetic Alphabet), known more commonly as pinyin, and in all foreign language books published in China since 1 January 1979 pinyin has been used, as well as being taught now in schools alongside the standard Chinese characters. For this work, however, I have chosen to use the older, and to my mind, far more elegant transcription system, the Wade-Giles (in modified form). For those now used to the harder forms of pinyin the following may serve as a basic conversion guide, the Wade-Giles first, the pinyin after.

p for b	ch' for q
ts' for c	j for r
ch' for ch	t' for t
t for d	hs for x
k for g	ts for z
ch for j	ch for zh

The effect is, I hope, to render the softer, more poetic side of the original Mandarin, ill-served, I feel, by modern pinyin.

It is not intended to belabour the reader with a whole mass of arcane Han expressions here. Some – usually the more specific – are explained in contect. However, as a number of Mandarin terms are used naturally in the text, I've thought it best to provide a brief explanation of these terms.

aiya!	a common expression of surprise or dismay
amah	a domestic maidservant
Amo Li Jia	the Chinese gave this name to North America when they first arrived in the 1840s. Its literal meaning is 'The Land Without Ghosts'
an	a saddle. This has the same sound as the word for peace, and thus is associated in the Chinese mind with peace
catty	the colloquial term for a unit of measure formally called a jin. One catty – as used here – equals roughly 1.1. pounds (avoirdupois), or (exactly) 500 grams. Before 1949 and the standardization of Chinese measures to a metric standard, this measure varied district by district, but was generally regarded as equalling about 1.33 pounds (avoirdupois)
ch'a	tea. It might be noted that *ch'a shu*, the Chinese art of tea, is an ancient forebear of the Japanese tea ceremony *chanoyu*. *Hsiang p'ien* are flower teas, *Ch'ing ch'a* are green, unfermented teas
ch'a hao t'ai	literally, a 'directory'
ch'a shu	the art of tea, adopted later by the Japanese in their tea ceremony. The *ch'a* god is Lu Yu and his image can be seen on banners outside teahouses throughout Chung Kuo

chan shih	a 'fighter', here denoting a *tong* soldier
chang	ten *ch'i*, thus about 12 feet (Western)
Chang-e	the goddess of the Moon, and younger sister of the Spirit of the Waters. The moon represents the very essence of the female principal, *Yin*, in opposition to the Sun, which is *Yang*. Legend has it that Chang-e stole the elixir of immortality from her husband, the great archer *Shen* I, then fled to the Moon for safety. There she was transformed into a toad, which, so it is said, can still be seen against the whiteness of the moon's surface
chang shan	literally 'long dress', which fastens to the right. Worn by both sexes. The woman's version is a fitted, calf-length dress similar to the *chi pao*. A south China fashion, it is also known as a *cheung sam*
chao tai hui	an 'entertainment', usually, within *Chung Kuo*, of an expensive and sophisticated kind
chen yen	true words; the Chinese equivalent of a mantra
ch'eng	the word means both 'City' and 'Wall'
Ch'eng Ou Chou	City Europe
Ch'eng Hsiang	'Chancellor', a post first established in the Ch'in court more than two thousand years ago
ch'i	a Chinese 'foot'; approximately 14.4 inches
ch'i	'inner strength'; one of the two fundamental 'entities' from which everything is composed. Li is the 'form' or 'law', or (to cite Joseph Needham) the 'principle of organization' behind things, whereas *ch'i* is the 'matter-energy' or 'spirit' within material things, equating loosely to the *Pneuma* of the Greeks and the *prana* of the ancient Hindus. As the sage Chu Hsi (AD 1130–1200) said, 'The li is the *Tao* that pertains to "what is above shapes" and is the source from which all things are produced. The *ch'i* is the material [literally instrument] that pertains to "what is within shapes", and is the means whereby things are produced... Throughout the universe there is no *ch'i* without li, or li without *ch'i*.'
chi ch'i	common workers; but used here mainly to denote the antlike employees of the Ministry of Distribution
Chia Ch'eng	Honorary Assistant to the Royal Household

chi'an	a general term for money
chiao tzu	a traditional North Chinese meal of meat-filled dumplings eaten with a hot spicy sauce
Chieh Hsia	term meaning 'Your Majesty', derived from the expression 'Below the Steps'. It was the formal way of addressing the Emperor, through his Ministers, who stood 'below the steps'
chi pao	literally 'banner gown'; a one-piece gown of Manchu origin, usually sleeveless, worn by women
chih chu	a spider
ch'in	a long (120 cm) narrow, lacquered zither with a smooth top surface and sound holes beneath, seven silk strings and thirteen studs marking the harmonic positions on the strings. Early examples have been unearthed from fifth century BC tombs, but it probably evolved in the fourteenth or thirteenth century BC. It is the most honoured of Chinese instruments and has a lovely mellow tone
Chin P'ing Mei	*The Golden Lotus*, an erotic novel, written by an unknown scholar – possibly anonymously by the writer Wang Shih-chen – at the beginning of the seventeenth century as a continuation of the *Shui Hui Chuan*, or 'Warriors of the Marsh', expanding chapters 23 to 25 of the *Shan Hui*, which relate the story of how Wu Sung became a bandit. Extending the story beyond this point, the *Golden Lotus* has been accused of being China's great licentious (even, perhaps, pornographic) novel. But as C.P. Fitzgerald says, 'If this book is indecent in parts, it is only because, telling a story of domestic life, it leaves out nothing.' It is available in a three-volume English-language translation
ch'ing	pure
ching	literally 'mirror'; here used also to denote a perfect GenSyn copy of a man. Under the Edict of Technological Control, these are limited to copies of the ruling T'ang and their closest relatives. However, mirrors were also popularly believed to have certain strange properties, one of which was to make spirits visible. Buddhist priests used special 'magic mirrors' to show believers the form into which they would be reborn. Moreover, if a man looks into one of these mirrors and fails to recognise his own face, it is a

sign that his own death is not far off. [See also *hu hsin chung*.]

ch'ing ch'a	green, unfermented teas
Ch'ing Ming	the Festival of Brightness and Purity, when the graves are swept and offerings made to the deceased. Also known as the Festival of Tombs, it occurs at the end of the second moon and is used for the purpose of celebrating the Spring, a time for rekindling the cooking fires after a three-day period in which the fires were extinguished and only cold food eaten.
Chou	literally, 'State', but here used as the name of a card game based on the politics of Chung Kuo. See 'The Feast Of The Dead' in Book Four.
chow mein	this, like chop suey, is neither a Chinese nor a Western dish, but a special meal created by the Chinese in North America for the Western palate. A transliteration of *chao mian* (fried noodles) it is a distant relation of the liang *mian huang* served in Suchow
ch'u	the west
chun hua	literally, 'Spring Pictures'. These are, in fact, pornographic 'pillow books', meant for the instruction of newly-weds
ch'un tzu	an ancient Chinese term from the Warring States period, describing a certain class of noblemen, controlled by a code of chivalry and morality known as the li, or rites. Here the term is roughly, and sometimes ironically, translated as 'gentlemen', The *ch'un tzu* is as much an ideal state of behaviour – as specified by Confucius in the *Analects* – as an actual class in Chung Kuo, though a degree of financial independence and a high standard of education are assumed a prerequisite
chung	a lidded ceramic serving bowl for *ch'a*
chung hsin	loyalty
E hsing hsun huan	a saying: 'Bad nature follows a cycle'
er	two
erh tzu	son
erhu	a traditional Chinese instrument
fa	punishment

fen	a unit of currency; see *yuan*. It has another meaning, that of a 'minute' of clock time, but that usage is avoided here to prevent any confusion
feng yu	a 'phoenix chair', canopied and decorated with silver birds. Coloured scarlet and gold, this is the traditional carriage for a bride as she is carried to her wedding ceremony
fu jen	'Madam', used here as opposed to *t'ai t'ai*, 'Mrs'
fu sang	the hollow mulberry tree; according to ancient Chinese cosmology this tree stands where the sun rises and is the dwelling place of rulers. *Sang* (mulberry), however, has the same sound as sang (sorrow) in Chinese
Han	term used by the Chinese to describe their own race, the 'black-haired people', dating back to the Han dynasty (210 BC – AD 220). It is estimated that some ninety-four per cent of modern China's population are Han racially
Hei	literally 'black'. The Chinese pictogram for this represents a man wearing war paint and tattoos. Here it refers specifically to the genetically manufactured half-men, made by GenSyn and used as riot police to quell uprisings in the lower levels of the City
ho yeh	Nelumbo Nucifera, or lotus, the seeds of which are used in Chinese medicine to cure insomnia
Hoi Po	the corrupt officials who dealt with the European traders in the nineteenth century, more commonly known as 'hoppos'
Hsia	a crab
hsiang p'en	flower *ch'a*
hsiao	filial piety. The character for *hsiao* is comprised of two parts, the upper part meaning 'old', the lower meaning 'son' or 'child'. This dutiful submission of the young to the old is at the heart of Confucianism and Chinese culture generally
Hsiao chieh	'Miss', or an unmarried woman. An alternative to *nu shi*
hsiao jen	'little man/men'. In the *Analects*, Book XIV, Confucius writes, 'The gentleman gets through to what is up above; the small man gets through to what is down below.' This distinction between 'gentlemen' (*ch'un tzu*) and 'little men'

(hsiao jen), false even in Confucius's time, is no less a matter of social perspective in Chung Kuo

hsien — historically an administrative district of variable size. Here the term is used to denote a very specific administrative area; one of ten stacks – each stack composed of 30 decks. Each deck is a hexagonal living unit of ten levels, two li, or approximately one kilometre, in diameter. A stack can be imagined as one honeycomb in the great hive that is the City. Each hsien of the city elects one Representative to sit in the House at Weimar

Hsien Ling — Chief Magistrate, in charge of a Hsien. In Chung Kuo these officials are the T'ang's representatives and law enforcers for the individual hsien

hsueh pai — 'snow white'; a derogatory term here for Hung Mao women

Hu pu — the T'ang's Finance Ministry

hu hsin chung — see ching, re Buddhist magic mirrors, for which this was the name. The power of such mirrors was said to protect the owner from evil. It was also said that one might see the secrets of futurity in such a mirror. See the chapter 'Mirrors' in The White Mountain for further information

hu t'ieh — a butterfly. Anyone wishing to follow up on this tale of Chuang Tzu's might look to the sage's writings and specifically the chapter, 'Discussion on Making All Things Equal'

hua pen — literally ' story roots', these were précis guidebooks used by the street corner storytellers in China for the past two thousand years. The main events of the story were written down in the hua pen for the benefit of those storytellers who had not yet mastered their art. During the Yuan or Mongol dynasty (AD 1280–1368) these hua pen developed into plays, and, later on – during the Ming dynasty (AD 1368–1644) into the form of popular novels, of which the Shui Hu Chuan, or 'Outlaws Of The Marsh', remains one of the most popular. Any reader interested in following this up might purchase Pearl Buck's translation, rendered as All Men Are Brothers and first published in 1933

Huang-ti — originally Huang-ti was the last of the 'Three Sovereigns' and the first of the 'Five Emperors' of ancient Chinese tradition. Huang-ti, the Yellow Emperor, was the earliest ruler recognized by the historian Ssu-ma Ch'ien (136–85 BC) in his great historical work, the Shih Chi. Traditionally, all subsequent rulers (and would-be rulers) of China have claimed descent from the Yellow Emperor, the 'Son of Heaven' himself, who first brought civilization to the black-haired people. His name is now synonymous with the term 'emperor'

hun — the higher soul or 'spirit soul', which, the Chinese believe, ascends to Heaven at death, joins Shang Ti, the Supreme Ancestor, and lives in his court for ever more

hun tun — 'the Chou believed that Heaven and Earth were once inextricably mixed together in a state of undifferentiated chaos, like a chicken's egg. Hun Tun they called that state' (The Broken Wheel, Chapter 37). It is also the name of a meal of tiny sack-like dumplings

Hung Lou Meng — The Dream of Red Mansions, also known as The Story Of The Stone, a lengthy novel written in the middle of the eighteenth century. Like the Chin Ping Mei, it deals with the affairs of a single Chinese family. According to experts the first eighty chapters are the work of Ts'ao Hsueh-ch'in, and the last forty belong to Kao Ou. It is, without doubt, the masterpiece of Chinese literature, and is available from Penguin in the UK in a five volume edition

Hung Mao — literally 'redheads', the name the Chinese gave to the Dutch (and later English) seafarers who attempted to trade with China in the seventeenth century. Because of the piratical nature of their endeavours (which often meant plundering Chinese shipping and ports) the name continues to retain connotations of piracy

Hung Mun — the Secret Societies or, more specifically, the Triads

huo jen — literally, 'fire men'

I Lung — The 'First Dragon', Senior Minister and Great Lord of the 'Ministry', also known as 'the Thousand Eyes'

jou tung wu — literally 'meat animal': 'It was a huge mountain of flesh, a hundred ch'i to a side and almost twenty ch'i in height. Along one side of it, like the teats of a giant pig, three dozen heads jutted from the flesh, long, eyeless snouts with shovel jaws that snuffled and gobbled in the conveyor-belt trough...'

kai t'ou	a thin cloth of red and gold that veils a new bride's face. Worn by the Ch'ing empresses for almost three centuries
kan pei!	'good health!' or 'cheers!' – a drinking toast
kang	the Chinese hearth, serving also as oven and, in the cold of winter, as a sleeping platform
K'ang hsi	a Ch'ing (or Manchu) emperor whose long reign (AD 1662–1722) is considered a golden age for the art of porcelain-making
kao liang	a strong Chinese liquor
Ko Ming	'revolutionary'. The Tien Ming is the Mandate of Heaven, supposedly handed down from Shang Ti, the Supreme Ancestor, to his earthly counterpart, the Emperor (Huang-ti). This Mandate could be enjoyed only so long as the Emperor was worthy of it, and rebellion against a tyrant – who broke the Mandate through his lack of justice, benevolence and sincerity – was deemed not criminal but a rightful expression of Heaven's anger
k'o t'ou	the fifth stage of respect, according to the 'Book of Ceremonies', involves kneeling and striking the head against the floor. This ritual has become more commonly known in the West as kowtow
ku li	'bitter strength'. These two words, used to describe the condition of farm labourers who, after severe droughts or catastrophic floods, moved off their land and into the towns to look for work of any kind – however hard and onerous – spawned the word 'coolie' by which the West more commonly knows the Chinese labourer. Such men were described as 'men of bitter strength', or simply 'ku li'
Kuan Hua	Mandarin, the language spoken in mainland China. Also known as kuo yu and pai hua
Kuan Yin	the Goddess of Mercy. Originally the Buddhist male bodhisattva, Avalokitsevara (translated into Han as 'He who listens to the sounds of the world', or 'Kuan Yin'), the Han mistook the well-developed breasts of the saint for a woman's and, since the ninth century, have worshipped Kuan Yin as such. Effigies of Kuan Yin will show her usually as the Eastern Madonna, cradling a child in her arms. She is also sometimes seen as the wife of Kuan Kung, the Chinese God of War

Kuei Chuan	'Running Dog', here the name of a Triad
kuo yu	Mandarin, the language spoken in most of Mainland China. Also rendered here as *kuan hua* and *pai hua*
kwai	an abbreviation of *kwai tao*, a 'sharp knife' or 'fast knife'. It can also mean to be sharp or fast (as a knife). An associated meaning is that of a 'clod' or 'lump of earth'. Here it is used to denote a class of fighters from below the Net, whose ability and self-discipline separate them from the usual run of hired knives
Lan Tian	'Blue Sky'
Lang	a covered walkway
lao chu	sing-song girls, slightly more respectable than the common *men hu*
lao jen	'old man' (also *weng*); used normally as a term of respect
lao kuan	a 'Great Official', often used ironically
lao shih	term that denotes a genuine and straightforward man – bluff and honest
lao wai	an outsider
li	a Chinese 'mile', approximating to half a kilometre or one third of a mile. Until 1949, when metric measures were adopted in China, the *li* could vary from place to place
Li	'Propriety'. See the *Li Ching* or 'Book Of Rites' for the fullest definition
Li Ching	'The Book Of Rites', one of the five ancient classics
liang	a Chinese ounce of roughly 32g. 16 *liang* form a *catty*
liu k'ou	the seventh stage of respect, according to the 'Book of Ceremonies'. Two stages above the more familiarly known *'k'o t'ou'* (kowtow) it involves kneeling and striking the forehead three times against the floor, rising on to one's feet again, then kneeling and repeating the prostration with three touches of the forehead to the ground. Only the *san kuei chiu k'ou* – involving three prostrations – was more elaborate and was reserved for Heaven and its son, the Emperor (see also *san k'ou*)
liumang	punks
lu nan jen	literally 'oven man'; title of the official who is responsible for cremating all of the dead bodies

lueh	'that invaluable quality of producing a piece of art casually, almost uncaringly'
lung t'ing	'dragon pavilions'; small sedan chairs carried by servants and containing a pile of dowry gifts
Luoshu	the Chinese legend relates that in ancient times a turtle crawled from a river in Luoshu province, the patterns on its shell forming a three by three grid of numeric pictograms, the numbers of which – both down and across – equalled the same total of fifteen. Since the time of the Shang (three thousand-plus years ago) tortoise shells were used in divination, and the Luoshu diagram is considered magic and is often used as a charm for easing childbirth
ma kua	a waist-length ceremonial jacket
mah jong	Whilst, in its modern form, the 'game of the four winds' was introduced towards the end of the nineteenth century to Westerners trading in the thriving city of Shanghai, it was developed from a card game that existed as long ago as AD 960. Using 144 tiles, it is generally played by four players. The tiles have numbers and also suits – winds, dragons, bamboos and circles
mao	a unit of currency. See yuan
mao tai	a strong, sorghum-based liquor
mei fa tzu	common saying, 'It is fate!'
mei hua	'plum blossom'
mei mei	sister
mei yu jen wen	'sub humans'. Used in Chung Kuo by those in the City's uppermost levels to denote anyone living in the lower hundred
men hu	literally, 'the one standing in the door'. The most common (and cheapest) of prostitutes
min	literally 'the people'; used (as here) by the Minor Families in a pejorative sense, as an equivalent to 'plebeian'
Ming	the Dynasty that ruled China from 1368 to 1644. Literally, the name means 'Bright' or 'Clear' or 'Brilliant'. It carries connotations of cleansing
mou	A Chinese 'acre' of approximately 7,260 square feet. There are roughly six mou to a Western acre, and a 10,000-mou

	field would approximate to 1666 acres, or just over two and a half square miles
Mu Ch'in	'Mother'; a general term commonly addressed to any older woman
mui tsai	rendered in Cantonese as 'mooi-jai'. Colloquially it means either 'little sister' or 'slave girl'; though generally, as here, the latter. Other Mandarin terms used for the same status are *pei-nu* and *yatou*. Technically, guardianship of the girl involved is legally signed over in return for money
nan jen	common term for 'Man'
Ni Hao?	'How are you?'
niao	literally 'bird', but here, as often, it is used euphemistically as a term for the penis, often as an expletive
nu er	daughter
nu shi	an unmarried woman; a term equating to 'Miss'
Pa shi yi	literally 'Eighty-One'; here referring specifically to the Central Council of the New Confucian officialdom
pai nan jen	literally 'white man'
pai pi	'hundred pens'; term used for the artificial reality experiments renamed 'shells' by Ben Shepherd.
pan chang	supervisor
pao yun	a 'jewelled cloud' *ch'a*
pau	a simple long garment worn by men
pau shuai ch'i	the technical scientific term for 'half-life'
p'i p'a	a four-stringed lute used in traditional Chinese music
Pien Hua!	Change!
p'ing	an apple, symbol of peace
ping	the east
Ping Fa	Sun Tzu's *The Art Of War*, written over two thousand years ago. The best English translation is probably Samuel B. Griffith's 1963 edition. It was a book Chairman Mao frequently referred to
Ping Tiao	levelling. To bring down or make flat. Here, in Chung Kuo, it is also a terrorist organization

p'o	the 'animal soul' which, at death, remains in the tomb with the corpse and takes its nourishment from the grave offerings. The p'o decays with the corpse, sinking down into the underworld (beneath the Yellow Springs) where – as a shadow – it continues an existence of a kind
sam fu	an upper garment (part shirt, part jacket) worn originally by both males and females, in imitation of Manchu styles; later on a wide-sleeved, calf-length version was worn by women alone
san	three
San chang	the three palaces
san kuei chiu k'ou	the eighth and final stage of respect, according to the 'Book Of Ceremonies', it involves kneeling three times, each time striking the forehead three times against the ground before rising from one's knees (in k'ou t'ou one strikes the forehead but once). This most elaborate form of ritual was reserved for Heaven and its son, the Emperor. See also liu k'ou
san k'ou	abbreviated form of san kuei chiu k'ou
San Kuo Yan Yi	The Romance of The Three Kingdoms, also known as the San Kuo Chih Yen I. China's great historical novel, running to 120 chapters, it covers the period from AD 168 to AD 265. Written by Lo Kuan-chung in the early Ming dynasty. Its heroes, Liu Pei, Kuan Chung and Chang Fei, together with its villain, Ts'ao Ts'ao, are all historical personages. It is still one of the most popular stories in modern China
sao mu	the 'Feast of the Dead'
shang	the south
shanshui	the literal meaning is 'mountains and water', but the term is normally associated with a style of landscape painting that depicts rugged mountain scenery with river valleys in the foreground. It is a highly popular form, first established in the T'ang Dynasty, back in the seventh to ninth centuries AD
shao lin	specially trained assassins, named after the monks of the shao lin monastery
shao nai nai	literally, 'little grandmother'. A young girl who has been given the responsibility of looking after her siblings

she t'ou	a 'tongue' or taster, whose task is to safeguard his master from poisoning
shen chung	'caution'
shen nu	'god girls' – superior prostitutes
shen t'se	special elite force, named after the 'palace armies' of the late T'ang dynasty
Shih	'Master'. Here used as a term of respect somewhat equivalent to our use of 'Mister'. The term was originally used for the lowest level of civil servants, to distinguish them socially from the run-of-the-mill 'Misters' (*hsian sheng*) below them and the gentlemen (*ch'un tzu*) above
shou hsing	a peach brandy
Shui Hu Chuan	*Outlaws of the Marsh*, a long historical novel, attributed to Lo Kuan-chung, but re-cast in the early siteenth century by 'Shih Nai-an', a scholar. Set in the eleventh century, it is a saga of bandits, warlords and heroes. Written in pure *pai hua* – colloquial Chinese – it is the tale of how its heroes became bandits. Its revolutionary nature made it deeply unpopular with both the Ming and Manchu dynasties, but it remains one of the most popular adventures among the Chinese populus
siang chi	Chinese chess; a very different game from its Western counterpart
Ta	'Beat', here a heavily amplified form of Chinese folk music, popular amongst the young
ta lien	an elaborate girdle pouch
Ta Ssu Nung	the Superintendancy of Agriculture
tai	literally 'pockets' but here denoting Representatives in the House at Weimar. 'Owned' financially by the Seven, historically such *tai* have served a double function in the House, counterbalancing the strong mercantile tendencies of the House and serving as a conduit for the views of the Seven. Traditionally they had been elderly, well-respected men, but more recently their replacements were young, brash and very corrupt, more like the hoppoes of the Opium Wars period
t'ai chi	the Original, or One, from which the duality of all things (*yin* and *yang*) developed, according to Chinese cosmology.

	We generally associate the *t'ai chi* with the Taoist symbol, that swirling circle of dark and light supposedly representing an egg (perhaps the *Hun Tun*), the yolk and the white differentiated
tai hsiao	a white wool flower, worn in the hair
Tai Huo	'Great Fire'
T'ai Shan	Mount T'ai, the highest and most sacred of China's mountains, located in Shantung province. A stone pathway of 6293 steps leads to the summit and, for thousands of years, the ruling emperor has made ritual sacrifices at its foot, accompanied by their full retinue, presenting evidence of their virtue. T'ai Shan is one of the five Taoist holy mountains, and symbolizes the very centre of China. It is the mountain of the sun, symbolizing the bright male force (*yang*). 'As safe as T'ai Shan' is a popular saying, denoting the ultimate in solidity and certainty
Tai Shih Lung	Court Astrologer, a title that goes back to the Han Dynasty
T'ang	literally, 'beautiful and imposing'. It is the title chosen by the Seven, who were originally the chief advisors to Tsao Ch'un, the tyrant. Since overthrowing Tsao Ch'un, it has effectively had the meaning of 'emperor'
Ta Ts'in	the Chinese name for the Roman Empire. They also knew Rome as Li Chien and as 'the land West of the Sea'. The Romans themselves they termed the 'Big Ts'in' – the Ts'in being the name the Chinese gave themselves during the Ts'in dynasty (AD 265–316).
te	'spiritual power', 'true virtue' or 'virtuality', defined by Alan Watts as 'the realisation or expression of the Tao in actual living'
t'e an tsan	'innocent westerners'. For 'innocent' perhaps read naïve
ti tsu	a bamboo flute, used both as a solo instrument and as part of an ensemble, playing traditional Chinese music
ti yu	the 'earth prison' or underworld of Chinese legend. There are ten main Chinese Hells, the first being the courtroom in which the sinner is sentenced and the last being that place where they are reborn as human beings. In between are a vast number of sub-Hells, each with its own Judge and staff of cruel warders. In Hell, it is always dark, with no differentiation between night and day

Tian	'Heaven', also, 'the dome of the sky'
tian-fang	literally 'to fill the place of the dead wife'; used to signify the upgrading of a concubine to the more respectable position of wife
tiao tuo	bracelets of gold and jade
T'ieh Lo-han	'Iron Goddess of Mercy', a ch'a
T'ieh Pi Pu Kai	literally, 'the iron pen changes not', this is the final phrase used at the end of all Chinese government proclamations for the last three thousand years
ting	an open-sided pavilion in a Chinese garden. Designed as a focal point in a garden, it is said to symbolize man's essential place in the natural order of things
T'ing Wei	The Superintendancy of Trials, an institution that dates back to the T'ang dynasty. See Book Six, *The White Mountain*, for an instance of how this department of government – responsible for black propaganda – functions
T'o	'camel-backed'; a Chinese term for 'hunch-backed'
tong	a gang. In China and Europe these are usually smaller and thus subsidiary to the Triads, but in North America the term has generally taken the place of Triad
tou chi	Glycine Max, or the black soybean, used in Chinese herbal medicine to cure insomnia
Tsai Chien!	'Until we meet again!'
Tsou Tsai Hei	'the Walker in the Darkness'
tsu	the north
tsu kuo	the motherland
ts'un	a Chinese 'inch' of approximately 1.4 Western inches. Ten ts'un form one ch'i
Tu	Earth
tzu	'Elder Sister'
wan wu	literally 'the ten thousand things'; used generally to include everything in creation, or, as the Chinese say, 'all things in Heaven and Earth'
Wei	Commandant of Security

wei chi	'the surrounding game', known more commonly in the West by its Japanese name of *Go*. It is said that the game was invented by the legendary Chinese Emperor Yao in the year 2350 BC to train the mind of his son, Tan Chu, and teach him to think like an emperor
wen ming	a term used to denote Civilization, or written culture
wen ren	the scholar-artist; very much an ideal state, striven for by all creative Chinese
weng	'Old man'. Usually a term of respect
Wu	a diviner; traditionally these were 'mediums' who claimed to have special pyshic powers. Wu could be either male or female
Wu	'non-being'. As Lao Tzu says: 'Once the block is carved, there are names.' But the Tao is un-nameable (*wu-ming*) and before Being (*yu*) is Non-Being (*wu*). Not to have existence, or form, or a name, that is *wu*
Wu Ching	the 'Five Classics' studied by all Confucian scholars, comprising the *Shu Ching* (Book Of History), the *Shih Ching* (Book of Songs), the *I Ching* (Book of Changes), the *Li Ching* (Book of Rites, actually three books in all), and the *Ch'un Chui* (The Spring And Autumn Annals of the State of Lu)
wu fu	the five gods of good luck. They are often depicted as five men clad in the red robes of officials. They confer Long Life, Riches, Welfare, Virtue and Health
wu tu	the 'five noxious creatures – which are: toad, scorpion, snake, centipede and gecko (wall lizard)
Wushu	the Chinese word for Martial Arts. It refers to any of several hundred schools. *Kung fu* is a school within this, meaning 'skill that transcends mere surface beauty'
wuwei	nonaction; an old Taoist concept. It means keeping harmony with the flow of things – doing nothing to break the flow
ya	homosexual. Sometimes the term 'a yellow eel' is used
yamen	the official building in a Chinese community
yang	the 'male principle' of Chinese cosmology, which, with its complementary opposite, the female *yin*, forms the *t'ai ch'i*, derived from the Primeval One. From the union of *yin* and

	yang arise the 'five elements' (water, fire, earth, metal, wood) from which the 'ten thousand things' (the wan wu) are generated. Yang signifies Heaven and the South, the Sun and Warmth, Light, Vigour, Maleness, Penetration, odd numbers, and the Dragon. Mountains are *yang*
yang kuei tzu	Chinese name for foreigners, 'Ocean Devils'. It also is synonymous with 'Barbarians'
yang mei ping	'willow plum sickness', the Chinese term for syphilis, provides an apt description of the male sexual organ in the extreme of this sickness
yi	the number one
yin	the 'female principle' of Chinese cosmology (see *yang*). Yin signifies Earth and the North, the Moon and Cold, Darkness, Quiescence, Femaleness, Absorption, even numbers, and the Tiger. The *yin* lies in the shadow of the mountain
yin mao	pubic hair
Ying kuo	can refer to both English, the language, and England, the country
ying tao	'baby peach', a term of endearment here
ying tzu	'shadows' – trained specialists of various kinds, contracted out to gangland bosses
yu	literally 'fish', but, because of its phonetic equivalence to the word for 'abundance', the fish symbolises wealth. Yet there is also a saying that when the fish swim upriver it is a portent of social unrest and rebellion
yu ko	a 'Jade Barge'; here a type of luxury sedan
Yu Kung	'Foolish Old Man!'
yu ya	deep elegance
yuan	the basic currency of Chung Kuo (and modern-day China). Colloquially (though not here) it can also be termed *kuai* – 'piece' or 'lump'. Ten *mao* (or, formally, *jiao*) make up one *yuan*, while 100 *fen* (or 'cents') comprise one *yuan*
yueh ch'in	a Chinese dulcimer; one of the principal instruments of the Chinese orchestra
Ywe Lung	literally 'The Moon Dragon', the wheel of seven dragons that is the symbol of the ruling Seven throughout Chung

Kuo: 'At its centre the snounts of the regal beasts met, forming a rose-like hub, huge rubies burning fiercely in each eye. Their lithe, powerful bodies curved outward like the spokes of a giant wheel while at the edge their tails were intertwined to form the rim.' (Chapter Four of *The Middle Kingdom*)

AUTHOR'S NOTE & ACKNOWLEDGEMENTS

Thanks must go to all those who have read and criticised parts of the many different drafts of CHUNG KUO over the thirty four years of its creating: to my good friends and 'Writers Bloc' companions – Chris Evans, David Garnett, Rob Holdstock, Garry Kilworth, Bobbie Lamming, Lisa Tuttle and Geoff Ryman – for honing the cutting edge; to John Murry – alias Richard Cowper – both for sharing what he knew, and for long years of patient husbandry; to my brother Ian, much-loved, ever-enthusiastic; to Ritchie Smith, dear friend, drinking companion and 'Great Man'; to Tony Richards, for friendship's sake; to Andrew Motion – for finding 'A Perfect Art' not so perfect and giving good reasons; and to my agents, Hilary Rubinstein, Clarissa Rushdie and Diana Tyler. Their comments and advice have helped me avoid many pitfalls and, without doubt, given shape to the final manuscript.

I would also like to offer thanks to Bruce Sterling for the inspiration given by his excellent novel, *Schismatrix*... and for five of his words, now embedded in my text.

I reserve special thanks for two friends whose encouragement, advice and criticism throughout have been invaluable. Brian Griffin for unerringly knowing (better than me sometimes) what I'm up to, and the late and much missed Robert Carter, not merely for the introduction to Wei Chi and his patient and astute reading of the emergent book, but for all the long years of friendship. To you both, *Kan Pei!*

To my long-time editors; Nick Sayers at New English Library, Brian DeFiore at Delacorte, Nic Cheatham at Corvus, Carolyn Caughey of Hodder-Headline, John Pearce and Alyssa Diamond over there in Canada. Thanks to you all for the many kindnesses, and for making the whole process of editing so enjoyable. Their patience, cheerfulness and encouragement were more than I could ever have hoped for.

To Christian Vander and Magma, for the music ...

Finally, thanks to my partner in crime, Brian Aldiss. If anyone's shadow lies behind this work, it's yours. This is delivery on the Planetarium speech that time!

David Wingrove
Spring 2017

CREDITS

The version of the I Ching or Book of Changes quoted from throughout is the Richard Wilhelm translation, rendered into English by Cary F. Baynes and published by Routledge & Kegan Paul, London, 1951.

The translation of Ch'u Yuan's T'ien Wen, or 'Heavenly Questions' is by David Hawkes from *The Songs of the South: An Anthology of Ancient Chinese Poems*, published by Penguin Books, London, 1985.

The translation of Miu His's *Bearer's Song* (from *Han Burial Songs*) is by Arthur Waley from *Chinese Poems*, published by George Allen and Unwin, London, 1946.

The translation of Meng Chiao's 'The Stones Where The Haft Rotted' and Li Shang Yin's 'Exile' are by A. C. Graham from *Poems of the Late T'ang*, published by Penguin Books, London, 1965.

The game of *Wei Chi* mentioned throughout this volume is, incidentally, more commonly known by its Japanese name of *Go*, and is not merely the world's oldest game but its most elegant. As far as this author knows it has no connection to the trigram of the same name in the I *Ching* – the sixty-fourth, 'Before Completion', but a playful similarity of the kind beloved of the Han might possibly be noted.

Finally, *The Game of Wei Chi* by D. Pecorini and T. Shu (with a Foreword by ProfessorH. A. Giles) is a real book and was published by Longmans, Green & Co. in 1929. It was, alas, long out of print, and I have Brian Aldiss to thank for my much-treasured copy. It was my fond hope that its use herein might some day lead to the re-publication of this slender classic, as proved the case.